10405232

"WHICH IS THE YOU, MISS MARISA?"

Tuan's voice was husky as he asked, "The sharp-tongued creature who can't stand to be alone with me for five minutes—or the silken thing that lay beside me in the night?"

"I didn't—" But her heart pounded wildly, and the denial didn't sound as forceful as it should.

His hands slid over her shoulders, and she willed herself to move but could not. Time seemed to stop as she submitted to his touch. He was too close, too male, too dangerous.

"Kiss me, Marisa," he ordered softly.

But she would not obey. To do so would reveal every sad secret of her lovesick heart. She swayed against him briefly and then, with a deep sob, turned and ran....

AND NOW...

SUPERROMANCES

As the world's No. 1 publisher of best-selling romance fiction, we are proud to present a sensational new series of modern love stories—SUPERROMANCES.

Written by masters of the genre, these longer, sensual and dramatic novels are truly in keeping with today's changing life-styles. Full of intriguing conflicts, the heartaches and delights of true love, SUPERROMANCES are absorbing stories—satisfying and sophisticated reading that lovers of romance fiction have long been waiting for.

SUPERROMANCES
Contemporary love stories for the woman of today!

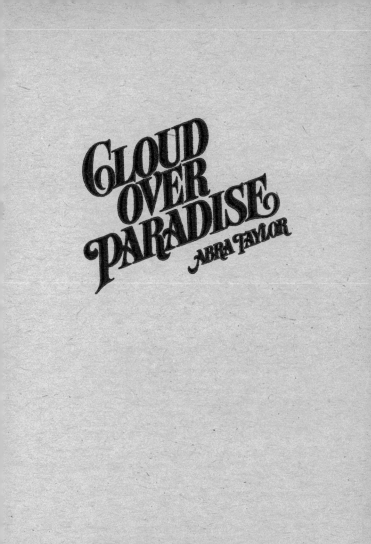

CLOUD OVER PARADISE

Abra Taylor

Harlequin Books

TORONTO · LONDON · LOS ANGELES · AMSTERDAM
SYDNEY · HAMBURG · PARIS · STOCKHOLM · ATHENS · TOKYO

Harlequin first edition, July 1981
First printing February 1981
Second printing March 1981
Third printing June 1981
Fourth printing April 1982

ISBN 0-373-70005-9

Copyright © 1981 by Abra Taylor. All rights reserved.
Philippine copyright 1981. Australian copyright 1981.
Except for use in any review, the reproduction or utilization of
this work in whole or in part in any form by any electronic,
mechanical or other means, now known or hereafter invented,
including xerography, photocopying and recording, or in any
information storage or retrieval system, is forbidden without
the permission of the publisher, Harlequin Enterprises Limited,
225 Duncan Mill Road, Don Mills, Ontario, Canada M3B 3K9.

All the characters in this book have no existence outside the
imagination of the author and have no relation whatsoever to
anyone bearing the same name or names. They are not even
distantly inspired by any individual known or unknown to the
author, and all the incidents are pure invention.

The Superromance trademark, consisting of the word
SUPERROMANCE, and the Worldwide trademark, consisting of
a globe and the word Worldwide in which the letter "o" is
represented by a depiction of a globe, are trademarks of
Worldwide Library.

Printed in Canada

CHAPTER ONE

"WAKE UP, MISS BLAKE. We've landed. *Wake up.*"

Strong fingers shook at Marisa's shoulder, lending emphasis to the words. She came awake unwillingly, out of restless slumbers during which even the call to fasten seat belts had been obeyed numbly in a sleep-drugged state. With a sense of deep disorientation she opened her eyes to the view of an airstrip and startling scenery beyond, where dark green mountains lumped against an incredibly blue sky.

"We're in Faaa Airport," came a disruptive male voice over the hubbub of other passengers deplaning. The man spoke in English, as he had earlier. His accent was American and bore no trace of the French that she knew was his mother tongue. "This is Tahiti. Come along, Miss Blake. I haven't a moment to waste."

Still groggy with sleep, she recoiled instinctively from the hard hand on her shoulder. Slowly her eyes left the plane window and swerved upward into a collision with eyes like the sky, the blue of them startling against the deeply tanned face of her new employer. The memory of the charade she had agreed to perform washed back like a returning tide, bringing wakefulness.

"I'm not going to bite you," came the man's sardonic voice. The grooves in his cheeks deepened briefly. "This is a business arrangement, remember? Now stop looking at me as though I were the original Dracula, and unstrap your seat belt. I have some matters to attend to in Papeete."

Still light-headed from the flight, Marisa loosened the buckle as instructed. She ran swift fingers through her hair, seized her large traveling handbag and allowed herself to be propelled into the lineup of passengers still crowding the aisles. She remained composed despite the several admiring glances she drew; she was not unaware of the effect her appearance produced. Silky shoulder-length champagne hair, long dark eyelashes, smoky green eyes, skin like melted honey—all these things had a way of drawing the eye. But Marisa was self-critical enough to realize that it was an effect produced not by any special arrangement of eyes and nose and mouth, but by her unusual coloring. She was not a beautiful girl, but she was a decidedly attractive one; it was a fact that she had accepted long ago, with gratitude that nature had been so generous.

At last they emerged from the DC-8 into sunshine so brilliant that Marisa had to squeeze her eyes partly shut. It was hot—too hot for the long-sleeved cream silk shirt she wore. But then, the Air

New Zealand flight had been hours late leaving Los Angeles; she had expected to arrive in Tahiti in the middle of the night.

"This way," said her new employer crisply. He seized her arm in a no-nonsense grip, making her feel self-conscious where the stares of others had not.

The man at her side steered her toward the gleaming modern terminal with a whirlwind impetuosity that she had come to expect of him in the few hours she had known him. The actual hiring had been done only yesterday morning, in a short but astonishing interview with this man's confidential secretary, an attractive woman who had made all arrangements with an efficiency and dispatch that left Marisa's head spinning. The secretary had delivered her to the airport last night and left her there with the assurance that her new employer would turn up before flight time.

Marisa had waited all night, on edge; and when the call for boarding finally came he had still not appeared. It was only at the last minute, as she hung back at the gates, that he had arrived—introducing himself and sweeping her through to the plane all in one breathtaking rush. He had given her no more than one unfriendly once-over, which seemed strange considering the unusual nature of the employment. Even on the long flight to Tahiti he had not remained at her side; instead he had vanished into the cockpit—but *that* was not so unusual, Marisa supposed, for a man who was a pilot and airline owner himself.

"Ah! Monsieur de Vigny! *Ça va bien? Quel plaisir de vous revoir!*"

The airport officials instantly recognized Marisa's new employer, a circumstance that greatly smoothed the entry into French Polynesia. It was only to be expected, she reflected. His company—Air des Iles, a South Pacific airline specializing in interisland flights—was headquartered here in Tahiti, and he would be well known at Faaa Airport.

Her passport, bearing the recent stamp of her stay in France, was quite in order; so were her various medical certifications and other papers provided by Monsieur de Vigny's secretary last night. While these things underwent the most cursory of scrutinies, Marisa watched her new employer surreptitiously.

Antoine de Vigny. Under the circumstances, she supposed, she would be expected to call him Antoine. It would seem strange—but then, it was not as if Antoine de Vigny was a total unknown, a man of whom she had never heard. Marisa's brother-in-law, Roger—husband of her sister, Sarah—had worked for Air des Iles for many years as manager of the company's small Los Angeles branch office. Or, at least, Roger had worked there until his untimely illness and subsequent death only ten days ago. Which, Marisa supposed ruefully, was the sad circumstance that had led to her being offered this remarkable job.

The Air des Iles owner was chatting now, briefly, with airline officials, his manner informal and far friendlier than it had been in his fleeting contacts with her. Even though he appeared totally relaxed, there was about him a dynamism, a sense of restless energy, that was quite overwhelming. Deceptively calm, Marisa decided wryly—like the eye of a hurricane. What an unsettling man he had turned out to be! There was the overpowering physical presence of him, for one thing—the breadth of those shoulders and the height that gave him a six-inch advantage over Marisa, even with her highest heels on; and she was by no means short. Attractive, too, if you liked the masterful male-animal type, with features just irregular enough to escape being too handsome, and deep facial grooves that ran like rivers down his cheeks. With that board-flat waist and those long powerful limbs, he looked more like an athlete than an airline owner. Or perhaps that impression was due to his deep tan: even his dark brown hair had been burnished by sun, giving it a look of vitality.

He was, she had to admit, a superb physical specimen. So why had she felt an instant, if well-concealed, antagonism toward him this morning? Perhaps it was those startling blue eyes, and the faint animosity she had sensed in him—almost as if he resented the necessity of hiring a woman, any woman, to perform the extraordinary charade of pretending to be his fiancée.

Or was it so extraordinary? Yesterday, during

the interview, she had spent some absentminded minutes wondering what earthly reason might necessitate the charade, minutes during which she had scarcely heard what was said for the swirl of speculation in her brain. But since meeting Antoine de Vigny this morning she had become convinced there could be only one reason—a woman. Some woman must have become too importunate; and no doubt Marisa's role was to help him divest himself of that woman.

"Come along, Miss Blake." Antoine de Vigny's crisp voice unsettled her brief reverie. Again her elbow was seized in a powerful grip, and she felt herself being propelled—no, swept—through the gleaming terminal building. She hurried to keep pace with those long athletic limbs. Everywhere there was a polyglot of faces and races: Tahitians, Chinese, Malays, Europeans, tourists from every corner of the globe. It was a very cosmopolitan crowd, and everything seemed to be color and confusion.

"Perhaps it's time I started calling you Marisa," he continued as they threaded their way through the busy terminal. "In view of our, er, engagement, first names seem appropriate. Oh, by the way—"

He came to a sudden halt, throwing Marisa temporarily off balance. He delved into the pocket of a lean mud-colored twill suit that was only two shades darker than his tan, and fished out a small object. He seized her left hand, and before she had time to realize what was happening, an enormous emerald sparkled on her ring finger.

"I can't wear that," she said in dismay, "even on a temporary basis. It's too big! Why, I might lose it, and I couldn't possibly repay—"

"It's insured," he cut in, and dismissed her protest with an offhanded wave. He resumed his headlong progress through the crowd. "I can hardly exchange it; it was bought in Los Angeles. Why else do you think my secretary asked for your ring size yesterday?"

Breathlessly Marisa hurried to keep pace. "I do wish she'd chosen something less extravagant."

"Don't you like it?"

"It's beautiful, but—"

"Then don't complain. It goes with green eyes," he said brusquely, surprising her that he should have noticed.

He explained their destination as he hurried her along. "We're being met in the Air des Iles lounge by one of my pilots, who also happens to be a good friend. He's American, an expatriate who came here some years ago, before it became difficult to settle in French Polynesia. Nowadays you need a permit, and it's not easy to get."

"Why are we meeting him?" asked Marisa, wondering if this other employee had been given responsibility for settling her into a hotel.

By now they had reached a door marked with the Air des Iles emblem. Marisa's employer pushed the door open and ushered her through into a large room plush with pale carpeting and comfortable lounge chairs. The room was empty.

"Damn," said Antoine de Vigny, frowning. "I hope he hasn't been delayed on an incoming flight. He's flying us on to Ta'aroa."

"Ta'aroa?"

"The little island where I live," came the dry answer as he closed the door of the soundproof lounge, instantly blanking out all the terminal noises. "That's where we'll be staying."

"Island?" A small sense of unease gripped Marisa. She came to a halt near the grouping of soft furniture and looked at her employer with troubled eyes. "I thought we'd be staying on Tahiti," she told him.

His dark eyebrows tilted upward with some surprise. "Surely my secretary explained?" he said.

"No," said Marisa, now decidedly worried.

"Hmm." The blue eyes remained on her, unfathomable for the moment. "That does surprise me. Very competent woman, my secretary—that's why I flew her to Los Angeles to help me sort out the chaos your brother-in-law's death created in our little branch office. It's not like her to neglect an important detail like that. Are you sure you were listening properly?"

"Perhaps I...." Marisa shook her head, straightening her thoughts and trying to remember exactly what *had* transpired in the interview yesterday. For the first ten minutes she had been answering a dizzying assortment of questions about herself—about the small Maine fishing village where she had grown up; about the death of her parents in a car crash four years ago, when she was eighteen; about her studies in France since then.

Marisa's father, a small-town lawyer, had not been a wealthy man. Nathaniel Blake had had a tendency to take on cases for the underdog, and a happy-go-lucky lack of interest in whether his clients—fishermen, many of them—could afford his services or not. Mostly it was not. Moreover, he had been given to investing in his clients' fly-by-night schemes—fish canneries that failed, patents for lobster traps that never worked. He talked constantly of the travel he could never afford to indulge in. If Marisa had inherited nothing else, she had inherited her father's taste to see the world.

But she had also inherited some of her mother's financial caution. Once she had acclimatized herself to the shock and grief caused by her parents' death, Marisa had cast about for some way to continue her education and support herself at the same time. Her older sister, Sarah, who was married and living on the West Coast even then, had offered financial help, but Marisa had been loath to accept it. By chance she had learned that tuition at the Sorbonne was free, though the number of students accepted was limited. As language study had always been one of her strong points, she had decided in that moment she would work toward becoming a translator. So she had applied to the

Sorbonne and was fortunate to be accepted because of her strong educational background. She had scraped together enough money for a round-trip ticket to France and enrolled at the Sorbonne with no real appreciation of the truly horrendous cost of living in Paris. In the end, over the years, she had had to accept a small amount of financial help from Sarah and Roger after all.

Then two months ago word had come that her brother-in-law had been hospitalized; the prognosis had been grave. "And you flew back to help your sister with her four children," the secretary had stated yesterday, bringing the questioning to a close. And for the rest of the interview, after the nature of the job and the salary had been mentioned, Marisa's brain had been in a total whirl.

"Perhaps I did misunderstand," she admitted now to Antoine de Vigny. "I was in a state of turmoil from the job offer. And I was tired, too—I'd only just come back from a camping trip with Sarah's two older children. I took them off shortly after the funeral, in order to distract them and relieve my sister—Roger's illness had been very trying for her. A pretended engagement, that's all I remember—for a period of one month, and with an enormous salary paid in advance. I don't deny I jumped at it because it sounded easy, and because I needed the money, and because I've always wanted to see Tahiti. But—"

"Well, no matter," interrupted Antoine de Vigny. "You'll like it on Ta'aroa. It's a beautiful island, a nice secluded Pacific paradise, unspoiled by hotels and—"

"Wait a minute," objected Marisa. "That puts a whole new complexion on this job. I thought I'd be staying in Papeete, in a hotel. But on a secluded Pacific island, with a man I hardly know...."

"Tahiti or Ta'aroa, does it matter?" The cerulean eyes looked down at her from a great distance, their expression now decidedly derisive. "You can be absolutely sure that no matter where we are, I won't take advantage of you. My need for an annulment is too pressing."

"Annulment?" Marisa puzzled briefly, comprehension for the moment eluding her. Then, as his meaning became clear, shock reverberated down her spine.

"Marriage is the usual goal of an engagement," he remarked dryly. "Ours will come a little sooner than most, that's all. Don't tell me you closed your ears to that, too?"

Marisa stared at him in total disbelief. "I'm sure I'd have heard *that*," she said at last, flatly.

"You'd better sit down," came the sardonic observation. Antoine de Vigny seemed wholly unperturbed by Marisa's evident dismay; his tall frame was totally relaxed, but there was about him an alert and disconcerting watchfulness. "Sit down, and I'll go through it once again," he said with exaggerated patience.

Marisa needed no urging. She sank into a deeply cushioned chair, legs like jelly from this latest shock, and from the distinct suspicion that she was being railroaded in some way.

"The marriage will be for one month only," he told her coolly, "to end in annulment when the time is up. I believe my secretary assured you there'd be no problem with sleeping arrangements."

"She did no such thing," Marisa denied.

"In that case I'll assure you now." His eyelids drooped briefly over a mocking blue. "You'll have a separate bedroom, Miss Blake. To all intents and purposes the marriage will appear to be real enough, but it will be in name only."

"Your secretary told me none of this!"

"Odd," he murmured with a small enigmatic smile playing over his lips. "She made all the arrangements herself—special wedding license, preacher, informing my family...."

Marisa's green eyes narrowed poisonously. "You'd better explain a whole lot more than that, Monsieur de Vigny. It seems I've been misled, and I want to know why. I'd never have come four thousand miles to marry a total stranger!"

He looked at her for a moment of silence and then dropped into a soft chair a short distance from Marisa's, stretching his long limbs lazily in a way that suggested satisfaction. He extracted a pack of cigarettes from his pocket and lighted one with a wooden match ignited on his thumbnail, then regarded her with veiled eyes through a haze of smoke.

"Exactly," he said in the softest of voices, after a long silence. "I didn't think you would."

Marisa's brain reeled from the implications. "You mean you deliberately tricked me into coming to Tahiti!"

"I'm afraid so," he said with a sigh so deep it could only be feigned. "But I'm sure you'll forgive me when I've explained why, and when you understand that I have no designs on your person. The job isn't so very different from what my secretary described. But time was of the essence, and I couldn't afford to let you say no. I need to get married at once, to someone with your special qualifications. Frankly, if my secretary hadn't found a woman with those qualifications I'd be desperate—damn desperate."

He stubbed out the cigarette, although it was hardly smoked, while Marisa stared at him, rage and resentment gradually replacing the sensations of deep shock.

"Then you'll have to be desperate, for I won't stay in Tahiti now!" With no very sure idea of her goal, she snatched at her handbag and struck out for the door.

He moved so swiftly she could hardly credit her senses. Like a jungle predator, she decided later, zoning in on its prey—but at the time she was far too startled to make any such comparisons. One moment he had been stretched indolently in a deep chair; the next he stood between herself and safety. His broad shoulders leaned against the door, blocking escape, and his eyes had turned mocking, almost amused.

"Where do you think you're going? You might ask a little more about the job—especially as you've already been paid for it."

She opened her mouth to make an angry retort, until the import of what he had said seeped through. The secretary had indeed given her a check yesterday—a very large check. The very size of it was part of what had destroyed her rational processes during the interview.

"I'll pay the money back, then."

"*Can* you?" he asked coolly. "I know a great deal about your affairs, Miss Blake. I suspect you've already given the money to your sister, Sarah, to repay her for all those years she and Roger have been giving you a helping hand. As I recall, all the time you studied at the Sorbonne you refused to accept anything more than nominal help—you earned the rest yourself and refused all offers of more. Now it seems to me that an independent soul like that would pay back borrowed money at the first possible opportunity, especially when her sister needed it. A total of five thousand dollars, I believe—not so much over four years, considering the cost of living in Paris. Does the amount sound familiar?"

Marisa clenched the strap of her shoulder bag for strength, while the color fast drained from her face. "You—you bastard," she whispered.

He smiled in a slow watchful way that did not

quite touch his eyes. "I think you'd better sit down again," he suggested imperturbably. "You look quite done in. Didn't it ever occur to you that such a large sum might be bait for a trap? A velvet trap, true—for I assure you, you'll come to no harm."

She glared at him venomously, unable to trust herself to speak.

"It might also occur to you," he added dryly, "that I have no interest in marriage, *real* marriage, to a total stranger. It won't be any more difficult for you than a pretended engagement would have been. Now won't you sit down and listen?"

Marisa, still speechless with fury, found herself being urged backward toward the chair she had abandoned such a short time ago. She reacted to his touch as if burned and despite her shakiness covered the distance without help. It was true; she would have to listen. She had little money in her purse, and her return ticket was in his possession. How *could* she have allowed herself to be snared into this situation—even with Sarah's encouragement, and assurances that Roger had thought highly of Antoine de Vigny!

"That's better," he said in a dry tone, once he had seen her settled in a chair. He himself remained standing this time, occasionally prowling the soft carpet that turned his footsteps silent.

"Now, Miss Blake, do a little more thinking about why you—you in particular—were chosen for this job. Surely it must occur to you that I have

other women acquaintances, so why would I hire a
total stranger? If you understand why you were
hired, you'll also understand why you can be quite
sure you'll come to no harm at my hands. Why *did*
you think you were chosen?''

She looked at him, hating him, hating the
bronzed face and the hard self-assured look of
him, hating the arrogance of his assumption that
she would fall in with his plans, hating most of all
the blue eyes that seemed to bore holes in her.

"I assumed," she said tightly, "that your
secretary had suggested me because she was aware
of Sarah's financial straits. There were a lot of
medical expenses to pay, and they weren't all
covered by the company plan. I supposed she
thought it would help the family in some way.''

"An act of generosity?" he suggested sardonically.

"Obviously I was wrong.''

"Obviously," he agreed with that maddening
imperturbability, seemingly immune to the venom
in her voice. "To be truthful, Miss Blake, I first
considered hiring you a week ago, and I would
have told you so if I'd been able to meet you. I'll
admit I was curious to meet you in person and
assure myself you'd be a suitable candidate for the
job. That's why I called at your sister's home the
day after the funeral.''

"She told me," Marisa said frostily.

"There was a dual reason for my visit. First, I
wanted to offer condolences to your sister, as I

hadn't been around to do so the day of the funeral. But I also wanted to have a look at you. However, you weren't there.''

"I took the children to the zoo that day," came the stony reply.

"I also returned the following day," he informed her coolly. "But by that time you'd gone off on your camping trip. Perhaps if we'd met I'd have been more honest with you about my intentions. But your absence gave me little choice, and as I needed a woman of your qualifications in a great hurry, I proceeded to make my plans.''

"And how," she asked tautly, "could you be so sure I was a suitable candidate—sight unseen?''

"When I failed in my efforts to meet you," he said without the bat of an eyelash, "I had you investigated.''

"Investigated!" Marisa gasped.

"I had to be sure I could use you." He stopped on the carpet just in front of her and looked downward with a half smile, apparently unbothered by any twinge of conscience. "I make it a practice to know about my employees, and that's what you are now—an employee. Ah, yes, Miss Blake, in the time you were away I learned quite a number of things about you—enough to assure myself that you would do very well as a temporary wife. So I had my secretary set about procuring your papers for entry into Tahiti. You don't really think she could have made all those arrangements in one day, do you? As it was, she had to use some pull.''

Damn him—damn the male arrogance and the presumption of him! How dared he have her investigated? How dared he assume he could sweep her along with no regard for her wishes?

"I suppose that's how you found out about my financial failings," she said cuttingly, "but it still doesn't explain why you decided to force marriage on someone you'd never laid eyes upon!"

"What difference do looks make?" His brows tilted upward mockingly. "I'll admit the wrappings are a pleasant bonus, but it's the contents that first piqued my interest. I needed a wife I could shed easily at the end of the month, by annulment—and it appeared you had a qualification that would make an annulment indisputable. It's a qualification not always easy to find nowadays, and certainly not here in Polynesia."

"What qualification?" she asked suspiciously, traces of color rising to her face.

"You were engaged once, for a short time, four months ago. Would you care to tell me why you broke off the engagement?"

"I don't believe that's your concern."

"Ah, but it is." Eyes totally enigmatic now, he pulled an envelope from the breast pocket of his suit and tossed it into Marisa's lap. With a start of recognition she saw her own handwriting. There was a French stamp on the envelope, and her sister's address.

Even before extracting the letter from the envelope, she suspected its contents. She glanced at the letter briefly, only long enough to reaffirm her guess. It was a letter she had written to her sister from France, shortly before Roger's illness. It brought back memories that were personal but no longer painful. She had long since come to the conclusion that the engagement to Philippe had been a mistake in the first place, the result of proximity and a need for male companionship. Because she spent all her spare time tutoring English to help pay for room and board, Marisa had not met many young men during her years in Paris. Philippe was a rising young business executive who wanted to brush up on his English: he had acquired Marisa's services, and the relationship had developed from there. In the letter she had told Sarah everything—the doubts concerning her fiancé, the decision to break off the engagement and the exact circumstances that had impelled her to do so.

Marisa thrust the letter into her purse with a gesture of defiance. "Do you always read other people's mail?"

He shrugged, retreated a few feet and folded his arms with an enraging casualness. "Not as a rule. But remember I was faced with the monumental task of putting our Los Angeles office into shape. Your brother-in-law was suffering the symptoms of his brain tumor in the last months before he was actually hospitalized. He threw nothing out, and he left everything in a state of confusion. My secretary had to go through a mountain of old correspondence, and that letter happened to be in the mountain. I presume it found its way to the Air des Iles office because it contained a change of address, and Roger needed the address to send funds. Why *did* you move to a different *pension*? Because your fiancé remained too persistent?''

She would not give him the satisfaction of admitting he had guessed the truth; instead she countered coldly, ''Your secretary shouldn't have given you the letter. I'm surprised she did.''

''She was aware of my predicament, and my pressing need to marry. She thought the letter might be of interest to me. And it was—for that's what gave me the idea I could use you.''

''I can't imagine what the letter told you,'' Marisa snapped, although by now she could imagine very well. Her lack of experience with the opposite sex had been spelled out clearly enough in her detailing of why she had become involved with Philippe in the first place. ''It was all rather personal.''

''The job is somewhat personal, too,'' he reminded her sarcastically. ''The letter told me quite a lot that suggested you would be useful. It told me you spoke French; that you were independent—beyond accepting small loans from your brother-in-law; that you were of marriageable age, and with no emotional ties at the time of writing. Shall I spell out what else it told me?''

Marisa's face was a study in stone, although the hectic stain of color betrayed everything.

"You broke off with your fiancé because you didn't believe in trial marriages, Miss Blake. It seems he was becoming too importunate; he wanted to take you to bed. Quite a natural urge, I would say," he added sarcastically, "now that I've seen you for myself. I consider it my good fortune he didn't succeed."

He paused, then continued in a soft compelling voice, "Virginity is a technical phenomenon that makes an annulment a foregone conclusion. Instead of the trial without the marriage, I'm looking for the marriage without the trial. Now do you see why you'll be quite safe with me? I don't intend to do anything to change your, er, state of grace."

"I can't know that, can I," she said sharply.

"Take my word for it. Normally I'd run a mile to avoid an untried girl like you."

"You might change your mind."

"I won't change my mind," he assured her. "I need that annulment too badly."

Her eyes narrowed. "Why do you want to get married at all?"

"Did I say *want*?"

"Need, then. Why do you need to get married?"

"I don't have to tell you that." All at once his expression became curtained, and once again she felt that indefinable air of hostility she had sensed that morning. His voice, too, became abrupt. "I've paid you very well for this coming month, and as I have no designs on your person, my motives are none of your concern.''

''I'll have to know them,'' she insisted frostily, ''or how can I know you're telling the truth? I might decide to go along with you if you explained the circumstances.''

A frown fretted at his brow as he considered her request. Then, as if struggling with a decision, he walked over to the huge plate-glass window that looked out on a view as imposing and exotic as Marisa had seen earlier from the plane window. For some moments he stood staring out of it moodily, his broad shoulders hunched against the serrated skyline of Tahiti, his hands thrust deeply into his trouser pockets. In outline his muscular frame now seemed as taut as a coiled spring.

''I need to get married because my father has issued an ultimatum. He wants me to find a wife by my thirty-fifth birthday. For very good and important reasons, I've decided to do as he asks. You don't need to know why—just take my word that it's absolutely essential. Moreover, he wishes to witness the ceremony.''

''Doesn't he trust you?'' asked Marisa acidly.

He turned back to the room and looked at her for a long bruising moment without commenting on her interruption. ''My father also lives on Ta'aroa, the island where I have my home. It's about forty minutes from Tahiti by air, close enough that I can commute to work. My great-grandfather started a small vanilla plantation on

Ta'aroa, and the de Vignys have lived there ever since. Recently I've been kept—" he paused, and started again "—kept too busy to go to Ta'aroa. I rent a small bungalow on Tahiti, but it's not really home. I need a holiday, and what better excuse than a honeymoon? You can think of it as a holiday, too," he finished dryly. "A paid holiday, no strings attached."

"There's a very important string attached," she contradicted, "and that's marriage. You say you won't take advantage of me, but how can I be sure? I have only your word that you want an annulment. I don't think I can risk it."

His hand ran restlessly through his hair, and he said irritably, "If you must know, there's another woman."

It was the first piece of news that Marisa had not found surprising. "A woman you want to avoid? Or—"

"A woman I want to marry," he said flatly.

"Why don't you marry *her*, then?"

The pause became a little too long, and Marisa received the distinct impression that he preferred not to answer. "She's not available at the moment," he admitted at last, curtly. The blue eyes were now decidedly antagonistic. "You're far too curious for your own good, do you know that?"

"I must know more," she persisted. "Who is this woman?"

Now his face became totally closed, his scowl so markedly unfriendly that his facial grooves turned

to frightening slashes. "Very well, I'll tell you this
much. My father issued his ultimatum six months
ago. Frankly, I've always avoided marriage like
the plague—so you can see it was a difficult decision. To tell you the truth, I procrastinated too
long. By the time I made up my mind to ask the
woman—her name is Yvonne, and she lives here
on Tahiti—I had left it too late. She had taken off
for a few weeks in New Zealand, and now I can't
locate her."

"And all this is supposed to reassure me?"
Marisa's voice traveled to the fine edge of hysteria. "A woman you couldn't make up your mind
to marry—along with the fact that your religion
probably doesn't permit divorce? I don't want to
be trapped into a loveless marriage!"

"Believe me," he frowned, "I have no intention
of being trapped into a loveless marriage, either.
As it happens, my religion does permit divorce—
Tahiti's largely Protestant, and my forebears were
Huguenots—but I don't believe in it. I want a
marriage in name only. If I'm to meet my father's
ultimatum, my need for an annulment is absolute."

"None of what you've said makes sense to me."
Marisa stood up, gathering her handbag once
again. "I can't go through with it."

"In that case I'll take my money back." He
moved alarmingly close, his face hard and threat-
ening and offering no quarter now. "I want it
now! If I can't get it from you, I'll get it from your

sister—one way or another. Rest assured I have
ways."

Oh, God, thought Marisa desperately. *Could* he
garnishee the Air des Iles pension that Sarah was
to start receiving soon, or one of the other sums
payable on Roger's death? What were the legalities involved? Not that it mattered; Antoine de
Vigny was evidently the kind of man who decided
on a course of action and legalities be damned.

"Make up your mind at once," he pounced,
sensing her momentary indecision. "We haven't
got all day. I want your answer before my pilot
friend comes through that door, which will be in
about—" He glanced at the thin gold watch that
nestled among crisp dark hairs on his wrist. "In
about one minute."

Marisa glared at him. "So you planned this little confrontation right to the very last minute!"

"Of course I did," he snapped. "Give me your
answer—*now*!"

Marisa's breath exploded on a note of total
frustration. "All right, you win," she fumed,
"but I won't pretend I like it!"

He turned affable with a change of mood that
was dizzying; his thunderous expression of seconds ago might never have been. "You don't have
to like it, but you do have to pretend," he said
genially. "Remember it's what I'm paying you
for."

The opening of the lounge door forestalled the
vitriolic comment on the tip of Marisa's tongue.

Quelling a havoc of rage and hatred, she turned in time to see a man enter—a bluff bear of a man, sandy haired and of medium height. He appeared to be in his late thirties. Although he wore no jacket, his pale blue shirt and crisp blue trousers were evidently a uniform, for they bore the Air des Iles insignia as did the flight bag he carried.

"Dooey!" exclaimed Antoine de Vigny. "Punctual as always."

"Well, 'Toine! Good to see you." The pilot came across the expanse of carpet and clapped his employer on the shoulder. He grinned with evident pleasure. "Welcome back! I was beginning to think we'd lost you to Los Angeles. Dammit, man, Tahiti isn't the same without you!"

"Tahiti will have to do without me for a little longer. I'm taking a month's holiday for my, ah, honeymoon." Antoine de Vigny gave a broad answering smile. It was the first time Marisa had seen him really smile, and in her present poisonous mood she found herself resenting that his even white teeth looked as healthy and well kept as the rest of him.

"This is the girl I mentioned yesterday, Dooey." Antoine gripped Marisa's arm and drew her forward, performing introductions. "Marisa, this is John Doonsbury—everyone calls him Dooey. He was my copilot years ago, when I first started Air des Iles on a shoestring, with only one small flying boat and a lot more nerve than business know-how. Dooey's the best damn flying-boat pilot in the Pacific."

"Bar one," grinned Dooey.

"How do you do, Mr.—"

"Please call me Dooey. Everyone does." The pilot smiled warmly, as if he had not noticed the stiffness in Marisa's voice. She was controlling herself, but barely.

That hated presence turned his attention to Marisa. "Dooey and I have some matters to look after, and it may take us an hour or so. For one thing, I'll have to confirm the arrangements my secretary made from Los Angeles. You can wait here." He looked at her closely, his eyes gleaming victory. "Probably a rest would do you good; you look quite...shattered. There's a small room—" he tilted his head toward another door leading off the lounge "—and a cot the pilots sometimes use. Hang the sign, and no one will disturb you. You'll find facilities for freshening up. Do you mind being left alone for a time?"

Marisa rewarded her employer with an uncompromising silence as Dooey started to walk toward the exit, his back now turned so he could not see the wordless outrage she expressed with her eyes.

"I'm not sure how long we'll be," Antoine de Vigny went on calmly, as if he had not noted her expression. "Communication from island to island can take a little time. Ta'aroa has a radio-telephone, and so do many of the other islands, but there has to be someone at the other end. We'll be back as soon as possible. Will you be all right?"

"I'm not made of glass, Monsieur de Vigny,"

she retorted in a low acidic voice, certain that
Dooey was now out of hearing range. Suddenly,
out of the corner of her eye, she noticed that the
Air des Iles pilot had returned across the soundless
carpeting; but it was too late to bite back the for-
mal term of address. "Antoine, I mean," she said,
stiffening.

"Relax, Marisa—Dooey knows the story. I
spoke to him long-distance yesterday, to ask him
to rearrange his schedule for today. I could hardly
lie to my best friend, could I? All the same, you'd
better start thinking of me as Antoine or you'll
make the same mistake when it matters."

Dooey grinned jovially. "Truth is, ma'am, all
his friends call him 'Toine." He retrieved his forgotten flight bag and elaborated, "Spelled T-u-a-n.
Sounds like 'Toine, t-w-a-n, except that Tuan has
other meanings in some parts of Asia. Means lord
and master, important man, that sort of thing. I
suppose you'll be calling him that, as most of us
do. Our mark of affection and admiration," he
said with a mock sarcasm and a make-believe bow
in Antoine's direction.

"That's enough, Dooey," Antoine replied with
a small frown that implied no rancor. "Wait for
me outside the door. I have something else to say
to Marisa in private."

He waited until Dooey had left and then raised a
sardonic brow. "Do you think you can manage to
call me Tuan?"

"Antoine is almost more than I can handle for

now." Her eyes dueled with his. "Does it matter?"

"Not in the least," he drawled. "Suit yourself. Perhaps you'll change your mind when we get to know each other better."

"I already know everything I want to know, Monsieur de Vigny, and I don't plan to become one of your admirers."

"Antoine," he corrected.

"Antoine, then," she said grudgingly. "Is that what your enemies call you?"

He rubbed strong sun-browned fingers around the back of his neck, a curiously weary gesture for a man who looked to be in prime condition. His voice became deliberately flat. "The day you stop hating me you can call me Tuan."

"I hope you have infinite patience," she replied meaningfully, drawing from him a return of the scowl that could be so unsettling.

"Less than I need for a sharp-tongued thing like you." His eyes betrayed a growing irritation. "I asked Dooey to leave the room only so I could apologize for my deceptions. I hoped you would understand I had very little choice in the time available. And now I apologize."

"Not accepted," she said airily.

"Dammit, Miss Blake—" He looked down at her with utter exasperation written on his tanned features. "I've apologized, and now I expect some efforts on your part. Please remember, you're being paid for this—a great deal of money, with very little asked in return. You're an employee, Miss Blake, not a judge and jury. I didn't deceive you very much; it's not so different from a mock engagement. And I'm as unhappy about the necessity as you are."

"Impossible," she retorted, finding a vengeful satisfaction in discovering that her taunts were getting beneath his skin.

His face tightened perceptibly. "I don't want a month of verbal fisticuffs. If you keep trying to goad me into losing my temper I'll do just that—and I warn you, you won't like it. Now start earning your money and earning it fast."

"Oh, don't worry. I'll keep a proper tongue in my head when other people are around. I can pretend to like you if I'm compelled to. And I am compelled to, aren't I? No matter how much it makes me suffer! I have no choice."

"That's right; you have no choice." He glowered at her. "And I don't give a damn whether other people are around or not, I want a little civility from you. I didn't bring you all this way just to have a sparring partner. I can understand that you resent being tricked, and I'm sorry for that. I can understand that you feel spiteful, and I'm sorry for that. But for God's sake, Miss Blake—Marisa—let's bury the hatchet."

"Bury it where?" she broke in, and her expression told him she had already picked a target somewhere between his eyes.

His eyes darkened dangerously, and thunderclouds built between his brows. For one frightening instant Marisa wondered if she had gone too far; she was sure from the clench of his fists that he wanted nothing more than to seize her and shake her like a rag doll.

But he kept his hands to himself, and gradually his face closed over, shutting her out. When he spoke his voice was controlled, quiet and lethal. "Remember this, Miss Marisa Blake, and remember it well. I hired you because I need a temporary wife. A *wife*—not a fishwife! From now on suffer all you like, but suffer in silence!"

He swung on his heel and slammed out of the room, leaving emotional wreckage behind him, and a stillness that was like the aftermath of a storm.

Marisa, shaking uncontrollably and feeling far more miserable than she would have thought possible, did exactly as he had ordered. She found her way to the private cot and spent nearly an hour and a half in solitary silence, suffering.

CHAPTER TWO

AN IMMENSITY OF BLUE PACIFIC stretched beyond
the window of the plane. For the first ten minutes
of the short flight Marisa had been too preoccupied
with her own turbulent thoughts, and with the dis-
quieting presence of the man beside her, to pay
much attention to the view. But now she turned to it
with some determination, if with less appreciation
than she might have felt under other circumstances.

The period in the waiting room had put things
back in perspective. It *was* only a job, and a highly
paid job at that; and surely as a man of some
standing Antoine de Vigny could be trusted not to
take advantage of an employee. He had always
been good to Roger; Sarah had told her that.
Marisa knew she must make the best of the month
to come, and not let her initial rage and resentment ruin her enjoyment of a part of the world she
had always wanted to see.

"You seem fully recovered now." The voice interrupted Marisa's preoccupation and dragged her
attention back to the interior of the plane, where
those bluer-than-blue eyes lay in wait. "Does that
mean you've accepted the inevitable?"

"I'm trying," Marisa said politely.

"Then you've accepted my apology?"

"I'm trying." That answer was harder; it was said with a decided lack of enthusiasm.

"I suppose I should also apologize for vanishing earlier today when we were on the flight from L.A. Surely now you can guess why."

"I suppose you didn't want me asking questions."

His mouth twitched briefly. "It would have been inconvenient. A crowded jet is hardly the place for a confrontation."

Briefly Marisa's eyes swept the empty seats in the passenger compartment of this compact but comfortable flying boat. "This is a large plane for two passengers," she observed stiltedly, because she did not want to discuss the fight that had taken place in Tahiti.

"True," he agreed, shifting his frame in the passenger seat that appeared too small for his length. "This boat's used for somewhat larger charters normally. In ordinary circumstances I'd be using my own plane for this leg of the trip, but as I've been away it's undergoing an overhaul. I'll pick it up next time I'm in Tahiti."

Since leaving Tahiti Antoine de Vigny had shed his jacket, revealing a short-sleeved white shirt and confirming Marisa's earlier estimate that the breadth of his shoulders and the condition of his physique were not mere tricks of good tailoring. Determinedly she tried to fix her eyes and her mind on something else—anything else but him.

"Don't you have any questions you'd like to ask about Polynesia?" he pressed. "With eyes that color you must have a few curious bones in your body."

She did, but she had not yet forgiven him enough to indulge in easy chatter. "I'll ask my questions later," she said with forced civility.

"Ah, Miss Marisa. Still so aloof? So cool and self-possessed, just as you were when I first saw you in Los Angeles this morning. Doesn't anything ruffle that smooth surface of yours?"

"Very evidently *you* did, this afternoon," she said stiffly, feeling anything but unruffled at this moment. After a day of travel she felt unbathed and weary, and her silk dress was badly creased— and that said nothing of her frayed nerves.

"Ah, but you managed to compose yourself very well by the time Dooey and I returned. Defenses all back in order; butter wouldn't melt in your mouth."

"That's what you wanted, isn't it?"

"Not quite this much," he said dryly. "I don't deny you give a man a perverse desire to shake that cool exterior and see what else he can find. So far I've seen only two sides of you—the smooth side and the abrasive side."

"You make me sound like one of those kitchen sponges," she said stiffly.

"More like a sea anemone," he mocked. "Looks like a flower and stings like a nettle."

"Perhaps in self-defense," she suggested tartly.

He laughed—the first time she had heard him laugh, and it unsettled her all over again. "Not the sea anemone," he said. "It's a voracious predator. It shoots narcotic needles into its prey and devours it alive. Very beautiful and very deadly— to other small sea creatures, at least."

"Surely you're not accusing *me* of those characteristics," Marisa said pointedly.

"Ah, for me the killer clam might suit better." His expression suggested self-derision. "Not nearly as pretty as a sea anemone, and much bigger. Now *that's* a trap for the unwary diver."

Marisa looked at him with some alarm, animosity for the moment forgotten. "Not in the lagoon on your island?"

"Don't worry, there are none on Ta'aroa; they're found mainly in the Indo-Pacific."

"What do they do—eat people?"

"No, just clamp onto a foot or a hand, and virtually nothing will pry them loose, short of severing their very tough muscles. They earned the name 'killer' because sometimes people drown when the tide comes in."

"Very comforting," she said, "when I'm the victim."

"Then perhaps the simile isn't so appropriate after all," he said mockingly, "for unlike the giant clam, I plan to let you go. Now, Miss Marisa, what else would you like to know about the Pacific?"

"Nothing," she said, her voice chilling over as she returned to a detached politeness.

"Such enthusiasm," he noted. "I take it you're not impressed with the Pacific."

Marisa looked down at her hands and tried not to see his. But they remained in view: hard, tanned, capable hands devoid of ornamentation, clasped for the moment around one knee. It seemed boorish to remain so distant when he was making efforts to set her at ease.

"I am impressed," she admitted, glancing upward through thick lashes and trying a not-too-successful smile. "I'm impressed by everything I've seen, but I'm still feeling resentful of the way you tricked me, the way you decided to use me—whether or not I wanted to be used. Oh, I know you're paying me, and I will try not to let my personal feelings get involved anymore. It's only a job, after all. I'll try to start thinking of you as an employer instead of a—a—"

"A scoundrel?" he filled in derisively. "Or a husband?"

"Certainly not husband," she said, escaping his eyes again.

"Certainly yes husband," he disputed, "in every way but one."

The conversation had taken too personal a turn. There was a moment of strained silence, which Marisa broke by changing the topic. Deliberately she switched to French, hoping the change of language would provide a change of mood. The four years of studying in Paris had given her an excellent command of French; in truth, she seldom noticed the transition from one language to another.

"How did you learn to speak English so fluently?" she asked.

"I'm half-American. I was born in the United States and I lived there as a young child."

"I thought your family had always lived on Ta'aroa."

"When my father married my mother, he moved to California for a few years."

"And you've retained your accent ever since childhood?"

"I also attended university in the United States, and that's where I learned to fly."

"I take it your mother is American," Marisa said.

"She was. She's not alive."

"Oh." There was a terseness in Antoine's voice that made Marisa wonder if she had touched on a raw nerve, so she added quietly, "I'm sorry."

"It happened too long ago to be sorry." His face turning to hers was now curtained. "She died when I was ten years old."

"That must have been very difficult for your father."

"It was an unsuccessful marriage," he said expressionlessly. "They were already separated— and my father had custody. By then he had moved back to Ta'aroa."

Marisa decided it was best to abandon that line of questioning and find more neutral territory. "Perhaps you'd better tell me a little about Ta'aroa, as we'll be arriving there soon."

At once he became more genial. "Best place in the world," he assured her. "It's a high island, not one of the low coral atolls you often see in picture books. Ta'aroa has a perfect lagoon—in other words, there's no channel through the coral reef. That means no sharks. It also means that no copra boats can call at the island, which keeps the place relatively untouched by civilization. Even the old vanilla plantation has fallen into disuse now that my father's no longer able to get about."

Marisa looked at him quizzically, but he went on without answering her unspoken question about his father. "There are no cars, no roads, no TV, no telephones—except for the one radio telephone at my father's house. If you want to go anywhere you get there by foot or by outrigger. Mostly we walk."

Marisa's mind still dwelt on the speculations about Antoine's father. Was he possibly in ill health? If so, that would account for his desire to see his son married. It seemed indelicate to ask if a terminal illness was involved, so Marisa put the question a different way.

"Why does your father want you to marry? You said he had good and important reasons. Is it because he's lonely, or wants grandchildren, or—"

She was totally unprepared for the way her employer's face closed over in response to her question. "I don't think you need to know anything about his reasons," he remarked bleakly, "or about mine. Whatever you may have guessed, you're mistaken. He's not dying, and he has no eccentric whim of wanting to see his line perpetuated. You don't need to concern yourself with the reasons for his ultimatum. You'll see very little of my father. He has his wife, and his house is at the other end of the island from mine. Now stop assuming things."

"But I only thought—"

"Don't do any more guessing, Miss Marisa, or you're bound to guess wrong!" Her brief protest had only angered him further, evoking something primitive in his expression. The facial grooves deepened ferociously. "You're an employee, and please remember that family matters are none of your concern. Confine your curiosity to other things. I'm not paying you to pry!"

Chastened, she clamped her mouth over the sharp retort she longed to fling back in his face. That he should accuse her of prying, even as he was sweeping her into a situation she had longed to avoid—*ached* to avoid! Why had she bothered to attempt a normal conversation with the man? He was impossible, impossible, impossible.

Even his next words, spoken a minute later when he had calmed down, did nothing to appease her now.

"I apologize for my tone of voice. You *are* an employee, Marisa, and I don't speak to my employees that way—any of my employees."

She turned politely veiled eyes in his direction. "I didn't intend to pry," she said evenly.

"Good. In that case we'll get along fine. Let's go back several steps in the conversation and start all over again. We were talking about the Pacific."

But Marisa was still simmering inside despite her cool exterior, and could not so easily dismiss the emotion-laden exchange of the past few minutes. "I don't feel like talking at all. I prefer to keep our relationship impersonal," she said indifferently, and returned to contemplation of the window.

An impersonal relationship indeed! She had known him only a matter of hours, and already she knew it would never be possible to have an impersonal relationship with this infuriating and domineering man who sat beside her. She sensed that he was a man who would always command strong emotions—loyalty or love or loathing, but never apathy. Even now, with her face turned away from him, Marisa remained supremely conscious of his nearness—of his overwhelming virility, of the leashed power lurking beneath the surface. *Love him or hate him....*

And because there was no other possible way to feel at this moment in time, Marisa abandoned herself to hatred. The smoky green eyes now cemented to the tiny window hardly saw the untroubled lapis lazuli of the Pacific, for the storms that raged inside. Several minutes passed before she realized that Antoine de Vigny was speaking again.

"I beg your pardon?" She turned to him coolly, as though she had not been envisioning, with relish, the sight of him being blown through an open hatch without benefit of parachute.

"I asked if you would like to see the approach to Ta'aroa from the cockpit. The copilot can come back with me. A break in my own rules, I'm afraid—but, you see, there are advantages to being the boss."

"Yes, I'd like that." For a moment she forgot to be angry with him; her pleasure in his suggestion registered on her face.

"Wait a moment, then." He uncoiled his long limbs and pushed his way to the low door that divided the cockpit from the passenger section of the plane. Moments later he returned, the copilot close behind.

"All arranged," he announced with a nod at Marisa. "But hurry. Ta'aroa is on the horizon now."

Within moments Marisa was strapped into the copilot's seat, all rancor temporarily forgotten. Dooey grinned a friendly welcome at her before returning his attention to the controls.

"Just in time," he exclaimed cheerily, squinting at an empty horizon. "We'll be into the approach soon, and you'd have missed the best view. See it over there?"

Marisa peered into an endless expanse of Pacific broken by nothing but the occasional cloud. "I don't see a thing," she admitted.

"That cloud dead ahead." Dooey nodded at a dazzling low-hanging powder puff of white that clung to the horizon. "That's the Ta'aroa cloud. Always the same—and always there. I'd recognize it even without my charts and instruments, just the way the old-time Polynesian mariners used to. A signpost in the sky! It's the Ta'aroa cloud all right."

"The Ta'aroa cloud?" asked Marisa with some amazement. "You mean it doesn't change?"

"Not much—except at sunset. Then it turns marvelous colors."

"And it stays with the island—it doesn't move along the sky?"

Dooey laughed at her amazement. "Some of the high islands in the Pacific have their own special clouds. A little trick of the trade winds. They press the moisture against the mountains in much the same way day after day after day, month after month after month...." Dooey glanced at Marisa again and grinned. "It's not as maddeningly monotonous as it sounds, unless you're the civilized type. Drives some city folk crazy after a while, always having the coco palms bend in the same direction."

Marisa laughed. "I won't be staying long

enough to lose my wits, thank goodness." She peered intently at the rapidly enlarging cloud and then exclaimed in sudden excitement, "I can see the mountains now!" And indeed, two jagged peaks shimmered suddenly out of the sea and the cloud that had concealed them until this moment.

"And you can see the reef," volunteered Dooey. "Look—that ring of white, like a necklace around the lagoon. The white's not the coral, it's the breakers battering against the reef. From here you can't see the waves, but on the windward side the spume can be quite spectacular."

But it was not the reef that commanded Marisa's attention. It was the color of the lagoon within the white circle. Or rather the colors: for here the Pacific blue changed to greens, brilliant gemstone greens, turquoise and aquamarine and emerald. She blinked, not believing what her eyes were telling her. Surely colors like this did not exist in nature, not on this scale!

"It's not true," she murmured, denying the evidence that lay before her like a silken scarf on the sea—and then she realized that she had not spoken out loud. But the American beside her, having seen reactions like hers before, laughed as though he had heard her unvoiced thoughts.

"It comes on you like that the first time," he said good-naturedly. "Tuan said you were asleep on the approach to Tahiti—that's why he thought you should come up front."

"I did sleep through the landing," she conceded. "And when we took off again I had other things on my mind."

"So I heard," said Dooey with total amiability and no tact whatsoever.

Marisa compressed her lips imperceptibly and turned her attention back to the approach. The island loomed out of the surrounding lagoon, growing closer with every second as the plane lost altitude. Individual coco palms were visible now, their fronds dipping to the invisible command of the wind. At the edge of the island a ring of sand shelved into the sea—not the black volcanic sand of Tahiti, but an unbelievable sunlit sand, whiter than white, separating the darker greens of the island from the jeweled greens of the lagoon. On the beach a collection of small human specks, brightly clad and brown skinned, waved excitedly at the plane's approach; Marisa could see several outrigger canoes being readied at the water's edge.

The plane barely skimmed the water's surface, bounced once lightly and knifed smoothly into the still lagoon. It taxied, losing speed rapidly. Suddenly Dooey cut one engine and the plane swerved around neatly in a one-hundred-and-eighty-degree turn, ready for takeoff. Then the other engine, too, was killed, and the plane shuddered to a halt.

"Welcome to Ta'aroa," grinned Dooey. "Grand place for a honeymoon, isn't it? Even a fake honeymoon."

"Do you come here often?" asked Marisa,

evading the direct response as she released her seat
buckle.

"I've been coming twice a week since the big
shake-up," he said cheerfully, without explaining
himself. "Somebody has to bring supplies and
mail, and it's months since Tuan's been on
Ta'aroa. Of course, in the old days when he used
to commute from here every day, he'd be doing it
himself."

Marisa struggled unsuccessfully with speculations about what might have kept Antoine de
Vigny away from his own home, while Dooey
went on with a blithe disregard for her silence.
"Sweet little machine Tuan's got, but on a flight
like this he'd usually come and take over this big
crate, just to keep his hand in. Today he declined.
I suppose he felt he had to keep you calmed down
for the wedding today—sorry, did I say something
wrong?"

Today! Oh, Lord, another shock for the
system. How many more nasty surprises did her
employer have in store? She had realized that the
ceremony must take place soon—very soon. But
she had expected some short respite, some time to
gather her thoughts and look over the situation in
Ta'aroa. But today!

"Dammit, I know I was born with my foot in
my mouth," cursed Dooey, "but this time I can't
think what I said wrong."

"I didn't know it was to be so soon, that's all."
Marisa regained her poise. "I certainly didn't

think it would be today, when it's already late afternoon.''

"Typical of Tuan," said Dooey in a wry tone of voice. "He has a way of not telling things unless he thinks people have a need to know. You'll get used to it! Now come along, for I'm to be best man and I have to get back to Tahiti before dark.''

By the time they reached the passenger compartment Antoine de Vigny was leaning out the hatch, enthusiastically hailing a handsome and sturdy-shouldered Polynesian man who had pulled the lead canoe alongside. Half a dozen outriggers, patched sails lowered, hovered on the lightly ruffled waters beyond.

"Ha, Lotu!" cried Antoine.

"Tuan! *'Ia ora na!*" The man Lotu grinned, his teeth ivory white in the dark café-au-lait face. After the Tahitian welcome, he switched easily to French. "Too long you stay away, Tuan! The parrot fish in the lagoon, they recognize your shadow—they are nervous already! See how they dart about! They know we go spearfishing soon, hey?''

"Soon enough, Lotu!" Exuberantly Antoine tossed a suitcase across to the fine-looking young Polynesian. Then, sobering on the instant as though he had just remembered why he was there, he turned and gripped Marisa's elbow to help her from the plane. His voice became guarded. "We'll go spearfishing—but not today. Today is my wedding day, Lotu.''

"So we have heard, yesterday, from the radio! And your *vahine*, you have brought her...?"

"This is Marisa *vahine*, Lotu." Antoine gave her a helping hand into the bobbing outrigger. "Marisa, Lotu is my good friend."

Ashore, whoops of pleasure greeted the small party of arrivals. Still half-numb from the impetuous sweep of events, Marisa watched for the most part in silence, murmuring only in answer to introductions. Someone dropped a garland of flowers—or, as the Tahitians called it, a *hei*—over her shoulders; and she saw a similar garland being draped over Antoine's neck.

With one part of her mind, in the confusion of excited chatter in French and Tahitian, Marisa noted the handsomeness of the people who had gathered on the beach. Unlike some of the Tahitians she had seen on the short stop in Papeete, most of the islanders here seemed to have a full complement of teeth; they flashed whitely against skin the color of oiled mahogany, visible evidence of a diet as yet unspoiled by bully beef and biscuit. Of the skin, too, there was a lot more in evidence than in Faaa Airport. Most of the islanders, men as well as women, were clad in the garments known as pareus, or colorful saronglike squares of cotton—some still store-bright, some grown mellow with sun and many washings in seawater. After a moment or two Marisa recovered from the initial jolt of seeing that most of the younger women, or *vahines*, wore the pareu casually draped over the hip, as did the men. The baring of breasts seemed to bother neither owners nor on-lookers, Marisa reminded herself firmly, so why should it bother her?

Of any man who might be Antoine's father, there was no sign. Nor from here was there any sign of the house he might occupy—or, for that matter, the house that might be Antoine's. From this part of the beach Marisa could see only a village of tiny palm-thatched huts, nestled sleepily into the shelter of the valley between the two mountains and half-hidden by a stand of banyan trees.

But now she had no more time to take in her surroundings. There was a stirring at the edges of the crowd, and the islanders fell back in a deferential manner to allow something—or someone—to pass.

The incongruous vision that now appeared on the scene consisted of four litter bearers with a burden that must have strained even the muscular shoulders of the young Polynesian men at the handles. Sitting on the litter was a woman of enormous bulk, clad in a voluminous Mother Hubbard dress of flamboyant calico. The woman's imperious brown moon of a face and the regality of her bearing suggested that she must be a person of importance on the island. As the litter bearers came to a halt, she rolled off the litter with a surprising agility and came forward to meet Marisa. Antoine performed introductions with great cere-

mony, then added a brief explanation in English
for Marisa's benefit alone.

"Uma is the queen bee of the island," he
told Marisa. "Direct descendant of Polynesian
royalty—you can tell by her size. In this part
of the world it's considered a mark of distinction. She has no real power, but to tell the
truth, all the other islanders are a little afraid
of her; you can see by the way they kowtow. Uma
laps it up. She expects her word to be taken
as law." He smiled directly at Uma and added
conversationally, knowing he would not be
understood, "Terrible old tyrant, to tell the
truth."

Throughout this Uma nodded and beamed, as if
fully comprehending that her preeminent role in
island affairs must be properly explained.

"*'Ia ora na,*" Uma said to Marisa with great
graciousness, and then switched from Tahitian to
French. "I welcome you. My island welcomes
you. My islanders welcome you." Uma made a
sweeping gesture at the assembled group standing
at a respectful distance, and Marisa wondered
with a glimmer of amusement whether she did not
consider them all her subjects.

"And my daughter welcomes you," Uma went
on, as her ponderous arm made a peremptory
beckoning gesture. "Maeva! Come."

At once a very pretty Tahitian girl, slender of
limb despite an advanced state of pregnancy, detached herself from the throng of islanders and

moved forward. She was a full head shorter than her imposing mother.

"Maeva will be your friend," Uma declared to Marisa, and then turned to Antoine. "You have asked, Tuan *tane*, that someone help your bride for a time, to teach her the manner of preparing food. I have decided it shall by my daughter."

Marisa glanced swiftly at Maeva's swollen stomach and started to demur. "Surely Maeva won't want to—"

"It is decided!" stated Uma autocratically, with a commanding flourish that suggested in part why the islanders deferred to her. "Until my granddaughter is born, Maeva has little to do."

Now Maeva spoke for the first time. "I am very willing," she agreed pleasantly in soft and excellent French. "It is my own idea, too. I have asked if I may help you."

Marisa smiled warmly, liking the look of the young girl with her square pretty face and her long flow of black hair. Maeva appeared to be no more than seventeen or eighteen; undoubtedly marriage and motherhood came early on the island.

"That's very good of you, Maeva," Marisa said, deciding not to argue the point in Uma's presence.

Uma looked pleased with the good impression her daughter had evidently made. Her face ballooned into a grin and she rubbed her astonishing stomach in a gesture indicating satisfaction. "It is well," she nodded, then summoned her litter bearers with a lordly wave, causing ripples of reaction to run through the folds of flesh on her arm. "Now I shall depart. You will follow."

"She could walk perfectly well," murmured Antoine for Marisa's ears alone as Uma's gargantuan bulk was restored to its perch. "But she enjoys being carried too much to try. Wonderful old despot—thinks she's living in another century."

Marisa turned to Maeva as soon as Uma had departed. "You say it's your own idea to help me, Maeva. Are you sure?"

"Yes, for I wish to learn the English," Maeva said eagerly. "Now I speak only a little pidgin. Like this: this one *vahine* b'long Lotu. This you understand?"

"Yes, I understand," Marisa replied in careful English, returning the compliment of Maeva's attempt. So this was Lotu's wife as well as Uma's daughter—and Lotu was Antoine's friend. Perhaps it would be good to have Maeva's companionship for a short time, until she learned the customs of the island. She switched back to French. "I hope you will also teach me some words in Tahitian."

"Mais certainement," Maeva agreed promptly, her brown face wreathing in pleasure. "Then we will be teaching each other, *non*?"

During this exchange Antoine called for several young boys by name and dispatched Marisa's suitcases and his own large flight bag toward some unknown destination, presumably his own home.

It seemed they themselves were to go in the opposite direction, following the departed litter.

"Come along, Marisa. My father will be waiting." With one firm hand tucked beneath Marisa's elbow, he guided her away from the colorful gathering of islanders.

Longingly Marisa looked over her shoulder at the fast-vanishing luggage. "Can't I go and freshen up first? I'd really like to change."

"You freshened up in Papeete hardly more than an hour ago," he answered offhandedly. "And does it matter what you're wearing? This isn't exactly a proper wedding with all the trimmings." And without further ado he set off along the beach in the wake of Uma's incongruous conveyance. Having no choice in the matter, Marisa hurried to keep up with him with the distinct feeling that she was racing headlong into disaster.

Dooey, together with Maeva and Lotu and an ill-assorted group of children and yapping dogs, followed some distance behind; and this small strange procession moved in a northerly direction along the sparkling white rim of the island.

Without breaking his pace, Antoine pointed to a spit of land farther along the beach. "You can't see my father's house for the way the shoreline curves, Marisa, but it's less than a mile away."

"It looks more like two," panted Marisa, breathless from the effort of keeping up with his long stride. Her high heels dug holes in the soft sand, destroying her balance and making every step an adventure in itself. "Why didn't we land closer to it?"

"The plane can't land in that part of the lagoon." Antoine came to a halt and glanced impatiently at her precariously shod feet. "Ridiculous gear! Take them off."

"I...." How she longed to refuse that authoritarian tone! But one glance told her that the sand was ruining the creamy leather. And so, inordinately resentful that he had been right, she slipped her feet out of the impractical footwear and followed as he resumed his loping walk. The warm sand tingled at her stockinged feet. Progress was somewhat easier now, even when a small dog, risking collision, darted in front of her, closely followed by a near-naked child. Close by, coco palms bent their fronds to the warm prevailing breeze; but here there was no shade, and Marisa felt the fabric of her dress clinging damply to her spine with the effort of keeping up.

And that forceful stranger who was responsible for all this, who was sweeping her along with no regard for her wishes, how dared he look so cool, so composed, so virile, so at home! In these exotic surroundings, even the *hei* of scarlet hibiscus that hung around his neck seemed quite in keeping with the man. No wonder everyone called him Tuan! A primitive name for a primitive man, the type of man who saw what he wanted and let nothing stand in his way...yes, it suited him very well.

"You might have told me a little more about the

wedding plans," she said tightly, venting some of her resentment. "You didn't even tell me when it was to be."

"As soon as we reach my father's house," he informed her somewhat belatedly. "Does it matter? It seemed like an unimportant detail."

Marisa glared at him, speechless for a moment. Moisture trickled down the nape of her neck and vanished into the folds of her dress. She slowed her stride.

"It may seem unimportant to you," she flared, "but I don't make an everyday practice of getting married."

"Neither do I," he said with a momentary tightening of the mouth. "Didn't I tell you I've always avoided it? Now move along, Marisa, or else pretend a little affection. The others are close behind. Dooey may know the truth, but Maeva and Lotu don't. They'll be upset if they see you looking at me like that. You give every appearance of hating me with every bone in your pretty little body."

"Appearances don't always lie," she retorted.

He glanced at her with distinct distaste. "I can stand a lot, but there's one thing I can't stand, and that's a poison-tongued female. I warn you, Miss Marisa, it brings out the worst in me."

"Is there anything best in you?" she stung back.

"Oh, for God's sake," he muttered. His hand shot out, and he grasped her elbow with something that might pass for a caress to the casual observer. But Marisa, submitting to his touch, could feel the fury in his fingers with every jangled nerve ending and every one of those bones he had just talked about.

And then, from behind a fringe of coco palms and the concealing curve of the beach, a bungalow came into view. It was a low, cool, tree-shaded bungalow surrounded by a jewel-green lawn where Uma's litter bearers were even now depositing their unwieldy burden. From the distance Marisa could see another woman, a graceful pareu-clad islander, greeting the imposing tyrant and settling her onto a sturdy chaise longue capable of supporting such a ponderous weight. That accomplished and the litter bearers dismissed, the younger woman turned toward Antoine and Marisa and came across the grass.

And Marisa took her first full look at the most beautiful woman she had ever seen in her life.

CHAPTER THREE

"Tania!" Antoine walked forward swiftly while Marisa slipped into her discarded shoes.

"Tuan! How good to see you. *'Ia ora na!*" Across the clipped emerald sweep of lawn, the woman Tania moved with a fine-boned grace that made every movement seem like poetry. Her skin, her costume and her long lustrous hair proclaimed at once that she was at least part Polynesian. But there was some other racial characteristic, something in the great melting eyes and the way the bones seemed to flow beneath her pareu, an air of fragility and complexity that set her apart from the squarely handsome, forthright women on the beach. Marisa, trying to place this elusive characteristic, was reminded of something Oriental, perhaps a Balinese dancer.

Despite the cordiality of Tania's greeting, there was a marked reserve in her manner toward Antoine, suggesting that their relationship was uncomfortable. But when she turned to Marisa, a smile warmed her brown eyes, and her voice, in educated French, was as liquid as her limbs. "And you must be Tuan's bride. Welcome to Ta'aroa."

Antoine put his arm around Marisa's shoulder
with a reasonable pretense of affection. "Tania,
this is Marisa Blake. Marisa, this is my stepmother."

Try as she might, Marisa could not conceal the
flicker of surprise in her eyes as she acknowledged
the introduction.

Tania laughed, a low quicksilver note. "And soon
to be your mother-in-law! Did Tuan not explain?
How like a de Vigny! Tuan, you are fast becoming
as impossible as—" Tania paused to brush some in-
sect, imaginary or otherwise, from her shoulder.
When she looked up again, her expression was
bland. "You must not run roughshod over your
new wife, Tuan. Why didn't you tell her about me?"

"Why should I tell her and spoil the pleasure? I
knew she would be delighted to discover that she
had a mother-in-law not a dozen years older than
herself, and one with an education similar to her
own." He turned to Marisa by way of explanation. "Tania studied at the Sorbonne, Marisa."

"Perhaps it's not my age that surprises
Marisa," murmured Tania thoughtfully. "But I
suppose that wouldn't occur to you, Tuan! Now
go along and leave Marisa to me. Your father
heard the plane arrive and is beside himself with
impatience. He's in his study."

"How has he been?"

"Full of sound and fury, as always! Today, of
course, is harder for him—so do try not to upset
him. And by the way, Tuan, happy birthday."

So today was Antoine's thirty-fifth birthday!
He had been closemouthed about that, as about
everything. At last Marisa realized the reason for
his haste. Today was the last day to meet his
father's ultimatum.

Tania went on, "Above all, he's anxious to
meet your bride. But that can wait a few moments.
Marisa will want to freshen up, and she must be
exhausted. Now go!" She shooed Antoine toward
the house and turned to greet Dooey and the
others who were coming along the beach at a more
laggardly pace. Children and dogs, having followed as far as they dared, had already vanished.

In moments a white-clad Chinese servant appeared with *citron pressé*. Uma watched as if
holding court while Tania settled the newcomers
into lawn chairs.

"Except you, Marisa! I want to take you inside.
I'll be with you in a moment."

Marisa was glad of the opportunity, with Tania
occupied elsewhere, to look around and collect her
wits. Near the small group of people on the lawn,
the bungalow stood, or rather spread, amid a
grove of fragrant fruit and flower trees—man-
goes, papaya, frangipani burdened with flamboyant blossoms. In truth, the bungalow was not
one building but several, each with a low thatch of
pandanus leaves. Tidy coral paths, dappled with
sun and shade, connected the buildings.

Antoine had vanished into the largest and closest of the structures, which, unlike the others, had

a wide veranda and a railing adorned with small
curiously carved wooden figures. Marisa edged
closer, sipping the icy lemon. In books on the
Pacific she had seen many pictures of tikis; she had
seen the real thing only in museums, under glass.

"They represent Polynesian gods." Tania,
having finished with the others, had come up
soundlessly behind Marisa. "Or rather, they *are*
Polynesian gods. Some people would say that the
wood is still living, like flesh and blood."

"I was wondering if they were authentic."
Marisa turned, her face animating in response to
Tania's interest.

"Oh, absolutely, quite the genuine thing,
although I don't believe in them myself. Perhaps I
have too much Malayan blood—or Chinese."

So that was Tania's heritage. Mixed, like that of
so many people on the islands. Marisa longed to
ask more questions, but already Tania had started
up the veranda stairs.

"Come along, Marisa; I'll take you inside. You
haven't been ashore more than half an hour, and
that means Tuan didn't even give you a chance to
comb your hair. Just like his father! Perhaps for
you marriage to a de Vigny will be worth the ag-
gravation, *n'est-ce pas*?"

Inside it was blessedly cool. The house was
designed to admit the prevailing breeze, and in
spite of lowered bamboo shades it gave an impression of air and light. Marisa followed her hostess
to a pleasant bedroom.

"Now," said Tania in a voice that was firm for
all its soft music, "I shall lend you a robe and take
you to the bathhouse. Yes, it's a separate house,
and so is the cookhouse! We're lucky on this
island; there's plenty of rainwater for bathing."

Marisa looked at Tania with dubious gratitude.
"But Antoine said we were to be married as soon
as we arrived. He'll be waiting—"

"Pouff! Let him wait. No woman should have
to get married after ten hours of travel! How
extraordinary that Tuan should think it possible.
The *misi*, too—the preacher—he will have to
wait."

"The preacher?" For the first time it occurred
hazily to Marisa that she had as yet seen no person
who might be qualified to perform the ceremony.
Perhaps he was in the study with the two de Vigny
men?

"Yes." Tania was looking at Marisa in a peculiar way. "Did Tuan not tell you? Yet his secretary
arranged all the details from Los Angeles yesterday. There is no preacher on Ta'aroa, and the one
on the nearest island was unable to come—a previous commitment, it seems. You are to be married by radiotelephone."

At Marisa's look of astonishment, Tania
laughed. "These de Vigny men, they have a way
of keeping things to themselves! To be married by
radiotelephone is not unheard-of in this part of
the world, with so few islands sprinkled over so
many million square miles of sea. A little unusual,

perhaps, but then everything about this wedding seems to be a little unusual. Not least that we learned only yesterday that there was to be a wedding—when Tuan's secretary sent a message.''

An unusual wedding! It was as well, thought Marisa, that no one on Ta'aroa knew how unusual.

LATER MARISA COULD HARDLY CREDIT the fact that she had indeed been married; that the ceremony that had taken place meant anything. Unusual? It had certainly been all of that. *Extraordinary* would be a better word!

Upon Marisa's return from the bathhouse she had found her dress laid across the bed, freshly pressed, its travel-worn look miraculously vanished. Bless Tania! There had also been a pareu of particularly fine and clinging silk, a soft sliver of cloth in deep jeweled blues and greens. Tania herself had arrived moments later to show Marisa how to use the garment, should she so desire.

''That's very good of you, Tania. But you see, I'm already dressed—and I'm afraid I'd feel far too self-conscious wearing no more than a square of cloth. Today has been quite difficult enough without adding worries that my dress might drop off.''

''Nonsense!'' Tania seemed amused. ''The pareu is quite safe if you tuck it together properly. I'll show you later. You can keep this one, and practice. It will look wonderful with your eyes.''

"Thank you. And I will wear it—sometime."

"We'll have to hurry now, Marisa. Tuan is getting terribly impatient. He told the preacher to stand by the radiotelephone at five o'clock, and that's half an hour ago. And Alain—Antoine's father—wants to meet you before the ceremony."

Alain de Vigny was waiting in the study, standing behind his desk and leaning on it with his hands propped on its cluttered surface. He was a tall man, more austere in appearance than his son, but with the same bone structure; the same grooves in his cheeks, grown more pronounced with age; the same blue eyes. Surprisingly, for a man who had lived in the tropics for most of his life, his skin was unsunned. Yet his shoulders and his arms suggested that he was in superb condition for his age. With no more than a distinguished streak of gray at his temples, he looked amazingly youthful for a man who must be at least sixty.

Antoine performed introductions, and Alain de Vigny inclined his head in a courtly gesture. Strangely, he did not move forward from his desk to take Marisa's proferred hand. "Welcome to the de Vigny family, *mademoiselle*," he said with a small distant smile. "I see Tuan has not lost his good taste. He always had an eye for—for a pretty woman."

"Thank you." Marisa skimmed a glance at Antoine and wondered what made his jaw tighten momentarily. "I'm flattered that you think I qualify, Monsieur de Vigny."

"Please call me Alain. And you must do more than qualify in Tuan's opinion, or he would not have chosen to—chosen you."

"I—" But Marisa stopped suddenly, belatedly aware that the elder de Vigny had not even been looking at her as he spoke. With a shock she realized that, despite his wish for his son to marry, despite his declared desire to meet the bride, despite the polite flattery of his words, Alain de Vigny was utterly indifferent to her. His gaze was directed to something or someone beyond Marisa's shoulder—Tania, perhaps—and there was something strange in his expression, some emotion fierce yet guarded.

But if there were uncomfortable undercurrents in the room, Antoine chose at that moment to ignore them. His voice betrayed impatience. "Shall we go? Surely the amenities can wait. I haven't flown four thousand miles to miss my own wedding."

"Of course," said Alain de Vigny stiffly, and lifted one hand from the desk. Then he halted. Marisa became more than ever aware of that strained air, that bond of tension that seemed to stretch from Alain de Vigny over toward the doorway where Tania still stood, a soft brown shadow.

Now for the first time Antoine's father swerved totally away from the desk where he had been leaning, and spoke to his wife in a savage voice. "For God's sake, Tania, why are you standing about? Go and see that the others are all waiting in the radio hut. Make yourself useful!"

Marisa had the distinct impression that had Tania been of paler complexion she would have blanched. The dark heavy lashes dropped. Had there been a glimmer of resentment there, or hurt? Marisa was not sure, and as Tania left the room it was impossible to tell what that reaction had been. Her eyes were like deep brown pools with a still surface.

Obeying some instinctive impulse, Marisa started to follow her hostess from the room; but strong fingers captured her wrist.

"You'll wait for me," said Antoine quietly. His face was impassive. If the strange exchange had disturbed him in any way, he took care not to show it. He turned to wait for his father without releasing Marisa.

And now, for the first time, Marisa began to understand, in part at least, the reason for Alain de Vigny's peculiar behavior. His hands left the support of the desk, and he started to move toward the door. It was a progress that was painful to watch. His left leg appeared to be quite normal, but his right leg dragged badly and on alternate steps seemed barely capable of supporting the tall strong body above it. It was a caricature of a walk, slow, awkward, lacking in dignity; the walk of a wounded animal.

Marisa noticed a walking cane leaning against the wall, half-hidden by the door, and wondered why Antoine did not hand it to his father. She glanced at him, the unspoken question in her eyes.

But Antoine appeared to ignore her, just as his father ignored the cane when he passed it a few painful moments later.

Slowly they made their way out of the main bungalow and along the coral path to the radio hut. Questions gnawed at Marisa's mind. Why had Antoine not told her more about his family? Why, on the flight from Tahiti, had he not warned her about Alain de Vigny's disability? About Tania? About *anything*?

And what were the strange undercurrents she had sensed—in Alain de Vigny, in Tania, in Antoine himself? Why had Antoine's father, so obviously crippled, scorned the cane—and why had he been angry with his wife? Why had he been so insistent that his son marry—and so disinterested in *whom* he might marry?

And, merciful heaven, what was she, Marisa, doing in the midst of all this? With a very real feeling that she had opened the original Pandora's box, Marisa entered the small and already overcrowded radio hut.

"Dearly beloved, we are gathered together...."

Nine people, including a woman of enormous bulk and the Chinese-Tahitian thumbing the console dials, in a thatched radio hut designed to hold three or four comfortably; and the tenth, a disembodied voice that came from some island perhaps a hundred miles away across the Pacific. Bamboo shades raised to encourage any extra wisps of breeze, and coco palm fronds stirring at the edge of vision. A mongrel yapping in the distance, and birds screeching and chattering not a dozen feet away. The smell of salt from the sea and vanilla from the land, mingling and bittersweet... tiny impressions, each graven in Marisa's memory, along with the sand-scuffed toes of her very best shoes, mocking the solemnity of the occasion. Somehow that seemed to symbolize everything, all that happened to her in the past few hours, all the disruption of her existence. And overshadowing everything else in the room, this thing she was about to do, this overwhelming man she was about to marry, a man she had met mere hours before....

"I, Antoine, take thee, Marisa."

A shaky awareness of the steely sun-browned fingers that gripped her own; of the hard-edged voice that had told her, so short a time ago, that she had no right to take an interest in his personal life. And now was promising to have and to hold, to love and to cherish....

"I, Marisa, take thee, Antoine."

The unreality of her own voice, as calm as though the words were not a bitter mockery, a lie, an affront to everything she had ever believed about the joining of two people together; as though they were, for better or for worse, the truth.

"... let no man put asunder."

Crackle, blur, static, fade....

Inevitably during the ceremony Marisa had been overpoweringly conscious of the man whose lips now brushed hers, the man who was now her husband, the man with whom she would soon share a roof—even though they would not share a room.

But with some other part of her mind, in the cramped hut, she had also become aware of the fact that there was one pair of eyes that had been directed not once at the bride and groom; one pair of eyes that might have been seeing a different ceremony altogether; one pair of eyes that never left the slender brown pareu-clad woman that was his wife. Alain de Vigny had moved only inches inside the door of the hut, as though unwilling to display his disability in front of the whole assemblage. During the ceremony he had not taken his eyes from Tania. Marisa had the distinct impression that he was remembering the occasion of his own marriage.

Tania invited the guests to join her on the lawn; Uma lumbered out first. Tania followed, and then others began to file through the door of the radio hut. Alone of them all, Alain de Vigny stayed rooted to his position, watching as his wife walked past him into the filtered sunlight. His eyes followed her hungrily where his feet could not.

Alain de Vigny was a man with an obsession.

CHAPTER FOUR

"I DO THINK you might have told me about your father and Tania!" Marisa flung the words at her husband of a few hours like an accusation. *Husband*...could it be true?

Now at last they were alone, and walking toward Antoine's bungalow, which lay, Marisa had been told, about a mile and a half south of his father's. The sun hung mere inches above the horizon; soon it would be night. Moments ago they had passed the beach where they had landed, and the village of nipa huts. Uma and her litter bearers had veered off in that direction, and so had Maeva and Lotu. Dooey, who had been anxious to reach Tahiti before dusk, had taken off in his flying boat some time before.

They had all dined at the home of Antoine's father. Marisa had scarcely tasted the meal for the sick sensation in the pit of her stomach. She could not get over the feeling that she had become a pawn in some twisted game—that her marriage was linked in some odd way to the events she had witnessed this afternoon, not least of all to the strange emotions that warred within Alain de Vigny.

If only Antoine had warned her of what to expect! Yet even now, confronted with the fact of his oversight, he seemed to react with annoyance.

"What on earth are you talking about?" he grated at Marisa.

Marisa glanced sideways and saw a tight warning in the set of her employer's mouth. He had told her not to take an interest in his personal life. Yet how could she help it when, for a time at least, his life had become so interlinked with hers?

"I mean what I say! You could at least have told me about your father."

"He had an accident, that's all. I mentioned that he no longer gets about the island. What else was there to tell?"

"About his leg, for one thing. That he's a cripple."

"He's not a cripple, except in his mind. He's a vigorous, healthy man. He's not yet sixty, and he has a strength that many men of forty would envy."

"Except for his leg!"

"Except for his leg—but he spends a lot of time exercising to keep the rest of his body in condition. Until his accident he could free-dive in the lagoon to a depth of fifty or sixty feet. I'm sure he could still do close to that. His arms and shoulders are stronger than ever."

"You forgot to mention that he doesn't even go swimming now. It's obvious that he hasn't been in the sun for months. Why, he wouldn't even join us on the lawn after the wedding.'' Yet while the wedding group had been assembled on the cool shaded grass, Marisa had been conscious of the slight stirring of bamboo blinds from the bungalow nearby. The suspicion that Alain de Vigny had been watching the party on the lawn had gradually become a certainty in her mind; it was this as much as anything that had spoiled her appetite.

"He joined us for dinner," Antoine pointed out, his long legs setting a grueling pace across the sand.

"He was already in the dining room when we arrived there."

"Is that so odd? He was already in the house. The fact remains that he joined us for the meal."

"He joined *Tania* for the meal. He hardly knew we were there." Marisa looked at Antoine with vexation. How could he be so blind where his father was concerned? "Although I can't see why he's so nasty to her. It's almost as though he were punishing himself, and her."

"Oh, for God's sake, Marisa. Keep your psychoanalysis to yourself! He worships the ground Tania walks on. And she adores him."

"I wonder," said Marisa reflectively, debating whether to risk Antoine's further ire by asking whether relations between himself and his stepmother were strained in any way. But before she had time to pursue the thought, the beach curved to a secluded inlet, and a small, beautifully proportioned bungalow came into view. It was built

over the edge of the water on pilings and connected to the shore by a wide platform like a
bridge. On the lagoon side the low pandanus
thatch extended over a spacious veranda that
would command a breathtaking view of the fast-
approaching sunset. In the stillness of evening, an
inverted mirror image of the building hung in the
turquoise waters of the lagoon. Marisa paused
mid-stride, inexplicably reluctant to move closer.

"Are you coming?" Antoine, too, halted, and
regarded her impatiently. "Surely you're not
waiting to be carried over the doorstep. Now that
we're no longer in public, I see no reason to pretend."

"You don't pretend so very well in public,
either," retorted Marisa, ill at ease for no reason
that she could determine, and unable to express
this except in antagonism. "You spent most of
your time talking to Lotu."

"He's my friend, and I haven't seen him for six
months." His tone told her he considered her
complaint childish. "Besides, you were talking to
Tania. I didn't want to interrupt. Now come
along."

"I was just admiring your home. Do you mind?
I'd like to stand here for a moment."

"I suppose I should be flattered, as I designed it
myself. But frankly, at the moment I'm too damn
tired—and I could use a drink." Irritably he raked
his hand through the dark vital thatch of his hair
and frowned at Marisa. "Well, follow at your

own pace. But remember, in a minute or two the beach will be black as pitch. The moon doesn't rise until later, and it will take your eyes some moments to adjust to the dark.'' And with a long loping stride he took off down the beach and vanished over the small bridge into the bungalow.

Marisa followed at a snail's pace, scuffing at shells with her feet. Before venturing along the beach for a second time she had once more removed her shoes. The white sand still held the heat of the day, and it tingled at her toes. How could it possibly be dark in a minute or two? It was barely twilight even yet. The sun was sinking only now into the limitless blue of the Pacific; the whole world glowed for an instant and then became an intense purple. Remembering Dooey's words earlier, Marisa dragged her eyes away from the ocean and turned to look at the Ta'aroa cloud. It still kept its tenuous hold on the land, wisping at the edges, unchanged in shape, mauve and magnificent. Marisa caught her breath.

And almost before she had time to exhale, she was swallowed in darkness.

She knew a moment of panic. Gradually, as her eyes became accustomed to the night, stars poked holes through the black velvet of the sky. Sanity returned, and she edged her way carefully toward the bridge that led to Antoine's bungalow.

"Marisa? Are you there?" The voice reached out, enfolding her in the night emptiness.

"I'm all right. I'm coming," she returned; but

already he had moved out across the bridge. There was a pale phosphorescence in the lagoon now, and Marisa saw her employer's broad shoulders outlined against it, solid, reassuring, yet somehow alarming in a way that set her pulse beating double time. He moved to within inches of her, the very bulk of him reminding her that she felt fragile and shaky after the events of the day. She hoped he would not touch her. She could not bear it if he touched her.

But he made no move to do so, only standing aside to let her pass and then staying close to see that she worked her way safely across the short span of bridge. Behind her she could hear the clink of ice in a glass; he had indeed made use of his time alone to concoct a drink. The sound of it followed inches behind her back, advertising his nearness like fingers down her spine.

Inside the bungalow it was pitch-black. Marisa hesitated a foot or two inside the entrance, losing touch once again with reality.

"Wait a moment while I find the switch," came Antoine's disembodied voice from somewhere near her. "We have electricity—there's a generator."

"Why didn't you turn it on before? It would have been a lot easier to find my way."

"Because I wanted you to see this."

From behind her Marisa heard the click of a switch. An eerie light bathed the room—not light from above, but light from below. Glowing over

almost half the area of the large room was an
enormous Plexiglas window set into the floor.
Through it underwater lighting illuminated the
lagoon beneath. Marisa gasped. Small gorgeously
colored fish darted with quicksilver suddenness as
their dark world was disturbed, then settled once
more into brilliant immobility.

"Well, Miss Marisa, what do you think of it?"

"I—why, it's beyond description." Marisa
wrenched her eyes away from the fascination of
the world beneath the water. The odd half-light
coming from below carved hills and hollows out
of the face that was at once husband and stranger.
Marisa swallowed, strangely disturbed. "I had no
idea," she said.

"Of course not. That's why I didn't turn on the
lights before. I didn't want to ruin the sight for
you." Now he moved about the room, lithe and
long limbed and silent, flicking other switches. The
sensation that had trickled down Marisa's spine
vanished with the return of more conventional
lighting. He turned to face her, eyes half-derisive.
"What's more, Miss Marisa, I was curious to see
you with your guard down—for once."

Marisa laughed breathlessly, once more in command of herself but still caught up in the pleasure
of the surprise. "Well, for once I'm delighted you
didn't warn me. You do have a way of never telling a body what to expect!" Now she turned happily to take in the rest of the room—the airy rattan
furniture, the warm earth colors, the superb

muted wall hangings. These, she later learned, were made of tapa cloth, the traditional Polynesian fabric beaten from the bark of the mulberry tree and stained with natural dyes in designs centuries old.

"It's all beautiful. I can't tell you how beautiful!"

"Don't try." For once Antoine was looking at her warmly, his eyes feathering into lines of amusement that were less sardonic than the mockery she had earned before. He stood tall and relaxed, his thumbs hooked into the belt at his flat waist. "Well, Miss Marisa, would you like a drink?"

"No, thanks, I'm far too tired for that. I...." Suddenly she became acutely aware of the fact that, other than exits to the outside, there were only two doors leading off the living room. One stood open and evidently led to the kitchen: she could see the gleam of modern appliances and the glow of a dark brown tiled floor. That left only one possibility. One door: one bedroom. And yet he had assured her the sleeping arrangements would cause no problem. Her face fell; she had been sure Antoine would have a larger house.

"I'll be sleeping in the living room," he said nonchalantly as if in answer to her unspoken apprehension. "I'll be quite comfortable on that wicker daybed. But I'll have to keep my clothes in the bedroom. There's no other closet space suitable, and besides, if I left them in here, Maeva

would be sure to notice. Things like that have a
way of getting back to my father.''

As everything seemed to have a way of getting
back to his father.... Marisa frowned, pulled
back to the unpleasant realities of her situation.

"Why do you care what your father thinks?
You've done as he wished now, haven't you—
found yourself a wife? Surely he doesn't take an
interest in your sleeping arrangements!"

"I'm afraid he does," came the cool reply. "I
warned you you'd have to keep up the pretense—
for a month or thereabouts. It's part of what I'm
paying you for.''

Marisa's mouth felt curiously dry. She touched
a tongue to her lips in a gesture that betrayed some
trepidation, although Antoine could not have
known this, for he had turned his back to her and
walked to the wide sliding glass doors that led
onto the dark veranda. There was something in
the tense set of his spine that told her he did not
want to be questioned any further on the subject
of his father. Why *was* he so secretive?

"It seems odd to me," she persisted, "that he
displayed so little interest in his new daughter-in-
law. He didn't ask me a single question all the time
we were there. I got the feeling he didn't much
care *whom* you married.''

"Frankly, I don't suppose he does," said Antoine with studied carelessness, and downed the
rest of his drink at a swallow. When he turned
back to Marisa his eyes were unfriendly again.

"But is it any of your concern? I don't think so."

"Well, I *do* think so. You can't throw me into a den of wolves without some explanation! Why, I felt positively afraid of speaking today, in case I should say the wrong thing."

He frowned. "You're not likely to have an opportunity to say the wrong thing again. I don't suppose you'll be seeing much of anybody but Maeva and Lotu and the other islanders—and me, as I'm on holiday. My father keeps pretty much to himself."

"And how about Tania? Is she supposed to bury herself alive, too?"

"Dammit, Miss Blake, mind your own business. My father doesn't put a leash on her. She's free to come and go as she pleases. If you try to get involved in Tania's life, you're making a mistake." Antoine poured himself another drink, a stiff one, and added rudely, "Why don't you go to bed? You said you were tired."

"Don't change the subject!" Marisa tilted her chin at him aggressively, annoyed by his evasiveness. Did he really expect her to face this next month with no knowledge of what she was letting herself in for? "Your father may not put a leash on Tania, but I noticed the things she was saying to Uma and Maeva. Asking about the village life—what was happening on the island. Why, she can't have seen anyone outside her own household for days."

"That's her business, not yours. So put aside

your idle curiosity.'' A muscle worked in that hard jaw. ''Do I have to remind you again that you weren't hired to take an interest in my family's foibles?''

''I can't help but be curious! And it's not idle curiosity. Your family's foibles have changed my life, for a few weeks at least. There are too many things you haven't explained to me. Why Tania is so cool to you, and you to her. So...polite and distant, as though you were strangers.''

''That's nonsense.''

Marisa felt the growing hostility of his abrasive response, but she could not stop herself now. ''And why she puts up with your father's ill treatment. He's very rude to her. Why, it's as if—''

''Tania is a grown woman,'' Antoine broke in, ''quite capable of taking care of herself. If you meddle you'll only make things worse. I try not to meddle, too. She has to work out her own problems.''

''If you'd tell me a little more, I might enter into the spirit of this charade with some enthusiasm. Why, I might even try to *help* you.''

''I've told you all you need to know. Now drop the subject.''

She disobeyed, stubbornly. ''You haven't told me why your father wanted you to marry, and why you agreed to do as he asked.''

And now she could see the anger building in his face. ''And I don't intend to tell you, either, for you're sure to misunderstand. Our family problems aren't your concern.''

"Why *did* you do as he asked, Antoine?'' Marisa tilted her chin high and swept her pale hair back with one hand. "What sort of a hold does your father have over you?''

"Marisa!'' Forcibly he jammed his glass down on a tiled coffee table and strode across the room until he stood before her like a wrathful god. He gripped her shoulders and shook her once, violently, as though she had been made of straw. "Do I have to tell you again? Don't pry!''

Under his hands she felt curiously limp, and she was unable to drag her eyes away from the face that loomed over hers like a thundercloud. That he had unintentionally admitted to the existence of family problems seemed unimportant now. She was conscious only of the race of her pulse; of the feel of his fingers digging into her flimsy sleeves; of the seclusion of this bungalow lost in the Pacific night. She was also dismayed that she had allowed her emotions to get so involved where she was obviously not wanted—and alarmed at the discovery that she was responding, unwillingly, to Antoine de Vigny's undoubted physical magnetism, to the sheer overwhelming maleness and nearness of him. And she was disturbed to think that he must be able to see the tremble of her lips, and sense the quivering of her flesh beneath his hands.

She moistened her dry lips with a tongue tip. "Please don't touch me. Paying me doesn't give you the right to touch me.'' But despite her words she swayed toward him involuntarily.

For answer his mouth found hers, fiercely. It was a kiss like no other Marisa had ever received, for this was an assault, not an embrace. There was a violence in the mouth that crushed down over hers, hunger or hatred or perhaps some emotion that was a melding of the two. Marisa felt her entire being tingling and turning weak beneath the brutal onslaught that pried her lips apart. His hand rose to tangle in her hair, winding into the silvery curtain to pull her head backward and force her into compliance. His tongue probed deeply with an intimacy and an ardor that grew as she failed to marshal her defenses. For the first few moments of shock she did nothing to resist, not even when he crowded her to a couch and came down over her body, his knees intruding between her legs. The heat and the hardness of his body blanketed her, overwhelmed her, crushed her into a temporary submission.

But then, as some peculiar and unexpected sensations began to surge through her uninitiated flesh, she regained her wits. What was she doing—what was she permitting him to do? During the moments when she had been too stunned to retaliate, his imperative fingers had somehow loosened the top buttons of her silken shirt dress, revealing too much of the smooth swell of her breasts. A hard, sensual, knowing hand intruded there now, too intimately. She wrenched her lips away from

his only to feel his mouth sink urgently onto her
throat. Then, as he slid downward on her body,
lips like fire scorched into the deep curve of her
breasts—the bronze of his face dark against the
pale soft flesh. The well-muscled length of him
pinned her to the couch. Marisa could feel the passion burgeoning in his man's body and, even more
frighteningly, in her own. Something was bloom-
ing deep within her, something that wanted him to
go on, something that turned her limbs to liquid
and made a mock of the feeble protests she had
begun to utter.

"Oh, God." Suddenly, in self-disgust, he freed
her. With another oath he rolled away from her
and flung himself to his feet. He turned his back
to where she lay, perhaps to conceal the rampant
arousal of his body.

For frozen moments Marisa lay shivering with
heart pounding violently and clothing in disorder.
Her wide horrified eyes stared at the tall tense
frame and the angry hunch of his shoulders. What
had she let herself in for? A month of this isola-
tion—a month of lonely star-swept Pacific nights
with a stranger of such vehemence and passion?
Not least of her distress was at her own reaction,
the temporary insanity that had turned her flesh to
butter at the touch of a man she had known for
only hours.

"How could you," she said shakily at last, as
she restored her dress to decency and struggled to
a sitting position.

"How could *you*," he grated savagely. "How could you allow me, encourage me even—"

"*Encourage* you!" Marisa went rigid with disbelief. "Why, how can you say such a thing!"

"Can you pretend you objected too much?" Antoine at last turned to face her, looming tall, the grooves in his face deeply etched with the effort of self-control. "With what I know about you, I would have expected a little more resistance. Thank God I didn't let you drive me over the brink!"

"Drive you—oh, you do twist things!" Now Marisa's fury and frustration equaled his. Her eyes sparkled with tears she refused to shed, turning them bright.

He raked restless fingers through the unruly pelt of his hair in a gesture that conveyed pent-up emotion. "How the hell could I let myself forget that I can't make love to *you*, of all women? Normally I'd see nothing wrong in taking what's offered. But not *you*! I'll be damned if I'll make love to *you*!"

"Offered!" Marisa was stunned. "I offered nothing. I want that annulment as much as you do—more, for this insane pretense of a marriage isn't *my* idea. How can you say I *offered*?"

His mouth twisted into a cruel line. "Oh, I recognize the signs. The tongue touched to the lips, the melting of the limbs, the stirring of the pulses, the trembling of the flesh—do you think I haven't seen those things before? I was angry, yes, but I'd never have kissed you if I hadn't seen all the signs of a woman wanting to be kissed! Good God, I'm not a bloody hermit. I've seen women in that state before.''

Marisa gasped and came to her feet, her entire body trembling with righteous indignation. ''Oh—oh—you're beyond belief! Are you through with insulting me? If so, I'll inform you that I have no intention of joining your—your *harem* of willing women. You don't appeal to me at all—in fact, I dislike you more with every passing minute. Since we met you've never stopped playing the masterful male, all dominance and drive and won't-take-no-for-an-answer. Frankly, I'm fed up with it. Today has been a difficult day, and you caught me with my defenses in disorder. That's why I didn't resist properly. I was too shocked to resist! If you thought I displayed a certain weakness you're quite right—I *am* feeling weak. I'm weak and shaky from too much contact with you, as though you were an infectious disease. A disease I'd rather not have!''

Throughout Marisa's blazing monologue the anger in Antoine de Vigny's face had gradually given way to something else—something smoky and quizzical and tolerant, almost amused.

''Are you trying to tell me in a backhanded way that you're attracted to me?'' Now his eyes gleamed with mockery, a circumstance that only added to Marisa's helpless rage.

''I am not!'' Her eyes changed from smoke to

fire. "I assure you you're not quite as irresistible as you think, no matter how many women may have thrown themselves at your feet—melting limbs, parted lips and all! I'm glad I have our marriage and the prospect of annulment to protect me!"

Suddenly he frowned again. But despite the slashes that briefly framed his mouth, his mood had changed to a milder one, and this time the frown vanished swiftly, "There are better kinds of protection," he suggested with that infuriating droop of eyelids that suggested mockery. "You might try going to bed—alone. It seems to me I suggested that when we first arrived here."

With those words he strode across the room, taking his tall frame to a safer distance. His fingers found a light switch at the bedroom door, and out of the black space beyond, a room materialized. It was an attractive space bathed in cool blues and greens, but for the moment Marisa was far too annoyed to appreciate its charm.

She gathered her handbag and shoes and stalked past him into the haven of the bedroom with all the dignity that bare feet would allow. In the doorway she paused and looked daggers at this disruptive man who for a time at least was her husband, the most exasperating and arrogant man she had ever met. "I hope there's a good stout lock on the door!"

"I'm afraid not. But you can be quite sure I won't come in. I have no wish to—"

"Consummate our so-called marriage?" she finished for him venomously. "Aren't you afraid I might come out in the middle of the night and attack you?"

"You haven't got the right equipment," he replied with a gleam of wry amusement, refusing to rise to this new bait. "Can you throw me my robe? I imagine you'll find it on the back of the door, although as I haven't been here for a while I can't be sure."

"What did you do—move out in too much of a hurry to take your clothes with you? Six months is a long time to stay away from your own home."

That earned a moment of unfriendly silence, but then he controlled himself again. "Just look and see if it's there," he said with exaggerated patience.

Marisa found a black cotton bathrobe and thrust it at him ungraciously. "Wouldn't you like your pajamas, too?" she asked frostily.

"Don't use 'em, normally. I've a brand-new pair for the occasion, though, out here in my flight bag."

She managed to stare at him stonily, despite the unsettling images his words conveyed. "Anything else you need? A blanket? You might find it useful for smothering yourself."

Surprisingly, he greeted her acid words without rancor. "Thanks, no, there are a couple of throws out here—one for over, one for under. In case you're still asleep when Maeva arrives in the

morning, I don't want her to see signs that
I've been bedding down out here. I won't need to
get in there until morning; there are primitive
facilities farther back on the beach—an old privy.
No good for shaving, though. But no doubt you'll
be awake at break of day, after such an early bed-
time.''

"Not early enough for me! I wish the evening
had ended half an hour ago.''

He ignored this new gibe. "You'll find your luggage in the dressing room. The bathroom has all
facilities, including rainwater—after swimming a
freshwater shower is a necessity. Be sparing with
the supply though. The cistern's designed for only
one person's use.''

"You mean you weren't in the habit of bringing
your *mistresses* here?''

He looked at her for a long penetrating moment. Once again signs of anger fretted at his
mouth, the mouth that could be so consuming and
so cruel all at once, the mouth whose memory she
could still feel on her own. His eyes, in the
upward-reflecting light from the lagoon, seemed
to have taken on a mirror sheen, almost like
quicksilver, so that she could see none of the emotions behind them.

At last he said, with a peculiar timbre to his
voice, "No, Miss Marisa. No, I haven't. Ta'aroa
is very special to me. When I come here I want a
home, not a harem. I've never wanted to bring a
woman to this island.''

"Then why did you have to bring me!" she flashed, and closed the door in his face.

And then, drained and trembling with the aftermath of so much emotion, she stood leaning against the doorjamb for several shaky minutes. At last her limbs found strength, and she started to move toward the dressing room.

It was then, from the soft pad of footsteps in the living room beyond, that she became aware of the fact that Antoine had not until now moved away from the other side of the door.

CHAPTER FIVE

AFTER A FULL NIGHT'S REST Marisa was at once wakeful when she heard the sounds of her employer clattering about in the early hours. Despite all the headlong happenings of yesterday—or perhaps because of them—she had slept the sleep of true exhaustion. Last night not even his unexpected vehemence of passion had interfered with her much needed rest. Much as she detested Antoine de Vigny, she had to admit to herself that it had been he who had brought matters to a halt. An annulment was his prime concern; he had made that crystal clear. And so, despite the lack of a lock, she had slept with reasonable certainty that he would not come through the door.

This morning he made no effort whatsoever to be quiet, and she was certain that he was deliberately trying to rouse her, perhaps so that he might obtain fresh clothing from the bedroom. Mulishly she ignored his none-too-subtle hints and burrowed her head in the pillow. Not even the sunlight streaming a striated pattern through the bamboo shade could make her want to face him this morning,

Chauvinistic, thoughtless, cynical, demanding, heartless, unpredictable, overbearing, maddeningly self-sufficient, far too sure of his own sexual attraction.... Marisa exhausted whole catalogs of sins and invented new ones. Even the pillow pressed to her ears could not muffle the infuriating knowledge of him moving about the living room. Annoying, arrogant, autocratic, she stormed silently, until finally she heard her hated employer whistle his way out the front door and along the beach with a cheerful disregard for melody.

The sounds of Maeva, softer and safer, finally brought Marisa out of hiding. A shower of sun-warmed water—sparing, as she had been warned—gave her some confidence to face the day and what it might bring. By the time Marisa emerged clad in a flowered cotton sundress, Maeva had already packed a picnic basket for later in the day and prepared a simple breakfast—papaya and great green oranges, surprisingly ripe inside; sliced fresh pineapple and crisp toast and steaming coffee. Guiltily Marisa watched the pregnant girl as she moved deftly about the kitchen, setting a small table.

"If you show me where everything is, Maeva, I'm sure I could cope with meals—breakfast at least." Then, remembering that this would leave her alone with Antoine in the mornings, she added quickly, "Well, perhaps it's best if you keep coming for a time. But really, I could teach you English without accepting your help."

"Pah! In the day I have nothing to do. Lotu is off pearling and spearfishing with the men. It is only at night that he wishes to be with me. Until Lotu's child is born, there is only Uma to need me during the day."

Marisa hid a brief glint of amusement. Perhaps Maeva's desire to come here, for part of the time at least, had deeper motives than the learning of English. No doubt Uma expected her daughter to dance attendance, as the other Tahitians appeared to do.

"When is your child expected, Maeva?"

The young girl shrugged. "One moon, maybe two? It will be born when it wishes to be born."

"Perhaps you shouldn't be on your feet so much."

Maeva looked at her with such total amazement that Marisa went on quickly, "And if Uma is used to having you around during the day, perhaps she'll miss you if you spend too much time here."

"I do not think so. Often I go and visit all day with my other mother."

"Your other mother?" asked Marisa with some puzzlement, wondering whether Maeva meant godmother or grandmother.

"Yes, the woman in whose belly I grew."

"But...." Marisa's eyes widened slightly. So that accounted for the enormous physical differences between Maeva and Uma; Maeva must be adopted. "Then Uma is not your real mother,"

she said, summing up this new piece of knowledge.

"Of course she is my real mother!" came the
blithe retort. "My other mother gave me to Uma
when I was four years old."

Had Maeva been an unwanted child? Impulses
to pity took root, but Maeva's voice was so
matter-of-fact, so cheerful, that it seemed inappropriate to commiserate.

"Why did your, er, other mother give you to
Uma?"

"Why not?" said Maeva philosophically. "My
other mother had many babies, more than enough
for herself. She is still making babies even now!
And she was sorry for Uma because Uma had no
children of her own. Perhaps you find this hard to
believe?"

"I certainly do," confessed Marisa.

Maeva smiled sympathetically at Marisa's perplexity. "You would not find it hard to believe if
you had seen Uma then. Uma was not so big," she
said, as if that explained everything.

"I don't see what that has to do with it,"
Marisa observed, now totally confused.

Maeva looked at Marisa with distinct pity, as if
she thought her slightly simpleminded. "Because
Uma was not so big, she was not so important
then. Since my father died a few years ago, she has
grown very big. Now there is no longer any reason
to feel sorry for Uma."

Inexplicably, this last thought caused Maeva to

sigh heavily, leaving Marisa with her head in a swirl from what seemed to be a total lack of logic. Conceding defeat for the moment, she changed the subject as she poured herself a second cup of coffee. "At least, Maeva, you could start showing me what to do in the kitchen. One of these mornings you might want to sleep late."

"Sleep late?" Maeva looked incredulous. "On Ta'aroa we rise with the sun. Our nipa huts have no electricity, as this house does. Besides there is much to teach you! Would you know how to husk the coconut? How to prepare *poisson cru* with lime juice and the shredded meat of a coconut, and what to do with taro root? I do not think so. On Ta'aroa we have few of the prepared foods found even on Tahiti. Have you ever sliced an octopus or marinated an eel?"

"Frankly, no!" smiled Marisa. "I'm not sure I want to, either! But breakfast doesn't look that difficult."

"Only because Tuan *tane* has not returned with this morning's catch. After his swim he went fishing at the reef with Lotu."

"Tuan *tane*?" questioned Marisa, unsure of the meaning of the Tahitian word, although she had heard it used yesterday.

"*Tane* means 'mister.' Mister Tuan," explained Maeva. "Such a fine husband he will be! Strong and straight as a tree! You are very lucky, *non*? He will make fine babies."

"Er, I'm sure," mumbled Marisa, digging into the skin of an orange.

"You like babies? Many babies?"

"Of course—three or four, someday. But—"

"You start a baby soon, maybe?"

Marisa ducked her head. "Maybe."

"Right away, hey?" Maeva seemed totally uninhibited in her persistence.

"Ah...." Marisa tried to swallow her embarrassment. It was impossible to take offense. To Maeva the whole matter of babies was as natural as walking and talking, and in her warm brown eyes there was nothing but frank, friendly curiosity. Marisa tried to avoid a direct lie. "I haven't asked Tuan *tane* how he feels about it, Maeva."

"Surely Tuan *tane* will want to make babies with you! For what other reason would a person marry?"

"I'm sure I don't know," said Marisa, hiding a small smile behind the rim of her coffee cup.

"Why don't you ask Tuan *tane*?" came a voice from the living room, and Marisa's coffee cup clattered noisily back onto its saucer. She whirled around, dismayed, in time to see him materialize in the doorway. He had not yet shaven. Stubble shadowed his jaw and gave him the look of a beachcomber, relaxed and rakish and damnably self-assured. A small smile played over his lips.

"How long have you been listening?"

"Only a minute or two." Antoine moved into the kitchen, wearing yesterday's clothes, hair still

damp from the swim. He handed Maeva a catch of
small fish strung on a string, and turned back to
face Marisa. His unnaturally blue eyes contained
more than a glimmer of amusement. "Good
morning—darling."

Marisa bit her lip to restrain the cutting remark she longed to make. With Maeva present
there was little she could do to protest Antoine's
use of the endearment—nor to stop him when he
leaned over for an instant and buried his face
in her hair. He smelled of salt and soap, tangy
and clean; and she hated him for it. He pulled a
chair to the table, ignoring the daggers in her
eyes.

"Forgive me for not waking you this morning,
sweetheart. I thought you would be quite, ah,
worn out after so much lovemaking last night."

Marisa's eyes widened, and she gripped the edge
of the table to steady herself. Maeva giggled,
delighted.

Under lazy lids Antoine watched Marisa's dis-
comfiture while he continued, "You were sleeping
so peacefully I didn't have the heart to disturb
you. Do you know you look like an angel when
you're asleep?"

Maeva was busy gutting the catch at the sink
and had her back turned now, but she was listening with obvious eagerness. Marisa's eyes gleamed
green poison at him, expressing the outrage she
did not dare voice.

"But no more angelic than the way you look

right now, *ma chère*. Perhaps I should not have left your side this morning, after all."

Marisa made a choking noise, signifying fury.

"Speak up, darling." Antoine dug into a plateful of sliced pineapple with obvious relish, but his eyes never left Marisa. "You mustn't be shy, my love, just because I've arrived. Why, you and Maeva were discussing making babies quite naturally a few minutes ago. Why pretend now? You weren't so shy with me last night."

"Oh!" gasped Marisa, unable to restrain herself longer.

"Now don't go all North American on me! You must understand, Miss Marisa, that making babies is a topic of endless fascination in this part of the world. Isn't that so, Maeva?" Maeva nodded pleasurably, and Antoine continued, "Maeva will be delighted to know that you plan a family so soon—and so will the whole village, for that matter. Three or four, I think you said?" He grinned at Marisa wickedly. Beyond his shoulder sounds of approval and merriment came from Maeva as she flipped a fish into hot oil.

"Please, Antoine," Marisa pleaded, weak with desperation yet daring to say nothing Maeva might understand. *"Please."*

"If that's what you've decided on, darling, you don't need to beg." Every bone in his long body proclaimed that he was enjoying himself hugely. "I'm quite willing. I agree with Maeva—I can't think of a better reason to get married than the making of babies."

Marisa's face flamed, and she wished the earth would open and swallow her—or him. "I don't want to talk about this," she said, trying once more.

"Neither do I," he concurred promptly. "Why talk when there are more satisfactory things to do?" With that he turned and spoke a few words in Tahitian to Maeva, who rolled her eyes, patted her swollen stomach and launched into a gale of suppressed giggles. Then swiftly and efficiently she transferred the fish onto white plates and set it on the table.

"Perhaps it's best if Maeva leaves now." Marisa begged him with her eyes. "I can clean up later. There's no need for her to stay."

"Strange, that's just what I suggested myself," replied Antoine with an odd little smile. "Run along, Maeva. We won't need you until this evening." He gestured at her stomach. "And take care of Lotu's baby, hey?"

With Maeva safely out of the way, Marisa at last exploded.

"How *could* you!"

"How could I not? The entire village would have been disappointed if they hadn't heard the outcome of the wedding night." In an obviously expansive mood, Antoine leaned back in his chair and eyed Marisa with satisfaction. He pushed aside his fish plate and lighted a Gauloise. His hair was very nearly dry now, bringing little highlights back to the dark brown. Somehow that irritated her—that springing, healthy hair and the indolent animal grace of that virile body. But it was the blue eyes, the mocking, maddening blue eyes, that annoyed her most of all.

"It was unforgivable!"

"Then forgive me or not as you wish." He shrugged, and his eyes swept her with open appreciation. "At the moment I am rather sorry—not for lying, but because there's a need to lie. You do look very enticing, Miss Marisa, with that injured-maiden expression on your face."

"Whether you were lying or not is unimportant! If you'd been telling the truth I'd have been twice as upset—for *every* reason." Aggrieved, Marisa jabbed at a piece of fish and pretended it was him. "What we do or don't do in bed is hardly a matter of public property!"

"Sorry, Marisa; that's the way it is on this island. I would have warned you before Maeva arrived if you hadn't been dead to the world this morning."

"So *that's* why you were clattering about!"

He tilted a dark eyebrow upward, revealing little paler lines at the edges of his eyes where the sun had not quite reached. "Oh, you heard me, did you? Well, actually it's not. I was hoping you'd wake up so I could get my bathing trunks and my shaving kit. But if I'd seen you I would have told you to expect Maeva's curiosity. Surely you noticed it yourself—she could hardly wait to lead you into a conversation about making babies. If I hadn't arrived she would have become a whole lot more direct in her questions. She'd think nothing of asking you for an opinion of my prowess in bed.''

Marisa gestured angrily. ''In which case I would have told her to mind her own business!''

Antoine's eyes searched her face intently. ''Would you?'' he said, suddenly serious. ''I don't think so. You knew Maeva was not being rude—not by her standards. Tahitians talk about making love as naturally and enthusiastically as they do it. You wouldn't have been unkind, and you wouldn't have disappointed her.''

''All the same—''

''I couldn't disappoint Maeva, either. She would have lost face with the other islanders if she'd gone back with no news.''

''What were you saying to her in Tahitian?'' asked Marisa suspiciously.

''I gave her a good reason to leave, that's all,'' returned Antoine, negligently tapping ash against a saucer. ''I was afraid you were about to lose control.''

''What reason?'' persisted Marisa. ''I don't like to think you were making jokes at my expense!''

His eyes turned evasive as he ground out his cigarette. ''First, Marisa, you have to understand about Polynesia. Things that sound crude in other parts of the world are—well, here they're as natural as breathing. Nothing was said at your expense."

"You told her you wanted to make love to me!" accused Marisa, certain of this although he had not admitted it. Once more, color started to creep above her collar.

"If you want to put it that way," he conceded with an equivocation that told her his words had been considerably more direct. "But I won't have to do it again. Maeva is satisfied that the marriage is certain of success now, as we're in such a hurry to, er, make babies. It was only a little lie, and it made her very happy."

"A *little* lie! I can't think of a bigger one. Why, I don't even want to be alone with you!"

Antoine ran lean brown fingers over the morning stubble that gave him a faintly raffish air, the look of an adventurer. "Why did you suggest Maeva leave, then?" he asked, his deliberate mildness not concealing the mockery beneath.

And to that, because she had no answer, Marisa responded with a stony silence.

IT WAS LATE MORNING before she and her unsettling employer spoke again. Or perhaps, thought Marisa, "crossing swords" would be a better description!

After shaving and changing, Antoine had buried himself with a book in a cushioned rattan chair; Marisa spent some time unpacking the suitcase she had been too distraught to attend to last night. Through all the morning silence she remained conscious of the fact that the islanders were probably all atitter with talk of what was going on here and now in this bedroom. The very thought of it curled her toes.

How could Antoine—how could he, how could he! Yet he had done so many things wrong, in Marisa's view, that this was only the last of a series. She supposed the days to come would prove no easier than the past twenty-four hours had done. Twenty-four hours? It seemed she had known him a lifetime. Already her emotions seemed entangled, in a way she could not quite define, with people she had known for only a fraction of time. Tania, Antoine's father, Antoine himself. In her mind she could sort out none of their relationships, nor her own part in them, if any. Tania...Antoine's father...Antoine. And the woman Yvonne...? Where did she fit in? Yvonne was too much of an unknown quantity, too insubstantial a figure for her part to be guessed. Would Antoine marry her someday when his present marriage was annulled? And if he loved her, why had he not been able to make the decision more easily?

Two hours of thinking on the subject produced all the success of a dog chasing its own tail. Her speculations asked more questions than they answered and left her brain tired and throbbing.

At last, feeling a need to get outside in the sun and air, Marisa changed into her bathing suit. It was a sliver of flamboyant pink, a bikini that had never given her any particular pause in the past, but now seemed decidedly indecent. With gratitude that she had remembered to pack a voluminous white terry beach robe, she found it and covered the indiscreet bathing garment.

She was on her way out the door when Antoine looked up from his book. "I wondered how long you'd hide. Is my company so abhorrent to you?"

"I'd prefer not to answer that question!"

"Where are you going?"

"Where do you think?" Her morning's vexation still sounded in her voice.

"The way you're clutching that beach coat around yourself, I'd have to say you're going for a swim au naturel. I'd swear you don't have a stitch on underneath."

"Guess again!" returned Marisa airily, and with a toss of champagne-colored hair she vanished across the bridge.

In seconds Antoine caught up with her, and his hard fingers curled around her wrist. "Sunbathing or swimming?"

Marisa shook her arm free. "Do you mind not touching me? I wouldn't want to be accused of seducing you! I'm going for a swim."

"I'd prefer you didn't go swimming alone." There was no mockery in his eyes now, only seriousness. "At least, not until you know more about the lagoon."

"I don't believe there's danger out there. I saw

the islanders swimming yesterday.'' Marisa
pushed past him and turned toward the silver strip
of beach away from the village. She had seen this
through the bedroom window and it seemed more
private than the main beach, where there appeared
to be a never ending flux of men, women, children, outriggers and animals. ''You yourself said
there were no sharks.''

''There are other things it's best to avoid.'' He
fell into step beside her, the rhythm of his long
stride easier than hers.

''You, for instance?''

His eyes narrowed dangerously. ''Save your wit
for another time, Miss Marisa, and try using a little wisdom instead. You're a good swimmer, according to my reports, but you're not accustomed
to swimming in the South Pacific, and it would be
just like you to strike out for the reef alone. If you
want to go swimming I'm coming with you.''

''That sounds more dangerous than the reef!''
Her green eyes glinted at him, but the anger in
them was now at least partially feigned. In truth,
she was uneasy about swimming alone in strange
waters. Nevertheless she went on, with more
bravado than she felt, ''I assure you I'll be quite
all right.''

''Today of all days, Marisa, the islanders will
expect us to spend together. And what will you do
if a giant grouper takes a notion to taste your
toes? One of those creatures weighs upward of six
hundred pounds, with a mouth like a medium-

sized cave. One of them swallowed Lotu's swim fins last year.''

Marisa slowed her stride. "Is that true?"

"Why would I lie? Giant groupers aren't vicious, as it happens, just curious—but their curiosity can do a lot of damage. And they're not the only curious inhabitants of this lagoon. Besides, the really fine swimming is out by the reef, where it's best to go by outrigger, and anchor. Otherwise you expend all your energies just getting there.''

Marisa came to a halt. After the events of last night she had vowed to herself that she would avoid this disruptive man, but fate was making mock of her intentions. She looked at him irresolutely.

The warmth of the sun, the texture of sand, the pulse of the surf, the sway of the coco palms, the bittersweet sea smells—they all seemed to be conniving together, these forces of nature, to make refusal impossible. She felt suddenly enervated. And Antoine, his expression for once grave and totally devoid of mockery—he, too, seemed as inevitable as a force of nature. The irresistible force and the immovable object...but it was a battle she no longer wanted to join. She was tired of fighting. It seemed easier to give in; she wanted to give in. And surely a swim would create no trouble. She sighed her acceptance.

"Truce?" he said, asking her to put it in words.

"Yes—truce."

"Wait for me here, then—in the shade of that palm grove. You shouldn't get too much sun all at once."

When Antoine returned some minutes later, it was by outrigger. He jumped ankle-deep into the water, beached the craft and came toward Marisa, sand clinging to wet feet. He had changed into a brief bathing suit, and the sun gleamed bronze on the cording shoulder muscles, on the long powerful tendons of his legs, on the flat waist, on the hard masculine line of his thighs. Hair darkened his chest and, more lightly, his forearms and legs. The bathing suit, patterned in blue and white, molded his figure closely. Marisa fought a compulsion to stare, and dropped her gaze back to the patterns she had been drawing in the sand with a stick.

"I brought the picnic basket Maeva packed." His voice forced her eyes upward. Standing above her, he seemed very tall, very male, a threat to equilibrium. "And I've brought this for you. You can keep it—you'll be needing it."

In his hand he held a man's straw hat, ancient and shapeless, beachcomber style. Without asking her permission he jammed it down at a rakish angle on Marisa's long silky hair.

Ridiculously happy all at once for such a silly reason, Marisa smiled up at him under thick lashes. "Thanks."

Effortlessly he pulled her to her feet. "Most women would ask how it looked on them. Aren't you going to?"

"Of course I am!" She followed him to the outrigger, sparing only a brief surprise for the discovery that all of yesterday's antagonism had so easily ebbed away. "I'm as vain as anyone. How does it look on me?"

"I won't tell you." He grinned at her easily, an even flash of white against tan, and held out a helping hand. "Why should I contribute to your vanity? Now watch your step. Stay away from those fishing spears."

In the belly of the boat, along with the picnic basket, was a miscellaneous collection of gear including swim fins and masks, fishing nets, a pair of binoculars, a spear gun and an old denim-blue shirt of light cotton that was evidently Antoine's.

"Have you ever gone snorkeling before?"

"Once or twice, but never in waters as clear as this," Marisa admitted. "I'm looking forward to some underwater practice out by the reef. What color is the coral?"

"Don't you know me well enough by now to know that I believe in surprises? I won't describe the reef to you." He pushed the outrigger away from the shore, wading behind it, and jumped in limberly as it came free of the sand. "Life without surprises is like the sea without salt."

Marisa, who had been trailing her fingers in a patch of jade lagoon, scooped up a shimmering handful of brine and tasted it. She made a face.

"Don't drink the stuff, for God's sake. It'll give

you a thirst—and I'll have to break out one of my other surprises.''

"Champagne?"

"How did you guess? Maeva thought we might have something to celebrate." He grinned at her, fully at ease, as though in his element. Why did that male arrogance seem less irritating now? His arm muscles rippled under the sun as he worked the paddle lazily and easily. Memories of last night, of the feel of those arms, came unbidden to Marisa's mind. She forced her eyes away from the sight of him and back into safe waters. Beneath the outrigger jade changed to emerald, and emerald slid into turquoise. A school of tiny silver fish appeared, hung in the balance for an instant, changed direction and streaked away as one.

"And we do have something to celebrate," he continued when she did not answer. "At least, I do."

"I can't think of a thing," murmured Marisa to a brightly stippled butterfly fish that happened by.

"Why, the fact that we managed to spend the night under one roof and not in the same bed. If it can be done once, it can be done again."

"Thirty times," she reminded him, still trailing fingers in the clear lagoon. In the sun and the salt-tanged air all desire to join battle had totally evaporated. Marisa was enjoying herself. And surely today, in broad daylight, no trouble would develop!

"Thirty times...." He frowned briefly, then returned to easy amiability. "Ah, I hope we don't have to keep up the charade that long. I don't deny I may spend a few restless nights. I *am* made of flesh and blood, and you're a very attractive woman, Miss Marisa. Damnably attractive."

Marisa glanced upward, not wholly displeased by the compliment. "Then perhaps you'd better get a lock for the door," she suggested.

He smiled easily and with total self-assurance. "If I put a lock on that door, Maeva would be sure to notice when she goes in to use the bathroom. Can't have *that* piece of news getting around the island. Besides, I can resist—when I have a good reason. And I have the very best reason in the world."

The annulment, of course. Yes, an overriding reason. Of *course* no trouble would develop.

MARISA'S HEAD BROKE FREE of the still surface in a shimmer of silver. Her pained lungs gulped air, and with it more salt. She grasped the edge of the outrigger and clung to it, recovering. Half a minute later Antoine emerged some dozen feet away. He stroked toward her, arms knifing the water with a skill born of long practice, and rested in the water, keeping afloat effortlessly with long lazy sweeps of his powerful arms. He pushed his mask upward, and his hair, gleaming from the sea, streamed droplets into his eyes.

"Are you all right, Marisa?"

She smiled between gulps of air, and nodded wordlessly.

"What did you think of the reef? Don't answer until you're able."

For a few moments more she fought to restore her labored breath. At last she gasped, "It's a...a—" now she struggled for a word to describe what she had seen "—a fairyland."

He chuckled, his breathing seemingly undisturbed by the long underwater swim. He used no snorkel, only a mask and fins. "I thought you'd like it. But you stayed down too long for your first try. Now are you sorry you let me bring you to the reef?"

"No." Gradually Marisa's breath began to return, and with it a consciousness of the inadequacy of her bathing suit, and of his, gleaming beneath the water. She covered the intrusive thoughts with words. "The colors...the shapes...those beautiful ferns...."

"They weren't ferns, they were just another kind of coral. And as for the colors—why, sometime I'll bring you out at night, and we'll dive with an underwater lantern."

"It can't be more beautiful!"

"Oh?" He smiled, a nonchalant knowing smile that told Marisa more clearly than words that the reef by night would be indescribably lovely. Yet how could it be lovelier than what she was seeing now, on her second dive, her third, her fourth? The dives were shorter now, more suited to her breath-holding ability, and interspersed with periods of just floating on the surface, breathing through the snorkel and watching Antoine dive down past the steep cliff face of the reef. In this silent and hauntingly beautiful world, time seemed to lose meaning and words seemed to lose significance. Pink, purple, indigo, silver, green—the names seemed too pale to describe the coral castles of the reef; even black became a whole new color. Drifts of many-hued fish floated by, and sunlight, catching on their scales, splintered into rainbows. Giant crayfish scuttled into dark hollows in the coral and waved warnings with great yellow antennae. Exotic open-petaled floral shapes suddenly folded in on themselves and then more slowly unfolded—sea flowers or sea creatures, the distinction seemed unimportant. Fingers of seaweed stirred, beckoning.

At last, exhausted, speechless, shivering from too much salt water and capable of not one more dive, Marisa allowed strong arms to help her back into the outrigger. She had expected him to paddle back to the strip of beach where he had picked her up earlier, but instead he raised the outrigger's curious claw-shaped sail to the breeze and set the craft in a southerly direction. He told her nothing of where he was taking her, and she did not ask. Time, she knew, would tell; Antoine would not.

Fifteen minutes later he beached the craft in a small secluded cove toward the windward side of the island. Despite the stronger breeze, this cove was sheltered by cliffs and coco palms and, on higher ground, a thick banyan stand. Soon they were sitting on hot sand behind a windbreak of trees, picnic basket between them.

Marisa, now more than amply covered by her beach coat, unpacked cold cooked pork and chicken, fresh fruit, a loaf of crusty French bread. She laid it all on an improvised tablecloth of over-sized leaves, while Antoine busied himself with the champagne cork.

It was a companionable meal. The things that had passed between them yesterday seemed for the moment forgotten in shared food and shared wine and shared remembrance of the reef. At last, hunger and thirst slaked, they cleaned up the picnic leavings. Then Antoine heaved a sigh of satisfaction and lay back on the warm sand with arms folded behind his head. Marisa remained sitting with her arms huddled over her knees, and tried not to pay attention to the long near-bare body beside her.

"Why don't you take off that beach coat? You look far too hot." His lazy inflections told her that his eyes were still open and upon her.

"I'm not hot," she lied. In truth, sun and food and champagne had done their work only too well. Warmth and languor prickled the surface of her skin.

"Coward," he said softly.

"I don't know what you mean," she lied again, pushing her toes into silty white sand. Not two feet away the blue-and-white bathing suit rolled onto one hip, facing her.

"Are you afraid of me, Miss Marisa?"

"A little." Another lie. . . or perhaps just an understatement.

"Do you know there's not a soul within two miles of here?"

She formed an "oh" with her mouth, but no sound emerged. Something was stuck in her throat, possibly her heart.

"Anything could happen in a place like this, Marisa."

Still no answer: but her head ducked down farther, hiding the curve of her cheek with a long tangle of hair. Her heart hammered.

"And that's why I brought you here today. To prove to myself that anything *can't* happen." The palm of his hand smoothed the sand that lay in the space between them. "You got under my skin yesterday, Miss Marisa. God knows why—I usually display somewhat more self-control than I showed last night. When I brought you to Ta'aroa I vowed to keep hands off. For your sake and for mine—or something would happen that we'd both regret."

Now his fingers poked indentations in the sand. "Well, I'm damned if I'll let you get under my skin again—and one way to make sure you don't is to make friends with you. There's been too much fighting between us; that's the problem. If we have to share a house for three weeks—or four—we can't keep fighting. Sooner or later some argument would end up in bed.''

He paused for a time, assessing the reaction she was trying to hide, but the curtain of her hair protected her. At length he finished, ''Friends?''

''Yes,'' she returned in a strained voice, unaccountably disappointed. And why? She wanted to fight no more.

''Good.'' He rolled away again. Once more he was lying on his back, long legs crossed, one thumb notched into the narrow line of his bathing suit. ''I don't deny it would be nice to make love to you, Miss Marisa, under other circumstances. But life has enough complications. I don't want making love to you to be one of them.''

''No,'' came the low reply in agreement.

''I'm sorry for the things I said last night. As we're to be friends I'll admit I was angry with myself, not with you.''

She nodded a wordless acknowledgment and wished she had not noticed the way the crisp forest of his chest diminished downward to his waist and below, then disappeared in a fine line beneath the brief bathing trunks.

''This is going to be a rocky friendship if it's all one-sided,'' he remarked sardonically. ''Say something, Miss Marisa.''

She forced the words, ''What would you like me to say?''

''Anything.'' His hand, resting on the flat of his stomach, moved upward and lodged idly against the dark tangle of his chest. Against her will Marisa wondered what it would be like to touch where his hand touched. . . .

She closed her eyes, facing at last the fact that this whole conversation would become much easier if she could not see. In her mind's eye, images remained. But at least now she could speak. "I'm sorry we've been fighting so much."

"So am I. This is much more comfortable."

She laughed uneasily, in something less than total agreement. "Like two old shoes?"

"One old shoe and one very pretty little shoe."

"A mismatched pair, in other words."

"Look, Marisa, I'm sorry we got off to a bad start. It's a hell of a thing to ask a total stranger to marry."

"Ask?" There was a faint sarcasm in Marisa's voice.

"Hire, then. I'd have preferred not to use such steamroller tactics, but under the circumstances I couldn't afford to let you say no. I was in too much of a hurry."

"If you hadn't been in such a hurry you'd not have hired me at all," she reminded him. "You'd have gone looking for your lady friend—what was her name?"

"Yvonne."

Yvonne. . . . But the thought of her was shadowy, without substance, as if she were a person not quite real. She seemed to have no relationship

to Antoine de Vigny, to Ta'aroa, to the things
Marisa had seen since coming here.

"Why didn't you go looking for her that last
week—instead of taking time to have me investigated? Surely in a week you could have found
her."

His voice became offhand, almost callous.
"Why should I? I won't go chasing after any
woman."

"It seems to me," said Marisa very slowly,
picking her way through the thought, "that if you
loved her enough you would have done just that—
gone after her."

It was Antoine's turn to remain silent, and eventually Marisa spoke again, finding that the silence
grew more intolerable with every passing second.

"Marrying me was a mistake—for me, and for
you. I've become a complication—whether you
like it or not, whether I like it or not. Was it so
very important for you to marry?"

His voice turned curt. "I told you of my
father's ultimatum. I don't want to talk about it."

"If we're to be friends, it would be easier if you
started telling the truth. Your father didn't care
whom you married, and I don't believe you did,
either." Now that she'd voiced the thought, the
truth of it came to her like a jolt. She opened her
eyes and turned toward Antoine with a wondering
expression. "You don't love Yvonne after all.
You never did. You would have been using her—
just as you're using me."

For a moment his face closed over: his mouth taut as a bowstring, his eyes a formidable barrier. Then he relaxed and laughed, and shook himself to his feet. "If we're to be friends, Miss Marisa, you'll have to stop making personal remarks. You're entirely too curious for your own good, do you know that? Well, I have no intention of satisfying your curiosity. I'm going for a swim instead. I suggest you join me; you look hot. And you don't have to hide under that tent anymore. I may be using you, but I'm not going to use you in the way you're worried about."

Without waiting for her, he set off across the beach at a lope and knifed into the green lagoon.

Marisa followed more slowly, dragging her feet. Her remarks, she admitted to herself, had been far too personal for a mere employee. Antoine de Vigny's feelings for other women were no concern of hers. And yet she was sure, as sure as if he had told her himself, that the shadowy woman Yvonne meant nothing to him. One more piece of the jigsaw. Would she ever understand him...and did she even want to?

After the exercise at the reef, Marisa was far too tired to swim; she did no more than dip her body at the water's edge. Here on the windward side of the island the lagoon was not mirror-still as it had been elsewhere. A mile away from the shore waves thundered against coral, spewing foam high in the air. A fraction of this fury spilled over into the lagoon, causing a swell that broke against the gleaming beach in little wavelets. In the distance Marisa could see a white speck that told her Antoine was swimming to the reef, and only halfway there. It would be some time before he returned. She toweled herself on the edge of her beach coat and returned to the sheltered place where they had eaten. Then, face down, head pillowed on her folded beach coat, she began to sort out her tangled thoughts.

Antoine. . . could she ever be friends with him, as he asked? She was not too certain. Today had produced all kinds of apologies; some only halfspoken, to be sure, but apologies all the same. She had already learned enough about her new husband to know that he was a man who told only what he wanted to tell. A man who could be angered by any intrusion on matters he considered private. That's what had angered him last night, and once before, on the plane, when she had questioned him too closely about personal matters. What was it that drove him to react that way—as if she had touched on a raw nerve? And what had driven him to marry when he so obviously did not do so of his own choosing? His father had some hold over him. . . but what was it? And Tania, Tania running through it all like a refrain; where did she fit in? Perhaps the solution to the riddle lay with her. Surely Antoine could not object if she were to visit Tania sometime soon; it was a natural enough gesture for a new daughter-in-law. Yes, perhaps Tania could shed some light on matters.

In the meantime the sun felt good on her back, and the sand clean and soft beneath her. She would see Tania soon, and then perhaps she would begin to understand. And on that thought she began to drift, drift, drift....

FINGERS TOUCHED A STRAND OF HAIR that had become tangled somehow in the edge of her mouth. Fingers brushed against her lips, easing the hair away, smoothing it back behind her ear. Long strong fingers that she knew could be hard and demanding, and for the moment were gentle....

She had been neither asleep nor awake when Antoine returned from the lagoon, only in that half-world between. Now after feeling his touch she was awake, all awake, awake and alive in every tingling inch.

"Marisa...."

She forced herself to remain limp, feigning sleep. The fingers lingered near her ear, scarcely touching, a contact so light it might have been imagination but for the coolness of his skin after the swim.

"Marisa."

The name had been breathed a little louder than before, and she continued to pretend, sure that he could not know she had heard him. But her stomach against the soft sand was rigid with effort. If she waited the fingers would go away. They must go away.

"Marisa." His voice was a shade louder this time; it was becoming harder to pretend.

The hand moved to her temples, smoothing small strands away from the skin. Her insides screamed.

"For God's sake, Marisa, don't pretend." The texture of his voice had gone rough, rough and soft at the same time, like toweling. "That's the worst thing you can do."

Her eyes came open, because pretense was no longer possible. Antoine had lowered his powerful frame to the sand beside her. He was close, so close that she could feel his breath warming her shoulder, so close that to move an inch would be to tempt fate. She lay perfectly still.

"It's time to go. I only came to tell you that. Oh, dammit, Marisa, if only you hadn't kept your eyes closed. You look so vulnerable that way."

Suddenly his mouth was on her shoulder, dry and hard. His hand traveled to her spine and lodged there lightly against the flesh. But through some effort of will he did no more. He lay perfectly still, perhaps—like her—sensing that movement, any movement, might only lead to more than either of them could handle. His very stillness seemed to compound the tension between them. Marisa scarcely dared to breathe. Her heartbeat felt immense; the ticking of a pulse in her throat seemed like the pulse of the surf against the reef.

When he spoke again, his voice was muffled

against her skin. "Get up, very slowly, and go to the boat, and don't let me stop you."

Carefully she began to inch herself out from under him, trying to make no enticing movement that would excite him further.

"Oh, God," he said thickly, and all at once she felt fingers digging into her shoulder, turning her unresisting body until her back was to the sand and her face turned to the sky. One hand and a knee pinned her into place; the other hand made a fist in her hair. The same kind of enervation that had seized her last night drained her body again today, afflicting her with a strange paralysis of the limbs. For the moment she had neither strength nor will to resist. She closed her eyes and waited for what she knew must happen.

It did not happen. The mouth she had expected to feel remained inches away, close enough that she could feel his ragged breath fanning her cheek. She became unbearably conscious of the tangled crispness of his chest pressing against her bared midriff; of the dampness of his bathing suit molded closely against her thigh; of the stirring surge of his body.

"For God's sake open your eyes," he commanded roughly. His knuckles brushed against her closed lids, and then, as if to escape the knowledge of her flesh, the hand was withdrawn. Her eyes were still closed, but she could sense what she could not see—the clenching and unclenching of a fist somewhere near the tangle of her salt-soaked hair.

"You have sand on your stomach—do you know that?" He gave a short throaty sound that was half moan and half laugh, and his fingers started to find and brush away the tiny diamond grits that had lodged against her skin. Marisa averted her head, eyes still tightly closed. It was for some reason a gesture more intimate than any that had come before, a gesture intimate to the point of physical anguish.

"Dear God, *sand*," he said in a hoarse unnatural voice, and his hand traveled to the valley between her breasts. There was a ferocity in his fingertips, as though they obeyed some command more imperative than common sense. For breath-stopping moments the long strong fingers brushed sand from the soft down of skin revealed by her bikini top, and then a thumb slid under the straining fabric and ran along its edge, skirting disaster.

Marisa lay tense and trembling, strangely incapable of flight or of fight, aware of the length of him and the strength of him and the maleness of him with every fiber of her flesh. The frail inches of damp fabric that lay between them were scant barrier at all. And when he loosened the front fastening of her bikini top and brushed one of the barriers aside, she still did nothing to resist. The palm of his hand, still cool from the swim, captured the curve. For a time it lay unmoving, merely molding the flesh; and then it began to brush achingly back and forth, smoothing the silken surface of her breast until the darker rise turned taut beneath his hand.

"Beautiful," he murmured huskily, "how beautiful."

She opened her eyes then. And his eyes lay in wait—smoking, slate blue, darkened with desire. The most primitive of urges was reflected there. The harsh heavy come and go of his breath, the thud of his heart where the broad bared chest tingled crisply against her breasts, the laden sensuousness of his mouth—they all told of passions barely leashed.

It was as if the opening of her green eyes had been a signal. With a groan from some deep well within, he lowered his mouth and claimed her lips, bruising them apart, invading the soft inner recesses of her mouth with a ferocity and hunger that left her flushed and faint and aware of her own womanhood as she had never been before.

And now his fingers moved to another barrier. Only inches of fabric lay between his hand and that most vulnerable region of her flesh. And through that last thin barrier he touched where no man's hands had touched before, sending shock waves reverberating through her veins.

It was as if that, too, had been a signal. Belatedly Marisa began to struggle against the encroachments of his hands, and perhaps against herself. With a moan she twisted her mouth away from his, and her fists began to pummel at the broad bronzed shoulders. Her bruised lips, now freed, began to voice shocked protestations.

"Stop—stop! You don't know what you're doing. Oh, oh—damn you! Stop!"

For what seemed an eternity but could have been mere seconds, his mouth sank fiercely onto her throat where a pulse beat erratically, and his fingers at her thighs only firmed their hold. For this brief instant he seemed oblivious of the wild tattoo her hands were beating, as though her struggles were no more than feeble wing flutterings beneath the hard virile press of his body.

"Stop, I beg you—*stop*!"

At last he listened to the drumbeat of her hands. With an oath he levered his now heated body away from hers and rolled swiftly face-over in the sand. "Go, for God's sake," he ordered in an unnatural voice. "Go while you can."

With a sob Marisa scrambled to her feet and ran to the outrigger, beach coat and bikini top forgotten in the need to escape at once.

Ten minutes passed before Antoine joined her. Marisa had restored some decency by now, with the light denim-blue shirt that had been lying loose in the bottom of the boat. Without comment he loaded the picnic basket into the outrigger and tossed the missing apparel and the raffish straw hat in Marisa's direction. Then, without so much as a glance at her face, he pushed off and raised the sail. It was a trip accomplished in total silence until Antoine's bungalow was once more in view.

"I suppose I should apologize," he said, his voice flat and unemotional. "I thought I was strong enough to stop myself, but it seems I was wrong. I suppose I should also thank you for preventing something that—that would create an irreparable situation between us."

"I don't think this month is going to be possible at all," Marisa said stiffly through lips that still burned with memories of his mastery. "You must realize I won't be able to stay now."

His face tightened. "You'll have to," he said abruptly. "If you back out now, you'll be leaving me in an impossible situation."

"Why? You've done as your father asked. He's even witnessed the ceremony. He wouldn't need to know about the annulment yet. Tell him I have to go home for a time, that there's an emergency—"

"I need a woman *here*, on Ta'aroa," he cut in roughly. "That's what he really wants. You'll have to stay."

"I don't *have* to," she said, staring fixedly at a point somewhere near the hard line of his jaw. "I didn't think there'd be a repeat of last night, not with you so determined to have an annulment. But now...well, I can't go on like this for a month, wondering every day whether I'll have to fight you off. Get the money back from Sarah if you must— I'll find some other way to repay her. I gave in partly because of your assurances that you were in love with someone. But you were lying about that. And now...."

For long seconds something like hatred built in his face. Then abruptly he lowered the sail, setting the outrigger adrift. He leaned over to retrieve the paddle from the bottom of the boat, and for a moment she could not see his expression. "I wasn't lying," he said tersely. "I am in love with someone. But sex is something else. Sometimes a man gets urges he can't control—dammit, Marisa, I'm not inhuman!"

With antagonism Marisa watched him straighten in the boat. " 'If you can't be with the one you love, love the one you're with'—is that it?" With a hand still too shaky for her liking, she pushed the tangled sweep of hair behind one ear. "In that case the one you're with had better not be *me*. I think it's time we called a halt to this whole charade, before something happens that makes the marriage binding. I'm not strong enough to keep fighting you off, and I don't need your money that badly. I'm afraid I have to resign as your wife. We can get an annulment right away."

His eyes narrowed; his mouth turned taut and dangerous. "I can't allow that," he said slowly but forcefully. "The die is cast now. I won't let you leave—and as you can't fly a plane, you have very little choice in the matter."

Marisa glared at him balefully. "Then I have no alternative but to tell your father the whole truth."

He had not yet started to paddle; the canoe continued to drift. But the tension in his powerful frame suggested that he found her threat totally unacceptable.

"In that case," he said, his hostile eyes holding her, "I'll have to use a small piece of persuasion I've been keeping up my sleeve."

Persuasion? But Marisa was too stubborn to put the question into words.

"I didn't want to use this unless I had to," he went on inexorably, "and I don't like to use it even now. It's to do with your sister, Sarah. I told you your brother-in-law left his personal affairs in bad shape—that he had been showing symptoms of his disorder for some time. For nearly a year he neglected to pay into the company insurance plan, a small matter that voids his coverage in the normal course of events. I have the power to, ah, change the normal course of events. The decision comes up in about a month. There's a matter of some thirty thousand dollars involved. Can you deprive your sister of *that*? You see, Marisa, keeping up this charade is essential to me—absolutely essential."

As he talked, his unfriendly eyes remained trained on Marisa, assessing her reaction. Her face had slowly drained of color beneath the light glow put there by the sun.

"That's blackmail," she said, swaying visibly.

"Only because you've driven me to it," came the unfeeling retort. "I can hardly get another woman to take your place at this point. I assure you I wouldn't stoop so low unless the necessity were absolute. In any case, I'm not quite as low as you think. I've already taken some steps to intercede with the insurance company.''

Oh, God, thought Marisa, what choice did he leave her now? Sarah certainly needed the insurance money; she planned to pay off the mortgage with it. At the moment her sister's financial position was difficult but not dire—but a blow like that would make it very hard to raise four small children.

"If I stay here," she asked desperately, "can you guarantee the insurance company will pay?''

"Go on with the charade and I'll pay out of my own pocket if necessary," he told her, his tension lessening as he sensed her surrender. "Now, do you still plan to speak to my father?''

"No," she conceded unhappily. "I promise I won't.''

He relaxed visibly and raised his paddle. "What happened today won't happen again," he told her in a dry tone, hostility receding. "I admit it was a mistake to take you to a place like that. I won't make the same mistake again. For the time being it's better if we pursue our friendship in public places.''

"Friendship?" Marisa's small laugh, like the shattering of a fine crystal, held traces of hysteria. Did he really expect her to be friends with him *now*?

Surprisingly, he grinned, his eyelids turning languid over an enigmatic blue. "Perhaps 'friendship' *is* the wrong word," he said, good temper now fully restored. He sliced into the glassy turquoise water with his poised paddle and struck strongly toward shore. "In public, Miss Marisa, it has to look like love."

Her green eyes splintered the space between them, but for the moment she stifled her sharp retorts. What was the use of words? As usual, this domineering stranger had swept her along with no regard for her wishes, altering her destiny for some twisted purpose of his own—a purpose for which he seemed prepared to expend limitless amounts of effort and money.

But what *was* that purpose?

CHAPTER SIX

IN THE FEW DAYS THAT FOLLOWED it seemed the charade of the marriage would fall into a bearable pattern. The frequent presence of Maeva and Lotu, and of other islanders, made it necessary to develop a working arrangement, a kind of surface camaraderie that hid from curious eyes the truth of their relationship. When others were around Antoine played the part of the devoted lover very well, and Marisa grudgingly allowed his attentions. At these times she even began to take a wary pleasure in her husband's presence, for his manner was easy and engaging and his conversation knowledgeable on a variety of subjects.

It was harder when they were alone. There, under a still surface, danger lurked, as Marisa had been warned it lurked in some parts of the lagoon. Despite the manner of impersonal civility they adopted by mutual agreement when alone, it was impossible to forget the things that had happened between them—that had nearly happened between them, not once but twice. Things Marisa was determined not to let happen again. To tempt fate a third time would be disastrous. So when others

were not around she maintained a polite distance.
Although Antoine still took her swimming each
morning, there were no more trips to private
coves; no attempts to question him on the subject
of his father or Tania; no conversation beyond the
required minimum. Each night, once the evening
meal was finished, Marisa retired to her bedroom
early, certain that danger lay only in proximity.
She did not emerge until morning returned, and
with it safety.

In those first few days of the supposed honeymoon her husband undertook daily trips to his
father's house—to use the radiotelephone, he told
Marisa. Once Marisa joined him and spent fifteen
minutes visiting with Alain de Vigny and Tania.
But the occasion was remarkable only for the
shortness of its duration, and the fact that it took
place inside the bungalow although it was a beautiful sunny day. Alain de Vigny had been somewhat less morose than on first meeting. Tania had
been quiet, her exotic beauty blending into the
background for the most part. And although
Marisa thought about the Polynesian woman a
great deal, she did not during those first days attempt a visit on her own.

Once, inadvertently, Maeva revealed several
things Marisa had not been told by Antoine.

"It is a good thing that Tuan *tane* is married
now, I think!" Maeva was chattering in her usual
effervescent way as she showed Marisa how to
squeeze the cream from ripe coconut meat—a li-

quid that was quite different from the milk of the green drinking coconut.

She encouraged Maeva with a simple, "Oh?"

"For this past year, always making excuses to be away from the island—this island he loves so much. *Aue!*" Maeva exclaimed, using the all-purpose Polynesian expression that conveyed woe or surprise or any number of emotions. "Before, he seldom spent a night away from Ta'aroa, for by plane it is not so far from Tahiti, yes? But for a year he has hardly been seen, and for six months not at all. Tuan *tane* has been an unhappy man, I think. Restless like the wind! A man much in need of a *vahine*, a woman of his own. Now he will not be so unhappy. There were women before, it is no secret, yes? For a man who is so much a man there are always eager women! But he does not need many women, that man, he needs one. Tuan *tane* is not like the men of this island. He is like his father—" Maeva groped for the appropriate expression in French "—a man for one woman."

"His father does seem to have eyes only for Tania," Marisa observed, giving in to the temptation to encourage Maeva's gossip. Her husband's angry refusal to divulge personal matters had only deepened her curiosity.

But Maeva's next words contained no special revelations, and privately Marisa wondered if they were accurate. "It is true! And Tania, she has eyes only for Vini *tane*." That was the islanders' name for the elder de Vigny. "*Aue!* Sometimes I think

Tania is all Malayan and Chinese, not Tahitian at all.''

Marisa was not sure what that last remark meant, but she let it pass. By now she was quite accustomed to Maeva's incomprehensible observations. ''Did Monsieur de Vigny bring Tania here as a bride?''

Maeva shook her head. ''Tania has lived here all her life. Vini *tane*, too—except for the years when he lived in America during his first marriage. Vini *tane* saw Tania when she was sixteen, and fell in love—a stroke of the lightning, *non*? He himself was much younger then, and here a girl grows old early! But he was content to wait. He sent her to school, first in Tahiti, then in Paris, and when she was finished he brought her back to Ta'aroa and married her. Such a handsome couple! So much in love! Always walking hand in hand along the beach, swimming at the reef... that was ten years ago.''

So Alain de Vigny had not been crippled at the time of the marriage: that answered one question. Maeva went on, adding to the small store of information, ''Since the accident, of course, I have seen Vini *tane* very little. For a time Tania would come to the beach without him. Now she does not.''

''When was the accident, Maeva? What caused it?''

''Two years ago. An octopus in the reef,'' said Maeva matter-of-factly. ''Sometimes there are little ones, but this was a big one, a very great strong fellow! They were swimming—Tania and Vini *tane*. Tania was careless. *Aue!* She could have lost her eyes if the suckers had found her face. Vini *tane* had no weapons, and he was too close to the coral, which cut him like a giant knife. It was a very great battle, *aue!* But in the end Vini *tane* won.''

Marisa had long since stopped shredding coconut and was now staring at Maeva in horrified fascination. "How, Maeva—as he had no weapons?''

Maeva shrugged. "A man without weapons can kill an octopus if he knows which part of its head to bite. A big bite between the eyes, and the octopus will die at once. Vini *tane* has strong teeth.''

Marisa, feeling sick, said nothing.

"This upsets you?'' Maeva looked at Marisa, puzzlement written in brown eyes that had remained until now unperturbed. "But why? It is very bad of Tania to be so careless, that is true, for she is not a stranger to the reef. And, *aue*, it is bad that Vini *tane* had no weapons with him. With a weapon he might have killed the octopus sooner and not been swept against the coral. But where there is bad, there is also good! Vini *tane* gained much *mana* for killing such a big wily creature. Even Uma has respect for Vini *tane*, and she is afraid of no one! And there is no woman on this island who does not envy Tania for being married to a man who has done such a thing. She is very proud of him, you understand? What is the English word for 'teeth'?''

And so, for the time being at least, Marisa learned no more from Maeva. A few more pieces had been added to the jigsaw, but there was still no hint as to why Antoine should have agreed to his father's strange request to marry; or why Alain de Vigny should have made it. And now there was a new thought to puzzle over: why had Antoine been so unhappy for so long? Maeva's words suggested that the disturbance had gone on for some time, certainly longer than six months.

It was on the sixth day of the mock honeymoon that Antoine announced he intended to spend a day in Papeete on some urgent business matters.

''I'll fly there tomorrow morning with Dooey, and I'll be back by nightfall—in my own flying boat. I hear it's ready now. You can come along for the trip if you want,'' he offered with disconcerting casualness. ''I'll be busy most of the day, but there are some fine shops in Papeete. You might like to buy yourself a decent straw hat.''

She glanced upward and saw the mocking tilt of his brow. ''I can manage with the one you gave me.''

''What, still no vanity?''

She bristled at the derisive tone in his voice. ''On the contrary. I know it looks awful! I have no one I want to impress, that's all.''

''There are other things to buy—shellwork, bas-

ketware. Surely you want something to remind
you of your stay. How about a pareu?''

Marisa studied her fingernails. ''Tania gave me
a pareu, and I still haven't had the courage to wear
it.''

''And why do you need courage to wear a
pareu, pray tell? It covers a whole lot more territory than a bikini. Could it be because the island
girls wear them with nothing underneath?''

''Of course not.'' She pretended a serenity she
seldom felt in his presence. ''I'm not used to those
tucks and folds, that's all.'' It was not true:
Maeva had demonstrated several times, and
Marisa by now knew perfectly well how to arrange
the garment. But she would not admit to Antoine
that he guessed the reason for her reluctance. ''In
any case, I don't think I'll come to Tahiti with
you. Shopping is not my favorite occupation.''

''I could meet you for lunch. And don't forget
there are movies, boat excursions to Mooréa,
sight-seeing trips—''

''I'll stay here. Do you mind?''

But if he did, he made no effort to persuade her;
and the following morning he took off with Dooey
in the flying boat, leaving—for some reason that
Marisa refused to examine—a sense of emptiness
behind him.

It was on this day, with her husband in Tahiti,
that Marisa at last decided to fulfill her pledge to
herself and visit Tania. Tania...who had preyed
on Marisa's thoughts so often that it sometimes

seemed she might hold the key to all of Ta'aroa's secrets.

Tania was in a lawn chair, reading. In a pareu of silky cotton, muted in coloring as was the tapa cloth in Antoine's bungalow, she looked lovelier than ever—a cool satin-skinned beauty on an emerald lawn, blending effortlessly into a background ablaze with frangipani and hibiscus and fragrant gardenialike tiare Tahiti.

Marisa hesitated at the approach to the bungalow, feeling vaguely out of place in her wraparound denim skirt and sleeveless blouse. A stranger in paradise...the thought came to her unbidden. Antoine had been right; it was a mistake to come here.

But then Tania saw her, and it was too late to turn away.

"Marisa! How nice of you to come." Tania put down the book and moved forward with a look of genuine pleasure, and moments later Marisa found herself seated in the shade of a feathery casuarina tree with a cooling pineapple drink in her hand.

"Tuan mentioned he would be going to Tahiti today," Tania smiled. "Did he leave on the plane this morning?"

"Yes, he did." Marisa swirled her glass and studied it. "Is his father at home?"

"Alain is in his study—but I'm sure he'd be pleased if you said hello."

"As he's working, I won't disturb him," returned Marisa promptly. In truth, she had been relieved at Alain de Vigny's absence. "Actually, I came to see if you'd join me this afternoon. I haven't explored much of the island, and I'm longing to walk up into the mountains. It doesn't look like a difficult climb, but I hesitate to try it alone. I'd be very grateful if you could come along as my guide."

A fleeting shadow passed over Tania's face, then resolved itself into a smile. "Why not?" she said, almost as if to herself. "Wait here a moment, Marisa, and I'll speak to Alain. He—won't object."

Why would he not object today, reflected Marisa, when it was only too clear that he did object at other times?

As they worked their way up slopes moist with ferns and waterfalls, and heavy with the odor of overripe bananas, Tania's chance remarks revealed only too clearly that she had not been on an outing such as this for some time.

Halfway up they reached a shady grotto where mosses and ferns mingled with wild strawberries and small blue flowers. Wild orchids of a dozen varieties clung to their aerial homes; heavy globes of fruit hung from a large-leafed breadfruit tree. "Let's stop here," Tania suggested. "It becomes less pleasant not far from here."

In answer to Marisa's questioning glance, Tania explained, "The mountain beyond here lies beneath the cloud. It's almost as though you pass a line...on one side, everything is green and flourishing; on the other, it is wet and brown and barren. Beneath the cloud, little grows. Even the grass is stunted.''

"It's hard to believe," murmured Marisa, turning to look at the Ta'aroa cloud. Light lacy fingers caressed the higher slopes, white, sunlit, incredibly beautiful. "I would have expected even more vegetation—a rain forest, almost.''

"Where there is a rain forest there must be sun, at least part of the time. Beneath the cloud there is no sun. But why worry about that? Enjoy what is here!''

They found a resting place on a fallen log cushioned with moss. Tania ran her fingers appreciatively over the soft gray green velvet surface. "Alain used to love this place. It hasn't changed at all.'' Her chocolate eyes, surveying the lovely grotto, sparkled with pleasure. "And do you hear that bird? He's singing the same song. But of course that's silly," she added quickly. "It can't be the same fairy tern after two years.''

"What a pity your husband can't come here anymore," observed Marisa, keeping to herself the thought that Alain de Vigny's handicap should not have deterred Tania.

"Yes, it is a pity. I used to hope....'' Tania paused, looking at the sea that stretched below and beyond, unbroken blue as far as the eye could see, save for the white-ringed reef. "But of course that was silly, too. What must be must be.''

"Wasn't there anything that could be done?" asked Marisa after a few moments of silence. "Doctors, specialists? They do such marvelous things nowadays."

"Sometimes I think the specialists did too much. It might have been better if he had lost the leg." Tania's voice was quiet, unemotional. "Then he could hardly refuse the use of an artificial limb, *non*? As it is, he will not give up hope. He refuses to become a cripple."

"To *become* a...." Marisa gave Tania a strange look. "But he *is* a cripple. Surely he must know that."

"To know it and to admit it are two different things. And in some ways Alain has been right not to admit it. The doctors said he would never walk again without a leg brace. He proved they were wrong. It costs him an immense effort of will and much pain, but he walks."

"He walks..." repeated Marisa, remembering that agonized progress she had watched and wondering if it could be dignified with the name of walking. "That's all right around your house, if he insists. But surely he would find it easier to move about the island if he wore a leg brace. Does he have one?"

"Of course."

"And wouldn't it help him?"

"Yes. He might even be able to come up here—with that, and a cane, and my help."

"Then—why doesn't he wear it?"

"Because he does not want to, you see."

"Why not? Surely it's better than—than missing all this!" Marisa swept her hand at the island and the ocean in an all-inclusive gesture. "*Why*, Tania?"

Tania's eyes directed themselves at Marisa, betraying nothing but a calm acceptance. "Because he does not want me to see that he is a cripple."

"Doesn't want you to—" Marisa stared at her in openmouthed amazement. "But surely to see him in a leg brace can be no worse than seeing him walk?"

"But he will not let me see that, either."

"How can he *help* it? You both live in that house, and—why, he didn't seem to mind walking in front of me!"

"No, he wouldn't mind walking in front of *you*. It's *me*. But I do see him walk at times—although I pretend not to. Mostly he makes sure I'm not around when he moves from place to place. Didn't you notice how he sent me away the other day? For himself, he might accept being a cripple. For me...well, that is another matter. But why talk about it? One must come to terms with these things. He wishes me not to see, so I pretend not to see. It is not so difficult."

Not so difficult...and yet there was something in the deliberately flat way Tania said the words that told Marisa it was difficult, very difficult indeed. She wanted to ask more, but it seemed impolite to press for details, so she sat in silence until Tania continued.

"And of course I do as he wishes, because the accident was my fault."

"Your fault? But—"

Tania shrugged. "I was foolhardy. I knew where the giant octopus had its lair, and I swam too close. Now such an accident would not happen, for when an octopus is found in the lagoon—unless it is a very small one—the men hunt for it at once. The islanders might leave it until it grew even larger, for better eating...but Alain insists. Or he used to, until I stopped swimming." Then, changing the subject adroitly, Tania asked, "And what of your little bungalow? Are you enjoying it?"

"Why, yes," Marisa replied quite truthfully. "It's very beautiful."

"I suppose Tuan will add to it now that he is married—or he will as soon as he owns it."

"Owns it?" Marisa could not hide her surprise. "But I thought...?"

"Didn't you know?" Tania looked at her with equal surprise. "Alain is having the property deed made over to Tuan as a wedding present. It seems strange that Tuan would not have told you, as it's your wedding, too. I can't understand—"

"Antoine tells very little unless he wants to," said Marisa quickly, looking for a way to cover up her abysmal ignorance of her husband's affairs. "I suppose I just assumed that he owned the land because he had designed the house. Perhaps he was saving the news of the present as a surprise. He's very good at surprises.''

"But that would be a very poor surprise if you already assumed he owned the land." Tania picked a piece of grass and nibbled at it thoughtfully. "I wonder what other things he hasn't told you?''

"So do I," admitted Marisa with a rush of relief that the pretense could at last be given up. "There are lots of things I've been longing to ask.''

Tania laughed. "I reserve the right not to answer, of course. But what things have you been longing to ask?''

"A thousand questions." They began to tumble out. "You've answered some of them already, for to be truthful, I had wondered about you and—and about Alain. But there are other things. Why Antoine has been unhappy for this past year. Why he's been spending time away from Ta'aroa—especially as he loves it so much. Why you're—well, cool to Antoine, for I don't have the feeling that it's dislike. Why he refuses to talk about his father, and about you, and about anything— Oh, Tania, I suppose I may as well admit it. I've been wondering why he found it necessary to marry me.''

"Why, because he fell in love, I suppose," said Tania gaily, but her evasive words revealed as much as they hid. "What other possible reason is there?"

Marisa struggled briefly with her conscience, and lost. She had promised not to speak to Alain de Vigny, but the promise had not included Tania. For reasons Marisa refused to analyze, the need to know the truth had become too deep to deny.

"He didn't fall in love with me, Tania. It's just a marriage of convenience—in fact, he's told me quite frankly that he's in love with someone else." There was no need, Marisa decided swiftly, to add more. That she had been chosen by Antoine's secretary, that she had not met him until the day of the wedding, and that the marriage was to be of limited duration only—these facts might only cause Tania to withhold information. So to some extent she would not be breaking trust with Antoine. "I also know that he married at his father's insistence," she added, "although I don't understand why Alain should have insisted...or why Antoine would have agreed."

With a movement that reminded Marisa of a ballet in slow motion, Tania turned her body on the fallen log until she was able to study Marisa's expression. Her own beautiful almond eyes were unreadable. She did not answer.

"Why, Tania?" persisted Marisa with a helpless gesture. "Please—I'm finding it hard to live with so many questions."

"But really, you have asked only one question," replied Tania very slowly. Her slender hands, graceful even in their stillness, lay at rest in her lap. "I did guess that it might be a marriage of convenience, for if you and Tuan were well acquainted you would hardly call him Antoine—very few people do. But I thought I also sensed something in you, something in the way you look at him—"

"I'm not in love with him," Marisa broke in, looking down quickly.

"No?" Tania paused, registering some small disbelief. "In any case, as you know of Alain's ultimatum you deserve the rest of the truth. Although surely you must have guessed it by now. Why don't you ask the one question you want to ask?"

Marisa, unable to do so, studied the pattern of light and shade that fell on her hands. Her misery was transparent.

"I see by your face that you hesitate to put it into words," said Tania at last. "As if by avoiding the words you might avoid the truth! Perhaps the truth will not be so hard to face as you think. Why don't you ask it, Marisa? Why don't you ask if Tuan is in love with me—and I with him?"

"Are you in love with him?" faltered Marisa, asking the half of the question that she could bear to ask, thereby surrendering at last to self-knowledge: the knowledge that she herself was in love. Helplessly, hopelessly, unhappily in love.

CHAPTER SEVEN

"No, TUAN AND I are not in love, and never have been," Tania answered levelly enough, but whether there was truth in those still brown eyes, Marisa was unable to discern. *Still waters run deep.* Tania was an extraordinary woman: serene, subtle, secret, exquisite. And Tania had known Antoine for a lifetime, as Marisa had not; as the elusive Yvonne had not.

Tania. When had Marisa begun to think of her as a rival? A rival more real than the shadowy woman Antoine had once claimed to love. Rival. . . that was the thought that had tugged at Marisa's subconscious, the clue that had first told her the unthinkable might be happening. For it was unthinkable that she should fall in love with a man who did not love her, who would never love her. In spite of Tania's cool denial, Marisa was certain that Antoine had married a woman he did not love because he could not marry the woman he did love. An unnatural passion for his father's wife: what other circumstance could possibly account for the things Marisa had learned since coming to Ta'aroa?

There had been no affair. Or so Tania told her,

and Marisa sensed that much was probably true. But that Antoine had married someone—anyone—as a buffer between himself and Tania was at once clear, even by Tania's admission.

"How can I explain to you, Marisa? A man like Alain turns inward when he denies himself the world. He broods. You must remember that he is nearly twenty-five years older than I. He used to forget that, and so did I, but now he refuses to forget." Tania sighed, a soft accepting sigh. "Nor can he forget that I am—what I am. Underneath all the fine schooling he still sees me as he first saw me—as an island girl, a Polynesian *vahine*. He forgets that I am part Malayan, and Chinese, too."

"What does that have to do with it?" asked Marisa in puzzlement, remembering that she had dismissed Maeva's remarks on the subject as unimportant.

"Everything." Tania's mouth curved in a Mona Lisa smile. "But of course you might find it hard to understand. In parts of Polynesia a man may still offer to share his woman with guests, or even strangers who look a little lonely. She is willing—and why not? It breaks the monotony of the days. Oh, it is not as common as it used to be, but it can't be denied that *vahines*, especially unmarried ones, can be remarkably free with their favors.

"But my mother was half-Filipino, brought up in a convent, and through her I inherited centuries of quite a different tradition. And my father: his mother was Chinese, and Chinese wives are notable for their faithfulness. Of course Alain is quite right to think of me as Polynesian, for that is what I am, in most things. But he is quite wrong to think I have been unfaithful. I have always been faithful in every way. If it were not for his accident, he would never have doubted it. I have given him no reason to doubt that I love him."

"Then, why—"

"Alain knows that what a person does with the heart and what a person does with the body are not always the same. Surely you must know this yourself, Marisa?"

Marisa did indeed know this, and Antoine himself had said it: *sex is something else.* Now she could no longer put off the question that had been uppermost in her mind. "And Antoine—what of him?"

"Alain is jealous of him, eaten with a jealousy so terrible it has changed all our lives. You must have guessed it. Alain sees himself as destroyed, as less than a man, which of course is not true. In Tuan he sees a younger version of himself, a whole man. For a year after the accident it did not occur to me that Alain felt that way; we had always been so close. If I had understood it sooner, Alain would not have become like a man obsessed.... It happened gradually, so gradually that I suspected nothing. At first, after the accident, while Alain was still recovering, he refused to allow me to swim alone. He would encourage Tuan to take me...to the reef for swimming, then on picnics, or even for a day of shopping in Papeete. He was throwing us together, torturing himself, and I was blind; I didn't see it. Why would I? I am, after all, Polynesian. Yes, he was right about that in one way! I take each day as it comes. I don't deny that I enjoyed the outings! Alain of course saw that; I didn't try to hide it from him. I used to come in bubbling with pleasure. And all the time Alain was waiting at the bungalow, struggling to walk again in my absence, forcing himself while the jealous thoughts were eating away at his insides. You can imagine the rest.''

Visions of Antoine and Tania gnawing at the mind: yes, that was something Marisa could understand only too well.

A year ago, it seemed, matters had come to a head. There had been an enormous scene; Alain de Vigny's jealousies, ugly for being so long repressed, had surfaced. Tania had responded by seldom leaving the bungalow; Antoine had responded by staying away from Ta'aroa as much as possible. But Ta'aroa was in his blood, and no doubt, Marisa added ruefully to herself, Tania was, too.

It had been an impossible situation. Finally, six months ago, Alain de Vigny had ordered his son off the island altogether, an order made possible by the fact that none of the family's land was in Antoine's name.

''He even threatened to sell Tuan's bungalow and all the land that goes with it,'' Tania told her with a small shudder. ''*Aue!* It was an unpleasant business, I assure you. Finally Alain agreed to deed the land over if Tuan took a wife.''

''Surely Antoine could have bought another property!''

''In the Society Islands one cannot buy land without all kinds of special permits. Polynesia for the Polynesians, they say—well, it is a good rule, most of the time. If Alain's grandfather had not bought the land two generations ago, even Alain would own nothing. And Tuan was born in the United States, so for him it is very difficult. He tried and was refused, because so much of this island is already in the hands of his own father. So you see, Tuan had no choice. He had to obey Alain's wishes or leave Ta'aroa forever.''

At last Marisa understood. Any wife, from Alain de Vigny's point of view, to take Antoine's mind off Tania. Not quite any wife from Antoine's point of view—but one who could be shed easily once the property was in his name.

''Tuan agreed but procrastinated,'' Tania went on. ''At length Alain set a deadline. *Et voilà*— Tuan found you.'' Tania gave a liquid laugh like the music of a waterfall. ''I think he has not done so badly for a man who did not want to marry at all. He will be happy with you! And you will be happy with him; Tuan will be a fine faithful husband. I, too, will be happier—for now that you are here, things are improving for me. Alain has become much more reasonable. Why, I even went swimming the other day, and there was no scene.

Now do you see that you have nothing to fear from me?''

But that was something Marisa could not see at all—not then, and not later that night, when she lay tossing restlessly in a bed that belonged to the man she loved, a man who lay only the thickness of one wall away. One wall, but it might as well have been a whole world.

PADDLES FLASHING, they had set out on the lagoon in the early morning—Antoine and Lotu, bronze skin and brown; both well-muscled men at one with the sun and the sea.

Marisa had watched Antoine go with the ache of new knowledge in her throat. No, not Antoine—Tuan. Lord and master. He was that now in her heart. She could not yet bring herself to use the term of endearment and familiarity, but in her mind he was now Tuan, would always be Tuan.

Nothing had changed since yesterday, yet everything had changed. Why had she felt it necessary to be positively nasty to him last night when he returned from Tahiti, and again this morning after Maeva had left? Why, why, why? It had not been because of Tania, not really. In that respect Tuan could help his feelings no more than she, Marisa, could help hers. He was to be pitied, if anything. Then, why? Possibly because her own defenses had seemed so pitifully fragile against his penetrating blue gaze. She had been sure he would see the soul in her expression, and as a result she had been decidedly thorny.

"Down with that breakfast, Miss Marisa," he said mockingly but good-naturedly enough, playing by rules established a week ago. "I have something different in mind for this morning."

"If it's a surprise—no, thanks," Marisa had responded, with a vicious dig at her grapefruit. "One more surprise and I'll scream."

Tuan's eyes had narrowed briefly and perceptibly, but if he felt the need to respond with equal acidity, he had hidden it well. His reply had been level. "In that case I'll tell you. I thought we might go over the reef in an outrigger. It can be done—it's just a matter of waiting for the right wave. It's quite a thrill, Marisa."

"The only prospect that thrills me this morning is the prospect of being alone. Can't you see I'm getting bored with you?" Untrue, untrue...but the total misery inside had to be told somehow, and as she could not tell the truth, what else was there to do but lie? Her voice had been like crushed ice. "Bored, bored, bored! Bored with Ta'aroa—bored with your company. Please, for once, spare me the thrill of it."

For an instant his face had gone hard and dangerous, and then he pushed his chair away from the table. "In that case I will," he grated, and stalked from the bungalow.

He had set off northward, toward his father's house; Marisa's eyes followed him through the kitchen window until his well-knit frame vanished around the curve of beach. Half an hour of self-recrimination followed, until at length, unable to bear her own company for another moment, she set off in the same direction. In cool yellow shorts and top, with binoculars swinging in her hand and her ridiculous straw hat jammed on her head, she arrived at the busy stretch of beach used by the islanders in time to see Tuan and Lotu set off in an outrigger. If Tuan noted her arrival, he gave no indication of it.

Marisa was sitting cross-legged on the sand, watching the fast-vanishing outrigger, when Maeva appeared.

"Tuan *tane* has gone alone this morning?"

The incredulous voice broke through Marisa's misery. She put down the binoculars and tried to smile. "Actually, Maeva, he's gone with your husband."

Maeva let out a delighted bubble of laughter. "Lotu is not my husband. Not yet! Maybe, if I have a boy child, he will ask me."

It was Marisa's turn to be incredulous. "But you said—"

"Ah, that is when I was trying my English. Perhaps it is different in English. I am Lotu's woman, not his wife. 'Belong Lotu'—does that make me his wife?"

"Not exactly," admitted Marisa, "I just assumed it." Now, remorseful that she had been too embroiled in her own problems to see Maeva's, she turned for a better view of the girl beside her. Maeva was smiling, holding an armful of folded fishnet. She looked placid, pretty, very pregnant, and anything but sorry for herself.

"Won't Lotu ask you if you have a girl child, Maeva?"

"Of course not," Maeva replied equably, as if no other answer could be expected.

"And what will you do then?" asked Marisa, trying to keep the pity from her voice. "Will you keep the child or will you give it to an orphanage?"

"Orphanage?" Maeva looked puzzled. "What is that?"

"A place for children who aren't wanted—who have no home."

"I have never heard of such a place! There is no child on this island who is not wanted. Already a dozen women have asked me if they may have my child, even if it has the bad luck to be a girl child. There are never enough babies to go around. But I will keep the baby if Lotu decides to marry me. If he does not, I will give the baby to Uma."

"To Uma—" Well, thought Marisa with relief, that was one solution. At least it was all in the family. If Uma had taken on one child, she might very well take on another. "Yes, I suppose that would be best," she said.

Maeva went on cheerfully, "Uma has been hoping for me to make a baby ever since my father built me my own hut."

"Your father?" Marisa puzzled. "But I thought he was dead."

"Uma's husband is dead," Maeva explained with infinite patience. "My other father built the hut three years ago, when I was fifteen. I no longer live with Uma. That is why she hopes for a girl child."

"A girl child—but I don't understand," said Marisa, confused all over again. "I thought you wanted a boy child so Lotu would marry you. Why does Uma hope for a girl child?"

"So Lotu won't marry me, of course!" Maeva promptly showed a flash of white even teeth. "How else could Uma get her own baby—unless someone else is generous enough to give her one?"

"Please, Maeva, you're going too fast!" Marisa's head was spinning from her first real glimpse into the complexities of Polynesian morality. "And why did your father build a hut for you?"

"So the young men of the island could court me, why else? For how should I find a husband without first showing that I can bear strong sons? But of all the young men," she added philosophically, totally unaware of the havoc she was wreaking with Marisa's sensibilities, "of all the young men who came to my hut I like Lotu best. Tall and strong and so much of a man—like the Tuan *tane, non*? If Lotu asks me to marry with him, I will say yes. But not too fast, for it is best to let a man wait sometimes, *n'est-ce pas*? Otherwise he will get too high an opinion of himself."

Marisa, groggy with the effort of following this logic, struggled to assimilate these new facts. In spite of the things Tania had told her yesterday,

Maeva's attitude to sex and marriage seemed quite incredible. Trying to appear casual, she pressed for more details. "Does every young girl on the island have a hut of her own as you do?"

"Once she reaches the right age, yes. Or at least, most do, those whose fathers care enough. *Aue!* I suppose it is the same in your country; there are men too lazy to look after their daughters properly. But I have a good father."

Marisa swallowed an impulse to hysteria. "And Tania—did she have a hut of her own?"

"I was only a little girl then, but I have been told that she did not. Did I not tell you? Tania is not entirely Polynesian. Her mother came from the Philippines. It must be very dull not to be Polynesian!" For the first time Maeva sighed heavily and then jumped to her feet, good humor at once restored. "Would you like to see some net fishing?"

What an extraordinary conversation, thought Marisa. And yet, with the sun and the surf and the sight of Maeva casting the net and the squeal of children playing sticks and stones nearby, it seemed less insane than she would have believed a week ago. True, even in other parts of the world bearing a child out of wedlock was not the stigma it once had been. Nevertheless, Marisa's upbringing had made her assume that Maeva was married...that Maeva would want to be married, and that Uma, too, would want her daughter married with a child's arrival imminent. No wonder Alain de Vigny had assumed that Tania would be unfaithful!

Yes, Marisa mused to herself, in this part of the world it was dangerous to assume anything, anything at all.

She found this out all over again moments later, when Maeva allowed her to try her hand at net fishing. It had looked easy enough—Maeva crouching at the water's edge so that the fish would not see her shadow, then effortlessly casting the net in a fluid graceful coil that parachuted outward before it hit the water; rushing knee-deep while she tightened the net with careful little tugs, then bringing a silvery shimmering burden to shore. Yes, it had looked easy. But try as she might, Marisa could not make the fishnet land with a hundred simultaneous little splashes as Maeva had done.

"The leads—the weights—they must hit the water all at the same time exactly, or the fish will very fast go away," explained Maeva for the tenth time.

Not that there were any fish to go away. Unlike Maeva, Marisa had trouble distinguishing between the glint of sun on the surface of the lagoon and the tiny movements that betrayed the presence of a school of fish.

By now it seemed to Marisa that half the islanders, and certainly all the children, were watching her, totally enthralled and no doubt secretly amused by the spectacle. She felt hot, exhausted, frustrated and foolish. Another valiant effort landed in a graceless tangle. And another.

And another. Finally she gave up with a rueful laugh, turning away from the water—and straight into a pair of strong arms that had last been seen paddling away from shore.

"Antoine!"

"I was wondering how long you'd keep it up." Tuan made no effort to hide the amusement that crinkled around his eyes, even from the others who stood about. His hands held her shoulders lightly and affectionately in a way that he would not have tried and she would not have permitted in private.

"Oh...!" Conscious of the fact he was laughing at her humiliation, she clenched her fists tightly and willed him away with her eyes. Where he touched, her skin tingled.

"Easy, Miss Marisa," he teased lightly, reminding her that this was no time to pursue any private feud. Without releasing her he turned and shouted a few words in Tahitian. Bodies started to scatter, leaving them more or less alone on this part of the beach. For the benefit of the few children who remained close enough to hear, he spoke in English. "You've been a good sport. I enjoyed watching you. For a young lady who was bored only a short while ago, you hid it remarkably well. And if it makes you feel better, net fishing is very difficult. I'm just as inept as you are."

Marisa relaxed, or at least made a pretense of it. But it was hard, with the touch of his fingers and the nearness of him, and she averted her eyes.

"I thought you were off with Lotu for the morning," Marisa answered, herself speaking English in response to his lead. Oh, why couldn't she control her fluttering pulses...why did he have to look so damnably attractive, so *male*! The cutoff jeans he wore over the well-remembered bathing suit did nothing to hide the powerful muscle structure of his thighs; and the short-sleeved blue shirt was totally unbuttoned, revealing more of the hair-roughened chest and the flat hard stomach than peace of mind allowed.

"I am off for the morning, actually. We came back to get a another man—Tupui, a young friend of Lotu's. They're waiting for me now. Do you want to come and watch the hunt? I promise you won't be bored."

"Hunt?" For the first time Marisa permitted herself a glance at his intent face.

"For octopus. We've been searching the reef over by my father's house, and we just spotted a large one—a real brute. It was at some distance and it got away from us, so now we're going looking for its lair. Octopus hunting is not a sport everyone would want to see, but I thought if you were truly bored...." His eyes holding hers were like blue patches of Pacific sky. "And as you don't want surprises, I'll describe it. Lotu will dive down and use his body for bait. Then when the octopus has a good tight hold on him, he'll— Why in God's name are you looking at me like that, Marisa?"

"How can you *use* Lotu like that!" she burst out, oblivious of the few people who remained within hearing range.

"Lotu, Tupui, some other man—what's the difference?" A deep frown now grooved Tuan's cheeks, but unlike her he did not raise his voice, and only the increased pressure of his fingers on her arms told her that he had reacted to her outburst at all. "Somebody has to be bait. The octopus won't come out of its lair for a dead fish—and it's something that has to be done, Marisa. It can't be put off."

Marisa simmered down enough that she was no longer attracting attention. "I don't doubt that it has to be done—but why Lotu? He's your *friend*, Antoine, and he could be blinded or mutilated or worse. You can't *use* people all the time! Maeva's child could be born with no father. Or even worse, with half a father—like yours!"

On her arms, the fingers branded her flesh with sudden fury matched only by the blue blaze of his eyes. With a swearword that made others in Marisa's memory grow pale, he pushed her away savagely and strode along the beach toward the outrigger where Lotu waited with a smile on his face.

Later, from a more private stretch of beach where Marisa had gone to be alone with her troubled thoughts, she heard the sounds of men returning from the hunt. Distant laughter told her that there had been no disasters. But even the knowledge that Lotu and his friend Tupui were unharmed could not dispel the coldness she felt inside.

"I had to be sure I could use you," Tuan had said on the day they had met. *Use you...use you...use you.* What demons had driven her to fall in love with a man who used people? Herself, the shadowy Yvonne, even his own father, and now Lotu—they could all be sacrificed. And for what? For a woman who must be an obsession in his life, as in his father's.

For it had not escaped her attention that the octopus sightings had been near Alain de Vigny's bungalow. "Why, I even went swimming the other day," Tania had said. The words had seemed innocuous enough at the time, but now they rang in Marisa's mind.

No wonder Tuan had been searching that part of the reef for hidden dangers. No wonder he had not wanted the octopus hunt to be put off. No wonder he was willing to use Lotu.

The aftermath of the day was anticlimactic. With evident disappointment Maeva told Marisa that the hunters had come home empty-handed. The lair had not been found.

"*Aue,*" she said sadly, "to catch such a creature would have earned Lotu as much *mana* as Vini *tane* himself. Even Uma listens when Vini *tane* speaks."

"Surely you wouldn't want Lotu doing such a dangerous thing!"

"And why not?" shrugged Maeva. "A man must be a man."

With no urging, Maeva began to reveal how the octopus hunt was undertaken. It seemed that the living bait would dive down with an enormous lungful of air, wearing a close-fitting pair of goggles over his eyes to protect this most sensitive part of the body. He would dangle himself temptingly in front of the lair until the horrible invitation was accepted and the octopus seized with several of its tentacles, crushing the bait in its viselike embrace. But the rest of the suckers still held the creature fastened to the wall of its lair, so now the diver's partner would come up from behind and with one tremendous jerk pull octopus and bait together free of the reef. Now the lungful of air played its part, enabling the first diver to float to the surface, shackled by those long sucker-studded arms that would ease their grip only in death.

"Please, Maeva, I don't think I want to hear any more," Marisa said. "It sounds too horrible."

"Horrible?" Maeva looked nonplussed. "It is horrible only if the suckers find an eye. To lose an eye is not so much, but *aue*, the pain may make a man lose his breath, too. And that is not good, for if he loses his breath he cannot float on the surface. And then how can his partner save him?"

"I realize the octopus must be caught," Marisa said to Tuan when Maeva left after the evening meal. "But surely there are other ways! Can't you use a spear gun?"

His brows tilted higher, mocking her. "What? And disappoint the islanders?"

"You can't let Lotu run such a risk!"

"Marisa, you don't seem to understand. Lotu *wants* to act as bait. If I try to stop him, he and Tupui and the other young men will merely go hunting without me. Lotu is a friend, not an employee. He's under no obligation to obey my orders."

She looked at him for a long stony moment, anger building at his callous acceptance of the risks to Lotu. "If you don't stop it somehow, I'll never forgive you, Antoine. Never."

"You break my heart, Miss Marisa," he murmured, his expression still derisive. Then he frowned, turning serious. "The best I can do is extract a promise from Lotu not to go hunting without me. And then... well, I'll do what I can. Will that satisfy you?"

"I suppose it has to," she said stiffly, standing up to depart for the privacy of the bedroom.

"Ah, Miss Marisa," he muttered sardonically, his narrowing eyes suggesting something like exasperation. "I don't believe I've ever met a woman so hard to satisfy."

CHAPTER EIGHT

DOOEY ARRIVED SIX DAYS LATER on one of his regular runs, bringing mail and supplies for the islanders, a briefcase bulging with papers that pressed for Tuan's attention, and a letter for Marisa.

News from Sarah. Strange how far away the United States seemed, almost as though it were another universe! Had she really been here only two weeks, Marisa wondered. Sarah wrote with little anecdotes about the children, who were at last beginning to adjust to their father's death; word of a new kitten that had been added to the household; other trivia. Part of the letter left Marisa puzzling for a time, and she made a mental note to ask Tuan about it, but in the end she did not do so at once, for by now she was avoiding her husband as much as possible. From the first she had felt off balance in his presence, but since the day he had gone to Tahiti and she had recognized her feelings for him, she had become incapable of normal communication. Silence remained her shield in the absence of other defenses.

She saw no reason to doubt her conclusions about her husband's feelings for Tania. If she

wanted more proof of his misguided affections she
found it in the things he had said during her first
twenty-four hours on Ta'aroa. "I am in love,"
had been his harsh admission when pressed for information. Yet the woman he loved was not the
woman he had claimed to love; Marisa was more
than ever sure of that. He had been lying about
Yvonne, and he had almost admitted as much
tacitly.

True, he spent little time at his father's house,
making the trip across the island only when he
needed to use the radiotelephone, ostensibly in
order to communicate with the office in Papeete.
But was it the radiotelephone that drew him there,
or was it Tania? Once Marisa risked asking him
why he didn't have similar equipment installed in a
more convenient location near his own bungalow.

"Perhaps I will someday." He had shrugged as
if it were a matter of total indifference to him.
"But for the moment I prefer to use my father's
equipment. As it is, I can always be reached in an
emergency, and that's quite often enough.
Ta'aroa is my retreat, and I don't want to turn it
into another place of business."

But was that the real reason, Marisa wondered.
Tania's revelations had made it clear that Tuan
could hardly visit his father's bungalow without
an excuse of some kind.

It was not possible for Marisa to avoid her husband altogether. Except for short dips by the shoreline, he still refused to allow her to go swimming

without him. In this he remained unshakable, and
Marisa's only recourse was to insist that all swimming expeditions take place in that part of the
lagoon frequented by islanders.

She did manage now to avoid him most afternoons, and for that the uncaught octopus was to
be thanked. Since the day of its sighting, Tuan and
a number of the young Polynesian men had taken
to diving early each afternoon in the area where it
had been seen. Perhaps it was too well camou-
flaged; perhaps it had been grazing at an unaccustomed distance from its lair; perhaps its
hiding hole was concealed by a peculiar formation
of the coral. For whatever reason, it remained
elusive.

And so, because of this circumstance, did
Marisa. Gratefully she used Tuan's after-lunch
absence to vanish into the interior of the island,
where she would spend the rest of the day in
retreat, not reappearing until the dinner hour.

On an early exploratory trip she discovered a
soft and pleasant valley where waterfalls coursed
down cliffsides green with ferns. The valley
became a favorite hideaway. Here, as in the place
Tania had taken her, there were blankets of moss
on fallen logs, and orchids spilling from aerial
homes, and large-leafed trees drooping shade over
shy wild flowers. A deep rock-strewn pool at the
base of the trickling waterfall became a favorite
place for washing away the morning's salt—not
only because the water was cool and clear, but
because it conserved the precious store of rain-

water at the bungalow. Marisa avoided nudity, conscious that her ablutions might be interrupted at any moment should Tuan decide to come looking for her. She was not foolhardy enough to run such risks. When she changed out of her bathing suit after rinsing her body, she always did so in a small depression in the cliff face—a shallow cave, really, which was almost totally concealed by ferns and trailing vines. Sometimes after bathing she would stay in this hidden place with a book, grateful for the seclusion it provided.

Today, curled into her private hiding place, she had long since changed out of her bathing suit and into a cool embroidered peasant blouse and dirndl skirt. Her newly shampooed hair was brushed and shining and nearly dry; the book lay open in her lap. At the moment it remained unread. She was absentmindedly picking the fronds from a fern and communing with her unhappy thoughts.

The crackle of twigs brought her out of her reverie. She froze into immobility and turned her eyes to the lacy vegetation to see what might have caused the unexpected noise.

The tall familiar figure moved into vision through the shield of greenery. Tuan...! Her heart hammered. There was no escaping now. Perhaps if she stayed very still he would go away. But no: he moved closer and seated himself on a fallen log at the water's edge. He was evidently unaware that he was being observed. He was no more than a half dozen yards distant, close enough that she could see the expression on his face.

It was not the face he reserved for her. It was neither mocking nor cynical nor indifferent nor remote nor scowling nor polite. No, it was an expression much more naked than any of those, an anguished expression, and at the sight of it Marisa's stomach contracted into a small cold knot of something almost like pain. She felt as if she had intruded on something personal, something she should not have seen.

If she needed more evidence of his unnatural passion it was to be found now in the naked anguish of that face. Words learned long ago came flooding back to Marisa: how well they described what she was witnessing now. *And I am desolate and sick of an old passion; yea, hungry for the lips of my desire....*

And no doubt he had been faithful to Tania in his fashion. A man for one woman, Maeva had said: but under the circumstances, Tuan could hardly be sexually faithful to the one woman he loved. No wonder he sought other releases; no wonder he felt urges to assuage his physical needs with any convenient woman, herself included.

The impulse to reach out and comfort him had to be restrained, so she remained silent, scarcely daring to breathe. After a few moments he squared his shoulders, as if shaking off the momentary weakness, and lighted a cigarette. He smoked it in moody silence. The tobacco odor drifted to Marisa's hiding place, mingling with the damp smells of fern and waterfall. Time seemed to stand still.

She closed her eyes and prayed for him to go away. And at last it seemed that he might: the sounds of movement brought her eyes open again. But with a shock she realized that he had no intention of leaving. He had unbuttoned his shirt and was even now shrugging his way out of it, revealing the powerful corded chest and its texture of matted hair. Shoulder muscles rippled into view. And now he was unbuckling his belt....

Again Marisa closed her eyes, feeling faint and panicky. Of course she might have known this would happen! Rinsing in fresh water was not her exclusive prerogative. Why else would Tuan have come to this secluded grotto? If it had occurred to her earlier, she would have braved the confrontation with him, but now it was too late. She could hardly reveal her presence after remaining hidden for so long.

By the time she had lost the struggle with her conscience and opened her eyes, he was already in the water. Hating herself, she watched, unable this time to close her eyes against his intrusive presence. Lazily he swam across the pool. His arms gleamed a polished bronze as they stroked out of the water; his firm hard flanks paled where his bathing suit had protected him from the sun. Near the other edge of the pool he paused, treading water for an instant, for he was still out of depth. His hand reached out as if to touch something on the water's surface, something Marisa could not see. Then, more slowly, he swam back across the pool until he was half a dozen yards away from the near shore.

Now he would leave; surely he must leave... but no, he remained in the water, standing waist-deep. He shook moisture from his head; raked his hair away from his brow; looked at his surroundings in a leisurely fashion, as if in contemplation; scratched his chest; took his time.

"All right, Miss Marisa, you can come out now."

The words came like a stunning blow in the face, driving her into a state of shock.

"I know you're there," he went on. "You can stop pretending. Or would you rather stay in hiding until I dress myself?" He started to move out of the water. "You can watch or not, suit yourself. I'm not particularly modest."

"No—please! Stay where you are," she begged through the screen of ferns.

"Indefinitely?" he asked in an arid voice. "I should have thought I had no secrets from you now."

"I wasn't watching!" she lied as she scrambled from her hiding place, face averted and flaming scarlet that she had been caught in the role of a voyeur. "Wait where you are, and I'll leave."

"Stay put!" he commanded in the kind of voice that stopped her in her tracks.

"I can't stay here now!" Although her back was turned to the water, visions of his wet and gleaming torso remained in her head.

"If you don't I'll walk out as I am and follow you—all the way to the bungalow if necessary. Would you prefer that? If we meet any Tahitians they won't even look twice. Nakedness means nothing on these islands."

"That's blackmail," she gasped, but she moved no farther away.

"Call it blackmail if you want," he said calmly. "But I think it's time you and I had a talk. For this past week you've been fluttering away like a wild bird every time I come near you. God knows, we had a few adult conversations during your first few days here, so I know it's possible. Sit down and we'll have one now."

"I can't have an adult conversation," she choked out, "with a naked man!"

"If that's not an adult conversation I don't know what is." His voice was deliberately wry.

Marisa struggled to calm her quivering nerves. "I'll keep my back turned while you get dressed, and then we'll talk."

"Thanks, but no, thanks," he said, making no effort to hide some amusement at her lack of composure. "I know you too well, Miss Marisa. You'll run the moment I get halfway into my trousers. I'll stay as I am, where I am, and you'll just have to let your imagination run riot. Now turn so I can see your face, and sit down on that fallen log."

He paused a moment, waiting for signs that she intended to obey. When he saw none, he snapped out, *"Now!"*

It took her about two seconds to do as he had asked. Face still stained with color, she adjusted her skirts against the log's surface while she tried to look at some imaginary point several feet from his shoulder. In truth, the water's calm reflective surface showed only mirrored trees, and concealed far more than a bathing suit would have done at this moment. But it was the knowledge of his nakedness that mattered, not the evidence of it.

"That's better," he said with some satisfaction once she had settled. "Now start talking. Start with what you're thinking about right now."

"Well, I'm—I'm upset," she stuttered, in a state of near panic.

"What about?"

"About this silly situation you've trapped me into."

"Trapped *yourself* into, you mean. If you'd said hello I'd never have taken off my clothes."

"You knew I was here all the time!" she accused him with her gaze still pinned to some non-existent object in space.

"I didn't know you were there. I didn't even suspect until I was already in the water and found traces of foam still floating on the surface. You don't find foam in a still pool like this unless someone has been using soap. What were you doing—washing your hair?"

So that was how he had known! Marisa remembered now the way he had reached for something in the water, something she had been unable to see. She cursed her own stupidity for not realizing the shampoo would be evidence of her presence.

"Talk!" he thundered, stirring the water a little as if to make good his threat of coming out.

Marisa jumped like a scared rabbit. "Yes, yes, I was—washing my hair."

"Even then," Tuan went on equably, as if the past small exchange had not taken place, "even then it was only an educated guess. If you hadn't come scrambling out like a child who's been caught at the cookie jar, I might never have known."

"Now you're making me feel foolish, as well," she confessed, trying to find a place to put her eyes.

"What were you doing in your little hide-away?"

"Reading." The trees, hanging upside down in reflection, shimmered a little; flesh gleamed through. Marisa closed her eyes against the images. "I like reading."

"Keep your eyes open, Marisa, or I may decide to come out anyway. I can't talk to someone who won't look at me. And why do you vanish in the afternoons? Do you find my company so distressing?"

"Yes," she said with a little burst of relief that his question had allowed her to tell the truth. Then she asked, "Are you going to keep me on Ta'aroa for the whole month?" Some of the agony of her predicament crept into her voice. "You said it might be less."

He remained silent for a moment before answering, and when he spoke his voice was almost cruel. "Did I? Then I was being too optimistic. Remember, I was forced into this situation, too. I obeyed my father's wishes because of something I wanted—something I still haven't got."

She knew he referred to the property his father had agreed to deed him, but Tania had told her that in a conversation she could hardly repeat. "What if you don't get this—thing—by the end of the month?" Marisa persisted. "What happens then? Will you force me to stay?"

"Do you want to go?"

"Yes," she said to his earlobe. The word hurt her throat.

"You can go," he answered callously, as though he did not care, "when the time is up. Not before. You haven't earned your salary until the month is over—and don't forget the matter of your sister's insurance."

For a moment Marisa's heightened sensibilities kept her from answering.

"I had a letter from my sister yesterday, and—and I thought maybe you'd changed your mind about that."

"What the hell do you mean?"

"She said something about making an appointment to see the mortgage company, in order to pay off the balance. I got the idea she might already have the insurance money."

"Then she's acting prematurely," was Tuan's

abrupt answer. "Now I'm tired of that topic. What book are you reading?"

"A book about the South Pacific—one I found on your shelf. Something about clouds."

"Like the Ta'aroa cloud? Don't look at the sky, Marisa."

"Yes—about how the shape of the island determines the shape of the cloud." She allowed her eyes to come into tentative contact with his. "But you know that."

"Did you know the cloud sometimes blows away when the wind shifts? Oh, it doesn't happen often. For most of the year the trade winds hold the cloud in place. But sometimes a great wind comes out of the northwest—a storm wind. No one is particularly happy to see the Ta'aroa cloud go. The storm winds can be fierce. They can uproot trees, tear roofs off houses, drive coconuts through concrete walls. An island, especially a low island, can be stripped bare in minutes."

A great wind...wasn't that what Tuan had been to her? A great wind that had laid bare her defenses and stripped her of her self-possession; a great wind that had swept through her life and altered it forever. A great wind that did not even know its own power. The irresistible force: hadn't she always known he was that?

"Fortunately," he went on, without remarking on her silence, "the winds don't hit every place every time. A storm can devastate one island and leave its neighbor unscathed. Men can live out

their lives in the Pacific without seeing a hurricane.''

"Have you? Seen one, that is?"

"Several times. But I'm a pilot, remember? I've
traveled more than most men. I've seen the winds,
and I've seen the aftermath, and it's not pretty.
But life has a way of regenerating quickly in this
climate. The scars of nature, even bad scars, heal
with time."

But would they? Marisa was not sure, and certainly as long as she stayed here on Ta'aroa the
healing process could not possibly begin. Moments like this only added to the impossibility.
The wind was still blowing through her life. Un-
consciously she shivered.

"Surely you're not cold?" he observed.

"No—but you must be." Her eyes trailed
downward, past the danger zone of the water.
"Why don't you let me go away and—"

"Why don't you say it? You want to escape."
Once again his tone suggested mockery. "And to
think when I first met you you looked too cool to
be true, as if you could cope with anything. And
now you can't even look me in the eye."

"You have a way of creating circumstances I
can't cope with."

"Relax, Miss Marisa. The situation isn't about
to get out of hand."

"It's out of hand already!"

He laughed unexpectedly, making ripples. "Not
quite out of hand—just snafu, as pilots say. Situa-

tion normal, all fouled up. By tradition it should
be you in the water, and me watching. I assure you
I wouldn't be as circumspect with my eyes. Now
talk, and stop staring at your fingers. Look at
me!''

As her head jerked back to the pool, the water's
surface rippled once more, deranging the glassy
reflection of trees and allowing a disturbingly
clear image. Again she felt the urge to hysteria.
''How long are you planning to keep me here?''

''I'm in no hurry,'' he drawled wickedly, then
added after a moment's reflection, ''On second
thoughts, I'll let you go—temporarily—as soon as
you promise not to avoid my company anymore.
No more running away, and no more silence! I
happen to like female companionship when I'm
on holiday.''

''I can't promise that!''

''You'll have to.'' Coolly he took a single step
forward, and Marisa picked up her skirts and ran.

In her haste she stumbled several times on hidden roots and then collided ignominiously with a
large rock. She gasped as she started to fall, only
to find herself saved—by a pair of very wet hands.

''You shouldn't have run,'' said an amused
voice as he restored her to balance, if not to
equilibrium. Shock and dismay robbed her of
breath as the tall body, overpoweringly male and
overwhelmingly naked, dripped moisture against
her clothes. Forcefully but not hurtfully he propelled her against the trunk of a large tamanu tree.

He trapped her there, now not touching her, with one arm on either side of her body and hands propped loosely against the tree trunk.

"I wouldn't have come out, Miss Marisa, if you'd had the sense to stay put. Did you think I was bluffing when I threatened to follow you?"

Marisa pressed herself against the tree, shrinking as far from him as she could. She dared not move, for to move would be to tempt retribution from those arms that were far too masterful to fight. Every part of her froze—even her eyes, which were riveted to the little droplets of moisture nestling in a bed of dark chest hair. She could not look up for those mocking eyes that lay in wait, and she could certainly not look down. As it was, shock had glued her eyelids open, and she saw far too much.

"Why, you really are in a state," he teased. "Have you never seen a naked man before?"

"Please...!"

"Blushing becomes you, do you know that? That was the first sign of humanity I ever saw in you—blushing."

"I don't think I ever blushed in my life until I met you!"

"Is that a compliment? If so, it's the first you've ever paid me."

Marisa managed, the feat of closing her eyes. "Compliment or complaint, does it matter? I don't like blushing. Now please...."

"Don't worry, I'm not about to touch, much as

I'd like to. I learned my lesson the first two days
you were here. Now will you make the promise I
asked for? I warn you, you'd better make it
soon—very soon—or I really will give you something to blush about. I have a very active imagination, Miss Marisa, and it doesn't take actual skin
contact to—"

Her eyes flew open again. "I promise," she
gasped at once.

"Not a moment too soon," Tuan remarked
dryly, stepping back at last, a move that had the
disconcerting effect of putting more of him in
view. "Now don't run," he warned, and turned to
retrieve his clothes.

He dressed without taking time to dry his body
properly, and moments later, decently if rather
clingingly covered, he returned to Marisa's side,
still fastening the snap of the cream denims that
now molded his muscular thighs.

"Now start living up to your promises," he said
coolly. "I'm going sailing this afternoon, and I'd
like someone to crew. You'll have to join me, like
it or not. Well, Miss Marisa, are you coming?"

"Yes, Antoine," she said—for her, very meek-
ly.

CHAPTER NINE

"Now that Maeva's taught me so much about Polynesian cooking," Marisa announced a few days later, "I'm going to make tonight's dinner all on my own."

It was breakfast time, and Marisa had chosen this moment to speak to her husband for the pure and simple reason that Maeva was present. In the past few days, the promise extracted by Tuan had done nothing to ease relations between them: the situation had in fact deteriorated. Marisa knew a large part of it was her own fault. Tuan had told her he could not stand poison-tongued females, and that, she admitted ruefully, was what she was fast becoming. His usual manner—one of dry mockery—turned her overly touchy; and her touchiness in turn brought out the worst in him— that swift anger that could strike with such whirl-wind suddenness and pass just as quickly. Now every private encounter seemed to lead to a fight.

And she did not want to fight about this.

"I thought I should try my hand at a meal," she went on, "as Maeva's time must be getting close."

"A good idea," Tuan drawled, "and probably

as good a cure as anything for—whatever it is that ails you."

Marisa ignored his gibe and turned to Maeva. "And I'm going to have company for dinner. I've chosen an early hour so that we can eat on the veranda before it gets dark. You're invited, Maeva—you and Lotu."

"Remember the pecking order on the island," Tuan interjected coolly in English.

"And your mother, too, of course," Marisa added quickly in French. "I'll walk by her hut after breakfast and issue the invitation myself."

Maeva accepted with alacrity, and Tuan smiled, satisfied. But the smile died on his lips as Marisa plunged on, now directing her words to him, "I'm also including Tania and your father."

He said nothing, but his face tightened perceptibly.

"I've already invited them," Marisa informed him. Her eyes met his directly, and in them was a challenge. "I sent one of the island boys over there yesterday with a note. Tania sent a short note back accepting."

"My father never leaves his own compound." Tuan spoke slowly, his voice taut with disapproval.

"Well, tonight he is leaving it. I suggested they try coming by outrigger, and evidently your father agreed to that. I knew you'd be pleased."

Tuan looked anything but pleased, although in Maeva's presence he made no more demur. Yet, seeing the expression on his face, Marisa began to regret yesterday's hasty decision to invite Alain and Tania. Why *had* she invited them? She had known even as she penned the invitation that to see Tania and Tuan together would be like salt water on an open sore. But Tania had mentioned that Alain had improved since Tuan's marriage, and in the end compassion for Tania had led Marisa to make the decision. Surely Alain de Vigny would improve even more if he could see the marriage working out? Tuan always managed to put on a good show in the presence of others. And for one night she herself could pretend—no, stop pretending. It would be no pretense now to let the love shine unshuttered in her eyes.

Later that day, in the half hour before the dinner guests arrived, she found herself regretting the decision all over again. It was not for lack of preparation. Marisa was dressed; the dinner was cooked; the table on the broad veranda had been set for seven and looked beautiful with silver and sprays of orchids.

But it was a time of day that Marisa always found trying, as was any time of day when her husband had to change his clothes. Not that she ever entered the bedroom when he changed; on the contrary, she made a point of remaining as far away as possible. But there was something agitating about the thought of him rummaging through closets where their clothes hung side by side in silent treacherous intimacy. And always there was some evidence of him afterward, sometimes a discarded sock, personal as a signature; sometimes a hanger replaced askew, dislodging one of her garments; sometimes a towel damp from his body; and inevitably the faint lingering scent of him, a tang of salt and soap and the lemon freshness of after-shave.

Yes, it was a difficult time of day... and more so today because of the evening that lay ahead.

The sound of the shower—that was the thing that always triggered the unwanted visions that kept intruding on her mind. Why *must* she keep seeing his nakedness as she had seen it that day? Her skin turned hot at the vision those shower sounds awakened, and she hurried to the veranda to spend some unnecessary time with the floral arrangements. The little beads of moisture in a bed of crisp body hair, the broad bronzed chest, the long bronzed limbs, the hard, virile, unbronzed flanks—

"Very pretty orchids," came a dry voice from behind her. "Is there some reason you've shredded one all over the tablecloth?"

Marisa's stomach took a brief roller-coaster ride. Swiftly she swept up the evidence of her distraction and tossed it into the lagoon; by the time she turned to face Tuan her defenses were very nearly in order. "I do wish you wouldn't startle a person like that," she said crossly. "Frankly, I was pretending the orchid was a certain acquaintance."

He raised his eyebrows in a way that suggested derision, and handed her one of the two drinks he had brought outside. "Ah, Miss Marisa, one of us can be likened to an orchid tonight, but it's certainly not me." His eyes trailed downward over the supple flow of soft printed silk that concealed skin but not curves. "Even clings like an orchid," he murmured mockingly.

"How thrilling," Marisa said caustically, "to be likened to a parasite."

He compressed his lips briefly, and some of the mocking light faded. "I was referring to the dress clinging, not the person. Certainly not the person. Now sheathe the claws, will you? I refuse to fight tonight. Oh, by the way." He delved into the trouser pocket of a white slubbed-linen suit that turned his tan to teak. The movement had the effect of straining the fabric over those powerful thighs, reminding Marisa all over again of what she did not want to remember.

"You left these in the bathroom," he said, fishing out two rings—the large emerald, and the narrow circle of smaller emeralds and diamonds that was her wedding ring. "You can hardly go without these tonight. Why did you take them off?"

"Wishful thinking," she remarked airily, avoiding his touch as she received the rings and slid them back on her finger. In truth, she had removed them for safety's sake during dinner preparations.

"Perhaps you shouldn't have planned tonight's dinner." His voice now bore distinct traces of exasperation. "It seems you have too much trouble pretending."

"I don't know what you mean," she temporized, swirling her glass.

"You damn well do," he disputed. "And as *you* invited the guests, the least you can do is put on a show. If you can't pretend you love me, at least pretend you hate me a little less."

"There's no reason to pretend before the company arrives."

"Good God—is it so hard? What *is* the matter, Marisa? Ever since the other day when I trapped you by the pool, you've been behaving like a cornered cat. If something's bothering you, get it out."

"Nothing's bothering me!" she lied. "Except a whole lot of little things. Your bathing suit, for one. If you didn't hang it in the bathroom, you wouldn't have to go in so often to get it. Besides, I don't like *seeing* it there."

"Next to yours?" His voice was sardonic. "Well, that's where it's going to stay, for I won't hang it in the living room. And if you're still asleep, well, I can always go without."

"Or you could go without the swim," she suggested irritably.

"Why should I? I always swim without bathing trunks when I'm alone—or even sometimes when I'm in less susceptible company." An amused blue

gleam grew in his eye; perhaps he, too, was remembering the scene. "Yes, Miss Marisa, I've
been quite circumspect—I haven't ignored your
tender sensibilities. Except for the other day, the
only time I've gone without was the very first
morning you were here."

"So much for my tender sensibilities!"

"Ah, but I walked to another cove south of
here, in case you should wake up." He grinned,
guardedly but engagingly. "Am I forgiven?"

The smile turned her insides to putty and made
a brittle retort impossible. She turned a little
and lowered her head so that her hair swung into
a silky curtain, hiding many things. "I'm being silly. There's nothing to forgive. It must
be a case of nerves—this masquerade is much
harder than I thought it would be, and I'm nervous about tonight's dinner. Of *course* your
bathing suit doesn't bother me. I can't think why I
said it."

He pounced on her earlier thought. "Harder
than you expected? In what way?"

"I—oh. . . ." Why must he be so perceptive, so
quick to move to the heart of the matter? "I'm
anxious for it to be over, that's all. It seems like
the longest month in my life."

"It hasn't been a month." His voice had grown
hard, and without looking at him she could feel
the frown. "You agreed to a month, and there's
still more than a week to go. If you back out now
you know the consequences." Abruptly he

downed his drink. "I'm not through with you yet."

"Using me?" she asked bitterly, her thoughts traveling briefly to the still unsuccessful search for the octopus.

"Using you..." he repeated after her, and raked his fingers through his hair angrily. "Oh, dammit, Marisa, let's start all over again. What is it about you and me that makes sparks fly? Surely we can behave like civilized people for a little longer. Especially tonight. My father's been better since the marriage, and I wouldn't want anything to cause a setback. That's why I was unwilling for him to come tonight. Can you pretend to be a woman in love—or do you hate me so much it's impossible?"

Unshed tears ached somewhere behind her eyes, turning the lagoon an impossible blinding green. "I can pretend," she lied.

"Then start pretending," he muttered, and moved closer—so close that she could feel the heat of his body and the grazing of his thighs on hers. "Here comes the outrigger now."

She turned her head and saw a white claw of sail cleaving the lagoon's turquoise mirror, moving slowly in the protected lee of the island. From this distance the pareu-clad passenger could have been almost any of the island women, but the unsunned skin of the figure at the helm was unmistakably that of Alain de Vigny. As the outrigger neared, an arm circled Marisa's shoulder, pretending affection in a way that turned her nerve endings to a silent scream.

"Now try a smile—in my direction. If you can't smile, then frown. Upside down."

The bantering lightness of her husband's tone made the smile at last possible, and she gave it to him tremulously.

"That's better. That mouth wasn't made for frowns, you know. It's made for something... quite different. Now don't shrink away from me just because I paid you a compliment. We can be seen quite clearly."

His nearness was overwhelming, washing over her until awareness of him was like a pain. She became totally conscious of the way his shoulders, at eye level, pressed against the cut of the suit; the way crisp chest hairs could be seen through the fine blue fabric of his shirt—mid-blue, a match for his eyes, so that she felt the eyes even though she refused to look at them. And at last, giving in because she knew she must, she sighed and sank into the curve of his arm where she had longed so often to be.

"Keep it up," he murmured, his lips winnowing the tendrils of silken hair at her temples. "Remember it's only a game of make-believe. Now keep playing the game...."

The outrigger docked at the base of the veranda, where for the convenience of swimmers a flight of steps led directly down into the lagoon. Tania, playing her own kind of game, stepped out

of the boat and drew Marisa skillfully into the interior of the house, not watching while Tuan
helped his father moor the outrigger and make the
difficult ascent.

By the time Marisa saw Alain de Vigny again,
he was already seated beside the dinner table on
the chair he would use throughout the meal. By
that time the others had arrived—Maeva and Lotu
on foot; Uma, larger than life, in her ubiquitous
litter. The litter bearers deposited the enormous
Polynesian woman at the base of the bridge that
led across the lagoon and then, leaving the litter
on the site for later use, departed. Uma made her
way across the bridge with a regal rolling gait,
dispensing smiles like alms. In truth, she was
remarkably spry for a woman of such girth, and
Marisa wondered with brief amusement whether
the litter was not more for prestige than for prac-
ticality, as Tuan had suggested.

Tuan was right about one other thing: his father
showed considerable improvement. Alain still
followed Tania with his eyes, but it was possible to
see what manner of man he had been before his
accident—witty, charming, urbane, volatile,
virile. As drinks were served on the veranda, he
seemed to improve even more, undoubtedly
because of the attentions Tuan was paying Marisa.
Tuan was playing his game well, and Marisa was,
too. Theirs were the little covert gestures of lovers
who long to be alone—the light body brushings,
the brief meetings of eyes or fingers; and even

when nothing touched, an awareness that crackled across space like electricity between opposing poles. Or so it appeared—and for Marisa appearances did not lie.

An hour of drinks and hors d'oeuvres and chatter seemed to put all the guests at ease. Through the preliminaries Alain de Vigny and Uma remained seated at the table, with chairs turned outward so that they were a part of the small group that milled around the veranda decking. And at last, with some sense of pride in an accomplishment that had taken her most of the day, Marisa produced several side dishes and a great steaming bowl of *pota*—a rich concoction of young taro leaves cooked with bits of pork and thick coconut cream. And it was then that she knew her dinner was destined to be remembered, but not for culinary achievement.

Maeva took one mouthful and a peculiar look came over her face.

With dismay Marisa watched her, wondering what dreadful mistake she might have made in the relatively simple recipe. With misgivings she took a bite from her own plate. But her own *pota* tasted adequate, and others at the table were not making faces.

Maeva put her fork down with total calmness. "I must go," she said, dabbing her mouth with a napkin.

"Maeva—is something wrong?"

"My time has come." Another brief spasm crossed the young girl's face.

"Eat," said Uma phlegmatically, downing an enormous mouthful. "When the pains start there is still time to enjoy. It will be hours before your girl child is born."

"Perhaps it will be a boy child," Lotu contradicted, but deferentially. He shot a proud pleased glance at Maeva, rewarding her for her announcement of imminence. As the prospective father, he seemed no more flustered than any of the other Polynesians present. For what event was more natural, more welcome, than childbirth?

"It will be a girl child—what else?" Uma decreed, for the first time looking put out, and paying no attention to Maeva's rapidly changing expressions.

"It wishes to be born at once," Maeva said more urgently with a strangled look on her face. She pushed her chair away from the table. "I must go."

Uma looked at her daughter with unconcealed moon-faced amazement. "But the pains only started," she said.

"They started this afternoon," Maeva now admitted, "but I wished to say nothing. I thought they might go away, or wait until after Marisa *vahine*'s dinner. But now—"

She doubled over, unable to walk, and all at once the Polynesians sprang into action. When a woman could not stand straight and walk to her own bed of labor, it was time for others to act.

"Come, Maeva," Lotu said solicitously, putting his arm around her shoulder.

"To the bedroom," suggested Marisa.

"No, to my own hut," gasped Maeva.

Moving with astonishing alacrity, Uma caught up with her daughter. She placed her hand briefly on Maeva's round belly, judging the hardness of it. "Carry her to the litter," she ordered, at once taking charge. "There is still time for her to reach her own hut. Then she will not have to walk home after."

"She wouldn't have to—"

But Marisa's protests were lost in the confusion of what was happening. Within seconds Maeva had been bundled out the front door and over the bridge, followed by all members of the ill-fated dinner party except Alain de Vigny. With cautious haste Lotu settled the mother-to-be on the litter.

Because of Uma's great weight, the litter was designed to be carried by four people. Although Lotu and Tuan might easily have managed the lesser burden of Maeva, they could not do so because of the placement of the handles. Uma and Tania did not need instruction. Like the two men, each woman moved to a litter handle and accepted a share of the load.

Marisa, who had brought up the vanguard when the small party erupted from the bungalow, started to protest that she would take a litter handle instead of Uma.

"Look after my father instead," Tuan ordered crisply, and with no further ado the odd assemblage moved off down the beach at a near trot. In the midst of her anxiety about Maeva, Marisa found a bubble of hysteria rising in her throat at the sight of Uma rolling away into the distance, carrying her own litter.

Well, she had seen many incongruous sights since coming to the South Pacific, but this was one sight that would linger in her memory always! She turned back to the veranda where Alain de Vigny waited and as she passed the kitchen spared a brief rueful thought for the wasted hours she had spent baking bananas, frying taro root into fritters and squeezing the cream of shredded coconut through cheesecloth.

Her father-in-law was stirring fretfully in his chair. "I don't suppose they'll be too long," he said. The frown that had been smoothed away during the past hour had returned to mar the otherwise handsome forehead.

"I don't suppose they'll come back at all," Marisa said absentmindedly, thinking of Uma and Lotu—and then realized Alain de Vigny's thoughts were with two other people entirely. "I imagine Tania will stay until the child is safely delivered," she added quickly. "And with the speed at which things appear to be happening, that may well be before sundown! Which do you think it will be—a girl for Uma or a boy for Lotu?"

But Alain's mind was elsewhere. Food pushed aside, he slumped into some world of inner purgatory, and for the next hour conversation was at best one-sided. He appeared to hear little of what

Marisa said, and his gloom deepened as the sun
dipped near the horizon, a great orange ball over a
blue blue sea.

"I'd better put this food away before it spoils,"
Marisa finally observed with false cheerfulness.
Alain did not even answer. His eyes were brooding
at the empty stretch of beach that led to the village
of nipa huts.

If the first hour had been difficult, the second
and the third became impossible. By the time
Marisa had cleared away the uneaten dinner a pall
of darkness had closed over the veranda. True, interior lights shone through the open double door
and cast some illumination on the outside, as did
the phosphorescence from the lagoon. But the
table itself was in deep shadow. Several times
Marisa suggested moving inside; Alain de Vigny
did not even seem to hear.

And at length, exhausted with unreciprocated
efforts and unable to think of one more word to
say, Marisa gave up and subsided into total
silence, by now nearly as depressed as her guest.
The venoms of Alain de Vigny's imaginings infected the very air.

It was nearly midnight before sounds were
heard and shadowy shapes seen approaching
along the now moonlit beach. With the same
agony of movement that Marisa had witnessed
once before, Alain de Vigny rose to his feet and
dragged himself toward the sliding glass door. Its
double width was already wide open to permit

cooling breezes full sway. He pushed aside the screens, also, but he did not enter the house. He remained on one side of the doorway, standing in the spilling light of the living room, his tall body held rigidly erect, his features contorted with the pains of the flesh and the poisons of the mind. His eyes were riveted to the entrance through which Tania and Tuan would soon walk. Marisa moved up to stand beside him in the wide doorway, her heart in her throat with apprehension.

"I'm sorry we were so long, Alain." Tania came across the living room quickly, graceful in the light fluid wrapping of her pareu, a serene smile concealing the worry that Marisa suspected lurked behind the rich chocolate depths of her eyes. Immediately behind her Tuan entered, tall, powerful, handsome, virile—unmistakably a man who might stir any woman's sexual responses. His shirt was rumpled; his jacket had been removed and was now slung over one shoulder, hooked by a thumb.

With every sick cell of her imagination Marisa lived through some of the torments Alain de Vigny must be suffering now.

Tania had reached her husband, and her slender hand came out, touching his arm. Now the worry crept through to her eyes. "Are you all right, Alain?"

"What time was Maeva's child born?" he asked in a sick thick voice.

"Soon after we left. But—"

With the suddenness of a striking snake, the back of Alain de Vigny's hand cracked across his wife's face in a stunning blow that caused a pained intake of breath, not only from Tania but from Tuan and Marisa, too.

Deep shock touched Tania's eyes. Swaying, she stared at her husband as if she had never seen him before. "Alain," she whispered as her hand crept up to touch her cheek.

For one moment of frozen outrage Tuan had remained rooted to the floor across the room. But now in several long limber strides he was across the space. He seized his father, a man nearly as tall as himself, and slammed him bodily and explosively against the door frame. Wind knocked from his lungs, Alain de Vigny emitted a deep grunt of pain and remained pinned in place like a puppet suspended by his son's avenging grip. His expression was one of deep and terrible numbness, as if he did not yet realize what had happened.

Tania, doubtless afraid that Tuan might lose control, flew to her husband's defense. She seized Tuan's broad shoulders and tried to pull him away. "No, Tuan, *please*—"

For the moment he ignored her; an unholy light glinted in his eyes. "If you ever do that again," he warned his father in a steely voice, "I'll thrash you within an inch of your life. I don't give a damn if we're not evenly matched. Hurt her and I'll—"

"Tuan!" Tania's voice was urgent, desperate.

"Alain's never done such a thing before. Please—
please!"

At last Tuan's hands relaxed their iron grip,
although the knuckles remained whitened with the
effort of self-control. Released, Alain de Vigny
stumbled and quickly regained balance against the
door frame.

"You'd better leave," Tuan ordered grimly.

Alain de Vigny, thoroughly sick faced, turned
to Tania, issuing with his eyes a silent plea and
perhaps a silent apology, as well.

"Excuse me, I have to attend to my hair," she
said, and vanished like an obedient wraith into the
bedroom. With a warning narrowing of eyes in his
father's direction, Tuan followed her, but returned in moments; evidently he had wished only
to assure himself that she was all right.

With no word spoken, Alain de Vigny made his
agonizing way to the outrigger. With no word
spoken, Tuan followed. It was as if neither man
could trust himself to speak.

In the end it was Marisa who broke the silence,
partially in hopes of oiling troubled waters. She
turned to Tuan, who like herself had remained
near the top of the flight of stairs that led down to
the water. At some point he had switched on an
outdoor light of which Marisa had been unaware;
it illumined the set faces of both the men.

"How is Maeva?" Marisa asked.

"She's fine," came the short answer. "No trouble with the birth. She's asleep now."

"Boy or girl?"

"Girl."

"Oh." Marisa felt a twist of disappointment for Maeva's sake. Now it seemed unlikely that Lotu would propose.

"There was trouble, though—between Lotu and Uma. That's what kept us so late. Fact is, the whole damn village was in on the spree. Everybody and his uncle had to have a say."

Now Alain de Vigny's bowed head came up. The tortures in his eyes told that he knew what a terrible thing he had done—a thing even more terrible than he had at first believed, because it now seemed that perhaps it had been done without just cause.

"Tania will tell you about it," Tuan told his father in a curt voice, as his stepmother emerged into the night and started down the stairs to the water's edge. The outdoor light caught the smooth golden sheen of her skin and the luster of her long black hair. Now her still almond eyes reflected nothing of the troubled depths within. Marisa watched her with an ache deep in her heart, an ache too deep to be mere envy. How beautiful Tania was—how fluid, how fragile, how exquisite, how extraordinary. No wonder the emotions of both father and son were bound to this woman in a fearful life-shattering way that was destroying the soul of one man and the heart of the other.

The good-nights were polite but strained, and soon the outrigger slipped silently across the still lagoon, its wake of green phosphorescence shivering through the wide silver path laid there by the moon. Tuan watched it go, and Marisa watched Tuan covertly, perturbed by the tightness etched into the clefts of his cheeks.

When the outrigger could no longer be seen he turned abruptly and headed inside for the liquor cabinet, followed more slowly by Marisa.

"Drink?" he offered.

Emotionally exhausted by the events of the evening, Marisa sank into a chair and nodded. Her head throbbed. "A small one. Gin and lime. What was the trouble between Uma and Lotu?"

Tuan handed her a tinkling glass. "Lotu told Maeva he wanted to marry her, despite the fact that it was a girl child. Uma was very angry—started exerting her authority."

"About what?"

"She doesn't want Maeva to marry. If Maeva marries, there goes Uma's chance of getting a child—Lotu wants to keep the baby. So Uma started throwing her weight around—figuratively, not literally. She can be a holy terror when she wants. She told Lotu if he wasn't enough of a man to produce a boy child, he wasn't enough of a man to marry her daughter. Things got pretty hectic, especially when Uma pointed out three other children Lotu has fathered by other *vahines*—all of them girl children."

"Good grief," Marisa said, with a little disbelieving sound that was not quite laughter.

"Ah, on this island that's not considered immoral. No man would consider marrying a girl until she had proved herself capable of bearing children—not necessarily his."

"Yet Uma married," Marisa said thoughtfully, "and Maeva once told me she had no children of her own."

"Yes, she did—once. Two little boys. They both died of measles."

"Measles?"

"The Polynesians are very susceptible to it, especially the purebred Polynesians, as Uma is. She nearly died of it herself, and a result was able to produce no more children."

"Poor Uma," murmured Marisa, feeling a swift stab of pity.

"It was a long time ago—twenty-five years ago, when Uma was about your age. Her grief passed long ago." Tuan frowned, downed his drink and poured another from a new bottle of Scotch. He had remained standing across the room, near the liquor cabinet. Although he had not been pacing the floor, there was a tension in that long body that suggested he wished to do so. Restless like the wind, Maeva had said once...and now Marisa understood why.

"The upshot of the evening's argument," Tuan went on, "is that Uma refuses permission for the marriage. The rest of the islanders sided with Uma. It was a free-for-all."

"And Maeva—poor Maeva! Giving birth, and

then having all these arguments swirling around her! Didn't anyone think about *her*?''

"Tania did; that's why she didn't come back sooner. And I stayed because Lotu needed an ally. The whole village seemed to think he had made an improper suggestion, wanting to marry Maeva and keep the child when Uma had been told she could have it if it was a girl child.''

Marisa's expression told of her perplexity at all things Polynesian. "I wish I could understand about all this trading of children," she sighed. "Maeva told me the islanders sometimes gamble for a child. It seems so incredible.''

"Not that incredible when you think of the way they live—out in the open, milling about so that they see each other every day. They're like an extended family unit. The children are minded by whoever happens to be nearest. You'll hardly ever hear a child cry, for the closest woman always scoops it up to comfort it—every woman as warm and loving and caring as the child's own mother. That's why they trade children so easily, and why the children don't mind. In the dialect used on this island, the word for 'mother' means any female relative at all.''

"All the same, T—Antoine, it seems odd. I think Maeva would probably like to keep her baby, and I *know* she wants to marry Lotu.''

"She *did* want to marry Lotu,'' Tuan corrected. "She's refused the offer. Lotu's lost face, and I think she's disappointed in him now.''

"Good grief—why?"

"Because he didn't win the argument with Uma."

"Oh, Lord," muttered Marisa, unnerved by the complications of island life. What had seemed on arrival in Ta'aroa to be a very straightforward and joyous community was taking on all the aspects of a circus run by madmen. "Can't something be done?"

"I don't know." A frown fretted at Tuan's brow. "You have to understand about Polynesia. In the old days great battles were won or lost on the strength of two men standing shouting at each other on the beach—whole islands, whole kingdoms changed hands on the outcome, sometimes without a drop of blood being shed. Lotu's defeat tonight was a very serious thing."

"Surely Maeva will change her mind by tomorrow?"

"It won't be that easy," Tuan informed Marisa glumly. "Maeva was in her hut all this time, of course, but she sent word out that she won't marry Lotu until he proves he's a man. She was quite adamant, and there were many witnesses—half the island women were crowded into her hut."

"After fathering four children it seems to me Lotu's proved more than enough!"

"I imagine Maeva doesn't want to marry a man who can be browbeaten by her mother. Tania tried to talk reason, but Maeva wouldn't listen."

Tania. And that was another matter that needed

broaching. Marisa spent some moments studying the pale polish of her fingernails, loath to bring up the subject and unable to look at Tuan now. "That's another thing we should talk about," she said finally.

"There's nothing to talk about."

"You can't pretend now that there's nothing wrong between Tania and your father!" She risked a brief glance at his face and saw it fully shuttered against her curiosity.

"That's their business," he said brusquely.

"You made it your business tonight," Marisa pointed out.

"What did you expect me to do? Stand by and watch?"

Marisa persisted, "I think you should talk to me about what's behind it, Antoine, especially as I'm sure it has something to do with why I'm here on Ta'aroa. Whatever it is, I'll—I'll understand."

"No, you won't," he said ferociously, his face grooving in that way that told her he resented her questioning. "My father doesn't like Tania out of his sight, that's all. In any case, it has nothing to do with why you're here. Nothing!"

"That's not true," she whispered, and turned cold at the look of fierce closed arrogance that came over his face. Then, braving on, "And why does it put you on edge when I ask questions?"

Tuan appeared to control himself, but with some difficulty. His eyes turned opaque, and he forced a small laugh. "It seems to me you're the one who's been on edge," he said dryly. "You admitted as much earlier. A case of nerves, you said—but you never told me why."

Marisa huddled her arms around herself and then took a steadying sip of her own drink—a concoction much more powerful than she had requested. Tuan usually poured drinks with a light hand, but not tonight. And it had not escaped her attention that he had deliberately turned the conversation away from the subject of Tania.

"*Why*, Marisa?"

"Oh...." Her eyes glued themselves to his belt buckle. "It's the climate...and the pounding of the surf...and that huge blue sky...and the way we're living here together, alone, day after day after day. It's...grating on me. That, and the wind that never stops blowing in one direction. Dooey said that drove some people mad."

With deliberation Tuan put his unfinished drink on the cabinet and moved slowly toward her. Eyes transfixed, she watched the belt buckle advance, supremely conscious of the hard tissue of flesh and sinew that lay behind it.

He pulled her to her feet and with a knuckle to her chin forced her to meet his gaze. His face was very grave, somehow older. "Are you trying to tell me that you have sexual urges? Or is there more to it than that?"

"No, I...." Resisting the force of his hand, she wrested her head sideways because she could not bear those eyes like probes, exploring the nakedness of her expression. "I suppose there are some...sexual urges involved," she admitted, confessing to that part she could bear to confess, because he must in any case be able to feel it in the quivering of her body. His hands had traveled to her upper arms, and his fingers were like brands on the vulnerable flesh.

"And that's why you've been so jumpy? Because you want to sleep with me?"

"No, I—"

His grip tightened on her shoulders, as if to squeeze the admission from her. "Don't lie," he said in a low vibrant voice that was like fingers on her flesh. His breath was too near and too warm and too male, and deeply scented with alcohol.

"No!" The cry was torn from her very soul, and she wrenched herself away, pulses pounding. With a sob and a last anguished look at his dangerously darkened eyes, she ran for the bedroom. She closed the door and leaned against it, half hoping he would follow, yet knowing if he followed it would be for the wrong reasons: that he loved Tania; that for him sex was something else; that she would be no more than a substitute; that marriage to this man, real marriage, would only break her heart....

She walked unsteadily to the bed and sat on its edge for a long time, watching the door. He did not follow. He touched her door no more tonight than he had touched it on other nights. No action could have told her more clearly that Tuan did not wish the marriage in word to become one in deed.

At last, heartsick, she donned her nightgown, a sliver of flesh-colored bias-cut satin, crawled into bed and turned out the bedside lamp. For a long time she lay in misery, racked by the unsatisfied cravings of her body and her heart, watching the narrow sliver of light beneath the door. Prowling footsteps and the clink of glass told her that Tuan, too, was still awake. Brooding, perhaps, over the night's events; wondering what scenes might be taking place halfway across the island between Tania and his father....

"Oh, Tuan, I love you," she moaned to her pillow in a voice so low it was barely audible even to her own ears.

And three hours later, when the enormous crash reverberated through the night, she had only just drifted into sleep.

CHAPTER TEN

SHE WAS AWAKE AT ONCE, sitting bolt upright in bed, heart pounding and nerves jangling. Had it been a part of a dream—that shattering noise that splintered the night? The lights were still on in the living room. She heard shuffling sounds, a muffled thud, then a low groan. Without a further flicker of hesitation she pushed aside her tumbled sheets and raced to the livingroom door, not giving thought to the inadequacy of her apparel.

Antoine was standing in the far corner of the room, close to the wide daybed. His eyes were glazed, his stance unsteady. He had removed shirt and shoes and socks. A trail of clothing littered the floor—clothing, and glass.

There was glass all over the place, the remains of the shattered sliding door. An emptied liquor bottle, also broken, resided among the paler shards. It took Marisa only seconds to piece together what must have happened: Tuan, driven by his own particular demons, must have hurled the emptied bottle at the door. What terrible emotions must have been aroused in him by the sight of his father's physical abuse of Tania!

"Wait, don't move!" Marisa cried, eyes now finding the bloodied floor near his unprotected feet.

It was as if he had not heard. His goal was bed, and in his state of inebriation he was apparently beyond reason. His eyes were turned in her direction, but there was no recognition in them; she might have been invisible. Even as she stood rooted to the floor, unable as yet to move to his aid because of her own bare feet and the barrier of broken glass that lay between them, his hands started to fumble with his belt buckle.

"Tuan, no," she whispered, eyes rounding as a new kind of alarm seized her. But his fingers, though unsteady, moved unerringly to the zipper and propelled it downward. With less success his thumbs caught at the waistband of his trousers and his underwear, too, and pushed at it where a dark arrowing of hair vanished out of view. For a brief moment he swayed and leered drunkenly, as if he had finally become aware of her presence, but it did not stop him in his intent. Fabric bunched into his hands, he pushed downward; and then, standing on one foot, he freed himself of the first trouser leg. The movement caused him to trip on the second trouser leg. He crashed backward, six foot two of drunken male animal, and the daybed broke his fall.

"Tuan!"

A deep groan was his only answer. He rolled over onto his stomach. Unconscious—some part of Marisa's mind informed her of this at once. He was unconscious, and unlikely to be capable of doing anything more for himself.

It took only seconds to race for a pair of light satin mules to protect her own vulnerable soles. With no heed yet for the broken glass, she crunched her way to the daybed. A brief glimpse told her there was not too much glass in the immediate vicinity, so she knelt down at once to examine his bloodied feet. At the moment only one foot was exposed; the other was still entrapped in a trouser leg. The cuts she could see were small, light surface wounds only. With some difficulty she managed to tug the last of his clothing free, exposing the other foot. There, too, to her relief, she found little damage. One small splinter of glass embedded in the heel appeared to be the major source of blood, and she pried it out painstakingly with her fingernails. That done, she sat back on her haunches. Now that she had assured herself the damage was slight, the knowledge of his nakedness unsteadied her. She found the light throw he used at night and drew it over his body, leaving the feet exposed because she had not yet finished attending to them.

She picked a careful path to the kitchen, finding and dampening a cloth with which to wipe away the blood. Tuan kept a well-stocked first-aid kit, and this, too, she located before returning to the living room.

Although she applied iodine liberally, he did not

even stir: apparently he was too far gone to feel its
sting. That done, she turned her attention to the
glass. It would not be possible to clean up all
the damage tonight, but she managed to pile the
larger, heavier pieces of plate glass neatly out of
harm's way; the smaller shards were swept up and
safely disposed of in the dustbin. She restored the
broom and dustpan to the cupboard where they
were kept and returned once more to the living
room. She turned off all lights except those that
gleamed greenly upward from the lagoon through
the Plexiglas window in the floor. Those she
would leave on in case Tuan woke and needed
light.

And then, hesitantly but impelled by some urge
deeper than reason, she walked back to the daybed
where he lay. He had rolled onto his back again.
The cover had worked partly free and lay loosely
over the board-flat reaches of his lower waist. His
chest lay fully exposed—that broad forested chest
she had so often longed to explore. To her eyes
and to her hand it was like a magnet. Obeying an
instinct too imperative to resist she knelt beside
the couch and touched—a feather-light laying on
of one hand, but it conveyed to her unbearably
sensitized touch the warmth and strength and
virility of his alcohol-drugged body.

He still did not stir, and perhaps that was what
robbed her of reason—the utter defenselessness of
the hard body that lay beneath her palm. What
wild unheeding need drove her to hover so long

over the sun-bronzed skin...to explore the well-loved contours of his face, the rivers in his cheeks, the strong straight nose, the brows, the temples, the closed unseeing eyes? There was a fine agony in her fingertips as she traced and probed the slightly parted lips—feeling the warmth of his mouth, the fanning of his breath, the moistures of him. She touched her fingertips to her own lips and tasted the taste of him. She felt the roughness of his jaw and the hollows in the deep strong column of his throat, and reveled in the textures of him. She drew the line of his collarbone, and then another line—a long, slow, compulsive journey that impelled her fingertips down the length of his chest to his navel and below, and when she could resist no longer, she folded back the light covering. And then her wanton eyes explored. Heat prickled over her skin, and some inner part of her turned to an aching void.

"Oh, God," she whispered, and then, abandoned in her need, she gave in to temptation—a total, abject, shameful surrender to the wild tremors of wanting that coursed through her flesh. Uncaring of consequence, she pushed aside the straps of her nightgown. The clinging bias cut slid easily over her breasts and her hips, and moments later, naked and shivering uncontrollably, not from cold but from the guilty knowledge of what she was doing, she stretched beside him on the daybed, her nakedness touching his lightly and sinfully. Where their unclothed flesh met, her body seemed to burn.

He remained oblivious of her presence. She took his inert hand and covered it with kisses, and still he did not stir. Unable to resist, she placed the hand on her breast—and then, for the first time, she felt a movement in his fingers. She froze beneath the slow erratic tempo of his touch. Breath held until she thought it would explode in her lungs, she waited for the unthinkable. He could not awaken. He must not awaken.

"I want you," he muttered thickly, his warm breath stirring where his head was bent to her throat. Or had she imagined the words? Even now it could not be said he was awake, or aware of the way his hand had begun to arouse her nipple— soothing, seeking, stroking, sending that terrible pulsating weakness through her lower limbs. It was as if the movement of those fingers was caused by some deep and devastating need of his unconscious self.

The hand grazed its way downward, over her belly and below, not knowing what trail of destruction traveled in its wake. For agonizing seconds the seemingly directionless fingers lingered, and then, just as the sliding hand halted, he subsided once more into some deeper oblivion.

She shuddered beneath the stillness of his hand. She knew she should move, but she could not move. The intimacy of his touch was without voli- tion or passion—but all the same it was ecstasy and anguish, pain and pleasure, heaven and hell, a bittersweet sinning too seductive to resist. Strange needs, unnamed and unfulfilled, pulsed through her limbs. Too long she lay there, beyond reason and beyond shame, quivering on the brink of discoveries she could not make.

At last he groaned in his sleep and rolled away, freeing her body but not her imprisoned senses. Driven, despairing, now wild with wanting and no longer caring if he woke, she turned and clung— clung as she longed to cling, kissed as she wanted to kiss, touched as she ached to touch, seeking out the secrets of his man's body and yet finding no release, because for her there could be no fulfillment, not tonight, not ever.

"Tuan, Tuan, I love you." A thousand times the whisper stirred against the tears with which she had dampened his face.

And when at last an unwanted dawn dispersed the lurking shadows of the night, she left her husband's side and crept back to her own bed, sickened and shamed by her own shamelessness. To the dull aching void deep within her had been added a terrible hopeless emptiness of the soul. How could she face Tuan tomorrow with the knowledge of what she had done tonight?

CHAPTER ELEVEN

THREE HOURS AFTER DAWN Marisa left the bungalow on soundless feet, sandals held in hand. Not
wanting to wake Tuan, she did not even take
breakfast—not that she was hungry in any case;
she was still far too distraught to think of food.
And should hunger overtake her later in the morning, it was always possible on this abundant island
to find something to eat. At the bases of the
banana trees ripe fruit lay rotting, free for the taking; there was more than the islanders could con-
sume.

Maeva's hut was her goal, and as Marisa had
been there before she had no trouble locating it. It
lay in pools of shade beneath the broad leaves of a
breadfruit tree. She stepped over the low lintel
that kept marauding pigs away, and went to the
open entrance. The door of plaited matting was
tied high with a length of sennit, admitting light
and air into the simple single room.

Maeva was seated on the bed, a wooden-framed
affair with a woven rope mattress, plain but not
uncomfortable. Her pareu was slung casually
around her hips, but at her breast was the beauti-

ful girl child whose birth had restored most of Maeva's natural slenderness. Several Tahitian women and children were clustered about, cooing admiration.

"Marisa *vahine*!" Maeva looked up, totally unselfconscious. "You see what a good baby I make? Her name is Terita."

There was no mistaking the pride and pleasure that shone in Maeva's square and pretty face. Marisa joined the ranks of admirers, genuinely fascinated and affected by the newborn's tiny curling fingers and closed eyes, and the rapacity with which that small mouth clutched at Maeva's breast. It was a distraction from her own troubled thoughts, and a welcome one. The large audience seemed to bother Maeva not at all. In fact, when sounds of a plane landing in the lagoon lured the island women away just as Maeva wrapped her baby and placed the swaddled child in a crude crib, she called after the scattering figures an admonition to return as soon as possible.

Marisa remained with Maeva, knowing it would only be Dooey with the usual supplies and mail, which arrived twice a week and always about this time of day. This morning she did not want to face Dooey's joviality, which—although she liked him—could be overwhelming at times.

"Lotu, he is the very proud father, too! *Aue*, he thinks this baby Terita very special. To see him, you would believe I had made a boy child!"

"No doubt she *is* very special for him," Marisa

smiled, "because she's yours." Briefly she wondered whether to broach the more sensitive matter of Lotu's proposal; Maeva's next words made the decision for her.

"You have heard that Lotu now wishes me to marry? I have said no."

"Yes, I heard that. I thought you intended to say yes, Maeva."

Maeva sniffed, and her chin turned stubborn. "I will not marry with a man who is afraid of Uma!"

"No doubt Lotu's just being respectful to your mother, Maeva, as all the islanders are. You do love Lotu—you told me so."

"Love—pah!" But something in Maeva's agate eyes suggested that the statement was less than the truth. "If he comes to lie with me in the night, I will not send him away. For how would I feel if he found another *vahine*? To make love with him, yes, but to marry...no. First Lotu must prove he is a man."

Marisa sighed, aware that no persuasions on her part would change Maeva's thinking. "Does that mean you'll give your baby away? Surely now you won't want to."

A fleeting spasm of discontent passed through Maeva's eyes. "I have promised Uma," she said more disconsolately, and then, brightening immediately, she turned to show Marisa a very pretty shell-and-flower arrangement that had been brought as a gift by one of the island women. To the smallest detail it was exactly the same as a hundred other shell arrangements Marisa had seen before, but she murmured the appropriate responses.

Sounds of the departing plane warned that Maeva's other visitors would soon return, and with a last wistful peek at the newborn baby, Marisa took her leave, hoping to give Maeva some few moments of peace. She managed to waste away most of the morning with a halfhearted inspection of the vanilla plantation that had been lying more or less fallow for two years. Although grasses and weeds had grown unchecked around the trees, the thick-stemmed vanilla vines had continued to thrive in their aerial homes, evidently needing no manual pollination. The presence of hummingbirds performing their gravity-defying act of midair suspension suggested nature's way of running things. The scent of unpicked pods was strong in the air, and last year's wasted crop crunched beneath Marisa's feet. Perhaps someday, if nature ever worked its healing magic on Alain de Vigny, the plantation would reclaim his attention.

At last, in early afternoon, when she felt she could procrastinate no longer, Marisa returned to the bungalow. She was sure Tuan would be up and dressed by now, and possibly—with luck—elsewhere. But fortune was not with her.

As she entered the bungalow he emerged from the bedroom, jaw clean-shaven and hair still damp from the shower. The faint grayness about his mouth suggested that he was still feeling the after-effects of last night's overindulgence. At the sight of Marisa he halted, and a deep worry line creased his forehead.

"Sorry about last night," he apologized at once. "I don't normally drink much at all. Can't remember doing a thing like that—ever before."

"There's no need to apologize." Marisa averted her gaze from the eyes she could not meet, but with the corners of her vision she still saw his expressions. "I suppose you had cause last night," she said in a low voice.

"Not cause enough for that kind of thing," he returned dryly, hand gesturing at the broken door. "Did I . . . do anything else I should apologize for? Anything, ah, ungentlemanly?"

"No."

Tension sagged out of his shoulders—those shoulders too intimately explored, too well remembered.

"Well, thank God for that," he said in a heartfelt voice. Hurt lumped in Marisa's throat at this fleeting evidence that marriage remained, for him, an abhorrent prospect.

"I was afraid I might have lost control. I seem to remember something—very hazy, all green light and silk skin."

"You must have been dreaming," she said quickly.

"You did come out and clean up the glass, though," he noted thoughtfully.

"I did it this morning," she lied. "I, er, when I came out to see what caused the noise last night, you were already asleep, and I didn't want to disturb you."

"Odd..." he frowned, and Marisa quickly intruded on his reflections lest they produce any part of the truth.

"Can I get you anything to eat? It's past lunch, and I don't suppose you've had a single bite."

"Good God, no. I'm paying for my sins today. But a few cups of good strong coffee wouldn't be taken amiss. Can't fly to Tahiti without clearing my mind."

"Tahiti?" Marisa had longed for his absence, yet now, curiously, she felt a deep stab of disappointment. She forced her eyes upward, meeting his, finding there an odd light she did not understand. "I didn't know you were going to Tahiti this afternoon."

"A little legal matter," he informed her with a half smile, and Marisa wondered briefly if his business concerned the transfer of property.

"Shall I expect you back for supper?"

"No, I thought—"

But in the moment before Tuan had time to complete his sentence, a call from the lagoon side of the bungalow intruded into the words. Turning, Marisa saw the triangular top of an outrigger's sail hovering beyond the veranda railing.

"It's my father." Tuan's face closed over, tightening into grim lines. Followed by Marisa, he went out the screen door and onto the decking overlooking the water.

Today Alain de Vigny was in the outrigger alone. He appeared gaunt and gray faced, his eyes hollow and haunted.

"Tania's gone," he said at once, with no preliminaries. His voice trembled with emotion. "Gone to Tahiti. She left this morning on the flying boat—with your friend."

Tuan's jaw worked as if with some volcanic inner anger. "After last night," he said to his father in an abrupt voice, "are you really so surprised?"

Alain de Vigny had the grace to lower his head penitently. "I've done nothing but regret my behavior since," he said in a muffled voice. Then he looked up again, and Marisa sensed that it cost him a great deal to swallow his pride in this way. "Help me, Tuan."

"Why should I?" Tuan ran tense fingers through his hair. "Why the hell should I? Tania's a grown woman. If she wants to come back to you, she'll come back to you. If not—"

The words lay heavily and ominously in the sun-drenched air, and it was in that moment that a terrible thought occurred to Marisa. Had Tuan been aware of Tania's plans—had he perhaps arranged to meet her this afternoon? Was *that* why he was going to Tahiti? But it was a nasty worm of a thought, and she tried to push it from her mind.

"Please," begged Alain de Vigny with the painful humility of a proud man brought low.

Tuan's breath exploded on an impatient note. "All right, then," he said tersely. "I was planning to fly to Tahiti this afternoon anyway. I'll bring her back when I locate her—if she wants to come. I'll promise nothing. After what's happened, it may take a day or two of convincing."

"You were ...." The suspicions that germinated in Alain de Vigny's head were plain to see, but he controlled them as if with an enormous effort of will. He looked away quickly, not finishing his sentence, and spent some awkward moments shifting his near-useless leg, using one hand to drag it into a more comfortable position.

Marisa stepped forward, a protective instinct more than common sense dictating her next words. She laced her arm through Tuan's in an open display of affection. "I'm going to Tahiti, too," she announced as cheerfully and naturally as possible. "We were just talking about it when you arrived."

"Indeed we were," Tuan said without the bat of an eyelash. His arm tightened over hers as if in a silent thank-you; his other hand came over and the fingers intertwined with hers, effectively preventing a withdrawal of the arm. "Tonight," he said calmly, "I have a dinner date in Tahiti with—with my wife."

Relief touched Alain de Vigny's eyes, only to be replaced by a new worry. "Then you won't be flying back before dark," he frowned.

"No. But I'll find out what I can about Tania

and contact you by radiotelephone. Have the
operator stand by toward sundown.''

"I'll stand by myself," Alain breathed
with emotion, and moments later the outrigger was once more working its way across the
lagoon.

"Do you think you'll be able to find Tania?"
Marisa asked, trying without success to extricate
her arm.

"I'm sure of it," Tuan answered with supreme
self-confidence. He smiled down at Marisa, but
his eyes remained totally unreadable—a fathom-
less blue enigma that revealed no part of his feelings at this moment.

"I hope you're not upset about taking me to Tahiti." Marisa hid behind a curtain of lashes and
fastened her gaze on the strong column of his
throat.

"I was just about to suggest it when my
father turned up," Tuan told her with a studied
casualness that made Marisa certain he was
not telling the truth. "Why? Don't you want to
go?"

Did she? No—not when there was reason to
think she was not wanted on the trip. And yet did
she want the man she loved to be alone with Tania
in Tahiti? Marisa struggled with herself for all of
two seconds. "Yes—yes, I would like to go," she
said, turning a tremulous smile in his direction.
"In fact, I insist upon it—whether you want me or
not.''

AFTER THE QUIET OF TA'AROA, the city of Papeete seemed hot, noisy, colorful and cheerful—all blaring horns, squealing brakes, big open buses laden with people and protesting pigs, and motor scooters with a death mission.

They had put Faaa Airport behind them a short time ago and were traversing the city in order to reach Tuan's rented bungalow. As the ancient taxicab braked to yet another halt in the late-day traffic jam, Marisa's eyes turned westward to Tahiti's sister island of Mooréa, where the horizon was broken by twin green spires scarved in ethereal white.

"Mooréa's cloud is like the Ta'aroa cloud," murmured Tuan at her side. "It's always the same."

Today there had been no mockery in his manner, and as a result Marisa's own defensive edginess had subsided. "It looks so beautiful," she remarked now, some wistfulness creeping into her voice. "So peaceful."

"For a girl who claims to like a little excitement in her life," he remarked without rancor, shifting his long legs so that they protruded into her vision and dragged her attention back to the sticky taxicab interior, "you seem quite prepared to do without."

Marisa, not fully at ease, laughed uncertainly. "This is a little *too* exciting!" she remarked as another motor scooter whipped through an impossible space between cars and careered off to the angry toot of the motorist who had just missed hitting it.

"Ah, we'll be at my place soon enough," Tuan assured her equably as the taxicab turned off the broad acacia-lined avenue and onto a quieter route. They moved quickly now, noise and confusion soon left behind. By this time Tuan's hangover seemed fully cured, and he was quite in command of himself and the situation—cool, self-assured, virile in a way that stirred Marisa's senses dangerously.

To give her hands and her eyes something to do, Marisa plucked at the pleated skirt of the dress she had worn for the short flight. At Tuan's behest she had brought a suitcase full of clothes: "enough for two or three days," he had instructed her and at the question in Marisa's eyes he had added, "in case Tania needs convincing. And don't forget we'll be eating out tonight!"

"Are you so sure Tania will be at your place?" Marisa asked now, paying particular attention to a nonexistent piece of lint on her skirt.

"Reasonably sure," he said confidently. "Unless she's lost the key. She and my father used to use the place quite often—before his accident," he added as an afterthought. "Here we are now."

The taxicab pulled up at a low bungalow, one of a row of similar rental units, all thatch roofed with walled gardens. In the near distance sun sparkled on water. A low carport was attached to the dwelling, and in it resided a racy red sports car whose make Marisa did not recognize.

Tuan ushered her through the door, depositing her suitcase as he called Tania's name. There was no answer.

"Perhaps she's in the bath," Tuan muttered. It was hot inside the bungalow, and he flicked on an air-conditioning switch before he vanished through a louvered door that evidently led into an adjoining bedroom.

Marisa remained behind, drinking in her surroundings. It was a pleasant bungalow, wicker and rattan and bright chintzes, with French windows opening onto a sunken walled garden where hibiscus rioted and palm trees swayed. Living room, one bedroom, utilitarian kitchen: so Marisa surmised from what she could see. And a bath, too—Tuan had mentioned that. The bungalow was charming enough, but without the individual stamp of personality that marked his place on Ta'aroa.

"She's not here." Tuan was frowning deeply as he emerged from his cursory inspection of the bedroom. "Perhaps I should have inquired more closely at the airport. I'd better make a few phone calls. You raid the kitchen for a lemonade—something stronger if you wish. There's a local woman who comes in; she keeps things stocked. Pour me one, will you?"

Marisa started toward the kitchen. "With gin?" she asked.

Tuan made a face. "I think I'll swear off for the moment," he remarked in a wry tone as he sat down by the telephone.

When Marisa returned with the iced lemon, he was deep in a conversation well larded with Tahitian words. She deposited the glass by his hand and wandered out to inspect the walled garden, clicking the door firmly closed behind her in order to keep the air conditioning at peak efficiency; too late she realized she had locked herself out.

So, resigning herself to the fact that she must stay outside while Tuan finished with his phone calls, she descended the flagstone steps into the lower garden, sipping the cooling lemon as she went. Great stone urns trailed splashes of floral color, and overgrown bougainvillea dappled shade over the terraced area. With the sun lowering somewhat in the sky, the worst of the heat was leaving the air, and Marisa stretched herself on a long lounge chair, first tilting the back high so she could enjoy the view of the garden.

More than an hour passed before Tuan emerged from the bungalow, worry fretting at his brow.

"Tania took off earlier today by flying boat," he told Marisa at once. "A regular Air des Iles flight to Pago Pago. It was a little hard getting information, because my regular supervisor is off sick. However, I managed to find out she's booked to fly on to the Philippines tomorrow morning. She has relatives in Manila."

"Will you be able to reach her?"

"The plane's scheduled to land in Pago Pago any moment now." He frowned, thrusting his hands into his pockets. "When it lands, Tania will be given a message to call—if that half-witted clerk manages to get through to Pago Pago before she deplanes. I imagine I'll hear within the next half hour if I'm going to hear tonight. Otherwise I'll set about trying to reach her in the morning, before she boards the flight for Manila."

Marisa paid minute attention to the gyrations of an ant. "Do you think you can talk her into coming back to your father?"

"Yes," he said briefly, brooding.

Perhaps Tuan faced this prospect with mixed emotions, but Marisa did not. "Are you so sure?" she asked hopefully.

"Sure enough that I booked a flight back from Pago Pago for tomorrow morning." Now he looked decidedly gloomy. "It means we may have to return to Ta'aroa sooner than I planned. Dooey's on other assignments now, up in the Marquesas, and all my other flying boats are booked. I'll have to take her home myself—if she agrees to go. I've been in touch with my father, too, to keep him informed."

Then, as if forcibly dragging his mind away from thoughts of Tania and Alain, he smiled down at Marisa—a strained and watchful smile, but it indented the paler crinkles at the edges of his eyes. "I also took time to make a few other calls— one of them for a dinner reservation. There's a

table booked for an hour from now, at sundown.
I'm sure you're ready for some good French
cuisine. You have exactly fifty minutes to get
dressed—no, make that forty. I have to get
dressed, too.''

"I can spare you more than ten minutes," she
promised lightly, putting her feet over the side of
the lounge chair.

"Take your time. Tonight I want to show you
off. Get your vanity out of mothballs, and fuss.''
He reached down to help her out of the chair and
she reacted too strongly, springing away as if
stung. His mouth hardened for an instant, then
relaxed again, and he withdrew his offer of an arm
with no offense taken. Instead he reached for a
hibiscus blossom and broke it off its bush. "Here,
wear this in your hair—over the right ear.''

"Why?"

"You'll find out later.''

"Surprises again?''

His lids drooped briefly over the enigmatic blue.
"Maybe," he said evasively, without elaboration.

The restaurant he had chosen was exclusive and
discreet. It was an intimately darkened room in
which extravagant floral displays formed fiery
centerpieces over snowy napery. The flowers vied
with the flaming pink hibiscus Marisa had tucked
behind one ear, and Tuan pushed the centerpiece
aside, baring the table between them.

"Flower's on the wrong side, but other than
that you fussed very nicely," he remarked approv-

ingly, his darkened eyes traveling slowly over the
smooth sweep of champagne hair and down over
a sun-honeyed expanse of skin to the long clinging
sheath of dusty-rose silk jersey that made it em-
phatically clear all Marisa's curves were in the
right places. She had chosen to wear the dress
against her better judgment, and admittedly for
the most primitive of reasons. Yet now, with his
gaze sweeping down to the shadowed cleft between her breasts, she felt undressed, regretting
her choice.

"And you did very well, too, in your ten
minutes," she said, prodding at a silver saltcellar
but seeing him beyond it—well-knit, immeasur-
ably masculine, immaculate in a white dinner
jacket.

"Oh, I think you gave me a little more than
ten," he smiled; and throughout the superb meal
that followed, he remained at his charming best.
Tania and Alain were not mentioned. As Tania
had not been heard from before they left the
bungalow, it seemed unlikely that she had received
the message to call. Marisa did not want to bring
up the subject of Tania's problems, and nor, it
seemed, did Tuan. Instead he concentrated on
anecdotes of Polynesian life—tales that filled
Marisa with a sense of the undulating sensual
rhythm of island life, the enchantments, the ab-
surdities, the languid days, the deep velvet nights.
In his voice she felt the soft seductive pull of the
island, luring her, lulling her.

As they finished the meal a shapely Chinese-Tahitian girl, long hair sparkling with flowers, moved to the scrap of a dance floor and performed an abandoned *tamure* to the beat of drums and the clap of hands. Her skirt of shredded bark shook wildly; her feathered bikini top quivered to the hot pulse of the music and the leaping of her blood. Her uninhibited performance seemed to add to, rather than break, the magical mood of the evening, and when Tuan's hand closed over Marisa's on the tablecloth, thumb probing absent-mindedly at her palm, she made no move to withdraw.

Too soon, it seemed, he glanced at his watch. "Time to go," he told her.

"Why, it's hardly past ten o'clock." But Marisa's objections were halfhearted. In truth, the exotic smells and sights and sounds had too well seduced her senses. She was half-hypnotized, and no longer on the defensive.

"Why are we leaving so early?" she asked as he led her to the parking lot.

His hesitation was brief, no more than a half-beat. "I said we might drop in to see someone a little later—before midnight."

"Then you're not going home yet," she remarked, once more complaisant.

For answer he only smiled indolently, strong teeth gleaming under the standard lamps of the parking lot. He opened the car door and helped her in. In silence he levered himself into the driver's seat and negotiated the car onto the road.

On one side of their route lay the moon-glittered lagoon, on the other the lumping dark shape of Tahiti's mountainous interior. It was a beautiful balmy night, and a breeze whipped through the open windows of the low-slung sports car. At Tuan's suggestion Marisa had brought a chiffon scarf, which she wore now loosely so as not to crush the flower. She tried without success not to think of the man beside her—not to note the way his knuckles folded around the steering wheel, the way the wind whipped at the dark disturbing hair, turning it disorderly. To distract her attention she examined the multiplicity of dials and instruments on the dashboard.

"Is that what I think it is?" she asked, pointing to what appeared to be a car telephone, indistinctly seen in the dark.

"Unfortunately, yes," he confirmed in a dry voice.

Some minutes later he pulled off the road on the lagoon side and braked to a halt, then turned silently in his seat to contemplate Marisa.

Under a full moon and a sky huge with stars, with the soft suck of the surf against the distant reef, she became unbearably conscious of his eyes upon her, and of the way his arm had crept along the back of the bucket seat, too close for comfort.

And when her heartbeat became too large for the night, she whispered, "Why have you brought me here?"

"To talk to you in neutral territory."

It seemed not so neutral to her, this haunting Tahitian night with its soft perfumes and sounds. "Oh, Antoine—"

"Ah, Marisa. Is Tuan still hard to get your tongue around?"

"Yes, I . . . ." For something to do she removed the chiffon scarf and twisted it in her fingers. It allowed her hair to swing forward, curtaining her face. "I hardly think our relationship has been friendly enough for that," she said in a muffled voice.

"It was friendly enough tonight."

"For public consumption. And with only ten days to go . . . ." She stopped herself, not wanting to think of that. "You still haven't told me why you brought me here."

"I think it's time to have a little truth between us. Your turn first. You can start, Marisa," he said, wreaking havoc with his cool pronouncement, "by telling me what *really* happened last night."

CHAPTER TWELVE

NUMB AND TONGUE-TIED, she stared at him, her heart exploding with an overload.

"The truth about last night," he urged. The headlights of a car lanced past, revealing a faint smile and enigmatic eyes.

"I don't know what you're talking about," she managed at last.

"Yes, you do, Marisa," he said coolly. His hard fingers found her jaw and forced her face to remain turned to his, although in the deep shadows of the car interior little could be seen. "You've been prickly as a porcupine for nearly two weeks now, but last night was different. First, at dinner—was that all pretense?"

"Yes," she said, trying without success to avert her face.

"Hmm. Then tell me about last night. The truth this time."

How could she tell him what she had done, or any part of what she had done? "If you think something happened you're quite wrong," she said with a dry mouth.

"Really?" His voice was sardonic, betraying his

skepticism. "You're lying to me, Miss Marisa. Your account doesn't tally with the few facts I know. And if you lied about one thing—"

"You were very drunk," she broke in, her heart thudding. "How can you remember anything? It's as I said. I saw you were asleep. I went right back to bed and—"

"Marisa!" The word was a command, and the fingers that were curled around her chin tightened their grip dangerously. "Don't lie!"

"I'm not lying," she lied again, shakily. "What are you afraid of, Antoine? That I . . . seduced you in the night? I assure you I didn't! I wouldn't dream of it! I'd die before I'd let this marriage become a reality!"

She could feel the frown she could not see as he lowered his hand slowly from her chin. "Perhaps I should tell you what I remember," he said slowly. "I may have been well beyond reason, but I have a clear vision of you emerging from that bedroom, dressed in not very much. Something silky and clinging and see-through, like a second skin. What color is your nightgown?"

"Black," she said stiffly, breathing relief now that he was no longer touching her.

"Liar," he contradicted softly. "Don't you think I have eyes? I've seen your night things hanging in the closet. You have two nightgowns— one a soft green like sea foam, and one—"

"Stop it!" she cried. "All right, I'll admit you were still conscious when I looked out. I was horrified when I saw you staggering about removing your clothes, so I ran back into the bedroom at once.''

"Then who," he asked disruptively, "put the iodine on my feet? It was done during the night. Ah, yes, Miss Marisa, I woke at dawn and managed to pull myself together enough to struggle into my pajamas—a concession to those tender sensibilities of yours. Or are they really as tender as you pretend?''

Marisa had turned rigid at the mention of iodine; it was something she had totally forgotten. "I suppose you put it on yourself," she said defensively.

Tuan sighed heavily. "Oh, you devious creature. Do I have to wring the truth out of you? You've trapped yourself in one lie too many, Marisa. The glass had been swept up, too. I remember a lot of naked skin—mine *and* yours— and the little physical evidence I have seems to bear me out.''

"I've told you, your memory's at fault!" she cried, growing desperate. "What is this, an inquisition? And what does it matter what you imagined? I've told you we didn't sleep together. Nothing happened, and I'm still intact. You can get your—your precious annulment, if that's what's troubling you!''

"So much on the defensive?" he murmured, now sounding amused. "You do seem determined to make things difficult, and I intend to find out why. If I can't get the truth one way, I'll have to get it another. Come for a walk with me, Marisa. Along the beach.''

"Anything you have to say you can say right here!''

"Some things can't be said in bucket seats," he said equably, pocketing his car keys. He opened the door on his side and an interior light switched on, clearly revealing the lazy grin that had taken possession of his mouth. His eyelids drooped, mocking her. "You're a difficult woman, Miss Marisa, but I don't intend to let you ruin my life with your evasions. It's hard to lie with the moon for witness. Come along and let's see how long you can keep up this fiction.''

"It's not a fiction," she declared, guilt sharpening her voice as he came around and opened the car door on her side.

"Don't keep me waiting, Marisa. I'm anxious to, er, drop in on my friend before midnight. He'll be watching for us, too. A short walk in the moonlight—what harm can it do? If you don't come with me, I'll have to believe you don't trust yourself in my company.''

"I'm not coming," she declared, digging in.

"Very well," he smiled, in a way that was far too self-assured for her liking. "I'll go on ahead. Join me.''

"Don't hold your breath," she warned tautly as he clicked the car door closed.

"Meet you at the beach," he instructed affably,

and took off at a quick pace, deserting her. Simmering, she watched him go, clearly revealed now in the brilliant tropic night with the moon delineating the long athletic limbs, the confident stride, the white evening jacket cut to lie easily over the powerful structure of his shoulders. His tall frame diminished into the distance. He neared the lagoon and veered eastward, and for a time his silhouette, no more than a speck by now, was visible against the moon-drenched waters beyond. Then he melted out of view altogether as a stand of coco palms intervened in her vision.

Marisa burrowed stubbornly into place and glared at the empty driver's seat with exasperation. How like him to take the car keys! How like him to assume she would follow at his whim! And why was he so determined to wring a confession from her? Perhaps he had some uneasy notion that the marriage had been consummated last night, despite her denials; that she intended to make things difficult in some way. Or did he just want an admission so he could prove his damnable male-animal superiority? So he could humiliate her? God knows she felt humiliated enough without being forced to confess, too!

The minutes ticked by, punctuated only by the occasional prick of headlights through the windshield. She considered walking back to town. But it was a long walk, and she had no money and nowhere to go. Even assuming she could find her way to Tuan's rented bungalow—and she was not sure she could—she had no key to admit herself. But she could outwait him; she *would* outwait him.

The intrusive noise that sounded from the dash-board of the car startled her. It was a low continu-ous burring, impossible to ignore. She switched on the car's interior lights and realized the signal was coming from the telephone. A quick glance at the dashboard clock told her it was very nearly eleven o'clock. She stared at the telephone, flexing her fingers as she wondered whether to answer; by the time she had made the decision and reached for the instrument the burring halted as suddenly as it had begun. She spent half a minute scolding herself for her indecision: it could very well, she realized, have been an emergency. Or it could have been the acquaintance Tuan had planned to drop in on, phoning to confirm plans. Or it could have been some woman friend; he evidently had plenty of those.

Well, it was too late now to answer. But she should inform him that someone had been trying to reach him; and so, with minor misgivings only, she let herself out of the car. On a last thought she slipped off the summery high-heeled sandals she had worn over bare feet and threw them back on the seat, knowing they would only impede her pro-gress along the beach.

As she left the road behind, the moon and the night became immense. The sky trembled with a thousand thousand jewels, and the lagoon glit-tered with a soft unearthly light. Beneath her bare toes the dark sand still held the warmth of the day. In a short time she turned eastward as Tuan had done, and the silence and the emptiness of the beach made her uneasy. She had expected him to be sitting at the water's edge, or at least to emerge from the trees at her approach. But he was nowhere to be seen. Frustrated, she called his name softly. There was no answer.

Searching the deep velvet shadows for clues, she walked toward the grove of coco palms where she had last seen him. Something gleamed bone white among the low bushes beyond the trees—his jacket, she was sure, and he was very definitely not in it. Had he fallen asleep or, heaven forbid, gone for a moonlight swim? Cautiously, and still calling softly, she started toward the jacket, passing through the dark pool of shadow cast by the bending fronds of a palm.

"Oh!" she gasped in deep shock as something hard and human circled her wrist in a compelling grip. Instincts to flight filled her with unreasoning panic and she tried to yank herself free, but the fingers only tightened their hold and she found herself jerked backward against a warm length of male.

"Why so surprised?" said a low and disruptive voice, stirring the back of her hair. "You came to find me, didn't you?"

His free hand brushed the bare skin at her shoulder, soothing away alarm, and when she continued to tremble beneath his hands, he released her wrist altogether. Nothing held her now but the lightest of touches at her shoulder, yet still she could not run. She was in a prison, a prison of her own senses. Awareness of his nearness and his maleness drained her limbs of strength.

"Which is the real you, Miss Marisa?" he asked huskily. "The sharp-tongued creature who can't stand to be alone in my company for five minutes—or the silken thing that lay beside me in the night?"

"I *didn't*—" But her heart pounded like a wild creature's, and the denial did not sound as forceful as it should.

His hand slid over her shoulder, intruding into the deep vee of fabric at her neck. His fingers felt for a pulse and found it.

"Revealing," he murmured.

"I—you startled me," she trembled out.

"Oh?" His fingers insinuated themselves more deeply below the verges of fabric, following the rise, finding the nipple and stroking it slowly, seductively, until it hardened to a taut and tremulous betrayal of her needs. "Very revealing."

She willed herself to move, but could not. Time seemed to stop as she submitted to his touch; not even pride could save her now. He was too close, too male, too dangerous, and the unfulfilled aches of last night came quivering back.

"Was it my imagination, Marisa?" His dark head dropped to the hollow of her throat, and the movement of his lips laid moist and maddening patterns on her skin. He pushed her hair aside and drew with his tongue a gentle persuasive line that traveled to her earlobe. "Tell me it wasn't my imagination."

"Why do you torment me?" she whispered.

"Why do you lie to me?" His hands and his mouth made inroads on her sanity.

"Why do you care?" she asked desperately.

His lips moved in her hair, a madness in the night. "Why do you respond?" he murmured.

"That's not response, that's... weakness." She closed her eyes in a silent prayer for strength. "I told you once, you turn me weak. I can't... fight you."

"Fight?" He gave a low husky laugh and released her breast. Hands gentle on her shoulders, he turned her to face him. The moon carved shadows into his eyes and into the deep rivers of his cheeks. He held her a little apart; then slowly he lowered his hands to his sides until he was not touching her at all.

"Kiss me, Marisa," he ordered in a low vibrant voice.

She was held by his voice and mesmerized by those night-darkened eyes. But she would not obey, she could not obey, for to do so would be to reveal every sad secret of her lovesick heart. She swayed toward him briefly and then, with a deep sob, turned and ran.

"Marisa—"

He caught her in two strides, still in the shadow

of the coco palm. A strong hand captured a soft
handful of her dress, and then the hands were on
her shoulders, whirling her around. Hard demanding fingers dug into her flesh. Hard demanding lips descended, taking what she did not want
to give and yet was helpless to withhold. And
then, as he sensed the softening of her mouth, the
pliancy of her hips, the lips were not so hard.

He led her a little way, as Tahitian lovers do,
close in the curve of his arm. Wordlessly they
melted into the secret low-lying bushes. Above
them palms swayed to invisible commands, but
here there was no breeze, only the moon for witness. His eyes were dark pools of desire, grazing
her, praising her, possessing her. His fingers
touched the tremble of her lips and the moon-
silvered hair and the flower in her hair; and with
no words to explain his actions, he pulled the
flower from her left ear and put it to her right,
fastening it slowly, letting his fingers brush erotic
messages against her ear.

"How beautiful you are," he murmured huskily, lowering her to the ground. "Oh, Marisa, you
make a man forget...I can't be rational now."

Nor could she be rational now. His warm breath
closed in, and his tongue probed a wordless command, and she obeyed because she could not help
but obey, opening her lips to permit the invasion
that was like liquor to her senses. The kiss was
deep, wine-sweet, narcotic, a joining of mouths
that destroyed all reason for both of them. His

hands surged over her breasts and her hips; her arms wound themselves around his neck and clung. And when at last he raised his head, she opened her eyes and found his eyes hovering above, drugged with desire.

"I want to touch you," he whispered. "I need to touch you. I need to know."

And then, taking his time, banking his own fires, he unfastened her dress, making love with his hands and with his mouth as he pushed the soft fabric to below her waist. His eyes smoked darkly. She could resist nothing—not the lips that trailed their tortuous way over her breasts and the valley of her breasts; not the hands that slid beneath the silken fabric at her thighs, touching but not taking.

"Am I mad, Marisa? Or did I touch you this way last night...?"

No, he had not touched her this way last night. This time his fingers were slow and knowing in their search—awakening her flesh, stroking soft commands, gentling her, preparing her for what must surely be. Against the curve of her hips she could feel the readiness of him, waiting only for her ultimate surrender.

She reached for his shirt and loosened the buttons, pushing it aside so she could feel the tautness of skin and sinew, the texture of hair. He groaned deeply as her fingers ran riot over the corded muscles of his shoulders. Where his hand tarried, a wildness of sensation quivered into being.

But still she wanted more. The needs that trembled through her ready flesh begged for a release she longed to find, could find only through him.

Helping him now—wanting to help and wanting to give and wanting to wait no longer for what seemed right and sure and as inevitable as the moon and the tides and the soft Tahitian night— she lowered her hands and slid the last frail barriers from her hips. And then she lay fully bared to his view—the moon-bleached limbs, the silk and the satin of her, the tremulous willingness of her.

She heard the harsh intake of his breath and felt the explosion of it against her breast. "So beautiful," he muttered against her skin. "So silver, so gold...how I've wanted to see you like this, to kiss you like this.... Oh, God, I *can't*...!"

And with a ferocity that left her trembling, he pulled himself upward on her body and kissed her deeply, intrusively, winding his fingers fiercely into her hair.

She gloried in knowing her nakedness aroused him so. But she wanted his nakedness, too, and so her hands began to trespass once again, telling him without words that she wanted him to be a part of her.

There was a sudden rigidity in his body—a terrible tension in the way his fingers tightened at her scalp. He wrenched his mouth from hers as if with great effort, freeing lips still bruised and tingling from the vehemence of his kiss.

"Don't stop," she whispered unsteadily. Abandoned in her need, she found his belt buckle and loosened it for him where the metal pressed coldly against her unclothed skin.

Groaning, he pushed himself away and buried his head at her waist, his hair dark against the moon-gilded flesh. "Not...yet," he managed jerkily. "Not...for God's sake...yet."

"What's wrong?" she whispered, suddenly sick with fear.

His voice was hoarse, his breathing heavy. "First we talk," he said.

"Talk—oh...."

The positive pain she felt deep inside her was not the ache of unfulfillment now. Memory washed through her like a nausea. "You make a man forget," he had said; and she had been forgetful, too.

The fragile magic of the night seemed to explode into a thousand fragments, each a painful reminder of the realities of her marriage. How could she have forgotten Tania even for a moment; how could she have wanted to consummate a marriage that could only end in heartbreak? Ill with humiliation, she tried to extricate herself, only to find herself gripped by hands like steel.

"No, I won't let you go so easily now," he said in a voice still thickened with desire. He inched upward on her body, controlling himself but not yet setting her free.

"Oh, Marisa," he murmured, seeing the look on her face, "do you think I've stopped because I don't want you? Don't you know it's been hell for me these past few weeks? God knows, I'm not a saint. That unlocked door has nearly robbed me of my senses.''

"That's sex talking," she said shakily, turning her head away. Inside her there was a sick urgency to justify her wantonness. "You want me the way I want you, and that's nothing to do with love. I—oh...." She squeezed her eyelids closed, willing the tears not to appear. "Please let me go. I'm ashamed of myself. So ashamed."

"Ashamed?" He gave a husky unsteady laugh. "Don't you realize this is the first encouragement you've given me? When you came to find me on the beach, I knew. If you hadn't wanted me, you'd have— What's the matter now?"

She had stiffened like a board at his words. "But that's not why I came to find you. It was the phone, the phone in your car—it rang."

"What?" Instantly alert, he rolled away and came to his feet. He hesitated for only a moment, looking down at her as he pushed his shirttails back into his trousers. "We'll talk at the car," he said, and took off along the beach at a lope.

Marisa's heart plummeted as this new guilt added itself to others. How could she have forgotten the phone call? And how could she account for her wantonness tonight, short of admitting her true feelings? Her hands were unsteady as she searched for her scattered apparel. It mattered little that Tuan, too, had admitted to attractions that had made these past weeks difficult. She had known of his strong sexual drives since her first day on Ta'aroa, and they had been total strangers then. His urges were as old as man's first mating; and no doubt, had they not been married, he would have seduced her tonight without compunction. But tonight, even tonight, some exertion of will had prevented him from taking what she had been offering so freely. And the final humiliation was that her shamelessness gave credence to his suspicions about last night.

Decency restored, if not self-respect, she started to leave the small clearing in the bushes. And that was when she saw the flower that had been in her hair, trampled on the ground. Stooping, she picked it up. It looked defeated and crushed— symbolic of everything she felt. As she left the grove of trees, she crumpled the fragile blossom in a fist and hurled the shredded petals against the bole of a coco palm. Well, attack had always been the best form of self-defense!

By the time she reached the car she had managed to put on an armor of prickly indifference that concealed the rawness of her emotions. From the distance as she approached, she could hear an indistinct conversation. He rang off just as she reached the passenger door and lowered herself into the seat, retrieving her shoes.

"I take it you managed to find out who was calling you."

It was as if he pulled himself back from a great

distance. "No trouble. My answering service took the call. It should have come through before, but there was some foul-up...the operator was trying to reach me on Ta'aroa." But he was still distracted; she could see that. Could the call have been from Tania?

"I apologize," she said coolly, "for not remembering why I went to find you. Frankly, you startled me into forgetting a lot of things. I'll admit my wits flew out the window—just as they did last night."

He went totally still; and now, she knew, she had his full attention.

"Yes, it's true," she admitted, turning to him with a fixed false smile that was revealed fleetingly by a car's piercing lights. "You weren't imagining. I *was* lying on the couch with you last night."

"I suppose I pulled you down," he said thoughtfully.

"It just...happened," she said, skirting the truth. "I didn't leave at once, as I should have done. You said you're not a saint—well, neither am I, it seems. I didn't admit it because I was ashamed, just as I'm ashamed of what happened tonight. I don't want it to happen again. I suggest we put an end to this ridiculous marriage before we make some terrible mistake."

He was so silent and so still, his reactions so concealed in the darkness of the car, that she started to talk again.

"Thank goodness one of us retained some sanity tonight,'' she said with a detachment that cost her dearly. "I'm grateful to you. If nature had taken its course, we'd both be regretting it now. I'm already regretting what *did* happen, and I realize I could have prevented it easily by confessing last night's lapse in the first place. There, you have my admission. That's what you wanted to know, isn't it?''

Again there was a little silence, but this time he broke it. "Yes,'' he replied slowly, with an odd timbre to his voice, "that's what I wanted to know.'' .

"My turn first, you said.'' She gave a laugh that was totally brittle; it hid the terrible hollowness inside. "Surely you didn't bring me here just to ferret out all my horrid little failings?''

When he spoke again, his voice had become abrupt. "No, I didn't. I brought you here to suggest a revision of the arrangement between us. In other words, I want to take you to bed.''

Marisa's stomach did a flop; her heart tied itself into a gigantic knot. So he *had* wanted to consummate the marriage. Oh, Lord....

"I wanted to be aboveboard about the whole thing,'' he grated harshly. "I wouldn't want to take undue advantage of your...horrid little failings. I'm asking for a rational decision, Marisa. As we both have sexual urges, it seems logical to—''

"To unite our urges like a—a pair of animals?'' she cried. "No, thanks! I don't want marriage

without love. The answer is no, no, no! I won't be
a legal sex object!''

Suddenly he switched on the car's interior light,
and his head snapped around until he had her fully
in view. His eyes became hard, his words hurtful,
his face a cruel mask. "Legal sex object? I don't
think you understand about Polynesia, Marisa.
Here a man can get all the sex objects he wants—
legalities be damned. The women are very willing.
It cost me a great deal to stop tonight, and you
might try to remember I'm in a state of considerable frustration. I'm not used to stopping at
the halfway mark! I did so only because I wanted
to give you an option, and because of that—that
damn virginity of yours. How you've kept it so
long I'll never know!''

"Oh!" Angry tears turned her eyes bright; it
was impossible now to pretend indifference. "If
you're feeling so frustrated, go and take it out on
some other w-willing woman—one who doesn't
mind being a substitute for someone else!''

His eyes blazed with a sudden fury, and for a
moment she thought he intended to strike her. But
he only reached for the interior light and switched
it off, then turned the ignition key viciously. He
drove home in total silence and saw her safely into
the bungalow, scrupulous now in not touching
her.

"I'm going out for a while," he told her, his
face set. "I may be late. Expect me when you see
me.''

"Are you calling on the friend you mentioned earlier?" she asked stiffly, conscious of the lateness of the hour.

"No," he said in a short voice, as she had known he would.

Suddenly all the fight went out of her, like straw from a scarecrow. She nodded wordlessly and watched him go, knowing even then that she would not see him again tonight; and that, not seeing him, she would not sleep.

It did not occur to her until a time after he had gone that with his cruel words at the beach he had been telling her his suggestion was not based only on a need for sexual fulfillment. Evidently he had some rational reason for changing his mind about marriage; some reason more compelling than mere desire. And yet that realization did little to dispel despair. Cruel visions intruded upon her mind, visions of twined limbs and willing lips and urges far more primitive than love. The emptiness inside became acute.

And I am desolate and sick of an old passion;
yea, hungry for the lips of my desire. . . .

CHAPTER THIRTEEN

THE NEXT DAY passed in an agony of apprehension, with no news of Tuan's whereabouts. Marisa spent the day wandering disconsolately about his rented bungalow, feeling alternately angry, depressed, despairing, humiliated by the events of the previous night and sick at heart for what seemed his casual abandonment of her.

The local woman Tuan had mentioned turned up in early morning, her mission today to water plants and apparently do very little else; she stayed no more than half an hour. A good-natured broad-bosomed Tahitian clad in a shapeless flowered shift, she introduced herself as Tehani and seemed not at all surprised to find a female in residence.

"Ah, the Tuan *tane*, he is always the lucky man," she grinned cheerfully after a frank appraisal of Marisa's assets. "And why not? Such a handsome, strong *popaa*! What *vahine* would not be proud to share his bed? You wish me to change the sheets?"

This placid assumption that Marisa was mistress rather than married woman did little to set her ap-

prehensions at rest, and through the day she found
herself with little appetite, although she did make
some halfhearted inroads into a box of soda
crackers. But when the shadows began to
lengthen, bringing the dinner hour near, hunger
began to gnaw at her. It was now about three
hours before sundown, and she was searching dispiritedly through the freezer compartment when
the sharp ring of the telephone sounded. Marisa,
who had spent the past two hours telling herself
she would not even answer if it did ring, at once
dropped a handful of freezer packages and ran.

She picked up the receiver with shaky fingers.
"Tuan?" she said at once.

But it was a woman's voice, crisp and efficient.
"This is Monsieur de Vigny's secretary," came the
recognized inflections. "I have instructions for
you, Madame de Vigny, from your husband. A
taxi will be arriving to pick you up within moments. You are to—"

"Where is Monsieur de Vigny?" Marisa broke
in impatiently.

There was a short but unmistakable hesitation
at the other end of the line. "He apologizes for
not contacting you sooner. You are to bring your
suitcase," the instructions resumed. "You will be
taken to Monsieur de Vigny's plane for the flight
to Ta'aroa. He wishes to return you there tonight."

"Oh, I—thank you."

Marisa managed to hide a sense of deep hurt

that Tuan had not seen fit to contact her personally even now. She was grateful for her restraint when the secretary went on, "Your husband has been involved in search-and-rescue work since dawn, *madame*."

Marisa's knuckles tightened over the receiver. "Rescue work?"

"He did not tell you because he did not wish to alarm you," the voice continued reassuringly. "There was an emergency with the Pago Pago flight last night. Radio contact had been lost, and so the problem became apparent only when the plane did not arrive at its destination. . . ."

Tania's flight! Marisa went cold with apprehension, hearing only snatches of what the secretary told her next. A gigantic air pocket. . . instrument damage. . . unable to send Mayday signal. . . forced landing on the sea. . . position not known. . . .

"Monsieur de Vigny, he flew out before dawn, and other pilots, too, on search missions. The flying boat was spotted at midday, drifting on the sea only an hour from Tahiti."

"My mother-in-law, Tania. . . ?"

"She is safe," the secretary assured Marisa in her pleasant and efficient way. "All passengers are safe, although some were injured in the turbulence of the air pocket—those whose seat belts were undone. Madame de Vigny was one of the lucky ones; that is why she is only now landing at Tahiti. Your husband has been busy since the

plane was found, bringing in others, the injured
first...."

Because of the limited range and capacity of the
flying boats available, Tuan and other pilots had
each flown several missions in the past twelve
hours, first searching, and then ferrying passengers back to Tahiti. At last Marisa satisfied her
most urgent questions and rang off, racing at once
to pack the clothes she had brought from Ta'aroa.
The taxi arrived just as she snapped the lid of the
suitcase closed.

Arrangements had been made for a launch to
take her directly to that part of the lagoon where
Tuan's flying boat was anchored. Tuan was
watching for her arrival and came to help her
through the hatch. Her heart lurched at the sight
of him. His face was drawn, his eyes haggard, his
jaw stubbled from a razorless day. He no longer
wore the dress shirt of last night. It had been
replaced by Air des Iles blue, rumpled and sweat
stained and evidently borrowed, for it appeared to
be a size too small: it strained across his broad
chest, and the top buttons were undone. The
greeting between them, too, was strained.

"I'm flying you and Tania back to Ta'aroa immediately," he announced as he leaned out to give
her a helping hand.

"Then Tania's going back to—" Marisa bit her
lip into silence as she ducked her head through the
opening into the plane's compact interior, and
Tania came into view.

"Yes, Marisa, I am going back," Tania said tiredly. Her eyes were exhausted, but she looked cool and composed after her ordeal. "I have already spoken to Alain by radio, to tell him so."

The next few moments were spent in quick but heartfelt condolences on the accident, and congratulations on the escape, while Tuan stood watching both women with dark unreadable eyes.

"Buckle in," he told Marisa impatiently at last. "We'll have to leave now if I'm to be back at Tahiti before dark."

"Back at Tahiti?" Marisa searched his face, concerned at the signs of sleeplessness and stress. "Surely you don't have to come back tonight? If you have to be here in the morning you could—"

"Dammit, I said I'm coming back tonight!"

Marisa opened her mouth and then closed it over her objections. It was clear to see that Tuan was very nearly at the end of his tether, his temper uncertain after the events of the past two days. She lowered herself into a seat without further demur and fastened her belt as he had instructed. Tears felt very near the surface; she herself had spent two sleepless nights. But others had undergone more trials than she, and the jealous imaginings of last night seemed petty in comparison with what Tania must have suffered, and Tuan, too. Doubtless he had spent last night at the airport, worrying and waiting for dawn; the phone call at the beach must have been to advise him of possible problems with the Pago Pago flight. No wonder he had been so abrupt in issuing his loveless suggestion that the marriage become reality. But why, with so much on his mind and so little need for a wife, had he issued it at all?

The answer to that puzzle came during the short flight to Ta'aroa, in a conversation with Tania.

"Perhaps you are wondering why I ran from Alain," Tania said quietly.

"I'm sure you had reason," Marisa replied.

"I did." Tania's beautiful face turned to profile, and her almond eyes trained themselves on the Pacific blue beyond the plane window. Today, clad in a high-throated silk cheongsam instead of a pareu, she looked Oriental rather than Polynesian. "But the reason is perhaps not what you think. I tell you this because I would not wish you to believe Alain had...mistreated me in any way the other night, after we left your bungalow. It is not in his nature to strike a woman, and I think he did it only because of...what he believed had happened. He was very distressed with himself, and I am sure he will not do it again. In any case, I would not have run for that reason alone."

Marisa maintained silence, knowing that Tania would continue; and after a moment she did.

"No—I ran from Alain for the same reason that I am now returning."

Tania's slender hand traveled to below her breast and rested there, and Marisa knew the reason almost before it was voiced in words.

"I told Tuan about this the other night when

Maeva's child was born," Tania went on in her
water-music voice, eyes turning back to the plane
interior. "I asked him to say nothing because I
have not yet told Alain. Perhaps I am afraid to tell
him, for fear of his...suspicions. I see you have
guessed, Marisa, and yes, you are right. I'm ex-
pecting Alain's child."

And Tuan's half brother. The revelation was
like a blinding lightning flash, and it no longer
seemed necessary to play guessing games. Marisa
knew what had driven Tuan to change his mind
about marriage.

IF NEWS of the missing Pago Pago flight had not
reached Marisa in Papeete, the same could not be
said of the island of Ta'aroa. Word had been
received last night, when the operator had been
trying to track down Tuan's whereabouts. A
veritable fleet of outriggers put out from shore as
the small flying boat droned in for landing an
hour before sundown. Marisa half expected to see
Alain de Vigny in one of the boats—after all, he
had twice dragged himself to his outrigger in the
previous two days—but oddly, his pale face was
nowhere to be seen. Perhaps, Marisa reasoned, he
did not want the islanders to witness the reunion
with Tania, which would doubtless be charged
with emotion.

The first outrigger to arrive alongside the landed plane was Lotu's. His face was glummer than it
had been on a similar occasion nearly three weeks

ago—but then, Marisa remembered dishearteningly, Lotu now had his own problems. She did not need to ask if Maeva had changed her mind.

Lotu's look of disappointment deepened when Tuan announced he would be returning to Tahiti at once.

"But, Tuan," he objected from his bobbing outrigger, "the octopus has been sighted this afternoon, by Tupui. It was grazing for food along the coral, and Tupui followed it. Its lair has been found. And as you wished to be present for the hunt—"

"I'll be back tomorrow afternoon," Tuan interrupted. "We'll go hunting when I return, I promise that. Now will you sail Marisa *vahine* to my bungalow? And you, Tupui," he called out to the occupant of another nearby outrigger, "please will you sail Tania to the bungalow of Vini *tane*? The women are tired—too tired to walk."

But it was Tuan who looked tired, too tired to fly. Marisa squelched the instinct to plead with him to stay. Doubtless under the circumstances he preferred not to sleep on Ta'aroa—at least, not without a woman of his own. Tania's pregnancy of three months was evidence enough that Alain de Vigny's accident had in no way impaired his virility. To lie alone in the night and to think of the person you loved in someone else's arms...it was a purgatory Marisa understood only too well.

"How is Maeva?" she asked Lotu in the few minutes it took to sail the distance to the bungalow. Already Tuan's plane was taxiing for take-off.

"She is well enough," Lotu said gloomily, with an unaccustomed lack of cheer.

"I saw your daughter yesterday morning. She's a beautiful child."

At which Lotu, strong and manly though he was, managed to look like a whipped dog; and Marisa quickly changed the subject.

What horrible tragedies seemed to be breeding on this secluded island, tragedies so great that Marisa felt thoroughly ashamed for the self-pity she had indulged in last night. Alain, Tania, Tuan and now Lotu and Maeva, too.... Involuntarily Marisa raised her eyes to the Ta'aroa cloud. How beautiful, how terrible, was love.

CHAPTER FOURTEEN

ANOTHER RESTLESS SLEEP.

This time Marisa tossed and turned and struggled in the lonely Pacific night with a decision that she realized she must make before she saw Tuan again. She knew her refusal of the previous evening could be retracted easily enough; with any encouragement whatsoever on her part, the marriage could now become a reality.

Would Tuan leave the next move up to her, she wondered, or would he repeat his loveless suggestion? The latter seemed likely. With Tania pregnant it would be doubly hard for Tuan to remain on Ta'aroa, unless he could vent his frustrations and forget himself in some woman's arms. Possibly a concern for Tania's well-being had motivated him, too: his stepmother's life would be considerably easier if Tuan's marriage of convenience remained intact.

And what would Marisa's answer be this time? She knew she must decide. Tuan had asked for a rational decision; and for her, no decision could ever be rational in his physical presence. Could she bear a lifetime of marriage contracted for the wrong reasons? Did she want half of him—or none of him?

It would be inconceivable to say yes; it would be impossible to say no.

When morning came she had slept, but not well; and the decision had not yet been reached. Her head throbbed, and she no longer wanted to think about it. She dressed herself dispiritedly in a sundress of embroidered cotton, ate a small and uninspired breakfast and looked about the bungalow for make-work, hoping to drive the demons from her head. But the bungalow had been thoroughly cleaned and polished yesterday; Tuan had made last-minute arrangements with two of the island *vahines* to come in during their absence in Tahiti. Now not a shard of glass could be found anywhere; even the furniture gleamed with new polish.

By noon she was listening for sounds of his plane; by midafternoon she was on the veranda watching the sky. Finally in late afternoon, not wanting to spend another minute in such self-indulgent anxiety, Marisa walked to Maeva's hut. Today there were no crowds. Now that the novelty of the new arrival had worn off, the other island women had gone about their usual business.

At Maeva's merry insistence Marisa administered an impromptu English lesson, most of it to do with the counting of small toes and fingers, and the naming of ears and nose and mouth and the tiny eyes that had by now opened like damp dark pansies in the tiny brown face.

"What is the word for 'open'? What is the word for 'pretty'? What is the word for 'love'?"

Maeva's questions tumbled out almost faster than Marisa could reply, and the answers seemed to cause much hilarity. But the visit served its purpose, for the balance of the afternoon passed agreeably enough.

"Do you think, Marisa *vahine*," Maeva asked when she had at last exhausted the lexicon of her daughter's anatomy, "that you and Tuan *tane* will make babies with blue eyes or with green?"

And there she was, dragged back to decisions she did not want to make. "I don't know, Maeva," Marisa said, looking down at the beaten earth floor and paying particular attention to a handsomely woven pandanus mat.

"Blue, I think," Maeva judged as she restored her now sleeping scrap of a daughter to the crude basket that served as a crib. "Vini *tane*, he made a baby with blue eyes, although his wife, the wife of long ago, she had eyes of gray. Or so it is said by Uma and others who were here."

"Oh?" Marisa glanced upward quickly. She had never wanted to ask Tuan about his mother; she knew no more now than she had known three weeks ago. "I didn't think Tuan *tane*'s mother ever lived on Ta'aroa," she observed, shamelessly probing.

"But she did, for a time," Maeva told her. "Vini *tane* brought her here when he was a very young man, for the first year after they were mar-

ried. Uma was only ten then, but she remembers
well. Uma says that wife was very beautiful, too,
but that Vini *tane* married her only because he was
lonely on Ta'aroa, and because he had reached the
age of marriage. Uma says he was kind to her, but
for her it was not enough. Uma says the gray eyes
were not content.''

''Not content?''

''She was not happy here, that one,'' Maeva
said. ''She used to spend much time in Tahiti. And
that made Vini *tane* unhappy, too. *Aue!* Some
men are strange.''

''Strange?'' Marisa puzzled. The chain of circumstances sounded unfortunate, but not so very
strange.

''He was unhappy to think of his wife with
other men,'' Maeva disclosed in a tone so matter-
of-fact she might have been discussing the
weather.

Of course! Ripples of shock were replaced by
floods of realization. No wonder the first marriage had not worked out! No wonder Tuan preferred not to talk about it! No wonder Alain de
Vigny, having lived through the infidelities of one
wife, expected the infidelities of another!

''Vini *tane* took that wife away from Ta'aroa a
year before Tuan *tane* was born,'' Maeva went on,
sublimely unaware of Marisa's reaction. ''Uma
says it was to keep her away from other men. But
why? He did not love her as he loves Tania. She
was unhappy, and the other men did nothing but

try to make her happy. Now you see why I said Vini *tane* is strange? He should have been glad to see his wife made happy.''

Maeva's idle flow of chatter went on for some minutes, with no more exceptional revelations. Her gossip could not be called malicious. Infidelities were discussed on Ta'aroa with great openness, even in front of children. Here adultery was an act as simple and free of guilt as sleeping or eating or going for a walk along the beach—and very often, Marisa had by now gathered, the direct result of the latter.

At last Marisa heard the sound she had been waiting for since noon—the drone of Tuan's returning plane. She stood up to go, quelling an urge to show unseemly haste. Maeva came to the door of the hut to say goodbye, and in the last short exchange of words Marisa asked, "Have you changed your mind about marrying Lotu, Maeva?"

Maeva's effervescent smile faded, to be replaced by a look of stubbornness. "No," she said.

"But I thought that now...." Marisa glanced back toward the crib and the tiny scrap of humanity that obviously held so much of Maeva's adoration. "Surely you want to keep Terita now?" she urged. "Oh, I know you promised Uma, but how can you bear to do it? You love Lotu, Maeva, and you love Terita, too. Doesn't it bother you to think of giving your baby away?"

Maeva shrugged without answering, as if it did

not; and with a last sigh Marisa turned to leave.
She was only several paces beyond the lintel when
Maeva's voice stopped her.

"Marisa *vahine*!"

She turned back and saw Maeva framed in the
doorway, shaded by the breadfruit tree with its
great pendulous globes of fruit. At the moment
the young pareu-clad girl had the placid brown-
skinned beauty of a Gauguin painting, an ageless
accepting quality that made her look older than
her years.

"What is the word for 'sad'?" asked Maeva
wistfully.

Marisa's throat lumped as she wended her way
toward the main beach, and not only with
thoughts of Maeva. The story of Alain de Vigny's
unhappy first marriage had crystallized her own
thinking. According to Maeva, it had been a loveless match. *But for her it was not enough....* The
poignant little words seemed to contain a message
that Marisa could not ignore. Not that she con-
doned the infidelities committed by Tuan's
mother, but it was difficult to be too judgmental
without knowing what that sad gray-eyed woman
might have suffered. A bride brought to a strange
land, with strange customs, only to find that her
new husband offered kindness but no love...who
knows what unhappinesses might have driven
Tuan's mother to behave as she did?

By the time Marisa arrived at the main beach,
Tuan's flying boat was taxiing slowly northward,

trailed by several outriggers. His evident goal was the sheltered cove where the plane was kept moored most of the time. The cove was not far from Alain de Vigny's bungalow, and Marisa knew it might be some time before she saw her husband, especially as he might stop in to see Tania and his father. Had Tania told Alain de Vigny of her pregnancy yet, Marisa wondered.

She decided to await Tuan's arrival on the main beach; it would be easier to remain impersonal in the presence of others. During the morning hiatus she had made preparations for the evening meal, and there was little to be done at the bungalow. So for a time she watched the island women collecting shellfish along the shore, and then spent some idle moments chattering with the woman whom she now recognized as Maeva's natural mother—an older and somewhat squatter version of Maeva, with a one-year-old slung casually at her hip on one side and a three-year-old boy tugging at her pareu on the other. Several older children played nearby, and although Marisa could not yet sort out which was which, she knew one or two of these belonged to the large brood of Maeva's natural brothers and sisters.

At last Marisa's attention was turned northward by the approach of two Polynesian boys—almost young men, really—coming along the beach with a burden that was a bizarre reminder of civilization in this primitive setting. Two near-naked teenagers carrying a large plate-glass door: how odd it

looked against a background of nipa huts and
flowered pareus and outriggers and palm trees!
Well, now she knew at least one reason Tuan had
elected to return to Tahiti. The glass door served
little purpose much of the time, but during a driving rainstorm it was a necessity.

The boys came to a temporary halt when they
sighted Marisa; evidently they had a message for
her.

"Tuan *tane* will not be home for a time," one
of them told her. "He says you are to dine if you
wish, and not to wait for him."

"Is he at his father's home?" asked Marisa.

The boy who had spoken grinned broadly. "No,
Marisa *vahine*. He is with Lotu and Tupui and the
other men, readying for the hunt of the octopus."

"Now?" asked Marisa in some alarm, with a
swift glance at the sun. "But it's so late."

"Not too late," came the blithe answer. "There
are still two hours of daylight. Tuan *tane* has
promised that if we carry this glass to his
bungalow, the hunt will wait until we return to see
it. Perhaps," he added proudly, "if more men are
needed, we will be allowed to take some part."

Marisa followed their progress to the bungalow
and saw the glass safely deposited near the door,
where Tuan would see to its installation later. She
could not dismiss a deep sense of uneasiness at the
news the boys had imparted.

"Did Tuan *tane* ask you to bring his spear gun
back for the hunt?"

"No, Marisa *vahine*," one of the boys said, looking surprised. "For what reason would he want a spear gun? In their outriggers the men keep spears and knives if they are needed. For the men of Ta'aroa it is no sport to kill an octopus with a spear gun." The lad glanced at his companion and bragged a little. "We killed a small one yesterday, Hiro and I. See what the octopus did?"

With great pride he held up one arm. On the inside of his youthful biceps, which had not been visible before, Marisa saw with a sick lurch that the skin had been torn away whole, leaving a large patch of raw flesh.

"Are you going to the reef in your own canoe?" she asked, aware that most of the young men of the island possessed a boat of some kind.

"Yes, Marisa *vahine*."

"Will you take me with you?" she requested urgently.

The boys exchanged a glance that implied indecision.

"Tuan *tane* promised long ago that I could watch if I wished," she said.

"But we must go at once, Marisa *vahine*," came the protest. "We cannot wait, for we promised to return at once."

"I'll only be a minute," she promised, "and then we can all go in Tuan *tane*'s outrigger if you like. That will save time."

The boys shrugged, conceding, and Marisa ran into the bedroom to change into her bathing suit.

Surely if she were present Tuan would see that a spear gun was used for the hunt? The spear gun was kept in the bottom of his outrigger, which was beached beside the bungalow. She was sure he would not mind the craft's being used; he himself had been teaching her how to handle it, and the two boys, like all Polynesian boys, would be thoroughly skilled in any matters to do with the sea.

Within moments she was ready, clad only in her brief bikini; with the two boys she set out at once. Tension built in Marisa as the boat clawed its way in a northerly direction, driven by the soft but steady trades. She checked the apparatus in the bottom of the boat. The spear gun was indeed there, along with a full complement of swim fins and masks and snorkel gear. No doubt Tuan planned to borrow such things from Lotu if he needed them, and his blue bathing suit would be in his flight bag from the Tahiti trip.

The waters were glassy-clear in that part of the lagoon where the outriggers of Tupui and Lotu and several other men had been pulled up on the reef. From the distance Marisa could see more than a dozen men gathered not far from the boats, standing on the coral ridge where it crested through the turquoise water. One figure held her attention: that powerful bronze frame, taller than the others, with the flash of blue bathing suit that contrasted with the pareus worn by the islanders.

Here there was not enough breeze to belly the sail, and as they approached the area where the hunt would soon begin, Marisa's young escorts picked up the paddles and stroked swiftly and surely toward their goal. Sounds of a developing argument came clearly across the water, and through the other voices Marisa could hear the authoritative tones of one she knew only too well.

"No, Lotu," Tuan was saying in a firm voice, holding out his hand. "Give me the goggles."

"Never!" Lotu's voice shook with anger, and as the outrigger drew closer Marisa could see that his face, too, showed signs of fury. In his hand he clenched a pair of old-fashioned underwater goggles of a type Marisa had seen the island men use on several occasions. With hand-carved wooden eyepieces and small dark bottle-glass lenses, they fitted closely into the eye socket. Although they produced a bizarre appearance rather like frog's eyes or a pair of Martian orbs, they had the advantage of being less easily dislodged than the larger modern masks that were now in general use on the island.

"I must do this," Lotu was shouting angrily above the general hubbub of men all calling advice and opinions. "Tupui has been promised the honor of killing the octopus, as it was he who found its lair. How can you take from me this other honor, the honor of being bait?"

"I promised I wouldn't let you do it, Lotu. Give me the goggles—now!"

For answer Lotu spat on the reef and jutted his chin out defiantly. "I have been friends with you for many years, Tuan, but this time, no. I, too, have made promises.''

In the general noise and confusion Marisa hardly remembered her own intent in coming here, and as she and her paddlers neared the chaotic scene the spear gun lay forgotten in the bottom of the outrigger. By now everyone was shouting at Tuan; it seemed that his words had aroused the ire of all the island men. The honor of being bait should fall to Lotu: that appeared to be the consensus.

Now Lotu and Tuan ceased their hostilities long enough to become aware of the near approach of Marisa and the two young lads. Lotu evidently took this as a signal that the hunt could begin as promised. He turned his back on Tuan, spat into the peculiar bottle-glass goggles and rubbed the spittle over the surface. Then, leaning forward from the reef, he dipped them into seawater in preparation for putting them on.

For one instant during which Marisa found all words and reason flown, Tuan looked directly at her—his face grim and set, his eyes holding hers as if no others were present.

Then, without a flicker of hesitation, he knifed into the green lagoon. He surfaced only long enough to draw a deep breath; if he heard the enraged shouts of Lotu and Tupui and every other man present, he chose to ignore them. With his lungful of air he streaked downward along the face of the coral reef, his long muscular body clearly visible in the limpid water. He knew his goal, and so—as clearly as if he had shouted it aloud—did Marisa and every other person present.

For a paralyzed instant silence and shock descended over the assemblage of men on the reef. Tuan had no swim fins and no goggles, and no partner was yet armed for the kill; the weapons remained in the nearby outriggers. Then came a shout, echoed by a dozen voices.

"Tupui! Hurry!"

A flurry of activity began as Tupui belatedly readied his own goggles and fins, while another man raced to the canoes and began a frantic search for Tupui's knife. It had been temporarily mislaid beneath a tangle of fishing nets, and precious seconds later a different knife was produced from a neighboring outrigger.

Marisa saw none of this, for by now her entire being—breath, body and soul—was concentrated on the living nightmare of what was happening beneath the water. Every detail was distorted but clear, performed in slow motion, horrible beyond imagining, to be imprinted forever in some hellish corner of Marisa's mind where monstrous memories were kept.

Tuan, still using the deep breath he had inhaled before his dive, was suspended in the glassy water about ten feet below the surface. He hung directly in front of a shadowed cleft in the coral reef, no more than thirty feet from where Marisa sat in the outrigger in a paralysis of fear. He moved past the cleft once or twice and then remained there, motionless but for the slow sweeps of one hand that kept his body from rising to the surface. The other hand served a different purpose: Marisa could see, through the crystal waters, that he had used that hand to cover his vulnerable eyes.

No goggles. In the scene of sick horror now being played out, Maeva's long-ago words came back: "It is horrible only if the suckers find an eye."

Suddenly Marisa saw Tuan's muscular body jerked against the reef, and with a dread too primitive for reason she became aware of the ugly thing that had done it—a huge tapering rope of a tentacle, studded along its length with whitish suckers. The tentacle had flickered around Tuan's naked spine with the speed of lightning, seizing with a suction whose power could be felt—to Marisa, at least—like shock waves through the water. The whipcord force had bound one of Tuan's arms to his torso, pinioning it completely and rendering it useless.

In her terror-stricken paralysis Marisa did not hear the splashes created by the simultaneous entries of Tupui and Lotu. But she did see Tupui slicing downward toward Tuan, knife clenched between his strong teeth, agile brown body ready for what must be done. Lotu remained on the surface, also armed for the kill; but Marisa was unaware of that.

In every millisecond now there was an eternity of anguish. Two more tentacles had whipped into place, joining the first in a stranglehold around Tuan's body. Each tentacle was as long as he—a ropy, ghoulish six-foot arm of grayish yellow shading to brick, as thick at the body end as a wrestler's forearm, as supple at the tapered end as a striking snake. The horrible embrace riveted Tuan against the reef, and although Marisa could not know it, the horny beak of the creature's mouth was now groping against his chest, seeking flesh. Nausea gripped Marisa, along with the kind of primeval horror man reserves for things not understood. She ached to scream through the water for Tupui to hurry, to do something, to act—but Tupui still hung in the balance several feet behind Tuan, waiting; and the scream that tore at the pit of Marisa's stomach never reached her lungs.

Time froze; but what seemed minutes might have been mere seconds. Even as Marisa watched, a fourth tentacle struck out like a whiplash, seizing Tuan's other arm and dislodging the hand that had been held protectively to his eyes. A fifth snaked out and corkscrewed sickeningly around his leg, its suckers clamping the flesh like gigantic suction cups.

And now Tupui acted. He had been waiting only until enough tentacles were in service that he himself might be reasonably sure of evading the creature's viselike embrace; to expose his own body to those arms would only increase the dangers to Tuan, for a man trapped by an octopus could not perform his part in the kill.

Hanging a full arm's length away, for three tentacles still remained to find a mark, Tupui took hold of Tuan's shoulders and jerked backward in one mighty and manly wrench that tore the octopus adrift from its fastenings on the coral. Two more of the tentacles thus loosened lashed around Tuan's body, their grip immutable. In the moment before he was totally immobilized, Tuan gave a powerful kick of the one leg that remained unbound.

He rose to the surface slowly but surely, trussed by the ugly creature. Somehow he managed to turn in the water until he was floating on his back; the movement brought the bulk of the octopus's body above the surface.

Tupui had followed Tuan's imprisoned body upward to the surface, but Marisa did not see that. In the terror of the moment she saw only her husband's bound torso and the ugly Medusa of a creature that held him in its death grip. Its bulbous mound of a head was clearly visible now, like some malignant growth rising from Tuan's chest and bristling with the misshapen protuberances that gave this sea monster such a forbidding aspect. To her horror now, the last long rope of a tentacle waved in the direction of Tuan's face, seeking one last vulnerable goal.

His eyes.

There was no conscious thought in her next action, nor did she ever know from what hidden well she dredged the courage. But in a burst of adrenaline she sliced into the water, aiming for the battle that took place not a dozen feet away. She surfaced at Tuan's head, and her hand flashed out to cover his face. Whether she succeeded, she never knew. She had the merest lightning impression of that long sucker-studded whip and then in the next split second her hand was lashed into place by hot clamps, and her head, too, where steel cables tightened around her scalp and her neck. Now pure primitive fear held her in its grip; it choked her, it engulfed her, it smothered her. . . .

But *fear* was too small a word for the brief vision she saw next. In a split second that took an eternity to happen, Tupui closed in from behind the octopus's head. Marisa did not see the brown hand that flashed into action, but she did see the great squat mound of a head being wrenched away from Tuan's chest and jerked upward. With some nightmare corner of her mind she caught a swift impression of a horny blood-flecked mouth and bulging burning eyes in a huge distorted face.

It was as well Lotu had already sliced through the water to her aid; for in the instant before Tupui's knife plunged, Marisa fainted.

CHAPTER FIFTEEN

A BLUE ENORMOUS SKY was the first thing she saw.
Sky, and then eyes.

Tuan's eyes. The blue was there. The lashes
were there. The lids were there. The little pale
crinkles at the edges were there. The eyes were
there.

Tears began to slide over Marisa's face, unwanted but unchecked. "It's all over," he reas-
sured her quietly, but the tears continued to flow.

They were in his drifting outrigger, to which,
she later learned, Lotu had towed her unconscious
body. At some point the two young Polynesian
boys had departed from the craft, and Lotu, too,
had been ordered away by Tuan; she was alone
with him now. Twenty yards away on the reef she
could hear sounds of jubilation; the canoe was still
close to the scene of the hunt. Tuan was sitting low
in the belly of the boat, and Marisa's head was
pillowed on his lap. The roots of her hair hurt.
Above her hovered Tuan's strong bronzed face
and his broad naked chest. His thighs and his wet
bathing suit cushioned her soaked hair.

Marisa's eyes searched his torso and clung to a

raw spot near his collarbone where the skin had been abraded, the site of the octopus bite. New waves of nausea washed over her, along with the tears she could not control.

"You're all in one piece, Miss Marisa." His smile was too grave to deepen the sunbursts around his eyes. "And so am I."

She could not yet answer, or ask the most horrible question of all, but he sensed what she needed to know.

"The octopus is dead," he said. "Tupui killed it in one blow between the eyes. It releases at once when it dies. Now do you see you needn't have worried? Tupui knew what he was doing. I was never in any real danger. But *you....*"

Despite the warmth of the sun she felt chilled. Taking breaths, even the shallow breaths she managed to take, seemed a herculean effort.

"It it hadn't been for Lotu's quick thinking, you'd have taken in an enormous lungful of water. As it was, he grabbed your hair and lifted your face just in the nick of time."

Her lips trembled where tears touched them, revealing the terrible weakness she did not want him to witness. She turned her head and buried her face against the narrow line of his blue bathing suit.

Only the sharp intake of his breath and the sudden fierce digging of his fingers into her scalp brought her to a realization of what she was doing. Swiftly she wrenched her tearstained face away and covered her abysmal confusion for the moment of thoughtless impropriety by attempting to struggle to a sitting position. She was unable to do so, but she managed to free herself from Tuan's support and lean weakly against the gunwale of the boat, as far from him as possible.

Tuan made no move to prevent her retreat. If he had appeared in command of himself only moments ago, he looked thoroughly shaken now. There was a pallor beneath his tan, and a grim compression of those hard lips; and for the moment Marisa was shakily grateful for the presence of others within hailing distance. Her gaze met his for one embarrassed instant and then fled. The tears flowed faster.

In moments Tuan had recovered his equilibrium. "You shouldn't have dived in," he said with a testy edge to his voice that had not been there before.

With averted head she nodded numbly, acknowledging this. Dizziness and nausea assailed her, and she felt humiliatingly close to fainting all over again.

"And why did you let yourself get so close to the octopus? It was a damn fool thing to do."

"I was afraid," she said faintly.

"All the more reason to stay away," he chided her roughly.

Marisa dashed her tears away, only to have them reappear. An enormous weakness had seized her entire being, a weakness so great she wanted only to cling to Tuan and weep out her fear and her love.

"Why did you do it?" he persisted.

"I was afraid," she trembled out again, unwanted visions chilling her brain and her body. "So afraid."

Her tears felt like fire, her face like ice. She began to shiver violently and involuntarily despite the heat of the late sun.

Suddenly a different kind of emotion touched Tuan's eyes. "I think I'd better get you back to the bungalow at once," he said, his brusqueness covering concern. "I think you're in shock—real shock. Here, put these over you."

He bundled her beneath some towels that were not entirely dry; they were the only coverings in the boat. Too enervated to resist, she allowed him to do as he wished. Then he reached for a paddle and yelled a hasty farewell word toward the group of laughing men gathered on the reef. With another access of nausea Marisa saw the sickening spectacle of the flaccid dead octopus whirling through the air. With great whoops of glee the men were flinging its lifeless body from one to another in a macabre game of catch.

Only Lotu remained apart from the others. He was squatting broodingly on a part of the reef much closer to where Tuan's outrigger was drifting. The expression on his face was quite visible from here; but with great tides of dizziness and nausea ebbing and flowing through her body,

Marisa was feeling too ill to understand as yet the dark accusation she read in those eyes.

The canoe broke into a breezier part of the lagoon and Tuan at last set the sail. As he moved about in the outrigger, Marisa forced herself to study his body for signs of the struggle. There were tiny red lesions here and there caused by the hooks attached to each of the octopus's suckers, and patches that might soon turn to bruises, but there appeared to be no serious damage. This knowledge brought relief but in no way served to diminish the violent shudders that now racked her body as she sat in a small damp huddle of misery and seasickness. How humiliating that her body should betray her like this; how terrible that Tuan should have to worry about her after living through such an ordeal himself.

"I'm sorry," she whispered through chattering teeth as he beached the outrigger and came to help her from the boat. He reached down to sweep her into the powerful circle of his arms, and her whole world reeled and tilted through a haze of tears. "I'm so ashamed of m-myself," she said.

His mouth tightened, and so did his hold on her body. "You spend too damn much time being ashamed of what comes naturally," he muttered. The peculiar timbre of his voice verged on savagery; then his tones became soothing again. "Now just relax. Rest and a good warm bundling up—that's the thing for shock."

He strode over the bridge into the bungalow,

cradling her as easily as he might have cradled a
helpless six-year-old.

"I'll walk," she tried to protest, but no words
passed her lips. In truth, her chilled and enervated
limbs were capable of nothing; Tuan had guessed
correctly when he said she was in shock. In the
bedroom he laid her limp and shaking body on
the bed and rolled her in a blanket at once. Then
he made a short detour into the bathroom, emerging with several large thick beach towels.

"You can't wear those wet things," he said.
He folded back the blanket briefly; and then,
with a gentleness that was incongruous for such
hard and powerful hands, he slid the damp
scrap of her bikini bottom over her hips and
off her feet. The top of the bikini was whisked
away with equal dispatch, baring all of her.
He wiped her body fleetingly with a cloth moistened in warm fresh water, and then dried her
thoroughly. Marisa permitted the intimate and
gentle intrusions of the towel because at the
moment she had no more strength than a baby;
but her own shuddering helplessness con-
tributed to a deep sense of mortification as she
submitted to his toweling of her breasts and
her hips and her thighs. However, there was
compassion, not passion, in his touch, and the
humiliation did not last long. Soon her nakedness was bundled beneath two warm dry blankets,
and she had been moved to the side of the
bed not dampened by the wet imprint of her bath-

ing suit. A towel was wrapped around her soaked hair.

Without another word Tuan vanished into the living room, returning moments later with a small glass of water. He supported her spine and pulled her head against his bare chest, his arm firm and warm against her naked shoulders, while she took a few sips. But the liquid did not bring the sliding tears to a halt, and she continued to shiver violently.

At last he laid her back on the pillow, stood up and regarded her tear-damp face with a perplexed frown.

"Did you eat any supper?" he asked. "Or lunch?"

"No," she admitted faintly. Her stomach still misbehaved, and she hoped he would not suggest that she try to take sustenance now.

He did not. "Oh, Miss Marisa," he murmured, "what am I going to do with you?"

Briefly he scowled down at the damp bathing suit he still wore. After no more than a moment's deliberation he slid it down over his hard flanks and kicked it away across the floor. He toweled himself vigorously and swiftly and lowered himself onto the bed beside Marisa; and because she was still white-faced and trembling with the aftermath of shock, he slid his long body beneath the blankets and gathered her in his arms, warming her nakedness with his own animal heat.

Gradually the shuddering stopped and the tears

dried against his comforting chest. How long she
lay pressed to him Marisa never knew; but as day
gave way to purple dusk, and purple dusk to
night, he still held her close. There was no arousal
in the embrace, only a safe haven from nightmare.
If Tuan felt desire at this moment, some strength
of will suppressed his natural urges; his man's
body remained quiescent, offering strength, not
love.

At last shock and the exhaustion of several restless nights claimed their due, and locked in the
warm strong circle of his arms she slept.

WHEN SHE WOKE NEXT MORNING only the imprint
of his head on the pillow remained to remind her
that all was not imagination. There had been no
nightmares, only a balm of deep and dreamless
sleep, disturbed now by the sound of low voices
from the living room.

The dizziness and the faintness and the nausea
had vanished. Marisa slid out of bed and dressed
without taking time to shower yesterday's salt
away, snatching the first things that came to
hand—a checked shirt and faded blue jeans. She
sat down briefly at the dressing table to run a
brush through her tangled hair and decided to tie
it back because the salt robbed it of luster. As she
looked in the mirror some instinct impelled her to
touch her finger to her lips. Why did they feel so
stung and warm—as if they had been kissed?

It was possible, she knew; in her exhaustion she

had slept deeply. The realization that Tuan might have caressed her sleeping body last night, much as she had once caressed his, filled her with a flood tide of love. How could she have thought yesterday that she would be willing to give up that part of her husband that could be hers? A half a man was better than none.

And in that moment when she touched her lips, she changed her mind all over again.

The murmur of voices had ceased before Marisa entered the living room. Tuan was alone and had just finished installing the new glass door; he still held a screwdriver in his hand. Tantalizing smells of coffee and bacon and buttery toast wafted from the kitchen, and Marisa sniffed with appreciation.

"Just in time," Tuan said with a smile, in the faintly sardonic drawl he used when he was in a good temper. His eyes slid appreciatively over her slender figure, bringing a becoming warmth of color to Marisa's face.

"How are you feeling this morning?"

"Quite recovered, thank you." Her eyes came into hesitant contact with his, and Marisa knew that he, too, was thinking of the intimacy of the embrace in which they had slept last night.

"No bad dreams?"

"No," she said. Her eyes escaped his only to come into contact with the masculine line of his thighs, hard and virile beneath close-fitting denim. "No dreams at all."

She shuddered briefly as memories of yesterday's nightmare returned to haunt her fleetingly; Tuan noticed the momentary revulsion.

"The octopus isn't an invention of the devil, Marisa," he said in a serious voice. "It isn't so horrible if you see it under other circumstances. Someday I'll let you watch a small one feeding—from a safe distance, of course. They can be quite beautiful and graceful and purposeful, gliding across the bottom, their colors changing in the light."

"I wish they didn't exist at all," she said.

"Then that would upset the balance of life at the reef—a delicate thing at best. The octopus is a predator, but it keeps other predators in check."

"I'll never like them," she said fervently.

"You don't have to like them," he assured her, "but you'll be less afraid of them if you come to understand them as the islanders do. Nothing like knowledge for dispelling fear."

Her throat constricted briefly. "Do you mean you weren't afraid yesterday?"

He laughed, scattering the hellish visions in her mind. "I'm human, too. Of course I was afraid—a little, before the octopus struck. But fear is easiest if you face it, and that's why I'll take you to watch a baby one feeding sometime. Do you think you could bear to watch?"

"I could try," she promised, adding in her own mind, *if you're there.*

"Now come along to the kitchen," he suggested affably, putting down the screwdriver and coming across the room to take her arm. "Breakfast has been ready for half an hour, and you've got some eating to catch up on. I'm looking after you this morning. No fresh fish, though—for once I didn't go spearfishing."

"Oh? But I did hear voices out here; I thought it must be Lotu." At his touch, something inside Marisa tingled with anticipation. If she had spent last night folded in his arms, would she do so again tonight?

"No, it wasn't Lotu." Tuan pulled out a chair and saw her settled at the table.

"Didn't he appear for your usual morning sport?"

"I'm afraid not," Tuan said levelly. "Lotu's not talking to me at the moment."

Marisa angled a swift glance at her husband and felt a stab of remorse. "Because of the hunt?"

"Because of the hunt," he nodded, retrieving two plates of toast and bacon from the oven where they had been keeping warm. "Don't worry; he'll get over it."

A great wooden bowl of fruit already decorated the table, and shallow dishes of freshly cut mango. Tuan poured coffee for himself and Marisa, adding cream to his own and a little sugar to hers.

"I remember now," Marisa said thoughtfully as she began to piece together yesterday's events. In the swift onward march of happenings and the horror of the hunt, she had quite forgotten Lotu until this moment. "He *was* very unhappy yesterday." She turned to look at her husband with wide worried eyes. "I'm sorry. I realize now I should never have interfered. When I extracted that promise two weeks ago, I didn't understand. I didn't know what it was like, how the island men felt about the hunt—and I certainly didn't know it would work out as it did."

"It worked out perfectly well," Tuan drawled with some amusement in his eyes. "You're still talking to me, aren't you? You mightn't be if I'd allowed Lotu to do as he planned."

"But. . . ." There was something else tugging at Marisa's mind, something that troubled the smoothness of her brow. At last it came to her, and her face fell as the simple truth revealed itself in a lightning flash. "Yesterday Lotu shouted that he had made promises, too," she said slowly. "To Maeva, of course—it must have been."

She could see that Tuan, too, now guessed what Lotu's words had meant. His mocking smile faded, to be replaced by a scowl of concern.

"Maeva's desire for Lotu to prove himself," he concurred gloomily after a moment of contemplating his coffee. Losing appetite, he shoved aside his plate of toast and bacon and lighted a cigarette. "Damn. I might have guessed. I suppose Maeva promised she'd marry him if he performed his role with proper aplomb—as Lotu certainly would have done; he's no coward. No wonder he didn't show up this morning."

"It's really my fault," Marisa admitted, sinking

inside to think she had caused a rift in the friendship of a lifetime. "I'll explain to Lotu; he'll forgive you."

"You'll do nothing of the kind," came the swift retort, and Marisa, taken aback, subsided into silence. She sipped at her coffee and picked at the toast and bacon, but her appetite, like Tuan's, had evaporated with the realization that yesterday's events might have dealt a cruel and crushing blow to Lotu's hopes—and undoubtedly Maeva's, too. Marisa was certain that the young Polynesian girl wanted nothing more than to marry Lotu and keep her baby, and only some streak of stubborn pride and her very public repudiation of Lotu prevented her from doing so.

"Who was here this morning, then?" Marisa asked at last, wanting to change to a less depressing subject.

"Ah Ling, my father's Chinese manservant." Tuan remained distracted; his manner was somewhat abrupt. "An invitation from Tania—for dinner tonight. I've accepted conditionally. Do you feel up to going?"

"Yes," she said, poking at her mango. The subject was not less depressing after all.

"Good; I'll let Tania know. Now will you excuse me? I think I'll go looking for Lotu."

He pushed his chair back and left the kitchen. Marisa heard him depart the bungalow and from the kitchen window saw his long easy body striding northward with a vitality less pronounced than

usual. What damage she had wrought with her interfering words two weeks ago! Would she have
tried to extract the promise from Tuan if she had
known how the islanders viewed the octopus
hunt—making a sport of danger, as men learn to
do when they must live on intimate terms with the
elements?

She sighed and decided that, notwithstand-
ing Tuan's directive, she would speak to Lotu
as soon as possible. And Maeva, too: that
much could be done immediately, this morning. Not that an apology would go very far toward solving the knotty problem of soothing
wounded Polynesian pride, but at least she
could absolve Tuan from blame in yesterday's
incident.

But speaking to Maeva was harder than Marisa
had imagined. Maeva was not at her hut this
morning; she was on the public beach, with her
small armful of four-day-old baby. It was
Maeva's first outing since the birth, and she was
surrounded by a covey of admirers—mostly small
children this time; the women of the village all appeared to be occupied elsewhere. Tuan was not in
sight, nor was Lotu.

Marisa decided she must confront Maeva at
once, for no more private opportunity might arise
for some time. Quickly and without preliminaries
she explained to Maeva the promise Tuan had
made, and why.

"So you see, Maeva, it's not Lotu's fault that

he failed to take part in the hunt. And it's not Tuan's fault—it's mine. Maeva, I—''

The words caught in her throat as she saw the look that came over Maeva's face. It was the same accusation she had read yesterday in Lotu's expression—an unforgiving hatred that turned Marisa cold inside, for she was very fond of Maeva.

"I'm sorry, Maeva," Marisa said in a heartfelt voice, but already Maeva had turned away, her brown back rigid beneath the long waist-length drift of straight black hair.

Oh, Lord, thought Marisa. Why had she ever tried to interfere in island ways that she did not understand?

Heartsick, she turned back to the bungalow, dragging her feet as she went. The sun seemed cheerless today. In her preoccupation she almost walked right by the figure seated on the beach beside Tuan's outrigger.

"Lotu! Oh—how nice to see you."

He rose to his feet at her words, a string of small fish in his hand. He looked patient and penitent, and thoroughly sad.

"Tuan's out looking for you now, Lotu," she said, recovering quickly from the unexpectedness of coming upon him. "Won't you come inside and wait for him?"

Lotu shook a negative with his hanging head.

"I'd like to speak to you anyway, Lotu," Marisa urged. And when he still refused to enter, she said swiftly, "It's about what happened yesterday, Lotu. First, thank you for saving me."

Lotu nodded and looked briefly surprised that she had mentioned it.

"But that's not what I want to talk to you about," she went on, and then explained some of the same things she had told Maeva. "So you see, it wasn't Tuan's idea to rob you of your part in the hunt. You must forgive him, Lotu. It was all my fault. You and he have been friends for a long time, and—"

"I have forgiven him already," Lotu broke in, still looking at the sand. "Here—I brought him a gift of this morning's catch."

He thrust the string of small fish forward into Marisa's hands and turned at once to walk away.

"Lotu!" The urgency in her voice stopped him. He turned reluctantly and retraced the few steps he had taken.

"Lotu, I know about your problem with Maeva," Marisa started as forcefully as possible. "She does want to marry you—I'm sure of it. All she needs is something to save her pride."

Lotu looked despairing. "What thing?" he said, spreading his hands.

Marisa cast about in her mind and seized on the first idea that occurred to her. "Tuan *tane* told me that Maeva was upset because you didn't win the argument with Uma. Do you think Maeva is more upset about that or about the octopus hunt? You've taken part in such hunts before."

"Yes," admitted Lotu, looking marginally hopeful. "Not for such a large creature, true, but—"

"Which is harder to face," asked Marisa suggestively, hoping to plant thoughts in fertile ground, "Uma or an octopus?"

"Uma," said Lotu fervently.

"Well, then," said Marisa.

"True," said Lotu, his chest swelling visibly. "Any man on the island can face an octopus of any size. But to face *Uma*. . . ."

"It will take some courage," said Marisa.

"It will take some thought," said Lotu, but already he stood taller and his mind was visibly at work. He turned away with a last absentminded word of farewell.

"Good luck," called Marisa to his departing back.

CHAPTER SIXTEEN

IT WAS NEARING DUSK when Marisa and Tuan headed for his father's home; the dinner invitation was not for an early hour. Marisa had voted in favor of walking the distance, partly because of curiosity to know the outcome—if any—of her suggestion to Lotu. She had not divulged that part of the morning's conversation to her husband. She suspected, rightly, that she would only be accused of interfering in island life.

But when they passed that busy stretch of beach occupied by the islanders, all was serene as usual, if confusion could ever be called serene. If Lotu had decided on a move, he had apparently not yet made it. Such an event would have reverberated around the island like thunder inside an empty drum. Perhaps a suitable occasion had not yet presented itself: Uma generally saved her public appearances for times when she could make a fitting entrance.

Lotu himself was on the beach, looking remarkably self-possessed tonight despite the fact that he appeared at the moment to be the butt of some misplaced humor. With the direct cruelty and

simplicity of children, two old women were calling out crude aspersions on his courage, his
lineage and his manhood. Some of what was
said Marisa could not understand, for it was
phrased in Tahitian. Others nearby were joining in the ribald laughter at Lotu's expense,
and Marisa marveled that he could remain so
cool under the circumstances. The scene brought
her to the conclusion that Lotu had decided on
a course of action, even if he had not yet taken
it.

Only Tuan's near approach brought the crudi-
ties to a halt. He exchanged a few words with
Lotu, and the two old women went on their way,
grinning and cackling gleefully. It was not the first
time Tuan had seen Lotu today—they had met in
the morning and mended fences—so the conversation was a short one. Within minutes it was over
and the busy public beach put behind.

"What were the old women saying to Lotu in
Tahitian?" Marisa asked.

"I don't think you'd want to know," Tuan
replied in a dry tone.

"But I do," Marisa persisted.

Tuan looked down at her and grinned wickedly,
his eyelids turned lazy with mockery. "Mostly
anatomical references—very direct ones, too.
Tahitians don't hesitate to use the words in public,
but they suffer in translation. Do you really want
to hear the exact words?"

"No," Marisa said, coloring slightly and turning her eyes back to the goal of the bungalow that would soon come into view.

Tonight Tuan's stride was more restrained than usual, considerably paced to Marisa's, which was slow despite the low sandals she wore. With one hand he carried a jacket slung over his shoulder for later use; the other hand was placed beneath Marisa's elbow. She could feel its warmth through the full sleeves of her soft silk shirt dress, the same dress she had worn for the wedding three weeks before. Later, in the night coolness, she would appreciate its long sleeves.

"I suppose Tania's fully recovered by now," Marisa said.

"She's resilient," came the noncommittal answer.

"I wonder if she's told your father about the pregnancy."

"Yes, she has." The brief reply told her little except that Tuan had seen Tania at some point today.

Marisa restrained the urge to ask how Alain de Vigny had taken the news. She knew she would find out for herself soon enough. Surely he must have taken it well, or there would be no dinner invitation for tonight! And as the pregnancy was now three months advanced, reaching back to a point in time when Tuan had been absent from Ta'aroa, and Tania spending all her time at home...yes, it seemed likely that Alain de Vigny had reacted well. Even the most unfounded suspi-

cions, like choking aerial vines, needed some twig
of truth to thrive upon. By Tania's own admission, Alain's previous suspicions had been given a
great deal to thrive upon—but how could he
suspect infidelity at a period in time when Tania
had hardly been out of his sight?

Marisa's guess proved correct: Alain de Vigny
had reacted to the news with pride and pleasure.
In his evident relief at having Tania restored to
him, he was treating her tonight with a considera-
tion and respect that told Marisa a little more
about the devoted husband he had been before the
accident. For the early part of the evening he
remained witty and charming and thoroughly self-
assured, perhaps in part because of the confirma-
tion of his virility. At first he showed few outward
signs of the inward twisting that had scourged his
life, and the lives of his wife and son, for these
past two years.

They ate on the lawn after dark, at a table
brought and set by the Chinese manservant. It was
all arranged smoothly by Tania in such a way that
it seemed hardly noticeable that Alain de Vigny
never stirred from his chair.

Tania had planned a Polynesian feast. Glossy
banana leaves were spread to serve as tablecloths;
sprays of waxy white tiare Tahiti spilled fragrance
into the air; lobster and baked breadfruit and
succulent roast suckling pig were brought wrapped
in little leaves, to be eaten with the fingers.
The moon had not yet risen. Flickering torches

were thrust into the lawn, lighting the scene and eclipsing the stars.

Two references during dinner turned Marisa uneasy. First, Alain de Vigny became fleetingly abrasive toward his wife when Marisa asked if Tania would be shopping for a layette in Tahiti. The second exchange was even more upsetting to Marisa, and it occurred when Tania happened to make the mistake of mentioning some small article purchased during a shopping trip that had taken place more than a year ago.

"That was the night you slept in Papeete," Alain burst in as Tania spoke. His voice trembled with a sudden and frightening violence of feeling.

"And so did I," Tuan interjected with deceptive casualness. "If you remember, father, there were readings of twelve on the Beaufort scale—hurricane weather. There was no way I could fly."

"And Tania spent the night in your bungalow." The accusation was compulsive, as though Alain de Vigny could not help himself.

"Yes," Tuan said coolly, "but I didn't. I've told you that before."

In the short ensuing silence suspicions chased each other across Alain de Vigny's white face, along with the flickering torchlight. "Where did you spend it, then?" came his driven question at last.

There was another uncomfortable silence. Tuan angled the briefest of glances at Marisa; she could have sworn he winced. "With a friend," he said, looking away.

"A woman friend?"

"Please, Alain, think of Marisa—"

"Yes," came Tuan's terse admission, edged with anger. "Shall I draw diagrams, too?"

"What was her name?"

"That's none of your damn busi—"

"I suppose you mean Yvonne," Marisa broke in as casually as possible, drawing a startled look from Alain de Vigny. Tuan choked, and even Tania looked surprised. Marisa smiled brightly and hoped the smile did not look as artificial as it felt. She turned to her husband. "Surely you didn't think I'd be jealous," she said with a feigned insouciance. "You told me about your relationship with Yvonne the first day we met."

"Yvonne," repeated Alain de Vigny thoughtfully. He cast one surprised and compassionate glance in Marisa's direction and turned to other matters. By this time Marisa felt distinctly sorry for herself, too; but at least the embarrassing exchange had accomplished its purpose. The sick jealousies and suspicions were put aside for the moment, and throughout the balance of the meal conversation remained innocuous.

After dinner, coffee arrived in steaming cups, and amber Benedictine in crystal liqueur glasses; and as the evening drew to a close, talk turned to the octopus hunt of yesterday.

"I hear it was a very good hunt, Tuan," said his

father. "Ah Ling gave me the details. Any after-effects?"

"Marisa suffered more than I did," Tuan remarked dryly, his hands cupped over a match. In the semidarkness his cigarette became a red glow, and Marisa's eyes followed it.

"I'm sorry about that." Alain de Vigny's gruff voice held a touch of something like apology. "It was good of you to keep at it, Tuan, until you found the creature. I must thank you."

"That's not necessary. In any case, Tupui found it."

"Of course you can forget what I said earlier about this part of the lagoon."

Undercurrents...undercurrents.... Marisa longed for the de Vigny men to explain themselves, and her wish was answered by Alain's next words.

"You can start swimming around here again, Tuan, any time you wish—as long as Marisa's with you," Alain de Vigny said, then turned toward Marisa with a strained smile. "Tania would enjoy your company, my dear, and you can be quite sure that this part of the lagoon is safe now. Two weeks ago I asked Tuan to check it thoroughly—and one thing that can be said for Tuan, when he does a job he does it well. Rest assured there'll be no more creatures of that size."

So the various searches had been undertaken at Alain de Vigny's request; perhaps she had been too hasty in her earlier reflections on the subject.

But before Marisa had time to think more about
the matter, a fat raindrop landed on her nose. And
another and another. . . .

"Run, Marisa!" Tuan commanded. The glow-
ing stub of his cigarette arced out into the darkness.
His hand arrived at her elbow in a compelling
grip, urging her to race for the bungalow. "Go
on! You'll get soaked. These tropical downpours
come and go in seconds."

Marisa started to obey the thrust of his hands,
and then halted when she realized he was not
following. She turned back to the tableau still
lighted by torches that had begun to hiss and sizzle
as water assaulted them. Tania was on her feet,
her usual serenity for once ruffled at nature's interruption of the evening. Alain de Vigny still sat
unmoving in his lawn chair, his face gaunt beneath
the flickering firelight. If he noticed the rain
splashing at his clothes, his hands, his hair,
nothing in the stony shadows around his mouth
and eyes betrayed it.

"Alain—" begged Tania with a small helpless
gesture. "Please come."

"Leave me alone," hissed Alain de Vigny with a
tight and frightening fury in his voice. "Damn
you, Tania—can't you see I don't want you here?
Now get out of the rain!"

"Father, that's enough." Tuan's voice held a
low warning: there was no mistaking its authoritative tone. A flame hissed and died, punctuating his
words. He gave Marisa a rough shove in the direc-

tion of the bungalow. "Get going, Marisa. You, too, Tania. I'll handle this."

Several more flames surrendered to the now pelting rain, but the electricity from the bungalow still shed some uncertain light on the scene, even through the wall of rain. Tania seemed frozen into immobility, torn between staying with her husband and obeying Tuan's directive.

"I won't go," gasped Marisa through the water that ran over her cheeks and into her mouth. "If you're all staying I'll stay with you. I won't be the only person to go inside."

Her words seemed to arouse Alain de Vigny to a new pitch of fury, as though she had been speaking for Tania, too—as indeed perhaps she had been. His face contorted with rage. "Curse you, all of you; leave me alone. You, Tania! Get the hell out of my sight! Leave me to my own damnation!"

"You can't speak to her that way!" Marisa burst out. Soaking now, with hair streaming lankly over her shoulders, she planted herself firmly in front of the chair where Alain de Vigny sat in the wet near darkness, tense and drenched and suffering some of the damnation he talked about. He half rose in his chair, rigid with a rage that was now directed at her as well as at Tania.

"Get away from here!" he bellowed. His untanned face gleamed under the driving water.

Perhaps it was the rain that gave Marisa courage—that driving wall of water that curtained the air between them. Or perhaps it was merely pent-up emotion from the past difficult days. She stood her ground.

"You have no right to speak to Tania as you do! Do you wonder that she left you? I wonder that she came back!"

The Chinese manservant was coming toward them now through the night and the rain, hunched and hurried and worried. He held a flashlight and an umbrella, already opened. Rivers of water coursed over its edges.

"Get away from here, you fool!" roared Alain de Vigny. "Get away, all of you!"

The startled servant thrust his offerings in Tuan's direction and scuttled away in the downpour.

"Come on, Marisa, you've said enough." Tuan kept the flashlight but handed the umbrella to Tania, who moved it over her husband's head, scorning its protection for herself.

"Yes, Marisa, please go," begged Tania, adding her plea to Tuan's. "You're only making things worse. I don't need your help."

"And I don't need yours!" Now Alain de Vigny returned to the real target of his rage. Passion and pain, a terrible naked pain, twisted his features. "Damn you, Tania, get that umbrella away from me. I'm not a cripple!"

"But you *are*!" Marisa was not crying; all the tears had been cried out of her yesterday. But the rain felt like tears, rivers of tears, releasing all

the deeply pent unhappinesses of the days gone
by. And now some of the surface things she had
been unable to say to Tuan came washing out like
topsoil in a flood. "You won't admit it, and Tania
won't admit it, and that makes you both cripples
in a way! Marriage isn't just sharing a bed, it's
sharing troubles, too. Will you still be pretending
when your child is born? Will you still be shouting
at Tania to get out of your sight—and then mis-
trusting her when she does? Oh, I can understand
why you would think Tania was having an affair
with your precious son. Yes, it's very clear what
you think! Well, they *haven't* slept together,
although God knows why not. With the way you
treat Tania, I'm surprised you didn't drive them
right into each other's arms—"

"Marisa!" thundered Tuan.

When, in the course of what was happening,
had he turned the flashlight on her face? Marisa
could no longer see her husband, but the beam of
light that impaled her through the rain told her
were he stood. She turned her eyes away from the
blinding light and back to where she knew Alain
de Vigny was still seated, although she could no
longer see him. A cold ball of fear lay in her
stomach now, not the kind of fear she had felt
yesterday, but a clammy fear of herself and what
she had said, and of what she still felt driven to
say.

"Do you know how many lives you've ruined?
You're lucky that Tania still loves you—that your

son still talks to you! You forced him into a love-less marriage, a marriage to *me*. I was never more than a convenience for him—he was using me to meet your ultimatum. It's been hard for him, and for me...."

She choked back admissions too painful for words, and changed directions, perhaps venting some of her own lingering distress from the conversation that had taken place earlier in the evening. The desperation rose in her voice.

"Do you think I'll try to keep him away from Tania? Well, I won't. Not for your sake—and certainly not for mine. I don't care if he sleeps with the whole d-damn female gender!"

The beam of light held her, accused her. She knew she had let Tuan down, and at the moment she did not particularly care. An icy unnerving silence had descended over the others. She plunged on, driven by forces as compelling as the torrential rain.

"You've caged Tania, and if you truly loved her you wouldn't do that. You can't make marriage a prison. You can't force love—you can only try to deserve it. You can't hold someone like...like an octopus with a stranglehold. *That's* why you're a cripple, Alain de Vigny, not because of your—your wretched leg!"

In the shocked void that followed, the rain ceased as suddenly as it had started, in the way of tropic cloudbursts. The cessation seemed by its very abruptness to be an act of violence. The sound of dripping grew loud in the darkness. Marisa started to shudder uncontrollably, suddenly conscious of her sodden clothes and the horror of the things she had said, things that could never be taken back.

Out of the black wet emptiness beyond her came Alain de Vigny's voice, low and tight and frightening in its intensity.

"I never want to see that woman again, Tuan. Get her out of my sight and off my property. Now! I want her off this island. And when she leaves Ta'aroa, Tuan, you leave, too."

CHAPTER SEVENTEEN

STARS HAD RETURNED with tropical swiftness even before Tuan and Marisa had dried themselves enough to attempt the journey home. Now, with the night air soft and warm and a pale luminescence christening the lagoon, the storm might never have happened. It might have been imagination, all of it, the storms of words as well, except for the tight sick feeling inside, and the still clinging clothes, and the unnerving silence of the man who walked beside her.

Tuan had covered her drenched clothing with his own jacket, still dry because he had not been wearing it on the lawn. When they reached the bungalow Marisa returned it to him wordlessly and slipped into the bedroom to change into dry clothes—not a nightgown; such a thing would have been inappropriate for the moment. And she could not yet go to bed: there was unfinished business to be settled. And so she dressed in the jeans she had worn that morning.

When she had finished, Tuan changed, too, emerging moments later in a navy turtleneck and lean dark cords that closely molded his thighs. The somberness of the outfit seemed to suit the night, for a menace still hung over the evening, with all the things that remained unsaid.

"I'm sorry," she said simply as soon as he appeared.

She had expected anger, and found none. There was no particular accusation in his eyes, only something smoky blue and indefinable that might have been remorse. They both remained standing, with half the distance of the room between them.

"I didn't realize you knew so much, Marisa, although I suppose my father's behavior made it impossible not to guess."

She nodded, acknowledging this. "I think I suspected on my first day here—because of that polite distance you and Tania always keep between you. And I knew your father had some hold over you. I guessed a lot, and Tania confirmed it all. She told me about the property deed—everything. It explained a lot of things."

"Then you know it's been like a sickness in my father's mind?"

"Yes." She studied the pattern of sleeping fish in the lagoon beneath the floor. "I know you haven't had an affair with Tania, if that's what you mean. If you had, I don't believe you'd be able to face your father at all. As it is, it must have been hard enough."

"Yes," he conceded curtly, confirming everything.

"That's why I jumped into the conversation earlier tonight with mention of Yvonne."

He was silent for a moment. "To protect me? I suppose that's why you offered to come to Tahiti, too."

"Yes."

Tuan's face tightened. "Then I was wrong to think you had other motives. No wonder you weren't interested in the...arrangement I suggested. Or were you?"

Marisa's throat hurt. How many times had she changed and rechanged her mind about that in the past two days? Two days! Tahiti was an eternity ago.

"No, I wasn't. I'm not," she said, making the decision all over again.

He was silent for a time; then he turned his back to her and walked to the door that led out onto the star-swept veranda. He pushed the glass aside and the screens, too, and stood there tall and tense in the night air. Beyond his broad shoulders the lagoon glittered under a rising moon.

"Did you mean everything you said tonight, Marisa?"

"Yes," she said, grateful that only his back could witness the naked anguish in her eyes. "Yes, except that I'm sorry I said it. I wouldn't want to make things more difficult for Tania—or for you."

Now the silence became strained like an elastic stretched too far, and at last Tuan snapped it. "I suppose it would be best if you did leave Ta'aroa altogether. In spite of what he said, my father has no power to make you go. But to be frank, I don't need you anymore. The business with the property deed is finished—I looked after it the first day I went to Tahiti, two weeks ago. You don't need to worry about your sister's insurance, either; it's been paid. You can leave on Dooey's regular trip. I can't ask him to come tomorrow; he has other charters. But he'll be here the day after, anyway. I'll contact him and tell him you'll be leaving then.''

How was it possible to be filled to overflowing with nothing but emptiness? Her eyes clung to the dark vital hair at the nape of his neck, memorizing the disturbing texture of it and the way it met his collar. Was it really all ending like this, as coldly as if they had been strangers? "You won't fly me out yourself, then,'' she stated tonelessly.

"I don't want to.''

"What will we do about the annulment?''

"It won't be any trouble. We'll talk about how to handle it when you leave. Not now—not, for God's sake, now.'' For a moment his voice became vicious.

"Will you apologize to Tania for me?''

"You can do that yourself if you want. Tomorrow is All Souls' Day, when the Tahitians remember the dead. My father can hardly keep her from joining the others at the graveyard tomorrow night, no matter what's happened. I'll be going, too—my grandfather and my great-grandfather are buried there. I'll take you if you like."

"Yes," she said in a still voice. And then, because there was one thing that remained unexplained, she added, "Why didn't you let me go two weeks ago? I wanted to go and you told me I couldn't. Yet the property was already in your name. There was no reason to—"

He swiveled back to face her, his expression harsh and frightening as it became when the clefts in his cheeks deepened into jagged lightning slashes. His voice was brutal. "Because I thought I could use you—why else? Now that you know the situation on Ta'aroa you can hardly fail to realize why I've had to stay away for most of this past year. As long as you were here with me—you or some other woman—my father would accept my presence. Well, frankly, I wanted to stay here a little longer. God knows I needed a holiday! With you gone—as you can imagine, I won't be able to stay. But I've accomplished my purpose all the same. The land's mine now, and someday, somehow, I'll be able to return. Yes, my dear Miss Marisa, you were very...useful."

Marisa's face had frozen at that moment when he turned, and somehow she managed to keep it that way for the three seconds it took him to slam his way out the front door and across the bridge.

THE DAY OF THE DEAD: it seemed appropriate for her last day on Ta'aroa. For Marisa it had been a day of living death. Tuan had not returned to the bungalow last night nor did he appear in the morning. Marisa packed; swam alone near the shore without pleasure; lay alone in the sun without feeling its warmth; ate alone without savoring the food.

She had come to the conclusion that she would not see him today when the door opened near dusk and there he was, taking her by surprise as always. He was still clad in yesterday's clothes, the dark turtleneck and cords, and his hair was damp from a recent swim. Sweat stained the cotton top; it was an outfit too hot for this time of day.

"I've come to get changed for tonight," he told her in a voice so remote it might have been that of a stranger. The employer all over again, Marisa thought sinkingly. Why had she ever allowed herself to believe anything else?

Tersely he told her that he had taken the day's meals with Lotu. Then, as he angled toward the bedroom, his glance skimmed over the casual clothes she wore. His eyes were as deep and distant and unreachable as the sky they resembled. "I'll only be a few moments. You'll have time to change, too."

"I wasn't sure you were taking me," she said.

"I promised, didn't I?" His voice became somewhat caustic. "As I recall, you wanted to apologize to Tania."

"Did she . . . have any trouble last night after we left?"

"I could hardly go and inquire today, could I?" he noted sardonically, and vanished into the bedroom. Marisa heard sounds of the shower running, and within minutes he emerged, still toweling his hair. He had changed into something cooler, but as depressingly dark as the clothes he had worn last night.

"Don't be long," he instructed brusquely.

Marisa's heart was leaden as she prepared for the evening ahead. With haste but no enthusiasm she rummaged through the already packed clothes in her suitcases for something suitable to wear. Mentally she discarded each dress as being inappropriate for the occasion, a day that seemed to be marked by a poignancy too deep for frivolous colors. The only garment that seemed fitting for the occasion was a dark evening cloak of forest green velveteen.

Finally, with no other choice, she pulled out the pareu that Tania had given her several weeks before. Its silky simplicity and dark jewel tones would be in keeping with the solemnity of a candlelight procession, and amid all the other women wearing similar garments she would hardly feel out of place. She wrapped the pareu around her naked body as she had been taught, noting with some detached part of her mind the sensuous slide of fabric on skin. If she was troubled by any self-consciousness at all, it was taken care of by the addition of the evening cloak.

Darkness had closed in like a shroud long before they reached the mountain-rimmed valley behind the village of clustered nipa huts. They climbed in silence. It was cool here on the rise of land where the graveyard lay, for a breeze drifted down from the cloud-capped slopes above. Tiny candles flickered in the gloom, hundreds of them, like small brave souls competing with the stars in the vastness of the Pacific night. They cast an uncertain incandescence over the white markers of the graves, markers that had all been whitewashed in honor of this day of the dead. Gatherings of flowers lay like pools of ruby darkness against the luminescent graves, breathing their evocative fragrances into the air. Voices, hushed by the velvet of the dark and the presence of the dead, murmured and mingled and became memories in the night, as though they had never been.

It might have been a dream, a soft, sad, insubstantial dream, but for the touch of Tuan's strong fingertips at Marisa's elbow, anchoring her to reality. In his other hand he held a lighted taper that defined the lines in his cheeks and carved changing hollows of his eyes. Marisa watched with a full heart while he laid flowers at the graves of his grandfather and his great-grandfather, fiery fringed hibiscus that glowed like dark red blood against the white.

Small groups of islanders stirred through the near dark, their progress marked by the quivering of candles and the shapes of shadows in the already shadowed gloom.

Uma passed, seated as always in regal grandeur. The sweating shoulders of her four litter bearers

gleamed like oiled mahogany under the light of the
large candle she held; theirs was a ponderous
burden to carry up a mountainside. And yet the
burden no longer looked incongruous to Marisa,
as once it had. Tonight Uma wore true dignity.
Her pareu of traditional tapa cloth lent distinction
where Western dress did not. Her majestic mountain of a body, her queenly bearing, her sorrowing
moon of a face—tonight it took little imagination
to place these things in another century. With a
sudden access of humility Marisa at last recognized that quality in Uma that caused the other
islanders to step aside deferentially and let her
pass.

Maeva walked several paces behind with her
newborn child, and did not look in Marisa's
direction. Lotu, too, was seen at a distance.
But Marisa sensed there would be no confronta-
tions here: tonight was not a night for petty
reckonings.

A shadow detached itself from the shadows of
other islanders, and gained definition by the light
of Tuan's candle.

"I hoped you would be here," Tania said in a
low quiet voice.

"I would always come for this night, if no
other," Tuan returned as quietly and steadily.
"Ta'aroa is where I belong."

Was Tuan trying to tell Tania the things he
could say in no other way, Marisa wondered. His
eyes were black enigmatic pools in the darkness,

and it was impossible to read anything there, but his mouth showed lines of stress.

"Of course." Tania seemed to accept the surface value of his words without looking for deeper meaning. "A man must have roots. Even Alain could hardly begrudge you this night. But surely you don't intend to do as he asks, Tuan?"

"Yes, I do. I'll leave in a few days, after I've closed up the bungalow."

"You know you don't really have to leave now. The bungalow is yours. Alain can't prevent you from staying here."

"I know that. But this time I don't really want to stay. It would be too painful under the circumstances."

"Under what circumstances?" asked Tania gently. "Nothing is changed—not really. Alain is a little upset, that's true, but his resentment will pass if you and Marisa stay out of his way for a few weeks."

There was an awkward silence, broken by Marisa. "I'm leaving tomorrow, Tania. We'll be getting an—getting separated. I'm sorry." She made a small helpless gesture, not sure why she should feel the need to apologize.

"I'm sorry, too, Marisa. Sorry for you and—" Tania looked compassionately at the face of the man who was her husband's son, worried frown touching her beautiful brow "—even more sorry for Tuan."

Unable to bear the look of tight white pain

about Tuan's mouth, Marisa broke in again, "And I apologize for all those things I said last night. I wouldn't want for worlds to make things more difficult for you, but I know that's just what I've done. Please forgive me."

"You said only what I should have had the courage to say long ago. Who knows? Perhaps some good will come of it. Now do you mind if I say goodbye? I must yet pay my respects to my mother's grave, and I don't want Alain to become anxious about my long absence." She laid a slender hand on Marisa's encompassing cloak. "Goodbye, Marisa. Please, for Tuan's sake—no, for your own sake—think things through before you leave tomorrow."

"I already have," said Marisa, lowering her head. There followed a swift exchange of goodbyes before Tania vanished like a soft brown wraith into the grouped shadows some distance away.

Tuan and Marisa remained on the hillside for perhaps another fifteen minutes, exchanging quiet greetings with others who arrived, or standing in silent shared communion. The tensions that had characterized most of the days of their marriage seemed for the moment to have evaporated, as if they were no more substantial than the ghosts of the past that hovered here among these white-washed gravestones.

Silent and still awed, Marisa allowed Tuan to escort her back down the twisting path and along the moonlit beach. When they reached the dark shape of the bungalow sleeping under the stars, he had still made no move to touch her. He moved ahead, switching on lights.

Marisa prepared herself a mug of warm milk while Tuan fixed himself a stronger concoction at the liquor cabinet. No words were exchanged. Slowly Marisa moved to the bedroom door. At the last minute she spun around to where Tuan stood, his back turned uncompromisingly in her direction. Her hand, emerging from the folds of the cape to carry the warm milk, almost clutched holes into the mug.

"Are you sleeping here tonight—at the bungalow?"

His voice was rough, bordering on rudeness. "No," he said. "I'll sleep on the beach, as I did last night."

"You can't—"

"Yes, I bloody well can!" He turned to glare at her.

She moistened her lips with full consciousness of what she was doing; of what she wanted him to do. Her voice misbehaved a little when she spoke. "I'm afraid I may have nightmares about... about the octopus. I did last night. Please, I'd rather know you were sleeping nearby."

What was that fierce blue fire that sprang into his eyes—was it anger, passion, some other emotion? It was impossible to tell, for at that moment an urgent banging came at the door.

"Monsieur Tuan! Monsieur Tuan—*venez vite!*"

Marisa recognized the voice as that of Alain de Vigny's Chinese manservant. He was still struggling to catch his breath when Tuan reached the front door. "Madame Tania...asks...that you...come at once," he panted. The Oriental face, usually impassive, was wild-eyed tonight; the normally spotless white coat was rumpled and sweat stained. Marisa was sure he had run all the way from the other bungalow. "Madame Tania...she needs you...."

"What's the matter, Ah Ling? Out with it! Is she all right?"

The servant nodded, still gulping for air. "It is Monsieur Alain...."

"What's happened? What the *hell* has happened?"

"He is gone."

"Gone where?"

"We have looked...we can find him nowhere. When Madame Tania returned from the graveyard he was gone." Ah Ling spread his hands expressively. "There are signs that he may have gone down to the lagoon, but he cannot be found—"

"Oh, God." Tuan's drink clattered noisily onto a convenient table. He strode into the kitchen, found a powerful flashlight and returned to the waiting servant.

"Is there anything I can do?" asked Marisa in a voice tight with alarm.

Tuan glanced back at her from the doorway, his face hard and set. Marisa did not need to ask what apprehensions troubled him; she knew. "No," he said swiftly. "I'll come back if I can—I promise—at some point in the night. But go to bed. For the love of heaven, don't be around when I get back."

And then he was gone into the night, a night that seemed suddenly cold and empty. Marisa stood transfixed in the doorway for several minutes, watching him vanish with Ah Ling, until she realized she was shivering uncontrollably. She pulled her cape more closely around herself and returned inside the bungalow. For a few moments she moved about like an automaton, switching out lamps and leaving only the underwater lighting to serve as a pale guide for Tuan's return. Then, feeling numb, she huddled into a high-backed rattan chair to wait, knowing that despite Tuan's directive she would not go to bed until she knew Alain de Vigny was safe.

What had she done... *what had she done?* Her actions since coming to Ta'aroa had wreaked such havoc with so many lives. So many lives....

Alain de Vigny. What manner of desperation had she driven him to with her compulsive words of last night? Where was he? Dead... drowned? The thought was not to be contemplated. He had not looked like a man inclined to commit suicide; his face was too strong, too obsessed, too rooted in pain and determination. But who could tell what went on inside a man's mind? *Oh, Lord,* she prayed, *let him be safe.* . . .

And Tania. What had she done to Tania's life? Tania, accepting her lot but unhappy with it all the same. Marisa knew that she had added to a burden that was already unbearable . . . had forced the unhappy woman into a position where she could no longer keep up the pretense that had allowed her, for this past year, peace of some kind.

Maeva, and Lotu. Surely if she had not forced Tuan to make promises about the octopus hunt Maeva would have accepted Lotu's proposal by now. Perhaps Lotu would yet succeed in winning Maeva over, if all went well when he faced up to Uma; but even so. . . .

And Uma. Suddenly, with a sense of deep uneasiness, Marisa envisioned Uma as she had last seen her. That noble colossus of a woman. That proud bowed head. Uma had been sorrowing tonight for the griefs of long ago: Marisa was certain of it. Oh, Lord. What damage might she have wrought with her spur-of-the-moment suggestion to Lotu? If Lotu won prestige, it would be at Uma's expense. And with a sudden flash of intuition Marisa knew that whatever move Lotu made, it would mean deep unhappiness for Uma. Why had it never occurred to her before now to consider Uma's feelings?

And Tuan. Most of all, Tuan. The very thought of him was a fist clenching at her heart. Without her interference he might have worked out his own salvation. Now he would not even be able to return to Ta'aroa. After last night's sudden storm he had not accused her of interference in his life—not with his eyes, not with his words. He had no need to: she stood self-accused. She knew she had not robbed him of happiness; he had never had a chance of that anyway. But she had robbed him of whatever sorry contentment he could find in life as long as he remained in love with his father's wife.

And as for herself? There was no easy way out. Annulment would not let her forget, or forgive herself. In her heart she was married to Tuan, would always remain married to Tuan, whether the marriage had been consummated or not. For her there was no forgetting, no forgiving, no drowning....

Still shivering with nerves, Marisa reached for the mug of now cooled milk she had laid on the glass-topped table beside her chair. Next to it lay Tuan's unconsumed drink. The light from the lagoon, glowing green from below, caught and splintered through the amber liquid, issuing a silent invitation. Without conscious decision her hand moved from the mug to the glass.

Although the drink was somewhat diluted now with melted ice, it was still too strong to be downed all at once. Marisa choked on a first large swallow and then sipped at it more slowly, in utter misery, hating the bitter stinging taste of the Scotch yet wanting its release.

In time the liquor did its work. The shivering

stopped; the warmth coursed through her veins. Soon her head nodded; she had not lied when she told Tuan last night's sleep had been disturbed by nightmares. Exhaustion claimed her after the wearing events of the past few days. She pulled her cloak closer over the naked feet curled under her. To forget, to drowse, to drown....

"MARISA...MARISA."

She came awake to the touch of his hands on her temple. She opened her eyes and there he was, bending over her, the green half-light from below casting a curious softness over his face. His eyes seemed very blue, oddly tender. His fingers, still cool from the night air, lingered lightly against her skin, then moved into her hair, smoothing it, then tangling in the smoothness.

"Marisa...God knows you should have gone to bed." His voice was rough and gentle and husky and harsh all at once. "It's been three hours...I was sure in three hours you'd have the sense to go to bed. Damn you, why didn't you have the sense?"

She was mesmerized by his eyes, by the feel of his fingers against her scalp. It seemed too much even to breathe. But the question must be asked. "Your father...did you find him?"

"He's fine. He was there when I arrived... he'd been swimming. Swimming, God help us! Tania suspected as much; she'd found his leg brace down by the water's edge. But she couldn't be sure in the dark, and that's why she sent Ah Ling.''

"His...leg brace?"

"Yes, he tried it. He was angry as hell that she caught him at it, though. I arrived in the middle of an enormous scene."

"Oh, Tuan." Her eyes were green pools of regret, reflecting jade from the lagoon. "I'm sorry. Three hours—it must have been dreadful for you, and for...for Tania."

"It's been hell, pure hell. For me, at least. But not because I stayed there. Didn't I tell you, Marisa, my father and Tania have to work things out for themselves? It's worse for Tania when I try to interfere. I left at once, as soon as I saw he was all right."

"But you stayed away so long."

"I stayed away from you." Suddenly his fingers moved out of her hair and found her shoulders, urging her to her feet. His face loomed very near; his mouth hovered mere inches away, a kiss away.... Marisa's heart pounded like surf on a stormy shore with the foreknowledge of what must surely come. Her lips, soft and unmistakably willing, parted to meet his; her eyes fluttered closed.

"Marisa, for the love of heaven," he said thickly, "don't you know what you're doing to me? You want to leave Ta'aroa; you said so. You want an end to this; you said so. Leave me now, just walk away from me...or I promise you won't go to bed alone."

Her eyes opened and his face swarmed into focus again, bending low over hers, so close that his breath mingled with her own. His eyes were darkened, his mouth twisted into a sensuous line, hungry for her and this time battling to deny the hunger. But Marisa could not deny her own hunger. At the moment she was without shame.

"Tuan, please kiss me...please."

She could hear the sudden rasp of his breath and feel the terrible tension in his fingertips. His hands moved to her collarbone as if of their own accord. She could feel him slowly parting the front of her soft cape and pushing the weight of fabric back over her shoulders. Slowly, compulsively, his fingers returned to the bared flesh below her throat. Slowly, brushing erotic messages into the skin, he explored the satin hollows; and then his hands were driven lower, to the soft swell of her breasts covered by the thin pareu. Feeling her response, he groaned and his breath grew heavier; his mouth twisted with something akin to pain.

"You know if I kiss you I won't stop there," he breathed.

His voice was thickened, his eyes heavy lidded with desire. The touch of him ignited fires in deep regions of her body, and she could sense the answering fires in his. The length of his body grazed her, growing in passion, growing in power—needing harbor, needing her.

To Marisa it no longer mattered that he loved someone else. It no longer mattered that he wanted her woman's body and not her woman's heart. It no longer mattered that he would give her only one part of himself; she wanted that part and she wanted it now.... ,

"Don't hate me," he muttered raggedly, trailing his knuckles downward to the flat of her stomach and below.

Nothing mattered now but need—her need and his need, the need that Tania could never fill. Nothing mattered, not even the losing of her last shreds of pride. ,

"Hate you?" she whispered, confessing everything with her eyes. She insinuated her hands into his waistband, freeing his shirt from its confines and letting her fingers stray upward against the good bare flesh beneath. "How could I hate you? I love you, Tuan."

"Oh, *God*!" And suddenly his mouth was on hers like an explosion. There was a wildness of wanting in the way he ravished her with his tongue and his ardent lips; a violence of need in the powerful contours that surged against her thin pareu. His fingers tore at the folds of the covering and it slithered to the floor, a dark forgotten pool. The cloak, too, succumbed to his impassioned hands. His palms flamed urgently over her body, remembering no restraints, obeying no command but that of driving need. Utterly abandoned now, she melted and clung and moaned her love and her surrender, a surrender that she longed to be complete.

"I love you so much," she whispered, even as he swooped her into the powerful circle of his arms and swept her toward the open invitation of the bedroom door. "I want you so much...."

And before he laid her all-too-willing body on the bed, he groaned hoarsely into the silvery curtain of her hair, "And I've wanted you...God, how I've wanted and waited and stopped so many times. But this time, heaven help me, I can't stop. Nothing can stop me now."

"I don't want you to stop," she murmured triumphantly, sinking her fingers into the texture of his hair and pulling his mouth down to invade her own. "I don't want you to stop...."

CHAPTER EIGHTEEN

LOVE AND PAIN. Did they always go together? Marisa lay tense and tingling in the curve of Tuan's arm, welling with hurt and with happiness. All was right; but all was not right. She had found no release for the needs of her body, for in the sword stab of the moment when he had made her his, the pain had prevented further pleasure. But Tuan had told her he loved her, and that had made the hurt worthwhile.

Tuan. At last she had called him that, as she had longed to do. The lord and master of her heart, now and for always. All the uncertainties, all the heartaches of these past days, had been burned away, and the needs of her still quivering flesh seemed unimportant now.

At first ardor had been everything. His lips had blazed trails of molten fire over every inch of her flesh until desire became a deep consuming void of wanting that could be filled only by him.

"I'll try not to hurt. Oh, God, Marisa, how I've wanted this...." His voice had been thickened by the passion he had reined in too long. Poised then, his mouth had taken hers, his deepening kiss help-

ing her through the moment of fierce rigidity that
followed the shock she could not quite conceal.

After that, though she had tried to respond, not
all the consummate skill of his caresses could draw
an answering passion from Marisa. But because
she loved him, she had pretended.

Later, storms spent, he had rained little kisses
over her hair and her eyes and her dampened
cheeks. He had murmured endearments huskily,
fingertips brushing away the moisture on her
brow. His body still covered hers, blanketing her
with heat. "Was it so very bad?"

"No," she had lied in a tremulous whisper. "It
was very good—because I love you, Tuan."

For a moment he had buried his face and held
his breath against her hair. She could feel the thud
of his heartbeat against her naked breasts. Then
the words had been choked out as if they were very
difficult to say. "I'm sorry, love. So sorry."

"There's nothing to be sorry for," she had murmured, twining her arms around his neck, exulting
that he cared.

Love. It was not mere imagination that told her
he had said the words a hundred times; each time
was branded on her memory. *I love you... I love
you... I love you....*

And when he had at last grown silent, she had
nestled into the curve of his arm and pretended
sleep, hugging the memories to herself.

That had been half an hour ago, but still she
could not relax. Beside her Tuan's virile body had

grown still, and she was sure he had succumbed to sleep. Without stirring she opened her eyes. He lay directly in her vision; she did not have to turn her head to see. No lamps burned, but moonlight filtered its silvery magic through the bamboo blinds, and a soft green diffusion of light came from the living-room door that stood ajar.

She knew at once he was awake. Oh, God why had she looked? For in that small sick moment the shadow of Tania fell across the night. It was there in his face—the small tensions of his mouth, the touch of regret in the grooves of his cheeks; and although his eyes lay deep in gloom she knew they were opened and turned to the ceiling. *And I am desolate and sick of an old passion; yea, hungry for the lips of my desire....* Why had she listened to the love lies of the mating game?

Unwittingly she held her breath, and perhaps that was what told him she was awake. He turned his head toward her; his unsmiling eyes were revealed by the somber light. Wordlessly he pulled her close. Wordlessly his mouth met hers. Wordlessly, in slow motion, he caressed her breast, soothing and stroking and gentling her.

His kiss was soft and deliberate, without the urgency of before. He asked; he did not demand. His lips brushed slowly; his tongue teased the outlines of her mouth until her lips parted of their own accord, offering what he would not take by storm. He probed, taking his time, tempting her into ardor. And when at last he sensed it in her mouth, he slid lower, and his lips found her breasts. He covered the them with kisses—nothing escaped the moist unhurried pillage of his mouth.

His hand roamed lower, too, and where it lingered passion grew—a slow sweet burgeoning of passion, like a wild rosebud unfolding in the warmth of the sun.

"I love you," he breathed as he claimed her once again.

This time there was no pain, only a rising, a flying, a floating free. . . .

And in the blinding shuddering moment when she found the ecstasy she had been seeking, the little love lies he whispered in her ears seemed right and beautiful and true all over again.

CHAPTER NINETEEN

DID FATE MEASURE OUT HAPPINESS only to make its coming catastrophies more cruel? And how could a day dawn with such promise and become such purgatory? Perhaps she should have guessed. Perhaps she should have seen it in the shadow that had touched her marriage bed last night. . . .

But when morning gold glanced through the bamboo blind, it seemed only to chase the night shadows away. Marisa stretched languorously, like a contented cat, and reached upward to encounter the depression on the pillow beside her head, still warm from her husband's head. This morning she had resolutely pushed all thoughts of Tania from her mind. Tuan had said the words of love, and that was what mattered for the moment. If she had less than all of his heart, she still had a great deal more than she had thought possible even a day ago. And if he was willing to say the words of love, then perhaps in time she would earn the full reality of it. She had the possession of his name; he had offered her love of a kind; surely for the present it was selfish to ask her fates for more.

"I love you, Miss Marisa. We can stay on Ta'aroa now... you know that, don't you?" Tuan had said this in the early predawn hours when they lay nested together. "Father will forget. He's angry as hell now, but the anger's doing something good for him, I'm not sure what.... Oh, God, there are better things to talk about. You, for instance...do you know your skin tastes like vanilla?" His mouth moved against a breast, touching, trailing, stirring her senses anew. "Like vanilla...."

They had slept briefly after that, but neither wanted to waste much time in sleep, and despite the long night of lovemaking they were both awake three hours after dawn. It had been arranged that Lotu, following the late ceremonies of All Souls' Day, would not arrive for the morning's spearfishing. Moments ago Tuan had gone to make coffee. He returned now bearing two fragrant mugs of it, wearing his black cotton bathrobe and nothing else.

He came to a halt in the doorway, tall, smiling, virile, vital. His eyes possessed her all over again; his mouth was sensual and self-assured. "I used to wonder what you looked like in the morning. Whether you'd be wearing your green nightgown or the other one, or—or what you're wearing now."

She pulled the sheet over her bare breasts with a morning modesty that told nothing of her abandon the night before. But her eyes remained undressed and told him everything he wanted to know. "Which would you prefer?" she teased with the confidence of a woman who knows herself wanted.

"Certainly not the sheet." He put the steaming mugs on a table and came down on the edge of the bed. "But it doesn't matter. I've memorized all of you, every inch of you.... Oh, Miss Marisa, we've got so much catching up to do."

She gasped briefly as his tanned hand slid beneath the covering and stroked the satin of her hip. "Oh, Miss Marisa, how long I've wanted to do this...."

And for a time it seemed that the coffee would be neglected altogether.

But several minutes later Tuan raised his dark head from her pale one and appeared to listen.

"What is it?" murmured Marisa, for she was already halfway to forgetfulness and had heard nothing.

"Damn." He pulled away from her, frowning. "It's Dooey...I'd almost forgotten." Now, by straining her ears, Marisa could hear the drone of an approaching plane. She laced her fingers around Tuan's shoulders, reveling in the good firm feel of his flesh and the hard muscles that tensed beneath her adventuring fingertips. "Can't you forget him? Maybe he'll just go away."

But the mood had been broken. "No, I can't forget him. And he won't go away, for I told him to arrange your flight to Los Angeles." Tuan unfastened her fingers, kissed them one by one and deposited a last hard kiss on the edge of her mouth. "But promise you won't move an inch—I expect to carry on exactly where we left off."

"I promise. But how long will you be? I can't stay in bed all day."

"Can't you?" His eyes teased her. "But that's exactly where I plan to keep you for at least a week. I'm taking another week of holidays, remember? One whole week, Miss Marisa, and I don't plan to tire of making love before it's over. I have three weeks of frustration to make up for! Afternoons we'll go to that secluded cove. Evenings we'll—"

"Sex maniac!"

"Say that again, darling, when I can punish you for it." By now he was doing up his belt buckle, and he cast a wicked grin in her direction. His teeth gleamed white against the bronzed skin, and his eyes, roaming over her half-hidden body, held marvelous promises of things to come. "Even though it's true where you're concerned. Now stop looking at me through those maddening lashes. It's absolutely essential that I go, and quickly, too. I have an errand to do before I see Dooey."

"An errand?"

"At my father's house. I'll explain later." He thrust his feet into soft suede desert boots. "I don't know how long I'll be—as I told you, it can take a time when you're trying to reach someone by radiotelephone. No doubt Dooey will come to the door. Tell him to wait—that I want to speak to him."

"Anything else?"

"Tell him there's no way that your pretty little body will be allowed to fly out of here today."

"I can't tell him anything if I stay in bed! You made me promise, remember?"

"On second thoughts, I release you. I don't want you greeting any man at the door with anything less than a full suit of armor." From the doorway he looked back, smiling, praising her with his eyes. "And stop looking so damn kissable. Any man would want to take you on first sight."

"Did you?" she asked, flirting outrageously from behind a curtain of lashes.

"Yes. And if you'd given me any good reason, I would have."

"I gave you several good reasons, on several occasions."

"By telling me you hated me with every second breath? Some kind of encouragement!"

"Oh, go away!" she laughed happily and breathlessly, and shied a pillow at the door as he vanished from sight.

And then he was gone, whistling tunelessly along the beach. Marisa, content in every bone, stretched and yawned and at once threw back the covers, exulting in the good fulfilled feel of her body. Today she would let nothing come between herself and happiness. But now she must hurry, for the drone of the plane had changed to a near thunder that hummed in the windowpanes, and before too long Dooey might be arriving at the door. She pulled up the bedclothes. Then she showered quickly, wasteful of rainwater today, and pulled the first thing she found out of the suit-case she had still had no time to unpack. It was a cotton skirt the color of new butter, and a sleeve-less top only shades paler. She knew it looked like sunshine with her hair, and that was how she felt—all shimmering and shiny and radiant inside.

By the time she finished dressing Dooey had still not arrived at the door; no doubt he had chosen to wait at the plane. She decided to make the short walk to the main beach herself, and deliver Tuan's message.

It was only a ten-minute walk, and as she ar-rived at the busy beach she saw that Dooey was only now being ferried to shore in Lotu's outrig-ger. As usual the islanders had arrived en masse at the sound of the plane. There was a milling noisy confusion of adults and near-naked children—the same kind of assemblage that had greeted Marisa on her first day in Ta'aroa. Supplies were being unloaded and mail from Tahiti was being dis-tributed.

Dooey jumped the last two feet to avoid the lap-ping waters, while Lotu beached his outrigger.

"Well, there you are," Dooey greeted her. His usually friendly face was somewhat more haggard than usual. "Wondered where you'd got to. Thought I might be able to avoid coming ashore today, but when you didn't appear—oooh," he finished, wincing and holding his hand to his forehead. "Agh, what a night! Thank goodness for copilots."

Marisa laughed. "Too much of a good thing?"

"Too much of a bad thing. That local beer is terrible." He looked around the beach. "Where's Tuan this morning? I should have thought he'd be around to kiss his little, er, wife goodbye. And where are your suitcases?"

Marisa paused, suddenly hesitant at the thought of telling Dooey that she would not be leaving Ta'aroa today. Tuan had contacted him only yesterday to make arrangements, and Dooey was sure to be far too curious about the change in plans. What had happened last night was too personal to be shared with anyone. Tuan would have to explain to his friend later.

"Tuan's at his father's house, but I don't suppose he'll be too long," she told Dooey. "And my suitcases are still at the bungalow. Come on back with me and wait there. I'll give you a cup of coffee."

"I could use that," Dooey said fervently, mopping his brow. A minor flurry of moving bodies attracted his eyes toward the Ta'aroa village. "Well, well, here comes Her Magnitude in person. First I'd better pay my respects."

Marisa turned and saw a sea of islanders parting

for the majestic arrival of Uma, who as usual had waited until there was a goodly congregation of people before putting in an appearance. Not far behind the straining litter bearers came Maeva, with the small bundle of her daughter cradled against her shoulder.

Uma's litter bearers deposited their impressive passenger. Spry despite her great girth, Uma rolled off, rose to her feet and moved forward, leaving the litter behind. Her atrociously bright tent of a Mother Hubbard dress did not endow her with the dignity of last night's tapa cloth, but in her mind's eye Marisa now saw that dignity and not the ludicrousness of cheap pink-and-red Lancashire cotton.

With a moonbeam of a smile Uma inclined her head, going through her ritual of greeting all arrivals at the island. " *Ia ora na,* Doo-i *tane,*'' she said. "I watched from my hut and thought you were not coming ashore today. Forgive me for being late in making you at home. Welcome to my island.''

Dooey bowed gravely, scraped and went through the appropriate responses, well aware that Uma thoroughly enjoyed her role of gracious hostess.

"You will take some *poe* with me, Doo-i *tane*?'' Uma offered magnanimously, even though the oft repeated offer was always refused politely. "Some coconut milk, perhaps? Or—''

Suddenly a great sound cracked across her

words. Marisa, and every other person on the beach, turned to its source.

Crack. Again that sound—and with sudden horror Marisa realized that Lotu was making his move. He was standing alone near a coco palm, separated from the cluster of islanders by perhaps fifty feet of beach, and in his powerful grasp he held Uma's litter. The remains of Uma's litter. Part of it had already splintered off against the tree.

Crack. It smashed again against the trunk of the coco palm, and another great chunk of carved wood flew off.

Crack.

Crack.

Cra-a-ack.

And while every islander on the beach stood frozen with disbelief, Lotu dropped the last pieces of fractured wood, dusted his hands and strutted to where Uma was standing.

Although Lotu was tall, Uma was as tall as he, and three times the weight. But at the moment Lotu seemed taller. He faced her squarely, arms akimbo, leaned forward from the hip and put on a stern expression. Uma looked benumbed, and utter silence gripped the onlookers. With thunder in his brow, Lotu pointed to Uma's feet.

"Walk!" he commanded, and swiveled proudly on his heel. Without so much as a backward glance he proceeded to obey his own command. He walked—no, swaggered—away along the

beach, leaving the flabbergasted crowd staring after his departing back.

"Lotu!" cried Maeva, and began to run after him, clutching her child. The cry broke the spell of silence, and all at once there was a babble of voices. For the moment Uma was ignored.

In that moment when all eyes were elsewhere, Marisa turned to look at Uma and realized every intuitive fear of last night. Uma's face had crumpled. As the other islanders gradually began to return their attention in her direction, the gargantuan Polynesian woman sank to the sand like a deflated balloon and hung her head in her hands. She was not crying, but her great shoulders heaved, sending tremors through the flesh. It took little imagination to realize the full extent of Uma's loss. Her hope of a child lost, her treasured litter lost, her prestige lost...everything lost by that one action of Lotu's. The islanders, too, realized these things, and one by one their voices grew hushed.

It was a tableau in misery, and Marisa's stomach flopped at the knowledge that her unthinking suggestion had brought it all to pass.

In that painful silence one person at last moved. It was Maeva's natural mother. She stooped down and swooped up the naked three-year-old at her side, and stepped forward. With great gravity she placed the boy child on Uma's ample lap.

"For you," she said solemnly, breaking the spell of tragedy. The three-year-old, with the adaptability of a child brought up in the total security of receiving love from every adult within his ken, started to play with the hei garlanded around Uma's neck.

And now Uma cried. Great round tears started to slide down that rotund face, but they were tears of joy, soon joined by a wreathing of smiles that was like the breaking of sunshine through a rain-cloud. Uma began to rock back and forth, crooning and hugging the child to her great melon bosom; and soon everyone was smiling and chatting and crying and laughing in the unutterable joy of the moment.

Well, it was a day for happiness after all, mused Marisa. With a singing heart she led Dooey along the beach toward the bungalow. Today the cloud that hung over Ta'aroa seemed to hold beauty and promise, not menace. How well things were beginning to work out! Lotu and Maeva reunited, for one thing. And Marisa was sure that Uma, with a fine boy child to console her, would no longer make efforts to hold Maeva to her promise.

And for others, too, things had taken a turn for the better. Alain de Vigny making efforts to use his leg brace and at last breaking the terrible con-spiracy of silence between himself and Tania—that, too, seemed hopeful. Surely once Alain began to lead a more normal life and tear down the walls that had cloistered him into a life of in-ner torment, his jealousies and sick imaginings would cease—just as Tuan had predicted. What was it Tuan had once said? In this climate the scars of nature, even bad scars, healed with time. Yes, Alain de Vigny and Tania would work out their salvation somehow, someday; perhaps even before their child was born.

And for herself. . . she hugged the memories of last night to her heart and refused for now to remember that Tuan loved someone else.

Unthinkingly she began to hum a lighthearted tune, and did not realize it until Dooey drew her attention to the fact.

"You seem very cheerful this morning," he observed with something less than his usual joviality. Evidently his hangover still nagged at him. "Is it because of that scene we just saw?"

"That—and other things." She wrinkled her nose happily. "The sunshine, for one thing. Isn't it a beautiful day?"

"Can't be the sunshine—that's there every day," he remarked with unaccustomed dourness. "So it must be the prospect of a flight with me. I should be flattered. Usually it's not expressed so tunefully."

"I have other reasons," Marisa said gaily as they reached the bridge.

"Must be the prospect of leaving Ta'aroa, then," guessed Dooey. "Though I can't think why! You've had a bloody good holiday out of this little escapade, haven't you? I say, that coffee smells like what the doctor ordered."

Marisa led him into the bungalow, happiness in

every swinging movement of her limbs. "How do you take it?" she asked, angling toward the kitchen.

"Black this morning," he directed; and moments later Marisa handed him a steaming mug. He sipped at it, nursing his hangover and seemingly recovering some small portion of his usual conviviality.

"Mmm, great coffee, this. Good for what ails me."

"I can't take the credit. Tuan made it before he went to his father's."

"What's he doing there—breaking the bad news to the old man?" Dooey chortled, tactless as always. "Or should I say the *good* news? That'll be a scene! Don't suppose he'll tell the whole truth, though." He winked at her knowingly. "Serves old stone face right, doesn't it?"

The turn of conversation had made Marisa more than a little uncomfortable, but she wanted nothing to interfere with the joyousness of her mood. She had no wish to discuss a marriage breakup that would not now take place. "I think he had some other business at his father's house. I'm not sure what, but it seemed urgent. He said he had to use the radiotelephone. Isn't that how he keeps in touch with the business end of things?"

But Dooey would not be so easily sidetracked from the topic, which, along with the coffee, seemed to be taking his mind off the morning hangover. "Trust Tuan to outwit the old codger! It's a good belly laugh, isn't it?"

"A good laugh?" Marisa's voice betrayed the beginnings of coolness, for she was growing annoyed with his somewhat callous treatment of the matter. Not that it was really Dooey's fault; he had no reason to think matters had changed during the past three weeks. He knew a few of the facts, but he couldn't know them all; couldn't know of the human emotions that had become tangled in what had started as a simple business arrangement. All the same, her vexation rose. "I don't suppose Monsieur de Vigny would find it amusing," she said pointedly.

"I don't suppose he would. But he'll never need to know the truth, will he? As far as he's concerned it'll just be another marriage on the rocks." Dooey took another swallow of coffee, insensitive to Marisa's rising annoyance. "Marriage on the rocks—that's a good one, isn't it?"

"I'd hardly call it a marriage on the rocks." Now she made no attempt to hide the coldness in her voice. "And really, I'm not sure I want to discuss it anymore. What's happened between Tuan and me is our own private business. No doubt he'll explain in time, as he's your friend. But I don't intend to."

"I say," said Dooey, belatedly growing alarmed at the tone of her voice. "I'm sorry. I seem to be treading on someone's toes. It's this hangover— my head's not on quite straight this morning. You haven't gone and fallen for him, have you? Don't answer if you don't want to; it's none of my business what cozy games you two may have been playing. Who could blame anyone for having an affair under the circumstances? But if you've fallen for him—I say, that's too bad. That does complicate things.''

"Nothing's complicated. It's all quite simple. And do I look unhappy? I assure you I'm not.''

"Good.'' Dooey heaved a deep sigh of relief. "It would be a shame, after Tuan arranged things so well. Can you spare another cup of coffee?''

As Marisa went out to the kitchen to pour it, his voice followed her. "Smart man, Tuan. He never did like nasty complications. And there's no complication quite as nasty as marriage when you're trying to avoid it! Clever idea that, about the phony preacher—''

The coffeepot, now fortunately empty, clattered into the sink.

"I say, you didn't scald yourself, did you?'' Dooey appeared at once in the kitchen door, but Marisa had her back turned to him, and he could not see the expression on her face.

"No,'' came a strange strained voice that seemed not to belong to anyone. Marisa was sure it was not her own: she was sure she could not speak. It was as though a battering ram had just delivered a crushing blow to her ribs and midsection.

"Good thing it was empty.'' Dooey picked up his refilled mug and returned to the living room, noticing nothing amiss. "I don't suppose he'd have met his father's ultimatum at all if the idea of a fake marriage hadn't come to him. Oh, his secretary got the special license all right, went through all the preliminaries—nothing like being thorough! Everything was quite proper until the end—until Tuan contacted the real preacher and told him he wouldn't be needed. Kept you waiting a time at the airport while he arranged it, but it was worth it, eh? Helluva good way to cut through the red tape!''

"Yes," came a faint answer from the kitchen.

"The stand-in was quite convincing, don't you think? My brother-in-law," said Dooey proudly as Marisa's face appeared in the doorway. It was pale beneath the tan, drained of blood, but the weeks of South Pacific sun concealed many things.

Dooey went on, "Mind you, he'd never fool you if you saw him, but that voice! Quite solemn and convincing—did he fool you at the time?"

"Yes." Again that peculiar voice that belonged to no one, this time composed but barely audible. Marisa walked past him to the bedroom door, moving like a robot.

"You looked so miserable that day. I'll bet you cheered up when he told you the news!" Dooey guffawed, and then held his head over a twinge of pain. "Oooh...shouldn't do that. Of course if you two hadn't been fighting like cat and dog, he'd have told you a lot sooner. As I recall, you tore quite a strip off him in the airport. That's when he decided to let you suffer a little."

Suffer a little. Suffer, suffer....

Dooey could see nothing but her rigid back in the bedroom doorway.

"You weren't mad that Tuan kept it from you till later, were you? He thought it would make a nice surprise—a little present for your wedding night, so to speak."

Mad? Yes, she had been mad...mad to think that Tuan wanted anything from her; anything but what he had always admitted to wanting. Anything beyond one stolen week....

Dooey glanced at his watch. "I say, he's taking a long time at his father's, isn't he? I did as he asked, laid on a ticket for the flight to L.A., and I'd like to see you settled in Tahiti before I have to take off again. I have a charter to attend to this afternoon. Shouldn't Tuan be turning up to say goodbye?"

Marisa turned in the doorway, facing the pilot. She forced her facial muscles into the facsimile of a smile, a smile somehow dredged up from the wreckage inside. Her voice remained steady, a stranger's voice.

"He said goodbye before he left this morning. He thought he might be delayed. He said if he was, we weren't to wait for him. Do you mind helping me with my suitcases?"

CHAPTER TWENTY

BEYOND THE WINDOW of the flying boat lay a
blinding blue world untouched by tragedy.
Although her eyes were turned in that direction,.
Marisa saw none of it—not the broad untroubled
Pacific, not the limitless sweep of blue sky, not
even the Ta'aroa cloud that was diminishing into
the distance until all that remained of the island
was a tiny, incredibly beautiful white powder puff
on the horizon.

Suffer a little. Why, in all these weeks, had
Tuan not told her the truth? Why...why? She
had asked him about the annulment only the night
before last. "We'll discuss it when you leave," he
had said. Surely that would have been the time for
him to tell her the truth, if he had never told her
before. If he intended to devise a torture he could
hardly have invented one more cruel than this.
Even if nothing physical had happened, even if he
had not claimed her body, even without the
memory of last night branding her flesh and her
brain, it would have been cruel to find out about
his deception at the very last minute. Did he
realize how cruel? Perhaps not...for until last

night he had had no reason to think that a silly ceremony would mean anything to her. She had revealed nothing of her true feelings until last night,
and then she had revealed everything.

That she had done so last night, so openly and
so unreservedly, made her burn now with shame.
"I love you, Tuan...I love you." Why had she
said those words; why had she thrown everything
to the winds...pride, reserve, modesty, chastity?
She knew he loved another woman. She had
known it all along, and last night she had willed
herself to forget.

Did it matter that he had offered words of love,
too, in response to hers? Words meant little. They
meant no more than the words that had been said
three weeks ago in a parody of a ceremony. Other
women had shared his bed throughout the years;
that had never been a secret. How many times had
he said those words, the words of last night, without meaning them? How many hundreds of
times— Oh, God, of course he had had to say
them last night; what else could he do when faced
with her own impassioned protestations? It was all
a part of the game of having affairs, a game she
had never wanted to play, still did not want to
play. Even last night she had known they were
love lies. Suffer....

He could have told her the truth last night. But
no. "This time...I can't stop," he had said in
that curious choked tortured voice. Perhaps it was
true, perhaps he could not have stopped himself

by then; she had led him on too effectively for that. But if she had known the truth, would she have led him there, to the point of no return?

The point of no return. "I don't want you to stop," she had whispered back to him in the night. Would her words have been different if he had, at that moment, told her the truth? Probably not, Marisa admitted to herself with painful self-knowledge. Undoubtedly not... for by then there had been not only Tuan to contend with, but the pulse of her own blood, the longing and the loving and the need to give that had grown so great during these past unforgettable days. Even knowing the truth, it would have been hard to say no, impossible to say no to her own heart.

Suffer a little. Suffer.

"One whole week... and I don't plan to tire of making love before it's over," he had said only this morning, in the sunlight, when reason should have returned. Another week.... There would have been no need for him to tell her the truth until the week was over. Another week? What was painful now would have been impossible at the end of another week. Impossible, insufferable... but to be suffered all the same.

True, he had shown some kind of twisted honor in the past three weeks. He had not intended to make love to her; he had told her so a hundred times in a hundred ways. She had thought it due to the need for an annulment, but now it was clear to see that his reason had been something else al-

together. If he had been totally without con·
science, he could have made love to her before last
night. There were so many times when she would
not have stopped him. That night on Tahiti, for
instance, when their lovemaking had seemed so
right, the conclusion so inevitable. "First we
talk," he had groaned as he pushed himself away
from her audacious hands. Had he intended to tell
her the truth that night? And then suggest an affair? It seemed likely. He had never mentioned
marriage, she now realized—he had spoken only
of honesty.

"I wanted to give you an option," he had said.
Had he warned her, subtly? "I never wanted marriage...life has too many complications...I
wanted to be aboveboard about the whole
thing...Miss Marisa, Miss Marisa, *Miss* Marisa. I
love you, *Miss* Marisa...."

Love lies. No, one love lie. One lie—one terrible, life-shattering, explosively simple lie. If
nothing else, she should have been warned by his
words: *sex is something else.* What a person does
with the heart and what a person does with the
body are not always the same. Hadn't she always
known that?

Yet knowing that, even knowing that, she had
been willing to settle for half measures. To settle
for half a man, the physical man only, a man who
would mouth the words of love without meaning
them, a man who would bring his body to bed and
not his heart.

And that was the true sin; her sin, not Tuan's. She had always thought that marriage should be nothing less than a total commitment for both parties. Yet faced with the decision, she had been prepared to settle for a marriage that was not. That it had turned out to be no commitment at all was perhaps only the mockery of a twisted fate. An enormous practical joke at her expense. A surprise. Tuan had always been good at surprises. A trial marriage that was all trial and no marriage at all. She had never been married, except in her heart.

Suffer, suffer, suffer, suffer....

"*Tiens*, are you all right?" The words were in French. "You're looking rather ill."

The voice returned her to the interior of the plane, bringing her eyes back from the window. It was the copilot who had come noiselessly back into the cabin, and he was looking at her anxiously. He was a young pale-haired Frenchman in a neat blue Air des Iles uniform.

"I could get you a glass of water," he offered with some concern. "Sorry I can't offer coffee or tea. Would a headache tablet help?"

"No...." Marisa tried a dismally unsuccessful smile. "I'm all right. It's just the altitude. I haven't done too much flying."

He gave her a rather peculiar look, as if he didn't quite believe her. But if he had more to say about her condition, he kept it to himself. "I just came back to see if you were all right, and to tell you to fasten your seat belt. We'll be landing in a few minutes.''

"Tahiti—already?" It had seemed a very short flight, perhaps because she had been lost in her thoughts. But a glance at her watch confirmed it; they had been aloft only twenty minutes.

"No, not Tahiti. We have to pick up another passenger. It won't take long, and then we'll be on our way again. Are you sure you're all right?"

"Yes, really I am."

He looked at her dubiously and then he was gone. Marisa turned her attention back to the window, watching without really seeing while the flying boat lost altitude and approached an island somewhat larger and evidently more populous than Ta'aroa. Its beaches were of dark sand, not the diamond-white sand of Ta'aroa, but other than that everything looked only too familiar—the clustered islanders watching the plane's approach; the swaying coco palms; the stained-glass lagoon.

Marisa kept her eyes open until the plane landed. Through the window on the far side of the plane she saw an outrigger approaching: seated in its bow was the man who was evidently to be the passenger. From here she could not distinguish him too clearly, for his back was turned, but he appeared to be a youngish man clad in a somewhat rumpled white suit. French, probably, from the look of him. He was leaning forward toward some other person in the boat, chattering volubly. Marisa had a sudden cold fear that he would be

one of those talkative persons who wouldn't leave
her to the privacy of her own thoughts. She
reached for the black eyeshade that was provided,
along with magazines, Air des Iles timetables and
other miscellany, in a pocket near her seat. By the
time the man came through the hatch she had adjusted her backrest to a reclining position, and the
eyeshade was firmly in place. The plane took off.

Air des Iles...air of the islands, spirit of the
islands, wind of the islands. That was what Tuan
had been in her life, a great wind blowing through,
a great wind that swept everything before it, all
caution and reason and conviction, a great wind
that ravaged and uprooted and demolished everything, and left in its wake a trail of destruction and
an awful sense of desolation.

The plane droned its way across an ocean she
could no longer see, putting distance between herself and Ta'aroa. Perhaps distance would help—
distance and time. There were the threads of her
life to be picked up. Did she want to go back to
France—to another year of studying and living
with a noisy happy French family, and tutoring in
all her spare time? Possibly a job would be better.
By now her bilingual skills should bring something, with luck a job involving travel, some position that would make it hard for Tuan to contact
her.

Or would he bother trying to contact her? "I
won't go chasing after any woman," he had told
her once long ago. Because no woman was worth

chasing except the one woman he could never have.

Why had she ever thought, even for a moment, that it might be possible to be married to a man who loved someone else? It would never have worked. Never, never, never...she had been mad to think it might. A life with only half a husband? Even Tania had more than that, for Alain de Vigny loved her, in his way, and Tania knew it. A marriage to Tuan would have soon soured. Before long the knowledge of his misplaced affections would have eaten away at her like acid, destroying her slowly but surely. No: better to escape now, to put the man and the memories behind her. Even if Tuan should do the impossible and come after her with some belated offer of marriage dictated by his conscience, it would be better to resist. Marriage to him would have brought nothing but misery in the end. Even today's harsh revelations, ugly and painful though they might be, were preferable to that.

"*Monsieur, madame*, we land in a few minutes." It was the voice of the copilot again. "Seat belts still fastened? *Ah, c'est bien....*"

Once more came the sensation of altitude swiftly dropping away, the brush with the lagoon, the knifing through water, the cutting of one engine, the swift turn, the sudden dying of the other engine. The plane rocked to a halt. Tahiti at last. Tahiti and safety.

Marisa removed her eyeshade and looked out

the window beside her, but from this vantage
point all she could see was a fringing reef and a
vista of blue Pacific. From here not even Tahiti's
sister island of Mooréa was in sight. She knew
something would be visible through the window
on the opposite side of the plane, but she could
not bear to look in that direction lest she meet the
eyes of the man who had been her fellow passenger. She remained in her seat, waiting. Now she
could hear the sounds of the hatch being opened;
voices in French uttering little civilities; the odd
word in Tahitian.

Her fellow passenger, like herself, had not yet
left his seat. Out of the corners of her vision she
could see his white-clad legs, although she kept her
eyes turned determinedly out her own window.
Other sounds intruded, sounds of someone coming through the hatch, into the plane. And
Dooey's voice.

"We'll wait in here," he said, and then she
could once again hear the closing of the door that
led into the cockpit.

Then into the edge of her vision another pair
of legs intruded. Long legs in tan-colored trousers. . . .

"Hello, Miss Marisa," said a well-remembered
voice.

CHAPTER TWENTY-ONE

HER EYES traveled up the legs and found the face. The shock was total, eclipsing reason. It was not him; it could not be him; she had gone mad; she had lost her senses. . . .

"Don't you have anything to say?" he smiled.

Slowly the color returned to her lips, and with it some sanity. This was no dream. This was Tuan in the flesh. The same sun-browned flesh: the same devastating blue eyes: the same little smile playing about his lips, grooving his cheeks. She squeezed her eyes shut briefly, but he remained.

"How. . .how did you. . .get to Tahiti?" she managed. "You didn't, you couldn't—"

"That's right, I didn't." He remained standing in the aisle, almost blotting out the man in the seat opposite. "You're back where you started, Miss Marisa. Back at Ta'aroa."

"Ta'aroa," she repeated numbly. But the shock of this was nothing compared to the shock she had just suffered. It only added to a sense of disorientation that was already stretched to its outermost limits.

"Yes, Marisa, Ta'aroa. You didn't think I'd let

you go, did you? I'm surprised you didn't recognize the cloud.''

Now, with her eyes trained in their new direction, she could see that what he had said was true. Past the line of those lean hips was the window of the plane, and beyond the window the beach was visible. It was white, gleaming white, Ta'aroa white.

"I...I had an eyeshade," she said in an unsteady voice. "How did I...did we...?"

"There's a radio in the plane, remember? You'd have been back a lot sooner if Dooey hadn't had another little errand, an urgent one. I didn't want him to waste time by—"

"Please, don't tell me any more." Desperately she wished the man in the opposite seat would leave. Or did she want him to leave? Whatever Tuan had to say to her could hardly be said with a stranger present. Apologies, protestations, recriminations...she wanted to hear none of them. She had managed, during what she had thought was the trip to Tahiti, to clothe herself in some tatters of self-control. If Tuan continued to talk, surely he would rob her of even those. So she tried to forestall him. "I don't want to know—I just want to go."

"Marisa, it would be better to say this in private, but—"

"You don't have to say anything at all," she broke in quickly, despairingly. "There's no need to apologize. You don't have to explain. I don't want you to explain. *Please* don't explain. I

understand everything, everything...." Her voice
dropped to an agonized echo of itself. "Words
won't change anything."

"Some words will. Will you marry me, Miss
Marisa?"

Another shock, a smaller one, followed by
numbness. Numbness and knowledge. Of course
he was only doing the honorable thing. He knew
how she felt about marriage—and she knew how
he felt.

"You don't have to," she said whitely, wanting
this whole nightmare to end. "It wouldn't work.
It's just more words."

"Is it? I love you, Marisa. I want to marry you."

"Please *don't*," she begged. "Don't go on
about it."

She turned her head away from him, unable to
bear this scene being played out to its ghoulish fin-
ish under a stranger's eyes. Why didn't that other
man leave? Why didn't Tuan ask him to leave?

"Dammit, Marisa, do I have to say it again? I
love you. I said it often enough last night. I said it
even before then, if you had cared to listen with
your heart. I love you. I love you. I *love* you."

"No more, please," she begged. How could he
go on this way with a stranger listening?

"I won't apologize for deceiving you because I
had the best of reasons. And I won't apologize for
what happened last night because I'm glad it happened. You wanted it to happen, too! I will
apologize for the way you found out we weren't

married; it wasn't what I had in mind at all."

She tried to make herself small in the seat, and prayed that the stranger could not understand English. She wanted to dematerialize and find herself somewhere else, anywhere else.

"Marisa, I want to marry you. How can I convince you? I can't think of any other words to say."

"I can," came a voice.

Now, for the first time, the man in the other seat spoke softly—in English, albeit accented. "Why don't you call the others, Monsieur Tuan? Two will be enough—the pilot and the copilot. They know part of the story anyway. There's no need for the islanders to find out what's going on. That can be our secret, hmm?"

Despite her wish to vanish altogether off the face of the earth, Marisa turned to the new voice as Tuan, responding to its suggestion, moved forward toward the cockpit. Her fellow passenger had swiveled in his seat, and for the first time Marisa had a good view of him.

"Permit me to introduce myself," he said with a twinkle in his eye that leavened the severity of his clerical collar. "My name is Jean-Paul Bénard. Tuan has explained everything, including the need for haste. He was on the radiotelephone to me when he heard the plane take off—a little prematurely, it is true, for he had not had time to give his pilot instructions. Ah, I see you will listen to me, but not to him! Well, you can believe everything he says. I've known your, er, husband for years. Take my advice, young lady, and just let it happen."

Let it happen. The swaying cabin of a flying boat was no less strange a place than the crowded radio shack where it had supposedly happened once before. There were fewer witnesses, true, but this time the deed was real enough. "Dearly beloved, we are gathered here together...."

And there she was again, in the teeth of a strong gale, a great wind that carried everything before it.

HALF AN HOUR LATER, still in a dream, Marisa walked into the bungalow ahead of her husband—her new husband. He had remained strangely silent since the moment they had parted company with the others back on the busy beach: perhaps it was due to the brief distraction that had taken place only minutes ago. When Jean-Paul Bénard had come ashore, to be greeted by a glowing Uma holding a small child by the hand and standing on two very competent feet, he had been happily collared by Lotu and Maeva, who wished to make arrangements of a nature that Maeva had described briefly and joyfully to Marisa.

"For the christening, I wish you to be godmother, Marisa *vahine*," Maeva had bubbled. "It will be done at the same time as the wedding—but not for one month, maybe two. It is good for Lotu to wait, *n'est-ce pas*? For I would not want to marry a man with a swelled head!"

"Oh, Maeva!" Marisa had laughed delightedly and breathlessly, but whether for her own happiness or for Maeva's was a secret known only to her own heart.

"Marisa, you silly, silly goose." As they entered the bungalow a pair of strong arms came around her from behind. Tuan had been patient for this moment only until they reached privacy. Now he forced her to turn within the circle of his arms and face him. Her eyes connected with a coffee-colored shirt at the level of his unbuttoned collar As he talked she could see the movements of his vocal chords within the tanned column of his throat.

"Capturing you has been like trying to capture a wild winged thing. You kept fluttering close and then darting away from me. Last night I thought I finally had you trapped. But I turn my back for one instant this morning and what do I find? You've flown the cage. And so hard to convince.... Didn't it occur to you, even once, that I might actually want you for a wife?"

"No," she said, addressing the collar and still unable to trust in the happiness he seemed to be offering.

"Then I have to assume you believed nothing I told you last night." A light kiss landed on her hair, and then he pulled back a few inches. "I meant every word I said. Look at me, Miss Marisa."

She did, and found eyes blue as sky looking into hers with a candor that could no longer be doubted. Candor and much, much more. But there were still too many things she didn't understand, too many uncertainties to be resolved.

"Do I look as though I'm lying?" he persisted.

"Not now." Her breath caught briefly as she remembered the terrible hurt and heartache of the morning. She buried her head against his chest so he could not see it in her eyes and in the tremble of her mouth. "Oh, Tuan, if I'd known. If you'd only told me the truth last night—the whole truth. Even if you had told me this morning—"

"How could I tell you last night? In the middle of making love to you? And don't tell me I shouldn't have made love to you. I'm a man made of flesh and blood and muscle and bone and feelings, not a plaster saint. Lord knows I felt wretched enough after I'd done it, but how could I tell you that last night? And how could I tell you this morning?" His hand stroked her hair, cradling her close. "I didn't want to put you through any more misery than necessary. I thought I'd contact the preacher, arrange for Dooey to pick him up and bring him to Ta'aroa, then confront you with the problem and the solution all at once. Marisa! I never had any doubts about wanting to marry you, not for one moment, not from the instant I admitted to myself that I really loved you, and that was long before last night."

"I didn't know," she whispered. "You didn't tell me."

He bracketed her head between both hands and propelled it backward to force her eyes to his. "How could I tell you I loved you," he said gravely, "before last night? A man doesn't throw away words like that on a woman who's looking icicles at him—or avoiding him—or calling her feelings for him 'horrid little failings'—or telling him she can't wait to get away from him. And those are the things you've been doing for the past two weeks, ever since the first day I went to Tahiti."

"Because I knew I loved you that day," she said simply. "I was afraid you'd see it."

"Oh, Miss Marisa, what a lifetime we've wasted." He laughed softly, his eyes gleaming triumph. "But no more...."

And he buried his mouth against hers for a few satisfactory moments. He started to draw her toward the bedroom, but Marisa resisted. If there was ever to be happiness in their marriage, there must first be honesty, complete honesty, and she knew she must confess.

"No, Tuan," she said. "First I have a confession to make—another horrid little failing, if you like. It's why I didn't believe you last night, why I still find it hard to believe—"

"Still? Stubborn woman! Why?"

"Jealousy."

"Jealousy!" He pulled back some distance, his face registering surprise and disbelief in equal parts. "Surely you're not jealous of my past? Marisa, if I could, and if it would make you happy, I'd turn back the clock—I'd turn back the universe. But I can't, and God knows you won't have reason to be jealous from now on. I want only one woman now—you."

"It wasn't that, not those casual liaisons," she admitted, twisting out of his embrace. She was filled with self-doubts now, and ashamed to admit fears that sounded petty in the telling. But say it she must, and put it out of her mind forever. "It was Tania. I thought you loved Tania. There seemed so many clues, so many subtle hints."

Tuan stared at her for a long moment, then raked a hand through his hair in a gesture that had more than a little desperation in it. "Marisa, you know that was all in my father's mind. Oh, God! It's been a sickness with him, a terrible sickness, and he's infected you, too."

"Which makes me no better than he is. Oh, I am sorry, Tuan; I know you didn't have an affair with her. I never thought that, not really. But I thought you *loved* her. I knew you loved someone, and she seemed the logical candidate. It explained everything, even why you would want to take me to bed. Because you couldn't have *her*...." Marisa buried her shamed face in her hands, for the thoughts sounded so mean minded now. "She's so beautiful, so...exquisite. I don't care who you loved as long as it wasn't Tania."

He remained silent and grave for a time, thumbs hooked into his pockets while he contemplated her distress. Finally he broke the silence, gesturing at a chair. "Sit down, Marisa. I'll start at the beginning—my beginning. Not from the first day we met. It begins before that. And if what I have to say doesn't lay your last doubts to rest—well, I suppose this marriage may turn out to be more difficult than I supposed.''

Marisa obeyed, perching tensely on the edge of the oversize rattan chair where he had found her last night. Tuan remained standing, his large vital body prowling the floor with that aura of restless energy he sometimes conveyed.

''I can't pretend I wasn't upset when my father made his twisted accusations a year ago. I was upset—damn upset. At the time he was still barely recovered from his injury and the operations that followed it, and I thought he'd get over his jealousies given time. I still think so. Even the smallest child on Ta'aroa could have told him how Tania felt about him! It's practically legend on this island—she's never had eyes for anyone but him. Somewhere deep down he knows that, too.

''So why did he start doubting her? You can probably guess most of the reasons. The lameness, the age difference, the enforced idleness, the turning inward, the easy ways of the island girls. But despite everything, the marriage has been a success—*will* be a success. This morning Tania was urging my father to wear the leg brace. Doesn't that tell you something? A month ago she wouldn't have talked about it, and he wouldn't have allowed her to. They'll work it out, Marisa. I told you that from the first. I believed it then and I believe it now. If I didn't tell you more about Tania and my father, it's only because their problem has nothing to do with us—has *never* had anything to do with us.''

"But you said he had good and important reasons for wanting you to marry," she reminded him. "So of course I thought their problems had a bearing."

"I said *I* had good and important reasons for doing as he wished, which isn't quite the same thing."

"But—"

"Hush, Marisa. I have to tell this in my own way." He came to a halt by the wide sliding doors that led out onto the veranda. Beyond lay blue sky and blue Pacific, blue as the eyes she could not at this moment see. "After that first scene I did my best to stay away and let things blow over, although I came back occasionally to see if my father had improved. Eventually, on one of those trips, he delivered his ultimatum. It was a hard blow, let me tell you. Ta'aroa has always been something special in my life. I won't deny that I toyed with the idea of marrying to satisfy my father. I wanted this property—but was I willing to enter into marriage with a woman I didn't love in order to get it? I decided I wasn't. Long before the deadline I had given up all thought of meeting his ultimatum."

"But you told me—"

He turned back toward the room, scowling, bringing back memories of other scowls, but somehow this time the facial grooves seemed less forbidding. "There you go jumping ahead of me, Miss Marisa! That comes later in the story. But I'll satisfy your curiosity one tiny bit before I go on. Yes, there is a woman named Yvonne, a very important woman in my life. You met her. She's my secretary.''

''Your *secretary*,'' Marisa repeated, stunned.

A glint of humor returned to his eye. ''I had to pull something out of the hat, didn't I? You were pressing me, pressing me so hard I had to invent something.''

''That doesn't make sense,'' said Marisa, her head in a spin.

''Let's back up a bit, then, and it will. I was prepared to lose Ta'aroa because I had never seen a woman I wanted to marry. And then I saw you.''

''But—''

''Stop and think a minute, Marisa. You've used your native intelligence to jump to a lot of wrong conclusions. Now try jumping to some of the right ones! You know what took me to Los Angeles, don't you?''

''Yes. Roger's death.''

''And having gone all that way, don't you think I'd go to the funeral?''

She stared at him with total incredulity.

''Yes, Marisa, I saw you that day. There's no reason you would have seen me; you were far too busy. I'll never forget the first moment you came into view: that marvelous corn silk hair of yours spilling forward over your face while you tried to console a small and very upset child, a child with hair the color of your own. God, I thought it was

your child! I can't tell you how I felt. Does it
sound incredible? Perhaps it is. But de Vigny men
have a way of falling in love like that—once,
violently and irrevocably. My grandfather did and
never regretted it, not through fifty years of marriage. My father did, with Tania—the moment he
saw her; and he fell so hard he was willing to wait
for her for seven years while she attended school
elsewhere. I felt as though I had been hit by a loco-
motive—and by a woman who wasn't available.

"I was sitting quite close to you, close enough
to fix you in my memory.... I left as soon as the
service was over, for I knew I couldn't bear to
meet you, and perhaps a husband I was prepared
to murder. To tell the truth, I wasn't thinking too
clearly. It wasn't until late that night that I realized it must have been one of Roger's children.
What other child would be at the funeral, and
upset? I knew you weren't Roger's widow; I had
met your sister once, years ago, and in any case
her picture was on Roger's desk. So who were
you?

"Who? I had to know. First thing the following
day I hired a firm of private detectives. I had the
answer within hours—who you were, that you
were single, some of the basic facts. I decided to
come calling. I owed your sister a courtesy call
anyway."

"And I was at the zoo," she said wonderingly.
"Oh, Tuan—"

He silenced her with a gesture. "I was quite prepared to try for a whirlwind courtship. It occurred to me that with luck I might win you and Ta'aroa, too—I still had a week to meet my deadline. I planned it as though I were a general planning a campaign to take a city by storm: theater tickets, reservations at fine restaurants, even jewels chosen to give to you at the right moment—including that emerald you accused my secretary of choosing.'' He turned his attention to her ring finger and added in a dry voice, ''I see you've managed to remove it since last night. Where is it—surely not turfed into the lagoon?''

''I left it in the bedroom,'' she told him with a pang of remembrance, ''with my wedding ring.''

He nodded, satisfied, and continued with his story. ''You know what happened after that. You vanished for the rest of the week. I felt angry, frustrated, cheated—not least because I had turned my whole schedule upside down in order to stay in Los Angeles. You spent a lot of time being curious, Miss Marisa—why weren't you ever curious about that?''

''About what?''

''About the fact that I would spend a week putting a small branch office in shape. Why should I? People can be hired to do that kind of thing. Air des Iles is a going concern in the South Pacific—I run hundreds of flights every week. The Los Angeles office is just one cog in the wheel, and a small cog at that—a convenience for tourists who want to arrange charters in advance. I went to Los

Angeles for the funeral because I had met your brother-in-law a number of times over the years, and I liked him, and I *do* take an interest in my employees, just as I told you. Good God—that little office practically ran itself anyway, or how do you think Roger would have·managed during the last months of his life?''

"I didn't think of that," she admitted.

"Anyway, you vanished. I hired more private investigators—three different firms. But you couldn't be located in any of the usual camp-grounds. I was desperate by then—damn desperate! And to tell the truth, I was resentful, too, because I wondered whether it wasn't a purely physical attraction, a trick of misty green eyes and honey-toned skin. I was resentful because you had turned my whole world topsy-turvy.''

"I know the feeling," she interjected ruefully.

"Resentful toward you," he went on, "and angry with myself for not being able to put you out of my mind. No woman had ever obsessed me like that. I knew almost nothing about you, didn't even know if I would like you, yet I was prepared to go to any lengths to get you. I think I almost hated you for that.''

So that was the reason for the antagonism she had felt when she first met him. Oh, Lord, could this all be *true*?

He frowned and paced the floor again. "By then I was badly torn between wanting to get you out of my system and wanting to sweep you away to the South Pacific. And all before I had met you! Then there was the matter of Ta'aroa, too—I didn't want to give up on that if there was hope. Three days before you returned from your camping trip I started to look for some way to pressure you into marriage on short notice, for of course a whirlwind courtship was out of the question by then. The investigators were told to look for anything, anything at all—and I flew my secretary out from Papeete to go through every last piece of paper in Roger's office. She spent two near-sleepless days going through armloads of files, looking for anything to do with you. You know what she found."

"My letter," Marisa said numbly.

"It took a little thought on the matter, but I soon saw how I could use it. You know the rest. It was a story invented out of whole cloth. I didn't give a damn whether you spoke French or broke a dozen engagements, or why... but I took the facts in the letter and used them."

"And I thought you were using me."

"I know you did. And I wanted you to—for I certainly didn't want you to guess the truth. I was sure you would if we met face to face... or that at the very least I'd frighten you off in some way. That's why I had my secretary do the hiring."

"Then you invented the business about Roger's insurance, too," she said thoughtfully.

"Not quite. What I told you was true enough— except that the matter had already been looked after. Roger's insurance was *my* insurance, that's all—so that you couldn't walk out on me at any point. Out-and-out blackmail, I admit, but by then I was ready to stoop to anything.''

But there was one thing he had not yet explained, one piece of deception that was hard to forgive despite all his admissions. Marisa looked down at her fingers. They looked naked, shorn of rings, and that reminded her of the moment she had removed them this morning—that moment of terrible hurt. "If that's all true,'' she said slowly, "then why didn't you go through with the real thing?''

He raked his hair; his broad shoulders tensed. "Oh, hell, I wish I had! I planned to, until the last minute. But stop and think how I felt. Resentful, angry, wanting to dislike you, almost wanting the detectives to find out something dreadful so I could actively hate you—and I think I did hate you at first. You were so composed, so controlled, so emotionally detached from me. How I longed to crack that cool blond surface of yours!''

"It's never been anything but cracked,'' she admitted unsteadily, "since the first day we met.''

"Underneath, maybe. On the surface it didn't seem that way. You disliked me thoroughly; I could see that. You seemed so brittle, so untouchable. That day in Faaa Airport I was tempted to put you on a flight home at once! If it hadn't been for the other matter, the matter of the Ta'aroa property, I might have done just that. Oh, I wanted you, and badly—but not enough to ruin both our lives for it. I decided then and there that there'd be no real marriage until I'd made up my mind about you.''

''A real marriage could have ended in annulment,'' she reminded him.

''Do you think so, Marisa—do you really think so? I had to have some barrier in my mind. If I'd been truly married to you nothing would have stopped me from making love to you. Even *hating* you wouldn't have stopped me. Physically, I wanted you too much. I thought I had enough willpower that I wouldn't take advantage of you under false pretenses. As it turned out,'' he finished with a wry smile, ''I was wrong.''

For a few moments Marisa studied the patterns of fish through the Plexiglas floor, and thought of the hurts and the doubts and the lies and the unhappinesses, and then put them behind her forever. She looked up, love spilling from her eyes, and smiled at him. ''Perhaps you have more willpower than you give yourself credit for. You certainly used it that night in Tahiti.''

''That wasn't exactly willpower,'' he admitted dryly, ''it was timing. There was a preacher waiting for us—until midnight. Don't you remember I planned to call on someone?''

''Yes,'' she said with new wonderment dawning.

''Why else do you think I took you to Tahiti? That night when I got drunk and hurled a bottle at the door—it was because you'd confessed to sexual urges, too, and it nearly drove me out of my mind not following you to bed. And then there were my hazy memories of the night. I had reason to think you were...weakening, and I wanted to be close to all the legal frills in case you thought they were important. By then I...didn't. That flower in your hair was frill enough for me."

Momentary puzzlement touched her eyes. "That flower...I'd forgotten about it. Did it mean something?"

"It's a Tahitian woman's way of saying she's taken." The blue eyes smiled down from a distance that no longer seemed too great to bridge. "Much more meaningful than a wedding ring in this part of the world. It tells other men to keep away—when it's behind the right ear. A primitive ceremony, if you like."

"So that's why you moved it," she murmured, marveling.

"After that night," he went on, "I was afraid nothing would stop me, not even a point-blank refusal on your part. That's why I flew back to Tahiti the following night. Why I nearly went out of my mind the night after...the night of the octopus hunt. Can you conceive how hard that was, sleeping with you in my arms? And I swear I'd have taken you the following night if I hadn't slept on the beach."

"Oh, Tuan," she breathed with emotion and sudden humility, realizing now what tortures he must have gone through. "And you say you have no willpower."

Now he moved closer to the chair where she sat, and hovered over it, tall and male and, as always, a threat to composure. "Do you still have doubts, Marisa—about anything?"

"No." At his urging she came to her feet, and her eyes told him that only love and trust remained. "No doubts at all."

His hands captured her face and turned it upward to his own. "It seems to me we were interrupted this morning in the middle of a very exciting scene," he said softly. The eyes crinkled encouragement at her. "Would you like to play it all over again?"

She laughed and nodded breathlessly, and turned weak inside as his mouth melted into her hair. "Oh, Tuan," she whispered to the strong bronzed throat, "I'm sorry for jumping to all the wrong conclusions."

His hands began a slow journey of discovery over her back and her hips. "Miss Marisa, my wild little bird," he murmured in the moment before his mouth closed over hers. "This isn't the wrong conclusion. It's the one I had in mind all along."

Yours FREE, with a home subscription to SUPERROMANCE T.M.

Now you never have to miss reading the newest **SUPERROMANCES**... because they'll be delivered right to your door.

Start with your **FREE** LOVE BEYOND DESIRE. You'll be enthralled by this powerful love story...from the moment Robin meets the dark, handsome Carlos and finds herself involved in the jealousies, bitterness and secret passions of the Lopez family. Where her own forbidden love threatens to shatter her life.

Your **FREE** LOVE BEYOND DESIRE is only the beginning. A subscription to **SUPERROMANCE** lets you look forward to a long love affair. Month after month, you'll receive four love stories of heroic dimension. Novels that will involve you in spellbinding intrigue, forbidden love and fiery passions.

You'll begin this series of sensuous, exciting contemporary novels...written by some of the top romance novelists of the day...with four every month.

And this big value...each novel, almost 400 pages of compelling reading...is yours for only $2.50 a book. Hours of entertainment every month for so little. Far less than a first-run movie or pay-TV. Newly published novels, with beautifully illustrated covers, filled with page after page of delicious escape into a world of romantic love...delivered right to your home.

Begin a long love affair with

SUPERROMANCE

Accept LOVE BEYOND DESIRE, **FREE.**

Complete and mail the coupon below, today!

- -

FREE! Mail to: SUPERROMANCE

In the U.S.
1440 South Priest Drive
Tempe, AZ 85281

In Canada
649 Ontario St.
Stratford, Ontario N5A 6W2

YES, please send me FREE and without any obligation, my
SUPERROMANCE novel, LOVE BEYOND DESIRE. If you do not hear
from me after I have examined my FREE book, please send me the
4 new **SUPERROMANCE** books every month as soon as they come
off the press. I understand that I will be billed only $2.50 for each book
(total $10.00). There are no shipping and handling or any other hidden
charges. There is no minimum number of books that I have to
purchase. In fact, I may cancel this arrangement at any time.
LOVE BEYOND DESIRE is mine to keep as a FREE gift, even if
I do not buy any additional books.

NAME   (Please Print)

ADDRESS   APT. NO.

CITY

STATE/PROV.   ZIP/POSTAL CODE

SIGNATURE (If under 18, parent or guardian must sign.)

This offer is limited to one order per household and not valid to present
subscribers. Prices subject to change without notice.

Offer expires February 28, 1983

PR20